Acme Time Trav

Volume 2

Gabriel and Ginny

By David Griffiths

Copyright © David Griffiths   2019

David Griffiths has asserted his right under the Copyright, Designs and Patents Act, 1988
to be identified as the author of this work

This book is licensed for your personal enjoyment only. This book may not be re-sold or given away to other people. If you would like to share this book with another person, please purchase an additional copy for each recipient.

Thank you for respecting the hard work of this author

CONTENTS

Book One 22

Coca-Cola Light 2

Iceland ready meals 14

The walk will do you good 18

So, what's her name then? 20

The Golden Egg 22

Where's the tea bags? 25

One Cool Customer 26

Can't stop thinking about her 27

Still staring at my chest then? 33

Someone to turn to 36

Fragments of what remained 38

Want to talk about it? 40

Who is Vicky? 41

I let him use my body as payment 44

Tricky one 49

It's getting cold 57

Walking to Ginny's house 62

You look very tired 66

Now that you've screwed me 69

Don't let them come to harm 73

Could you really do that? 76

So, you're going on your own then? 78

What about Moth? 80

I think we can eat later 82

Don't use him all up 85

What if it's raining? 87

He tasted pretty good 92

Do you fancy crumpets?   94

Yummy looking   96

Fancy some chips?   99

Where would we park it?   105

I meant 'when' Barney   108

Book Two   113

Where is he, the little shit?   113

I think I really frightened him   118

A small glass of white wine   120

Stay calm, boyfriend   123

A vista of stars   127

Proximity alert   132

A vague murmur in her sleep   136

Because I can't be hurt   139

If he dies   141

Sent a 'nudge'   144

Just use small thrusts   147

Why wouldn't they wish to help you?   150

This bit looks a bit barren   152

An insect trapped in resin   154

There's a storm coming   157

Please pick her up   159

Will you ever forgive me?   162

If it gives you any comfort   166

I can't even be strong for you   168

One less thing   170

Still bloody itches   174

Dead for forty years   176

Book Three   179

Told you it wouldn't do any harm   179

Not without getting squished   183

Ship noticed them   185

They might be finished tomorrow   187

What's the worst that could happen?   188

Being given unction   **196**

Why would he lie   200

There're worse ways   204

God-forsaken shithole   208

Docking time in one minute   210

Don't you think that's a bit strange?   212

Welcome back, sunshine   216

I think I can answer that   225

It's a fucking death sentence   229

We'll think of something   232

It's good to see you back, Ginny   233

I've always fancied going to Seville   240

Comfort from their proximity   243

Maybe now wasn't the time   249

A view to a tragedy   259

Where did that flyer come from?   261

The only good thing that fucker did   263

What if he doesn't?   265

A memory for your holiday   271

Life can be a bitch sometimes   276

No introductions are necessary   278

In Baltimore   280

Do you think you could catch one?   283

Rolling hills with moo cows   286

It's bought us time   287

He very much enjoyed his job   288

So fucking hard   290

I'll keep us safe   294

Someone a long time ago   296

I guess it's over   308

Book Four   309

You did get rid of the bad guys   309

It's what we said we were going to do   311

I'm Mary, John's wife   314

We've come to see you   316

Barney's wedding day   319

Want to talk about it?   320

Who is Vicky?   322

It's nearly that day   324

His wife survives him   327

Dead all these years   334

About the Author   341

Acknowledgments   344

Other Titles Available   345

Getting Book Reviews   346

BOOK ONE

Coca-Cola light   Thursday 13th July 2017 9:15 pm

Clacton Pier

It was dusk, and the lights in Clacton-on-Sea were clicking on. It had been a warm day, but a light cloud had thickened up and the onshore breeze gave a chill to the air. Gabriel had cycled down to the pier, leaving his bicycle chained to the railings lining the promenade. The pier was closed at this time of evening, but the local kids could easily scale the security barriers, and often congregated there. Gabriel sat with his back to the wall, next to the entrance to the children's ride called the Tea-Cup Enchantment. A Coca-Cola machine was sited next to the entrance. It was still switched on. It cast a pale pink glow onto the semi-dark pier, with its cobwebbed Victorian girders and peeling wooden slats.

"Are you alright, Gabriel?" Vicky asked.

Gabriel stared, transfixed by the Coca-Cola glow.

Gabriel hadn't wanted to go back to his mum's flat. He had needed somewhere quiet. Somewhere to have a private conversation. He had needed somewhere quiet to understand the 'thing', the 'device' strapped to his wrist.

NOTE if you are interested in how Gabriel came to have this 'thing' strapped to his wrist, please download a copy of Acme Time Travel Incorporated - Volume 1

"Gabriel ... are you alright?"

He had often come here. It was often quiet here. Sometimes other people turned up. Some were his friends, others not. Boys brought their girlfriends here. Drunks and druggies brought their own personal forms of entertainment. If you wanted space, you could find it here.

"Gabriel ... if you are concerned someone else might hear me, I can provide you with a tiny ear-piece. Only you would hear me. Do you wish me to do that?"

Gabriel considered the suggestion. He hadn't really given the idea any thought, but Vicky's suggestion made sense.

"Yes please, Vicky. That would probably be a good idea."

"Hold out your hand please, Gabriel, palm facing upwards."

Gabriel did so.

Instantly he felt as if something very tiny had been placed on his hand.

"Insert it into your ear, Gabriel ... either one. Whilst you are wearing it, I can talk to you purely through that device."

Gabriel picked up the tiny device. It felt like a piece of putty, soft and moldable. Tentatively he pushed it into his right ear. He sensed it beginning to mold itself to the shape of his ear. Soon it felt very secure and not uncomfortable.

"Does that feel ok, Gabriel?" Vicky asked, her voice sounding remarkably close and very distinct.

It felt as though he was wearing a set of expensive headphones.

"You won't need to speak loudly to me, Gabriel. I will hear your faintest whisper," advised Vicky.

"Yes, that's great Vicky," Gabriel replied, but he felt the terseness in his own voice.

"Gabriel ... Gabriel. I sense something is wrong. Is there a problem? Is it something I can help with?"

"There's something you're not telling me, Vicky."

"I thought John and I had explained everything. How I arrived, how John found me, how I cured him, why I am afraid to teleport, how I have helped him over the years, how ..."

"I think that's the bit that's missing," interrupted Gabriel. "When John said he wanted you to accompany me, you weren't just upset at leaving a friend. There was something else. There is something else. What is it, Vicky?"

Vicky seemed to sigh.

"Unless I stay in physical contact with John, his medical condition will rapidly deteriorate, probably over a period of a few weeks. His original catatonia will probably return first, meaning he will shortly lose the power of movement and speech. His mind will still be active, but with no power to act or react to stimulus. Then, when John cannot move of his own volition, or communicate with those around him, it is likely he will begin to suffer from the effects of dementia. I have kept it at bay for many years, but it will rapidly overtake him. He will become confused, forgetful, angry ..."

"And he won't even be able to communicate his feelings to anyone, will he?" Gabriel said, horrified.

"No, he will not," Vicky said.

"And he might be like that in a few weeks?"

"Did you realise," said Vicky, "that John's wife, Mary, she herself suffered from dementia for many years. I could have helped her, staved off the illness, but it would have required for me to be constantly attached to her. It was both John and Mary's tragedy that both needed me to be in permanent contact with them, to maintain their health. A decision was needed; which one I should assist. John wanted me to help Mary, but Mary won … and I helped John. So, I helped John, and John watched Mary's dementia take her away from him. He loved her and cared for her, past the point where she comprehended who he was. It ground his soul into the dust. I didn't think he could bear it."

"And now John has given himself up to that same fate," said Gabriel.

"I think he sees no better outcome," said Vicky forlornly.

Gabriel stared into the pale glow from the Coca-Cola machine, as if looking for wisdom.

· · · · · · · ·

"If he had had another device, another device such as yourself, then both John and Mary might have been helped," Gabriel mused.

"Perhaps that's true, Gabriel, but I would not have been able to request another STU device. They designed me with the facilities to request 'equipment', for clients to use on their tours, but I could not request another STU. You should understand STUs are expensive pieces of equipment. Each client is assigned one, solely for their personal help whilst on a tour. We are not 'given away free' like a toy to a child."

Gabriel pondered on Vicky's words.

"But if your time travel function worked, why didn't you take John to your future time? He could have asked for another STU for Mary."

"Gabriel. You must understand I am an employee of an enormous company who operates in the very high-end luxury market of personal time and space travel. The clients who go on the space/time tours are very, very wealthy, and they pay vast sums of money for the privilege. I do not believe ACME INC would give away a STU as a free medical assistance facility."

"But … maybe …," Gabriel said.

"Let me illustrate the point," said Vicky. "I remember an occasion where an ACME client was on a tour when his son became extremely ill. The client's wife and son had remained at home ... partly because of the boy's ill-health. The boy became gravely ill, and the client's wife contacted ACME, asking if ACME would help her son using their medical facilities. It was well known that ACME had one of the best medical centres available anywhere. As she said, if anyone could save her son, it would be ACME's MEDI-CARE facility."

"So, what happened?" Gabriel said.

"ACME refused to help her son. They argued that contractually, the client, her husband, had full health cover with them, and if anything should happen to him whilst on tour, ACME's full medical resources would be put at his disposal. Unfortunately, his wife and son had no such covering agreement. ACME insisted they would not provide medical services outside of their legally bound contract. They said they feared for any legal repercussions in the event they offered their services, but the patient died anyway. They refused to be moved on the issue."

"And?"

"And the son died," Vicky said.

"But ... surely ...," Gabriel said.

"ACME was prepared to take a very strong stance on that issue," Vicky explained, "to safeguard themselves against similar situations. They realised there would be a strong media backlash, but they stayed firm. They stayed firm until the media frenzy died."

"So, you think," said Gabriel, "that even if it had been possible to teleport John into the future, they would not have offered him a second STU?"

"On the evidence available, I would suggest it would be highly unlikely they would have given him a STU. The boy who died ... his mother ... she put forward an extraordinarily powerful case to ACME INC. She argued they had the medical technology to help him. She had even got one of ACME's medical staff to confirm to her that ACME definitely had the equipment necessary to save her son. Even with that information, and with the weight of the media behind her, she could not get them to help her son."

"Why on Earth would they choose not to ...?" Gabriel said, stopping as he heard footsteps on the pier's wooden planking. He looked up to see Rebecca walking towards him. She was about his own age, but, if he hadn't already known that, her heavy make-up would have made it difficult to guess her correct age. She had on a tight low-cut top, with a short skirt and high heels that clicked on the wooden slats. She had two boys in tow, walking slightly behind her. Rebecca always had boys in tow. Gabriel recognised these two; Pete and Slammer. They were probably about Gabriel's age. They were both big guys. They worked out a lot. He'd seen them about, but he'd never spoken to them. They both seemed to hang around playgrounds ... the ones grudgingly sited near grim tower blocks. They would haul themselves up and down on the climbing frames, building up impressive sets of muscles. Adolescent girls would stand around and admire them. Gabriel hadn't seen them fight, but he reckoned they probably relied a lot on intimidation. The exercises these guys did were good for lifting heavy weights, including themselves, but they didn't necessarily improve your chances in a fight.

Unless they got in a lucky blow ... in which case you were probably fucked.

"Hiya Gabs," called Rebecca, "watcha doing?"

"Just hangin'," Gabriel called back.

Pete and Slammer caught up with Rebecca.

"Evening, nig," Pete said.

Slammer chuckled to himself.

Gabriel didn't really want to engage any of them in conversation. He found in any prolonged conversation, Rebecca would eventually become abusive. And he saw from Pete's opening words, he probably hadn't had a fight all night and was probably looking for one now.

"Not seen ya about," Rebecca sneered. "You too good for us, nar you gotta job then?"

Pete sidled up beside Rebecca and began stroking her bottom, looking up and sneering at Gabriel as he did so.

"Always pleased to see you, Rebecca," Gabriel responded.

He was feeling strangely emboldened tonight. In such a situation he would typically have been tongue-tied by now. His nerves in front of girls would always get the better of him. In strange contrast, however, he had no nerves when confronted by guys looking for a fight. It was a learned response. He had been raised ... well ... more dragged up, in some tough areas of London. He realised full well an open display of nerves would only worsen the situation. And he knew he was a fit guy, quick responses, and light on his feet. He understood the value of avoiding being hit; once you were down, it got a fuck sight worse after that point. He also knew from direct experience, if you got the chance, stop the other guy before he got one in. And definitely stop him from getting any more in.

"You're not being a smart-arsed cunt are you, Gabs?" Rebecca said.

Gabriel heard a whispering in his ear – "Are you ok with this?" Vicky said.

"I'm fine," Gabriel whispered back.

"Hey nig," said Pete. "Don't you know you should show some respect to white girls?"

Gabriel pondered on the fact neither Pete nor Slammer had ever seen him fight. He and his mum had only moved up from London last November. They might well have seen Gabriel wandering about, but he guessed they knew little about him.

Other than that he was mixed-race.

"I can help get you out of here," Vicky said, with an air of worry in her voice.

"How are you gonna do that?" Gabriel said. "I thought you couldn't …"

"Talking to yourself ain't gonna help you nig," Pete said. "Not unless you think playing a moron's gonna …"

"Shut the fuck up, Pete," Gabriel said. "I'm trying to listen to somebody."

Pete turned to Slammer. They seemed to reach some unspoken agreement.

"I can …," Vicky said.

"I think it'll have to wait," Gabriel said.

Behind him was a section of the pier that housed reels of cable, spare parts for the rides and old chairs needing fixing. He turned and walked past the Coca-Cola machine and on into the darkened section of the pier beyond.

"Where the fuck you going?" Rebecca quipped.

Gabriel's boots crunched over the years of accumulated debris. He felt a cobweb brush against his face. He waited until his eyes got used to the darkness.

He heard footsteps behind him. Heavy footsteps.

At his feet was a metal bar, over three feet long, about one inch thick. They used it, amongst other things, to pry the roller-coaster rides back onto the tracks.

He knelt and picked it up.

He heard the footsteps behind him stop.

He turned. Pete was standing about three feet away from him. Slammer was standing to Pete's left, and slightly behind. Gabriel reckoned Slammer would wait to see what happened. It probably seemed to him like a forgone conclusion anyway, so he would probably be in no immediate hurry to join in.

Also, Slammer hadn't joined in any of the banter, which sometimes suggested no genuine desire to engage.

"Ok, nig ... let's ...," Pete said, taking a step forward.

Gabriel watched as Pete's left leg came forwards. He saw Pete plant it firmly on the ground. It was perhaps a foot in front of Gabriel. He was cocking his right arm back. He seemed to take his time about it. Pete was all about intimidation. He wanted you to realise you would get hurt. It was, Gabriel guessed, intended to be the forerunner to a heavy roundhouse punch to Gabriel's jaw.

Gabriel swung the metal bar into Pete's solidly planted left leg. He aimed for the knee. He felt the bar crunch into the bone. He let the bar's momentum lose itself completely in Pete's leg. He stepped back, bringing the bar up and diagonally across his chest, left hand low, right hand high.

Pete had collapsed to the ground. He was shrieking in pain. He didn't seem to know whether to bend his leg against his chest or whether to keep it straight.

Gabriel ignored him.

Slammer hadn't moved.

"Hit him, you fucker," Rebecca shouted.

Gabriel assumed this was a cue for Slammer.

Slammer smiled, more to himself than to anyone else.

"I should call it in," Slammer said to Rebecca. "I think the show's over for tonight."

Slammer turned and walked away. "Catch you around, nig boy," he said.

Gabriel heard him. He didn't think Slammer was being abusive. Rather, it sounded more like ... almost like a sense of respect.

"I'll get you. I'll fucking get you ... you cunt," Pete snarled at Gabriel.

Gabriel looked down at Pete. He swung the metal bar again; a big, lazy strike.

It crunched down onto Pete's right shin.

Rebecca stood watching, horrified.

Gabriel knelt and picked up some rags.

He wiped the bar down ... threw it into the darkness.

He heard it crash down ... into the mounds of cables, chairs, broken rides.

He turned and walked away.

"You bastard," he heard Rebecca shout.

Gabriel half-turned. "See you around, Rebecca," he said. "Shame Slammer didn't hang around, eh?"

"You ...," she began.

"He thought the show was over," Gabriel said, chuckling. "He didn't realise there would be an encore."

Iceland ready meals   Friday 14th July 2017 7:35 am

Gabriel's mum's flat - Clacton

Gabriel rolled himself off the old sofa that was his bed. As he got up, an exposed spring tugged at his shirtsleeve. He stopped, slowly un-hooking the fabric from the curl of steel. He couldn't afford to damage what few presentable clothes he had.

His mum was still asleep. She wouldn't get up until midday. He got washed, dressed and switched the kettle on. He rummaged in the sink to find the cleanest-looking mug for his morning coffee and gave it a quick scrape round with a metal washing-up scourer. Gabriel tried to keep his thoughts calm, but he always found searching through a sink piled high with dirty pots made him deeply unsettled. He would try to keep the place clean, and he would wash the pots every day for weeks on end, but if he ever stopped, he would find his mum would push dirty pots into the sink again, as if they magically cleaned themselves. It wasn't as though she was otherwise busy. She would exist on £1 meals-for-one from the Iceland shop (she never shopped or cooked for him ... he had been fending for himself for years), and inevitably she would throw the rubbish in the sink or the bin, neither of which she cleared out.

The kettle boiled, and he made himself a strong black coffee. He sometimes liked to have black coffee, but today he had forgotten to buy milk. He had looked, but the milk sat in the fridge didn't look too promising.

"Good morning, Gabriel," Vicky whispered. "You might want to fit the earpiece; in case your mother wakes up."

"Morning Vicky," he whispered back, pulling the tiny earpiece from a zipped compartment on his wallet.

"I need to do some research on my story idea ... the one about care support for families back in the 1920s and 1930s," Gabriel said. "I guess you might be able to get me some information I could use."

"I can do that, Gabriel. How would you wish to view it?"

"Erm ... I don't really know. What sort of things are you able to do?"

"Well ... present it in the form of a television documentary, for example."

"We don't have a TV," said Gabriel, looking around at their bleak flat, with its jumble sale and second-hand shop furniture.

"... or display it on any flat surface," said Vicky, "for example ..."

Immediately the wall behind him shimmered. A section of the faded yellow wallpaper became creamy parchment on which a series of old photographs and textual descriptions scrolled upwards.

"The old photographs look so clear," observed Gabriel. "I don't think I have ever seen old photographs with that level of sharpness before."

"That is because I am using a great deal of visual enhancement," Vicky explained. "The photographic material I have pulled back from the stock archives, but I can enhance it to a far greater degree than your current technology would allow."

"It looks so sharp; you almost feel you are there. Is it possible to make the screen even bigger?"

"If you wish, I can make the visuals fully immersive. Would you like to see an example?"

"Yes please, Vicky."

Suddenly Gabriel was standing on the pavement of a busy town.

"This is Coventry in 1932," explained Vicky.

The street was a busy thoroughfare, with cars passing and people walking up and down the pavement. On the other side of the road, a woman was walking along with a child, a boy of 12 years of age.

"Why don't you cross the road and see the woman with the child," suggested Vicky.

Without thinking, Gabriel checked no traffic was coming and set off across the road. It was only when he was halfway across the road; he realised he was walking into an old piece of video footage.

"How am I doing this?" Gabriel asked. "How can I walk around an old piece of video?"

"My graphic enhancement features enable me to 'build up' what you would have seen from the original material to hand, Gabriel. If you notice, I am also providing olfactory information to supplement the visual information."

"Sorry ... what does ...?"

"I am providing smells that would probably have been present then. I can turn that feature off, it seems unnecessary or unpleasant."

As Vicky spoke, a man got into a car next to where Gabriel was standing. As he opened the door of the car, Gabriel caught the faint smell of the wood and leather interior. The starter turned, and as the engine caught, a puff of bluish smoke caught in Gabriel's nose and throat. Gabriel was about to ask Vicky to turn off the 'smell feature', but he saw the woman with the boy getting closer to him. The boy was shrieking intermittently, but for no obvious reason. It appeared the woman had fashioned a leather harness for the boy. It tied around his waist, like a belt, and crossed over each of his shoulders. Each of the crossovers attached to a circlet of leather, which was fastened around his neck. The woman held onto a leash, and this was attached to the leather belt. It looked a little like she was walking a dog.

As the woman and the boy progressed up the pavement, coming towards where Gabriel was standing, Gabriel saw other pedestrians giving the woman a very wide berth. Typically, they avoided looking at her. Most cast a quick and furtive glance at the boy. They were finding it difficult to hide their unease at seeing such a thing.

As they got close to Gabriel, Gabriel stepped aside to let them pass.

The boy's eyes caught Gabriel's ... glittering and cavernous. Spittle dripped from the boy's mouth. The boy's mother wiped him automatically with a piece of cloth.

As the pair passed immediately in front of Gabriel, the boy looked directly up into Gabriel's eyes and shrieked. The noise seemed to come from the very depths of the boy's soul.

"Vicky? ... shit, shit, Vicky, Vicky?"

Instantly the visual was gone, and Gabriel was sitting in his mum's flat. His morning coffee was in front of him. He took a large gulp.

"Sorry Gabriel. Perhaps we should stick to the first type of presentation. I was trying to find relevant material, but maybe ..."

"That's ok, Vicky. Don't worry. I just wasn't expecting it to be so real, so vivid."

"Ok, Gabriel. By the way, I don't know if you are aware, but you can change my voice pattern, change my name, and change my personality. It's all part of the client service. What would you like?"

Gabriel thought for a minute.

"Did you give John these choices, Vicky? Are your current features John's choices?"

"Yes, that's right. He selected these features 70 years ago."

"Well, Vicky. It seems to me it would be ungracious of me to request you change after so long. You seem fine to me."

"It's nice of you to say, Gabriel. All right, I will stay just like this."

"Anyway, I had better get off to work ... Barney will wonder where I've got to. He waits for me to make the first cuppa, so God knows what he'll do if I'm late."

The walk will do you good   Friday 14th July 2017 morning

The distance from Clacton to Frinton was slightly over 7 miles, using the normal route for cars. It would take a car about 20 minutes to get there. By bicycle the distance was only 5.5 miles, and Gabriel could cycle that in about 30 minutes. It was a straight route along the coast, down Kings Parade and along the back of Frinton Golf Club.

Gabriel kept the bicycle Barney had lent him in his mum's flat. It wasn't safe to keep it outside, even if he chained it to something. At 8:45 am he had pushed it down the hallway and nudged the flat door open with the front wheel.

Thirty minutes later and he was cycling through Frinton, near to the Gazette office, when he heard a girl's voice calling his name. He stopped and looked around. The young girl he had seen at John's care home was standing across the street. She was smiling and waving at him. Instead of the grey smock she had been wearing the previous day, she was wearing a T-shirt, denim shorts and hiking boots with fluffy green hiking socks. Her legs looked long and tanned ... but not from sunbeds, he guessed. She looked like she walked a lot. Also, when he had seen her the other day, she had tied her hair in some sort of ponytail, but it was loose today. Her hair was long and very blonde. As she walked towards him, a slight breeze ruffled her hair up and around her face.

"Oh God, what was her name," Gabriel muttered to himself.

"Her name is Ginny," Vicky whispered back to him.

Gabriel started. He had forgotten Vicky was listening to him.

Ginny was crossing the road, walking over towards him.

"Hello Mr. News Reporter," she called out.

As she got closer, he saw her T-shirt had a quote on the front, saying

> **Don't let anyone**
> **drive you to madness**
> **The walk will**
> **do you good**

Suddenly Gabriel was aware she was watching him looking at the writing on her chest, and he flushed with embarrassment.

"Seen something you like?" she said, with a cheeky grin.

"Your T-shirt ... it's very ...," Gabriel mumbled.

"I printed it up myself," she chuckled, "using one of those 'print your own T-shirt' things."

She was smiling expectantly at him, and Gabriel couldn't remember if he had told her his name when he had seen her at the care home. Maybe he had, or maybe she had forgotten it.

"You going somewhere important?" she asked, her eyes sparkling at him.

"I'm … er … I'm going into the office, er … the newsroom," Gabriel said, feeling his old familiar nervousness with pretty girls overwhelming him.

"Your name's Gabriel, isn't it?" Ginny stated. "I asked John after you left the other day."

"Did you?" said Gabriel, unsure what to think.

"I'm not working today, so I thought I would come and look around the town for a bit," she continued. "I might stop around lunchtime and have a coffee and a sandwich over at the Golden Egg."

She pointed at a little coffee shop over the road.

Gabriel felt he should say something, but he wasn't sure what.

"What time do you have lunch?" Ginny asked.

"Erm … about 12:30 usually," Gabriel croaked. "For about an hour."

"Ok," said Ginny. "I'll see you in there about 12:35, and you can tell me what an exciting morning you've had."

"Uh … fine," said Gabriel, but even as he was speaking, Ginny had spun away and was walking down the street. He watched as she strode away, a strong, purposeful stride, her hips swaying gently, her hair gently moving to the turns of her body. She had gone twelve feet when she turned back to him, pirouetting lightly on the balls of her feet.

She gave him a cheery smile and a wave, and off she went again.

"I wonder how she knew I would still be watching her?" Gabriel muttered under his breath.

Maybe Vicky didn't hear him, or maybe she thought he was being rhetorical.

In any event, she didn't reply to Gabriel's question.

So, what's her name then? Friday 14th July 2017 10:30 am

The Gazette Office – Frinton-on-Sea

Gabriel sat at his desk, staring at his laptop screen. He didn't seem to be quite able to focus on the matter in hand (which was to research mental health care in the 1920s and 30s). He had typed into Google the search words 'Mencap history' and it had come back with an item labelled 'Mencap's history and timeline'. Apparently in 1946 a woman called Judy Fryd was trying to get recognition and support for people with children with learning difficulties.

So that was in 1946.

And John Cullen had been born in 1917.

And 29 years later, somebody was trying to get support for people looking after children with learning difficulties.

He barely imagined what John's mother had gone through to look after John, with no support other than from her friends and family. He would have to …

"So, what's her name, then?" Barney called across the room.

Barney was sitting with his second cuppa of the day. Gabriel seemed to make most of the teas now. Not (as Barney explained) because Gabriel was an office flunky, but because out of the two of them, Gabriel definitely made the best cups of tea. Barney very much relished a good cup of tea, and he would always give Gabriel fulsome praise for his efforts.

Carefully dunking a Digestive biscuit into his tea, Barney tried again.

"So, what's her name, I don't remember you saying?"

Barney smiled an innocuous smile at Gabriel, who was looking cornered.

"She's called Ginny."

Barney pondered on this.

"Short for something, is it?" Barney wondered, as if to himself.

Gabriel gave a 'don't know' sort of shrug.

"Old, fat and ugly, is she?" probed Barney.

Gabriel looked uncomfortable but saw Barney didn't mean any harm.

"Probably got warts as well," suggested Barney, chuckling.

"She's very … well …," Gabriel mumbled.

"Tell you what, Gabriel. We need some more tea bags. When you go for lunch, why don't you take twenty quid out of the tea fund? Get another box on your way back. And if you need to buy her a coffee and a sandwich, you might use the change from the twenty quid. That all right?"

Gabriel smiled over at Barney. He'd never had a Dad, or at least no one who had owned up to the responsibility. He wasn't sure if Barney had ever had kids, but he felt like Barney was taking on a stepdad role.

It was a marvelous feeling.

The Golden Egg   Friday 14th July 2017   12:35 pm

"Bugger, bugger, bugger."

The coffee shop was not far enough from the office to use his bike, so he thought a fast walk would do it.

There was probably nowhere to chain his bike to, anyway.

And then it was 12:35 pm and now Gabriel was running down the High Street.

He was a few minutes away from the coffee shop, but he really didn't want to upset Ginny. He didn't even know the girl, but he wouldn't want to make her cross with him. He imagined her sitting there alone in the coffee shop, looking at her watch. It's 12:40 pm, and the waitress has been over twice asking if she wants to order anything. Each time Ginny has pointed to her watch, giving that 'he'll be here in a minute' look, but finally, giving a wry smile to the waitress, she gets up to go.

12:42 pm and Gabriel gets to the door of the Golden Egg.

Ginny is sitting at a table for two, looking out of the window. She is smiling to him and beckoning him to go in.

"I've already ordered myself a coffee. Sorry ... I didn't know what you would like to drink."

"Sorry I'm late," Gabriel muttered.

"Somebody wanted to take that chair," Ginny said, pointing at the other chair at her table. "I said no. I told them you'd be here in a minute."

Gabriel realised he was feeling hot and bothered from his dash down the High Street. He felt flushed and stupid. Not the entrance he was hoping to make.

"I'm glad you could make it," she said. "I wondered if you might be too busy to meet me here."

Gabriel smiled awkwardly.

"Or you might have forgotten."

Before Gabriel had the chance to say anything, Ginny called over to the waitress.

"Hi, Sally. Can we make an order?"

The waitress heard her and walked over.

"So, he turned up, eh?" the waitress said to Ginny. Obviously, they were friends.

"Just as good looking as you said, eh?" Sally continued.

Ginny looked back at her friend, with an expression Gabriel could not decipher.

"Anyway, what do you guys want?" Sally asked. "Just a drink, or are you dining?"

"I wouldn't mind a cup of tea and a cheese and onion sandwich on brown bread," Gabriel said, but stopped suddenly, looking very self-conscious.

"Sorry," he spluttered. "Ladies first … you order please Ginny."

"Quite the gentleman, eh?" Sally said, smiling pointedly at Ginny.

Ginny turned to Gabriel and gave his left hand a pat, as if to soften his embarrassment.

Gabriel startled and almost pulled his hand away from the shock of her touch. He realised his hand had shuddered, and he guessed Ginny would have sensed it, but he rested it calmly back on the table.

Ginny re-settled her hand, leaving it resting lightly on his. "A cheese and pickle sandwich, please," Ginny said to Sally.

"White, brown or granary?" Sally said, chuckling to herself.

Gabriel saw she was amused about something, but he couldn't make out what.

"Brown please," said Ginny. "That would be nice. Thank you."

"I've got it," Sally said. "Be back soon. See you later, Ginny."

Ginny turned back to look at Gabriel. Keeping hold of his left hand, she ran her fingers up his wrist.

"Isn't that John's old watch?" she asked.

"He gave it to me," Gabriel said, perhaps a little too strongly. "Honestly … he gave it to me the last time I saw him."

"I know," Ginny said, smiling. "I asked him where it had gone, and he said someone else needed it."

Gabriel nodded.

"Funny thing to say about an old watch, don't you think?" she continued.

"How do you mean?"

"Well ... a watch is only used to tell the time but saying someone else needs it (she held her hands up as if to put quotes around the words 'needs it'), well, that makes it sound like it does more than just tell the time."

Gabriel looked both startled and awkward.

"Well, don't you think so?" she asked.

"It's only a watch," he said unconvincingly.

She put her hand back on the old watch, running her fingers over it, as if she were caressing the case and the dial.

"It feels funny," she said, "as if it's not really that shape at all. As if it is pretending to look like that, but really it is something else."

Gabriel looked at the watch. He felt foolish in her presence, as if she had outsmarted him on something he should have known about.

Ginny let her right hand stay on Gabriel's wrist, but with her left hand she leaned over and stroked the side of his face.

"I'm sorry, Gabriel. People say that I, well, that I sense things that aren't there."

Gabriel sat motionless. He didn't want her to move her hand away.

"People also say I'm too tactile," she continued. "Touching things, touching people. You'll tell me if I make you feel uncomfortable, won't you?"

Gabriel felt her hand pressed lightly against his cheek. The warmth of her fingers seemed to make his skin feel alive, feel vibrant. She smelled of a summer's day; she smelled of apples and peaches.

"I'm sorry," she said suddenly, taking her hands away from him. "I didn't mean to make you feel uncomfortable. I should learn not to do that."

She put her hands palm down firmly on the table, as if to restrain them, in case they should try to touch him again.

"Put your hands on hers," Vicky whispered.

Gabriel reached out his hands, gently enclosing each of hers within his own. He smiled at her, and she looked up and smiled back. The most joyous and welcoming smile he had ever seen.

"Well, this is nice, isn't it?" said Sally, carrying a tray on which was a cup of tea and two plates of sandwiches.

Where's the tea bags? Friday 14th July 2017 2:10 pm

The Gazette Office – Frinton-on-Sea

"So, she turned up, eh?" queried Barney.

"Er ... yes, she did, thanks," replied Gabriel.

"Had a nice time, did you?"

"Lovely thanks."

"Much to talk about, it being a first date and all?"

Barney chuckled quietly to himself, whilst fumbling around for something in a desk drawer.

"And you got the tea bags?" asked Barney, almost unable to contain himself.

Gabriel looked up. The tea bag purchase had completely slipped his mind.

"I'm sorry," apologised Gabriel, getting up to get some.

"Not to worry," said Barney. "I thought you might forget, so I nipped out and got some myself. Fancy a nice cuppa?"

One Cool Customer   14th July 2017   5:55 pm

Gabriel cycled his way back home to Clacton. He was meeting Ginny that night at the Horseblanket, a little wine-bar on Clacton sea front.

Barney had asked Gabriel if he had asked her out, and Gabriel had said yes, but explained it was Ginny who had asked him out. As they were leaving the Golden Egg coffee shop, she had simply said she had the evening off, and she would meet him at the Horseblanket at 8pm.

She had taken it for granted he would come, and she had put her share of the coffee shop bill down on the table, kissed him politely on the cheek, smiled to her friend Sally and skipped out of the door.

"You're one cool customer," Barney had said, laughing good-naturedly.

"I tell you what," Barney continued. "You know you don't get paid until next Friday, but I went to the bank today, and I can't be arsed going there again. Are you ok if I pay you now? Oh, and I've slipped in a bonus for your care-home storyline. Is that all right with you, mate?"

So, Gabriel, who had never had a date with a girl before, not only had one tonight, but he also had some money to buy her a drink.

Can't stop thinking about her   Friday 14th July 2017   6:15 pm

Gabriel got off his bike and pushed it up the steps into his mum's flat. He left it in the hallway, along with all the rubbish his mum seemed to collect. She seemed to collect junk from everywhere and leave it lying about. Gabriel's mum's ways really ground him down. He needed to find a place of his own; if he could only get enough for a deposit and a regular salary to cover the rent. Barney seemed pleased with his work, and that gave him hope, but he wasn't sure his work on the paper justified keeping him on. He thought Barney might only keep him on for a short while, and after that what would he do?

"Are you going to tell Ginny about me?" Vicky asked.

"Are you home, mum?" Gabriel shouted, knowing it was highly likely she would be out at this time of day.

As he expected, there was no answer, and Gabriel made his way into the kitchen. As he had expected, there was no food of any description. He had shopped yesterday, so there should have been stuff left, so God knows what she had done with it. It wasn't like she ever cooked anything. Not unless you considered putting boiling water into tubs of Pot Noodles to be cooking. "For God's sake," he mumbled to himself, getting himself into the frame of mind to do another shopping expedition.

"So, are you going to tell her about me?" Vicky asked again.

Gabriel paused in his food deliberations to have this conversation that was evidently important to Vicky.

"I don't know," he said. "What do you think about her?"

"She seems very nice … very kind," Vicky proffered. "I think she likes you a lot."

Gabriel pondered on Vicky's words. He hadn't been sure what to think, and he felt he was too inexperienced to make a clear judgement.

"I think you're right, Vicky. She … well … she excites me."

Gabriel felt his cheeks glowing.

"I can feel your heart rate is going up, Gabriel," Vicky said. "Are you all right?"

"I'm not used to girls who … well … I'm not used to girls, full stop. But Ginny … well, I can't …"

"Can't what?"

"Can't seem to stop thinking about her."

"Oh," Vicky said.

Gabriel pulled out the rucksack he used when going to get some shopping.

"Shall I provide you with some food?" Vicky asked.

"Sorry ... what do you mean?"

"Well, as I mentioned before, I can request stores and equipment to my location."

"What sort of things?"

"Well, food supplies for example."

"Isn't that stealing?"

"Well, I think there is an argument to say that, as you are my client, and since I was designed to provide for the needs of my clients, I think I would be doing the job I was built to do."

"That all sounds very plausible," agreed Gabriel, "and to be honest, it would intrigue me to see what you can do."

"Ok. I will request a standard three-day traveller's food pack. Clear a bit of space on the table next to you."

Gabriel pushed some rubbish to one side. He stood up to watch.

There was a faint shimmering in the area he had cleared, and suddenly a container appeared. It looked like creamy plastic, semi-transparent, with various packets stacked snugly inside it.

"There is a small green button on the top of the container, in the middle. Press that and it will open," advised Vicky.

Gabriel saw the green button. He pressed it gently. There was a vague hissing noise, and the container peeled itself open. It was like watching flower petals slowly open.

"They designed these ration packs to be tasty, nutritious and exceptionally light to carry. Take one out. There are food sachets and water sachets. The water sachets are all pink. The food sachets are pale green, and they each say what they contain. Each food sachet makes up a single meal for one person. Each of the sachets has a trigger to activate them. The trigger on the food sachets activates a cooking process."

Gabriel took out a pink sachet.

"These water sachets are empty," Gabriel remarked. "They are flat. There is nothing in them."

"That's for reasons of weight, Gabriel. The trigger on those sachets activates a process to pull the necessary chemicals from the air to re-constitute water. Try it. Press the button on the side, then lay the sachet down."

Gabriel did so, and the sachet started to purr. Over the space of a few seconds, the sachet expanded. The sachet glowed a pale green colour.

"Ok, it's ready," said Vicky. "There is a small teat at one end of the sachet. You can either suck on that or squeeze the sachet into another container."

Gabriel picked up the sachet whilst looking around in the kitchen for a clean cup. Not finding one, he put the end of the sachet into his mouth and sucked on the teat. The water was icy. It was delicious. It was like he would have imagined water would be like coming from a mountain stream.

"Wow ... I didn't realise water could taste so nice," he said.

"Try one of the food sachets," suggested Vicky.

Gabriel took one at random.

"You can use the container sides as a plate if you like. If you hold one of the container sides, it will disconnect itself from the rest of the box."

Gabriel did as suggested, laying the container side on the kitchen table. Placing the food sachet on the top, he pressed the activation button. As with the water sachet, it made a soft purring noise. After half a minute it glowed a pleasant pale pink. A small tab extruded itself from next to the trigger button, blinking with a soft red light.

"Pull on the tab," suggested Vicky. "It will peel open."

Gabriel pulled gently at the tab, and the sachet opened, revealing a pale creamy paste. Steam rose from it slowly.

"It looks like mashed up chickpeas," suggested Gabriel.

"There is a small pack of cutlery in the container," said Vicky. "Give the food a try. It is supposed to be quite nice."

Gabriel looked in the container, and sure enough, there was a packet with a spoon and fork. Presumably, the food sachets contained nothing that needed cutting up. He took out the spoon. It seemed to be a semi-rigid plastic. Noticeably light and extraordinarily strong. He scooped up a small portion of the creamy paste and put it in his mouth.

"Wow. This stuff tastes incredible. It seems to have many flavours in it. Nothing like I would have imagined," Gabriel said.

"Remember, Gabriel," said Vicky. "ACME INC clients have paid vast sums of money for their time and space tours. They only expect the best. You are eating food designed for those customers. And this food, the one you are eating now ... this is their travel pack food. Designed to be stored in a backpack ... and eaten on the move."

"It's amazing, anyway," Gabriel said.

"I'm glad you like it," Vicky said.

Gabriel pondered as he ate the food.

"Vicky?"

"Yes? "

"Did you get these sorts of things for John? Did he understand you could do this stuff?"

"Yes, he did, Gabriel. He was fully aware of what my features and functions are. I think that is why he gave me to you."

"You remember when Ginny said she thought you didn't feel right, somehow?"

"Yes, I remember that, Gabriel."

"What do you think she meant?"

"I think she had recognised the difference between my actual physical form and my holographic representation."

"What?" Gabriel said, scooping up another mouthful of the creamy paste.

"Well ... this form you see in front of you ... it is just an image I thought would be acceptable when I first arrived."

"So, this old watch isn't really you?"

"No. Would you like to see my actual physical form?"

"I suppose so," Gabriel said, sounding nervous. A sudden image of a garish spider-like creature strapped to his wrist suddenly made him feel very apprehensive.

The air around his left wrist shimmered briefly, revealing a dull matte black band, one-inch wide, quite thin, with no visible markings on it. He touched it. It felt rubbery. It felt vaguely warm.

"It's made from plasteel," said Vicky. "Very, very strong, but with flexibility. They decided it would be the ideal material. Very well suited to the purpose."

"Why was I not able to feel what you are really like … when I put you on?" said Gabriel.

"The technology used to create the effect is registered as HOLO-FORM," said Vicky. "It isn't simply a localised physical representation. The technology generates a hologrammatic field which expands out roughly sixty feet from the object itself. It will influence anyone within that field's range to believe in what they see, even when they touch the physical object itself."

"So why could Ginny tell there was a difference?"

"I don't know," said Vicky.

"So, can you leave the form looking like it is now, but with a clock face on it?"

"If that is what you want. Would you like a traditional clock face, or a digital display, or …?"

As Vicky spoke, the simple black band went through a series of transformations, with various configurations of time and date appearing.

"That one," said Gabriel. "Yes … leave it looking like that, please."

Vicky's physical form now kept the simple matte black surface, but with slightly depressed luminescent green dimples for the hours and slightly raised faint pink hands depicting the time.

"Is that all right?" asked Vicky. "You can display whatever you wish."

"That's fine, thank you," replied Gabriel.

"Anyway Gabriel," said Vicky, "as I was asking before, when you meet Ginny tonight, are you going to tell her about me?"

"I don't know," replied Gabriel. "I haven't known her for long at all. I can't guess what she would do if I told her. Maybe she would tell her friends, and that would not be good."

"I imagine it would not."

"And she probably has lots of friends. She seems to be outgoing. I mean, she knew the waitress in the coffee shop, and …"

"Would you want to tell her," asked Vicky, in a way that struck Gabriel as being understanding of his thoughts.

"I think I would like to tell her," he said. "I think I would like to tell her everything. Everything about me … but … but I don't understand why."

"I think you have had a lonely life," suggested Vicky.

"I've had loads of mates," Gabriel said, somewhat defensively, "but nobody I felt I could really get on with."

"I think that's why John gave me to you, Gabriel," Vicky said.

Gabriel pushed some old magazines off a kitchen chair and sat down.

"How do you think he is?" said Gabriel.

"Who?"

"John. How do you think he will be? Will he have got worse yet?"

"I'm not sure, Gabriel. It's difficult to say, but as the days pass, he will surely deteriorate."

"Maybe if we went to see him … check his condition. Maybe that way if we went to see him every few days …"

"I'm not sure that is what he wanted," said Vicky. "I suspect he wished to stop having any further treatment that would extend his life. He had a hard life. Better than he might have expected, but losing his child, and then losing Mary to dementia … it was hard for him. I am sure if he had had the choice, he would rather Mary had been well, even for a little longer, so he might have continued to enjoy her company."

Gabriel pushed his spoon through the remaining creamy paste in the sachet.

"I think if he could change anything, it would be in his past; not to look for any pleasures in his future," Vicky said.

Gabriel stood up, picking up the empty food and drink sachets and shoving them into a black waste bag. He took the food pack container and shoved it behind the sofa bed that he slept on. He couldn't imagine his mum finding it, not when she didn't see all the rubbish already littering the flat.

"I'd better get going," he said. "I'd like to get to the Horseblanket before Ginny does. I don't want her to think I'm late for every meeting we have."

Still staring at my chest then? Friday 14th July 2017 7:50 pm

The Horseblanket was quiet at this time in the evening. The newly re-configured watch on his wrist told him it was 7:50 pm. He had already gone inside, checking if she was there yet. Then he had come back outside and sat on a low wall next to the entrance. He heard the club's background music playing through small speakers set up above the entrance. It wasn't loud, but sufficient to show to passers-bye what to expect when they went in.

"Your heart rate is going up quite a lot," said Vicky.

"She might not turn up," said Gabriel.

"Are you worried she won't, or are you worried she will?" queried Vicky.

 Gabriel didn't answer.

"Here she comes now," said Vicky, and Gabriel saw her off in the distance, coming towards him. She had a different T-shirt on. She had replaced her shorts with a pair of tight-fitting jeans. She still had on the hiking boots he had seen her in earlier. She had tied her hair up in a single ponytail. It swished from side to side as she skipped her way along the pavement.

"She never seems to just walk, does she?" Gabriel said.

"Sorry Gabriel," said Vicky. "Was that question addressed to me, or was it merely an observation you were making?"

"I mean, she always seems to sort of skip along," said Gabriel, not answering Vicky's question. "It's like she has too much energy to just walk like the rest of us."

As she got closer, he saw her T-shirt had the words printed

>   **Should I be**
>   **a warning**
>   **Or**
>   **an example?**

"Still staring at my chest?" she said, laughing.

Before Gabriel had the chance to get flustered and embarrassed, Ginny stood in front of him, raised herself up onto her toes and pulled his face down to hers, kissing him lightly on the mouth. She took his hand and pulled him into the doorway of the club.

. . . .

He had bought her a drink, feeling especially important. She had chosen half a pint of draught lager. He had asked her if she wanted one of the club's fancy cocktails, but she had politely declined. He thought she was quietly chuckling to herself, but he wasn't sure because of the noise of the music. He got himself a pint of an indifferent draught bitter and they went outside into the seating area at the back of the club. They had labelled it a smoking area, but it was the only place with comfortable seating and quiet enough to talk.

She found two rattan chairs. She pulled them together around a small wooden table. They were the only ones in this seating area now, and Gabriel suddenly felt very self-conscious. He couldn't think what to talk about.

"I see you've stopped wearing John's old watch," she said.

"Well, er …," Gabriel mumbled, caught off-guard by her observation.

"It looks very expensive," she said, "but I thought having John's watch as a gift meant a lot to you."

"It does," Gabriel replied.

Ginny looked quizzically at him.

"So that's why you're not wearing it?" she said.

She took hold of his left wrist and ran her fingers over the black plasteel band.

"Just a minute …," she said, looking shocked. "This is the same … it's the same thing I felt when I touched John's watch."

She pulled her hand away suddenly, looking very frightened, as though she couldn't understand what she was seeing or feeling.

She stood up, pushing her chair back as she did so. The table rocked; her drink toppled. Gabriel grabbed it and steadied it.

"I've got to go …," Ginny said. "I've got to go now."

Gabriel had no idea what to do, but he stood up with her.

"Tell her," said Vicky urgently. "I don't understand how but she seems able to see behind the hologram. I don't know how she is doing that, but it is frightening her."

Gabriel stood stock-still. He seemed to have lost the power of movement, and as he stood there, he saw Ginny turn to go.

"Tell her," repeated Vicky.

"Ginny. Ginny, stop, please," he said.

"I'm sorry, Gabriel," she said, "but there is something about you that frightens me. I'm sorry, but …"

She turned and made her way out through the bar.

Gabriel sat down again. He was too stunned to see Rebecca coming over towards him until she was standing right in front of him.

"So, you bought me a drink, eh?" Rebecca said, pointing to Ginny's glass of lager.

Gabriel looked up and groaned inwardly. He looked around to see who Rebecca was with. There was nobody in the immediate vicinity. At least nobody who looked like they might be with Rebecca.

"Pete's not up and about yet," Rebecca said.

Gabriel stared past Rebecca. Maybe Ginny would come back and …

"He's asked his mates to come see you," she said.

"Yeah?" Gabriel said. At this point in time, he didn't really care.

"Yeah. Pete's not someone to forget things like that," she said.

"No, I guess not," Gabriel said.

"Yeah … you'd better watch your …"

"Sorry, Rebecca," Gabriel said, "but I can't be arsed listening to you right now."

He stood up and walked out.

Someone to turn to   Saturday 15th July 2017   7:50 am

Ginny's shift at the care home started at 8 am, and so she got there at 7:50 am, just to be sure. She walked up to the main entrance and punched in the access code. It was a code only known by the staff. They changed it every week.

She walked down to the staff room and pulled her work smock out from her locker. She wasn't much looking forward to the shift, but she thought it would take her mind off Gabriel. She hadn't really been able to get any sleep all night, thinking over how he had looked as she had left.

He had looked so ... what ... so shocked, so desperate, so misunderstood.

And so sorry he had inadvertently scared her.

And then she had walked away from him.

Well, ran away to be more precise.

She had walked home with her mind in turmoil. She had been looking forward to the evening with him. She realised he was very shy and very inexperienced. She guessed he came from a difficult background, but she could also see he was a sweet boy.

And he looked like he might really care for someone. He didn't look like the other boys around the town. They were all full of bravado, keen to show off to their mates. You couldn't go out with one and feel safe. They were on the pull, and with them that easily ended in violence.

But she was sure that wasn't true of Gabriel. She couldn't imagine him going back to his friends with sordid tales of conquest.

But something really had frightened her as she had sat with Gabriel. She didn't understand what it was, but she had recognised those feelings before. When they told her to get the hell out, she reckoned it was wise to do so. But looking back, it wasn't Gabriel who had triggered the emotion. He wasn't even aware of what the problem was.

But she had jumped up and ran anyway, even though ...

And she realised she had probably hurt him a great deal.

"You ok, Ginny?" Monica asked.

Monica was fifty years old and had been working at the care home longer than Ginny. She was Ginny's co-shift worker today, and Ginny always got on with her.

They made each other laugh.

"Things on your mind?" Monica pressed on.

"Oh, you know ... boys ... that sort of stuff."

"Somebody been unkind to you?"

"No, it's not that," replied Ginny, "it's just that he frightened me."

Monica looked angry.

"I used to be with someone who gave me that shit," Monica snarled, "and I can tell you now ... you don't need to put up with it. If you want, I can ..."

"No, he's not ... well, I can't explain it," interrupted Ginny.

"You tell me if you need some help, love," Monica said, sounding genuinely concerned. "I understand only too well what it's like. Nobody needs that shit."

"Thanks Monica," Ginny replied. "If I need to, it's good there's someone to turn to."

"Anytime love," Monica said. "Any time, day or night. Do you understand? Day or night."

"Thanks Monica. I really don't think this boy would ever hurt me, but thanks for the offer, anyway."

Monica looked over at Ginny. She remembered that back when she was being hurt, she never thought it would continue being bad.

She had thought it would be all right.

She had thought if only she said the right things, did the right things, he wouldn't be angry with her ... be so angry he had to lash out ... lashing out at her until she cried and screamed.

It had taken the support from a good friend of hers to get her out of the situation.

She didn't think she could have done it on her own. She didn't want a sweet girl like Ginny to be trapped in a desperate situation with no one to turn to.

She made a promise to herself to keep an eye out for the girl, just in case.

Fragments of what remained   Saturday 15th July 2017 9:45 am

John heard the quiet knock on his door and guessed it would be Ginny.

"Please come in," he said.

"Is it ok if I tidy round a bit?" she asked.

John kept his little flat tidy himself. He dusted round and emptied the bins himself. He didn't cook for himself anymore, so he was grateful to accept the meals the care home provided. Mainly, though he was pleased to see the staff members, for the company they gave him. The other residents at the care home were extremely limited in their capacity for social interaction. They were often very tied up within what remained of their minds, offering occasional glimpses into who they were or what they had done, but these fragments popped up too infrequently for him to converse with them in any meaningful way.

Ginny put her little tray of cleaning gear down on the floor and pulled out a cloth and a squirty bottle of multi-surface cleaner. She squirted a few drops onto the cloth, then set about cleaning his shelves, carefully moving his odd bits and bobs around as she worked.

"Did you ever meet up with Gabriel?" John asked innocently.

Ginny looked over at John, and John saw tears welling up in her eyes.

"He seemed so nice, and … and you gave him your watch, and …," she said brokenly.

"What's the matter, Ginny?" John asked, suddenly very confused.

Ginny sat down on one of the two dining chairs. She began sobbing.

"I don't know," she mumbled, "he had your watch, but there was something about it, and then he … "

John walked over to where Ginny was sitting and tentatively put one hand on her shoulder.

"Did Gabriel show you my old watch?" he asked, "and did he tell you anything about it?"

"He was wearing it the other day," she explained, "but now he is wearing some fancy new thing. It's very modern, but that's not what worried me."

"What is it?" asked John.

"I touched your old watch, yesterday, when it was on his wrist," she explained, "but it felt very odd ... I can't explain why. And last night I touched the new fancy watch he was wearing, and somehow it felt like ..."

She looked alarmed to be recollecting the experience she was describing, and John sensed the tension in her.

"Ginny," John said, "I have given my old watch away, and I don't think it is any longer my place to explain about it, but somehow you have noticed something that ... well ... something that I didn't think anyone could."

Ginny turned in her chair and looked up at John's face. She saw the care in his eyes. She trusted him.

"I think you should go back and see Gabriel," John said.

Ginny looked alarmed, so he continued.

"Ask him to tell you about the watch. Tell him I asked him to. Tell him it's ok for him to do that."

"But what ...?" Ginny said.

"Ask Gabriel. Please tell him it's all right. Tell him he has to trust someone."

Ginny stood up and gave John a hug of thanks.

"Oh, and Ginny. Please tell him I am feeling all right at the moment."

Ginny looked confused.

"He might be worried," he said. "I'm sure Vicky will have told him everything, and that would be sure to alarm him."

"Who is Vicky?" Ginny asked, but John was wandering off to his bathroom. She reminded herself to find out about Vicky later.

Want to talk about it?   Monday 17th July 2017 morning

The Gazette Office - Frinton

Barney looked over at Gabriel, who had been sitting staring morosely at his laptop all morning.

Barney had been making the tea himself all morning. It was a job that normally Gabriel took pride in doing.

"Want to talk about it, Gabriel?" Barney asked worriedly.

"Nothing to talk about, Barney."

"You never know," Barney replied, feeling even more worried.

"I think I've blown it," Gabriel said. "And I don't understand why. I don't know what I should have done. I don't even …"

"I'll buy you a sandwich and a pint at lunchtime, mate," Barney offered, and Gabriel grunted in assent, but Barney took no consolation from it.

Who is Vicky?   Monday 17th July 2017 5:30 pm

The Gazette Office – Frinton

Barney and Gabriel got back from a solemn and quiet lunch. Barney had bought Gabriel a cheese and pickle sarnie and a coffee. Gabriel had said he wasn't in the mood for alcohol, so they had sat there watching the world go by.

It looked as though someone had sucked the life out of him.

Back at the office, Barney stopped trying to make conversation, to let Gabriel mull over whatever it was he didn't want to talk about. It was obvious to Barney what it would be, but if the lad didn't want to discuss it, there was no point in trying. Eventually he would mention it, and then, well, maybe Barney could offer some sort of advice.

Or just consolation, if that was all that was left.

At 5:30 pm Barney said he was finished for the day. "Whatever you've got left to do today, I'm sure it will keep until tomorrow," he said, in as jocular a tone as he could muster.

Gabriel flipped down the lid of his laptop, then stood up and picked up his jacket and rucksack.

They both made their way down the stairs, Barney first, opening the door that faced onto the High Street. He ushered Gabriel out, locking the door behind him.

As Barney turned to go, Gabriel muttered "Oh bugger … forgot my bike," but as Gabriel fumbled for his own set of office keys and turned to go back up to the office, he saw Ginny standing on the pavement, facing him.

Barney saw the young woman standing directly in front of Gabriel. She was looking upset, and Gabriel was looking flustered.

"Well, I'd better get going," Barney said, but then he leaned over and whispered into the young woman's ear, "he's a good lad, and I wouldn't like to see him upset."

As Barney made his way off down the street, Ginny turned to watch him go.

"What did he say to you?" Gabriel asked.

"I think he likes you," Ginny replied.

"I guess so," Gabriel replied.

"Who is Vicky, Gabriel?" Ginny asked. "Does she work with you?"

Gabriel looked more confused than ever.

"I spoke to John on Saturday. He said Vicky has probably told you everything, and it might have alarmed you."

She saw the glimmer of comprehension in Gabriel's face.

"Oh, and John said to say he is feeling all right at the moment, so you shouldn't worry."

Gabriel nodded in understanding.

"So why should he be telling me these things, Gabriel? And who is Vicky?"

Gabriel stood silently, wondering what he might tell her.

"Also, he said it's all right for you to tell me about the watch, whatever that means," Ginny said.

"Well ...," Gabriel said.

"Oh, and something else, he said," continued Ginny. "He said you should trust someone."

Gabriel felt a sense of relief.

"Let's find somewhere to sit down," Gabriel said. "I need to explain some things to you."

Ginny looked unsure.

"That's if you want to," he mumbled.

Gabriel turned, and set off slowly, walking down the High Street. He wasn't sure if Ginny was going to come with him. He looked furtively to his side and saw Ginny turning to catch him up. Gabriel had put his hands into the pockets of his jacket, but then Ginny caught up with him and he felt her pushing her hand into his jacket pocket. He felt her small fingers squeezing into the pocket alongside his own. He stopped walking and turned to face her. She looked as though she had been crying all day, and Gabriel felt his heart go out to her.

"Gabriel," she murmured, looking unsure what his reaction might be.

"Ginny ... I'm deeply sorry if ... well ... I realise you got scared. I've been thinking about you, worrying about you for, well ... for all the weekend. I understand we hardly know each other, but I wanted you to understand I would never ever hurt you."

"I've been thinking about you, as well," Ginny replied.

"Well, I think we need to talk about it," continued Gabriel, "and now you have spoken to John, well ..."

Her eyes were glistening, and she looked like she might cry at any moment.

Gabriel reached out and put his arms around her, hugging her tightly.

Ginny leaned forward and nestled against his chest, wrapping her own arms around him.

A passer-by looking over smiled at them as they cuddled on the pavement. He noticed Gabriel's face light up, unaware it was Gabriel's first smile of the day.

I let him use my body as payment   Monday 17th July 2017 early evening

Outside the Gazette Office – Frinton

"I've got a return bus ticket," Ginny said.

"Where to?"

"Back to Clacton ... that's where I live," Ginny explained.

"Oh."

Gabriel didn't like to mention he had come on his bike that day. True, he sometimes caught the bus to work, but only if it was raining.

"Yeah, that's fine," said Gabriel. "Let's go catch the bus."

The bus stop was only a few minutes' walk, and at this time of the evening there would be many people using the service. They saw the queue forming already.

Ginny got a seat. It was next to the aisle. Gabriel stood next to her, holding on with one hand on the back of her seat, the other on the handrail above. As the bus pulled away, she looked up and gave him a smile.

The bus trundled its journey back to Clacton.

"I didn't even realise you lived in Clacton," Gabriel said over the noise of the bus engine and the general hub-hub around them.

Ginny saw an old lady on an adjacent seat turning her head to catch their conversation.

"I live in a sumptuous apartment on the sea-front, owned by a very wealthy old man," Ginny replied, grinning.

Gabriel felt his jaw drop.

"I let him use my body as payment, instead of rent," she continued.

The old lady coughed and looked as though she might be about to choke on something.

Ginny half-turned towards the old lady.

"Wine-drop gone down the wrong way?" said Ginny concernedly, then turned to look up at Gabriel.

"Don't worry, Gabriel. The old guy won't be in. It's your turn tonight."

Gabriel looked as though he didn't know what to say.

"Just joking, Gabriel," she said.

Gabriel laughed a sigh of relief, feeling he ought to be savvier, more aware of Ginny's sense of humour.

"Yep, just joking," she repeated. "He will be in really, so you'll just have to take me in turns."

Ginny fell about laughing in her seat. A middle-aged woman sitting in the seat in front of Ginny had also heard the conversation and began chuckling to herself.

The 'next stop' sign on the bus showed 'Clact. Rail. Stn', and somebody nearby muttered to the man sitting next to them something about it being a quick trip.

"Yeah, I hadn't realised we had come so soon," the man replied.

"Happens to the best of us," chuckled Ginny, reaching up to press the button to tell the driver to stop.

· · · · · · · ·

As they got off the bus, Gabriel looked at Ginny to see what she planned to do.

"Sorry about that, Gabriel," Ginny said. "I saw her ear-wigging, and I couldn't resist."

"That's ok," Gabriel replied, strangely proud Ginny could come up with funny, if slightly disturbing repartee so easily.

"I think we should go somewhere quiet, if that's ok?" she suggested. "I think we need to talk about things."

"Where do you think?" replied Gabriel. He wasn't sure how this 'conversation' would work out, and he didn't want to push Ginny away again.

"There's an old shelter on the cliff-top, a short walk down from the Pier," suggested Ginny. "It gets busy during the day, but it will probably be quiet in the evening."

"Sounds like the sort of place for young lovers," quipped Gabriel, but instantly regretted saying it.

"Well, let's go see, anyway," said Ginny. "If it's busy, we'll find somewhere else."

As they walked the short distance through the town, down towards the Pier and the cliff-top, the evening sky darkened, with the likely promise of rain.

"Feels like there's a storm coming," Gabriel said.

"How do you mean?" Ginny replied.

"It's when the sky darkens, and you get these little breezes starting up."

Ginny looked at Gabriel curiously.

"Have you ever noticed?" Gabriel said. "Sometimes you might walk down the street, and suddenly a breeze seems to lift a few leaves. They just spiral up. Not like when it's a windy day or anything. It's like a little tornado. They just seem to suck up stuff from an exceedingly small area."

"And you think that's a storm front, do you?" Ginny chuckled.

Gabriel looked sheepishly back at her.

"I think that's why I'm starting to like you such a lot," Ginny said.

Before Gabriel responded, Ginny lunged up and gave him a quick kiss on the cheek.

"Come on, let's get to the shelter before the big storm breaks," she said, chuckling quietly.

From the Pier they saw the Victorian shelter fifty yards away. A couple were sitting in one side of it; on the side that looked out to sea. Ginny looked as if she was going to suggest somewhere else, but as she considered it, a slight drizzle began to fall. Instantly the couple in the shelter got up and made their way to their car.

Ginny tugged Gabriel along and they sat down in the old shelter where the couple had recently vacated.

"The seat's still warm," Ginny noticed.

"Ginny?" Gabriel said. "You remember you were asking about Vicky."

"Yes," Ginny replied cautiously.

"Well, you remember the watch that John had. The old watch he used to wear?"

"Yes, I know the one you mean, Gabriel."

"Well, that watch is an electronic device. One that came from the future."

Ginny looked at Gabriel with a very sceptical look.

"Is this a joke, Gabriel, because if it is …"

"John found it seventy years ago," continued Gabriel. "It came here by mistake, and after John found it, it stayed with John. It helped him. It cured him. Before it helped him, John couldn't talk, he couldn't do anything."

"Gabriel!" Ginny said, warningly.

"I realise this is difficult to understand, Ginny. I hardly believed it myself. But this is what John meant when he told you to tell me I needed to trust someone."

Ginny gasped, recollecting her conversation with John.

"John gave me his watch, Ginny. This is it on my wrist."

He held his arm out in front of her, pulling back the sleeve of his jacket.

"That's not John's watch," she said.

"It is, Ginny. This is John's watch. He gave it to me as a present. It is the most valuable thing he has, and it keeps him in good health. It stops him from relapsing into his former state of catatonia."

"So why doesn't it look like John's watch?"

"It's a device from the future. It can assume the shape of whatever it wants. It's a thinking machine, Ginny. It has a voice. It has a personality."

"And my name is Vicky," the STU said. "I'm incredibly pleased to meet you, Ginny. I'm sorry I scared you before."

Gabriel clutched Ginny's hand tightly, seeing the tension and apprehension in her face.

"I use a holographic generator to assume the shape that you see. Without it, I'm simply a matte black plasteel band. Can I show it to you, Ginny? That's if you don't mind, Gabriel?"

"Go ahead," Gabriel said.

Ginny said nothing. Gabriel sensed her tension.

The watch on Gabriel's hand seemed to shimmer slightly, resolving into the old-style watch John had worn.

It shimmered again, revealing a matte black circlet enclosing Gabriel's wrist.

"This is my natural form," Vicky said. "And now I will change back to the shape Gabriel chose."

Ginny tentatively reached out and touched the watch, feeling the contours, trying to imagine the basic shape underneath it.

She laughed. "That's amazing," she said.

"What's amazing, Ginny, is that you can detect that this holographic image isn't real. For most people, the image I send overrides most people's senses, both visual and their sense of touch."

"So why ...?" said Ginny.

"I don't know. It's as though your sensory perception ... your touch saw past the holo image. You felt the actual shape underneath. And that I think is what frightened you."

Ginny stared at Gabriel's wrist, at the shape Gabriel had chosen.

"It's very uncommon, believe me," said Vicky.

"Are you all right, Ginny?" Gabriel asked.

"I'm ... I'm ... well ... I suppose ...," said Ginny.

"It is a lot to take in, is it not?" said Vicky.

Ginny looked out to sea.

"Are you ok?" Gabriel said, almost in a whisper.

Ginny turned and looked back at Gabriel, then looked down at the watch.

She smiled.

"I'm sorry, Vicky," Ginny said. "I guess I must seem very rude. As you say, it's a lot to take in. But, yes, I'm pleased to meet you. But it's so hard ... so hard to take in. It's like something from ... from Star Wars or something. It's ... well ..."

"It's a pleasure meeting you," Vicky said.

Tricky one   Monday 17th July 2017 8 pm

The old Victorian shelter - Clacton sea front

Gabriel smiled to hear Ginny conversing with Vicky. She was asking questions he hadn't thought to ask. She had asked how the space and time travel company that Vicky represented had come about.

"It's complex," Vicky said. "And lengthy as well."

"Well, can you sort of summarise it a bit?" Ginny said.

"I will try," Vicky said. "I suppose it began when the Earth ran out of its basic mineral wealth."

"I guessed we would screw it up eventually," Ginny said.

"Well, anyway," Vicky said, "there was the beginning of shortages, and no obvious way to provide substitutes. Suggestions had been made to send rockets into space to identify alternative sources, but no single country, or group of countries, were prepared to invest in such a huge undertaking. Eventually, in the year 2053, a consortium of exceptionally large companies formed the Space Exploration Group, SEG as it became known. Participating companies paid vast sums of money into the venture to reach other planets, extract their mineral resources, and then ship them back to Earth."

"As soon as 2053?" Ginny said.

"It was in 2053 it became obvious," Vicky said. "As Blahnik famously said, 'Mankind hasn't hit the brick wall yet ... but we can all see the bloody thing.'"

"Sounds like he was pissed off," Ginny said.

"I believe he had been trying to get a common agreement amongst world leaders for quite some time," Vicky said. "It took a throwaway comment at the end of an international symposium to get the sound-bite he needed."

"Well ... I guess if he finally got the message across ..." Ginny said.

"I suppose so," said Vicky. "And SEG realised there would not be a short-term solution to the problem ... so they thought they had best get started."

"So, was there interplanetary travel and time-travel available in 2053?" Gabriel asked. "It doesn't seem that far into the future."

"No ... not at that point in time, Gabriel. There had been advances in rocket propulsion, robotics etc, as you would no doubt expect. But there was not the capability to reach other planets and ship back mineral resources. Not in any workable timeframe, anyway."

"So, what did they ...?" said Gabriel.

"They decided to build spacecraft, 'probes' they were called, which could begin searching for planets capable of yielding the required mineral resources," said Vicky.

"It wasn't a fresh idea," said Ginny. "We're already sending out probes ... right now."

"That is true, Ginny," Vicky confirmed, "but the probes being sent out now are severely limited. They are limited by the time they will take to complete their missions, and their payloads are tiny compared to those sent on the SEG probes. The SEG probes had the capacity to search out planets with the required resources, and at which point they would place beacons on the ones found suitable. The beacons would identify the locations of the mineral deposits. The probes would then move on, repeating the process elsewhere."

"Sounds a lengthy process," said Gabriel.

"That's right," said Vicky. "They envisaged it would take years. Remember, they never considered this was going to be a short-term process. There was no 'quick win'. Many of the people who originally signed up agreements to join SEG anticipated they would be dead before anything tangible was found."

"I wonder how many people would do that these days?" Ginny wondered.

"So, anyway," continued Vicky, "as the probes were searching out suitable planets, improvements in rocket propulsion systems allowed fleets of mining vessels to be built and sent to the designated planets. The improved rocket motors meant the mining vessels got there faster. Improved robotics meant mining sites could be built without having to send real-live engineers, and within a brief space of time, shipments of extracted product were being transported back to the Earth. By 2083 there were three mining planets operational. Each planet could make three-monthly shipments back to Earth."

"So, it took SEG thirty years before it had products to sell?" Gabriel said.

"And at that stage," said Vicky, "the cost of extracting the product and shipping it back to Earth was very substantial. It appeared to have been massively under-estimated in the original costings. Many people thought the entire project had been a ghastly mistake ... an attempt by the original SEG board members to gain great reputations ... to be regarded as the saviours of mankind, when in practice they had brought their original companies to their knees, deep in debt, and SEG looked as if it would suffer the same fate."

"It sounds as though the entire space venture was a misguided …," Gabriel said.

"And perhaps it would have foundered at that point," said Vicky, "but such a massive undertaking as SEG's creates … creates secondary waves let's say. The entire enterprise had generated interest … interests which sparked off technological advances in other areas. An improved rocket propulsion system was discovered. It was called Ramstat, and it massively reduced the time for shipping products back to the Earth. It also meant that live people … engineers typically, might be shipped out to maintain the off-world mining colonies. Shortly after that, a French company called CrYO-GEN developed a means by which they could put people on long space flights into a state of suspended animation. Their products, known as CrYO-PODs were installed on all SEG spacecraft. So, suddenly, space flights were shorter, and with the advantage that you slept through the entire voyage. These factors really helped SEG to recruit engineers willing to act as maintenance crew on their extraction sites."

"But we still haven't got into time travel," Ginny noted.

"No, Ginny, and in fact that particular invention came about via a strange route."

"How do you mean?" Ginny said.

"Well, SEG-COMMS, a sub-division of SEG had been given the task of developing a faster means of communicating between SEG's Earth base and the off-world sites. They came up with a system which they called WORM-LYNK. That would have been in 2135. WORM-LYNK exploited inter-stellar wormholes for the transmission of data. It enabled the almost instantaneous transfer of high volumes of data across very great distances."

"But what did that have to do with time travel?" said Gabriel.

"What indeed?" said Vicky. "Research into a faster means of transporting things (and people) across vast distances had been under way for many years, but, in 2156, a thirty-five-year-old Spanish technologist called Sofia Carvallo saw the means of using the now quite old WORM-LYNK technology; using it as a means of not only transmitting data but also objects. She was working independently for a small techno-comp in Seville when she saw the potential for using this old technology. ACME INC contacted Sofia, and she agreed to join them. She joined their staff in April of the year 2157. She started with a massive amount of funding, and with seemingly limitless technical resources and equipment."

"In the year 2159," continued Vicky, "with the resources supplied by ACME INC, Sofia Carvallo built a prototype machine that used WORM-LYNK technology to ship not only data but also inert objects across large distances. By 2162 Sofia Carvallo's team had improved their prototype, such that not only inert objects but, crucially, 'warm bodies' could be transported safely. ACME INC realised they were ready to market this new shipping method. They formed a new subsidiary company, which became known as ACME-SHIPPING."

Vicky paused.

Gabriel and Ginny waited for her to resume.

"Anyway," Vicky continued, "ACME-SHIPPING got an agreement with SEG to replace their fleets of spacecraft with the new WORM-LYNK instantaneous matter transfer service. That would have been in 2164. Within several months of installing ACME-SHIPPING's transmitter/receiver equipment, the off-world extraction processors were shipping their product back to the Earth as soon as they had extracted it."

"And we still haven't got to time travel," Ginny observed.

"No," said Vicky, "but we very nearly have. It was after the ACME-SHIPPING transport processing had been fully implemented that Sofia Carvallo's team noticed that some shipments didn't arrive instantaneously. Some arrived with slight delays. Her team investigated this anomaly. They found that the WORM-LYNK process could be configured to use time as a variable. They found it was possible to make a shipment appear with a delay … a delay of minutes, days, even weeks. And interestingly, they found that the objects shipped were not affected by the delay. Further investigation showed they could send shipments which …"

"Got there sooner?" said Ginny excitedly.

"Exactly that," said Vicky. "They got there … before the time they were sent."

"Time travel," said Ginny.

"And found out by accident," observed Gabriel.

"Probably not the first time that somebody discovered something by accident," said Vicky a little tersely.

"So, then what …?" said Ginny.

"ACME INC saw they had discovered something … something monumental," said Vicky. "There had long been an interest … by the general public that is, in the off-world mining planets. SEG had set up its own tourism sub-division to cater to the interest, but ACME INC saw that with space/time travel, there was an amazing opportunity to tap into that market. And it would be an unbelievably valuable market. The people interested in such an offering were fabulously wealthy. They could, and would, pay vast sums to use such a service."

"I guess they would," Ginny said.

"So, ACME INC considered how it should best provide such a service. They set up a team of people tasked with identifying places, or more precisely times and places, both on the Earth and off-world, where wealthy tourists might wish to visit. An exceptionally large undertaking, as you can imagine."

"I suppose so," said Gabriel.

"Sounds like a marvellous job to have had," remarked Ginny. "I didn't see that advertised, the last time I was in the Job Centre."

"Why ... do you think 'time and space explorer' sounds more interesting than working in an old people's home?" said Gabriel.

"I shouldn't be too critical," Vicky said, "since that was where you two met."

"That's true," Ginny said, and she gave Gabriel's hand a squeeze.

"Anyway," Vicky continued, "ACME INC looked for places their potential clients might wish to visit, and for all the selected times and places they logged their spatial coordinates."

"How do you mean?" Gabriel asked.

"Well, if you are going to teleport to somewhere ... somewhere in time and space, you need extremely specific coordinates. That is because the Earth and the respective off-world planets are continually moving through time and space. If you wish to teleport to another planet, you need to be aware of precisely where that planet is at any specific point in time. In addition, you also need to know where the location you are aiming for is physically situated on that moving planetary object. And as if that weren't complexity enough, geo-physical activities on a planet, such things as earthquakes for example, can be big enough to affect the angle of the planet's rotation, or the rate of its spin. ACME INC realised they would need to keep a data store of all the coordinates related to all the potential places a client might wish to go. And they would need to keep that list of coordinates updated continually."

"Sounds like a vast amount of work," said Gabriel, "and that's what they presumably would have needed to do before they even marketed the service."

"Indeed. That is the case," said Vicky. "ACME INC realised they needed to get their coordinates information correct, because the implications of getting them wrong were too terrible to contemplate."

"How do you mean?" Gabriel said.

"Well ... if the coordinates were wrong, you might teleport someone into space, into a mountain, into anywhere. And their potential clients would be wealthy and important people. In the event of a client not returning from a tour, they were the kind of people who would have families, friends or business partners who would be capable of bringing massive pressure on ACME INC for compensation. They would be the kind of people who would probably bring a company to its knees."

"And no-one would want to use such a service again, not after such an incident," said Ginny.

"Yes," said Vicky. "So, you can see why getting the coordinates correct was so important."

"I guess you have got to get them right ... or ... don't do it at all," said Gabriel.

"And then there was the problem with the teleporter technology," said Vicky. "Sofia's team had built teleports to be used for shipping enormous quantities of extracted minerals. The teleport devices themselves were massive. If they intended to transport individual clients, they needed something smaller. Something much smaller."

"What, do you mean something that fits onto your wrist?" Ginny said.

"Exactly like that," Vicky agreed. "Sofia's team worked on the development of these personal 'space / time units', STUs as they became known. They released the first viable model onto the market in October 2175."

"And are we looking at one right now?" Ginny asked.

"Well ... a slightly later model, anyway," said Vicky. "And," she continued, "you should realise the idea was tremendously successful. ACME INC was inundated with potential clients wishing to use the service. Even though the price of such tours was 'upon request', this did not deter the very wealthy from putting in immediate orders for tours. ACME offered its clients the option to travel to anywhere ... anywhere on the Earth or any of the off-world mining planets, with a timeframe plus or minus 250 years. We, that is STUs, issued teleports to those locations, looking up the coordinates from a database used to store that information. And in addition, we issued requests for 'supplies', which might comprise food and equipment. Equipment meant such things as clothing, weapons, conventional transport ..."

"How do you mean, 'conventional transport'?" Gabriel asked.

"Well, for example, we could request a small Ramstat flyer, suitable for getting about on a planet's surface, we could even request a modularised space-craft. That way we ..."

"A space-craft?" said Ginny. "Wouldn't they be so big that ...?"

"A space-craft from the era of my manufacture would have no similarity to the ones of this era," Vicky said.

"But why would anyone request a space-craft," Gabriel asked, "if they could simply teleport to somewhere straightaway?"

"ACME INC offered many things," explained Vicky. "They did not limit the needs of their wealthy clients. They assumed they might well wish for ... well, wish for anything. So, ACME INC provided ... everything."

"So, we've got to the part where time travel has been developed," said Ginny. "Now, how do you explain how you came to be here. Something went wrong, didn't it?"

"Yes, Ginny. You are correct. And my best guess is the database of coordinates was corrupted. When I tried to teleport my last client ... well, my last 'official' client, I think the coordinates they gave me were incorrect."

"How could that be ...?" said Gabriel.

"I don't know," said Vicky. "They house the coordinates database in a very secure place. It would not have been easy for someone to get to it."

"And why would someone do such a thing, anyway?" Ginny asked.

"Again, I do not know," said Vicky. "It may have been industrial espionage. ACME INC's time travel business impacted heavily on other businesses. Perhaps ..."

"But if someone has broken the coordinates database, how is it you can request things ... and they get here ok?" said Gabriel.

"When I submit a request for an item, I specify my own spatial coordinates. All STUs are aware of their own spatial coordinates. A request process does not need to reference the coordinates database. ACME simply sends the requested item to where I am at that point in time."

"But when you teleport ... when you try to take a client somewhere else ...?" said Ginny.

"When I teleport, I use my own spatial coordinates as my start point, but the coordinates database sends me the coordinates for the specified destination."

"And that is where the problem occurs?" Gabriel said.

"I believe so," said Vicky. "It appears the end point coordinates being passed back have been corrupted."

"But," said Ginny, "the problem that caused you to arrive here ... that happened a long time ago. Maybe they have fixed the coordinates database. Maybe it isn't a problem anymore."

"That may be true, Ginny, but the only way to try it out would be to try to teleport somewhere. And if it hasn't been fixed ..."

"Tricky one, eh?" Gabriel said.

It's getting cold   Monday 17th July 2017   10:30 pm

The old Victorian shelter - Clacton sea front

The rain had settled into a steady downpour, with thick clouds hiding any light from the moon. Waves tumbled sand, and small pebbles up and down the beach.

Ginny and Gabriel sat quietly in the darkness.

"Hug me tighter please, Gabriel," Ginny said. "I'm getting cold, and it's too wet to set off home. I'd be wet through in no time."

"Back to your fancy flat on the sea-front?" said Gabriel, wrapping his arms around Ginny, hugging her against his chest.

He smiled quietly in the darkness.

"Can I provide you with a warm and waterproof coat, Ginny?" Vicky asked.

"What ... really?" said Ginny, snuggling into Gabriel's warmth. "I remember you said you could do that stuff, but I didn't really think ..."

"It is what I do," Vicky said. "I provide for my client's needs."

"Well I guess so," Ginny replied, "but what sort have you got?"

Instantly a glowing panel of light appeared in the darkness in front of them. On it were jackets and other items of clothing. The images slowly scrolled upwards.

"You can point and drag to control the display," Vicky advised.

"What ... like Smart TVs?" Ginny said.

"Possibly," said Vicky, unsurely.

Ginny tried various hand gestures. The display scrolled up and down.

"I think you have got the idea," said Vicky. "I remember it took a long time for John to get the idea how to control my visual interface ... but he had never seen or experienced the technologies that you probably use every day."

"I guess so," Ginny said.

"Anyway, please point to anything that you like," said Vicky.

"Wow ... there's some cool stuff," said Ginny. "I really like the steam punk styles."

"It was a style which became very popular at the time of my manufacture," said Vicky. "My client, the one before John ..."

"You mean the one who died?" interrupted Gabriel.

"Yes, that one," continued Vicky. "Anyway, he bought shares in the company that developed the steam punk couture. It made him very wealthy. Wealthy enough to buy an ACME INC tour."

"Didn't do him much good though, did it?" remarked Gabriel.

"Hey. How about that jacket? That one there," Ginny said, pointing, "but how about in green?"

"You can change the colour as and when you wish," Vicky advised. "It is one of the CHAMELO range."

"Well, if that's possible, I would love one of those," said Ginny excitedly.

"Ok, I will request one," said Vicky, and instantly a soft glow appeared on the bench to the side of where Ginny was sitting. As the glow dissipated, Ginny and Gabriel noticed something had appeared on the bench. It was enclosed in a transparent compression bag. Ginny lifted the bag and tugged at the seal. There was a faint hiss, and the bag opened to reveal the jacket Ginny had requested. Ginny pulled it out and slipped the jacket on. Instantly it molded itself to her form.

"Feel under the left lapel," said Vicky. "That's where the Chameleon controls are."

Ginny felt under the lapel, finding a small button. She pressed it gingerly. A panel on the right sleeve lit up on which was a colour selection facility. It offered a colour palette, plus an option to select some standard patterns. She tried out several, and the jacket responded instantly: a seascape, a cloudy sky, a field of corn swaying in the breeze.

"Some of those things hurt your eyes," Gabriel suggested.

Ginny pressed an option shown as an image of a lizard. Instantly the jacket adopted the colouration of where she was sitting. Anyone walking past her would have been hard pressed to see her ... well, her upper body wearing the jacket, anyway.

Ginny laughed and picked a pale green from the standard colour palette, and the jacket adopted the colour she had had in mind from the start.

"I think that will do nicely, thanks Vicky," she said.

"I don't suppose you want a hug, now you have a nice warm jacket?" Gabriel said.

Ginny leaned back into his arms, snuggling up to him, nuzzling her face against his.

"A warm jacket isn't everything," she said. "A fancy spaceship would be better right now. Something we could use to fly us back home in this rain," she said.

"I will see if there is one available, if you like," said Vicky.

"Can you really do that?" said Gabriel. He wasn't laughing.

"ACME INC imposed no limits on its clients. The clients paid for all items requested anyway, so it was not a problem," explained Vicky.

"But we don't have any money … not even the money to pay for a jacket," Gabriel said.

"I think ACME would bill my last official client's account," Vicky explained.

"But he's dead," Ginny said.

"But ACME INC aren't aware of that, are they?" Vicky said.

"I suppose not," Ginny said.

"Vicky?" Gabriel said.

"Yes, Gabriel."

"A spaceship … a spaceship would be huge, wouldn't it? said Gabriel.

"Yes, they are big … but you might be surprised to know that they come in a modular format. ACME don't know what will be requested specifically, so spacecraft are provided 'tailored to fit'."

Ginny laughed. "What, like furniture from IKEA, do you mean?" she said.

"I am not sure, Ginny."

"Wouldn't it need a launch pad and everything?" queried Gabriel.

"No," said Vicky. "A launch pad would not be necessary."

"So, does that mean we could get a spaceship … and use it to fly to another planet?" asked Gabriel.

"Yes, that would be possible, Gabriel."

"Wow," said Gabriel, "but wouldn't it take years to get to another planet?"

"The journey time would only be days or weeks," explained Vicky, "but even if it took a long time, each spacecraft is equipped with CrYO-PODS. You could be in a CrYO-POD for years and awaken feeling refreshed, as if you have had a good night's sleep."

. . . .

"What's on your mind?" Ginny said.

"How do you mean?" said Gabriel.

"You look ... you look troubled."

"I am worried about John," Gabriel admitted. "As Vicky said, without her continued medical assistance, he is likely to lapse back to his previous state in a very short while."

"And?" said Ginny.

"Maybe if we got to the future ... to see the people at ACME, well, perhaps they would give us a STU for John. I couldn't bear to think of John lapsing back, unable to speak or move," said Gabriel.

"Gabriel," Vicky said. "I think I have explained that ACME are unlikely to grant you another STU. Experience would suggest that ..."

"Yes ... I understand that Vicky, but I still think it would be worth a try," Gabriel said.

Ginny sat quietly, thinking about what Gabriel had said. She felt awful that she had been so pleased when Vicky had got her the CHAMELO jacket, forgetting the actual cost that was being exacted on John to give her that opportunity.

"I'm sorry Gabriel," Ginny said. "I think I'd forgotten the consequence of John making this gift to you."

"To us," Gabriel interjected.

"Ok, to us," said Ginny. "Well, I think I'd forgotten that whilst we sit here requesting coats from Vicky to keep us warm and dry, John's health is getting worse."

"Ok," said Gabriel. "No worries. We have remembered now, and I would like to do something for John. Something before it's too late."

"But Gabriel," Ginny said. "Even if ACME will give us another STU, if someone has corrupted the database of coordinates, I can't see how we could remotely get to the future. It seems more likely we would die trying. Are you willing to take that chance?"

"Gabriel?" Vicky said.

"Yes, Vicky."

"If it's ok with you, I would like to shut down for a little while. I think I need time to process some things."

"Oh, sure Vicky ... I didn't realise you went off line," said Gabriel.

"Well, it's a feature you can request. You might not always want me to be aware of all that you do ... in every minute of your waking day."

"Sure Vicky. I understand," Gabriel replied. He felt his cheeks burning in the darkness.

"If you need me urgently, you can just tap me lightly."

"Ok Vicky."

"Or I can register if your pulse rate escalates dramatically ... but you might not want me to pick up on that one."

Ginny chuckled and squeezed Gabriel's hand.

"No ... perhaps you're right, Vicky," Gabriel said. "Ok, catch you in the morning."

"Goodnight," Vicky said.

Gabriel and Ginny sat quietly for a moment.

"Come on Ginny. I will walk you home," Gabriel said.

"You don't even know where I live."

"Time to find out."

Walking to Ginny's house   Monday 17th July 2017 11:45 pm

"Did you realise Vicky could turn off?" Ginny asked.

Gabriel and Ginny were walking into the outskirts of Clacton. Gabriel had not known where she lived until five minutes earlier. She lived about half a mile from his mum's flat. They walked along the pavement, avoiding the puddles left by the rain, which had now mercifully stopped.

"No, I didn't realise that. Neither Vicky nor John mentioned it."

"Do you think she needs to power down now and again?" said Ginny.

"I don't think so," said Gabriel. "I think she wanted to give us some time alone together."

"I guess that for a ... what did she call herself ... an artificial intelligence unit ... one designed to learn and develop from contact with clients, well, if your usual client contact is ten days, but then you stay with somebody for seventy years, well, perhaps you become sort of ...," Gabriel said.

"... become more human?" finished Ginny.

A van came down the road, close to the kerb where they were standing. Gabriel tugged at Ginny's arm to stop, seeing a puddle in the road ahead. They stopped, and the van's tyres sent a small plume of water up onto the pavement where they would otherwise have been standing.

Ginny smiled to herself in the darkness.

They resumed walking.

"It's just around the corner," said Ginny.

"Oh, ok," said Gabriel, somewhat disappointed. "I thought it might be further than that."

Ginny looked at Gabriel and laughed. "Do you want to come on up? It's only a small flat, and I share it with another girl, but she's away for a few days. You can come and have a cup of tea before you set off home."

Gabriel looked at Ginny, unsure what to do.

"If it's not too late for you," she said, chuckling.

Gabriel looked at the time read-out on Vicky, but suddenly perceived that checking the time might be the wrong thing to do.

"It's quarter to midnight," Ginny said, in a tone Gabriel could not make sense of.

"For God's sake, Gabriel," Ginny said, in mock exasperation. "We might travel in space sometime very soon. If you are bold enough to do that, you should be bold enough to go back to a girl's flat."

Gabriel laughed in a self-conscious way.

"Come on," Ginny said, pulling Gabriel up a small flight of stairs up to her flat. "I'll put the kettle on."

Ginny pulled out a key and opened the door at the top of the flight of stairs. Gabriel noticed the door had a yellow post-it-note stuck on it that said

> **This flat belongs**
> **To Ginny and Moth,**
> **If you're not a friend**
> **Please bugger off**

"Who is Moth?" Gabriel asked.

"It's short for Mothwell-Barrett. Elizabeth Mothwell-Barrett. Apparently, she got called Moth at school, and it sort of stuck."

Ginny pushed open the door to the flat and felt along the wall to her right. He heard a switch click, and the room became dimly lit by the glow from a small table lamp and a set of fairy lights.

Ginny rushed around, quickly picking up things and pushing them behind cushions on the sofa.

Gabriel stood mesmerised. He hadn't been in a girl's flat before. He hadn't known what to expect but had guessed it would be tidier than his mum's flat.

Ginny turned to Gabriel and gave a shrug. She looked a bit embarrassed to have to tidy up a mess, but Gabriel couldn't really see why she was concerned.

"Sit yourself down," Ginny called as she made her way into what Gabriel assumed would be the kitchen.

An old sofa took up most of the space in the small living room in which he was standing. It was very old, with stuffing poking out of the seams. It faced towards a charity-shop sideboard, on which were a small pottery horse and a relatively small flat-screen TV. The small table lamp sat on top of the sideboard, to one side of the TV. A string of Christmas fairy lights were taped to the picture beading. The tiny lights were slowly repeating a phase of brightening up and then slowly fading away.

Gabriel heard a tap being turned on, and water filling up what presumably was a kettle.

"I find those fairy lights a bit …," Gabriel said.

"I'll adjust them," Ginny said. "They get on my nerves as well. Moth likes them like that, but … I think if I were here a lot, they would probably drive me mad after a while."

Ginny came back into the room and bent down over the top of the sofa to adjust the fairy lights. Gabriel watched fascinated as Ginny scrambled and bent over the back of the old sofa.

The small bulbs brightened and then settled down to a steady glimmer.

As she stood up, Ginny caught him watching her.

"Fancy some tea?" she asked.

·········

Gabriel and Ginny sat cuddled up on the sofa. She nestled on his chest. They had drunk their tea and then sat and snuggled.

"I'm not working tomorrow," Ginny said. "You can sleep over, if you want, and catch a bus to work from here."

Gabriel felt his heart rattling in his chest. He wondered if Ginny heard it as well.

"Anyway, time for bed," Ginny said, struggling to get up from the sofa.

"I'll get you a blanket … will you be ok on the sofa?" she said, walking off into her bedroom.

"Yeah, that would be fine," Gabriel said, smiling.

Ginny peered back from the bedroom doorway.

"You really would be pleased to sleep on the sofa, wouldn't you?" she said.

"Sofas are fine," replied Gabriel. "They're what I'm used to."

"You're a nice, boy … do you realise that?"

"How do you mean?" said Gabriel.

"Well … not everybody would …"

"What do you mean?" said Gabriel again, not understanding where the conversation was going at all.

Ginny chuckled to herself.

"Look, Gabriel. I understand you're good with sleeping on sofas and such, but I thought it might get cold in this room tonight."

Gabriel stared at her in confusion.

"I think we'd be warmer if we both slept in here," she said, pointing to her bedroom, "if that's ok with you?"

Gabriel sat staring at Ginny. His body seemed to be incapable of movement.

Ginny skipped over to him, laughing, and pulled him up from the sofa, leading him into her bedroom.

You look very tired   Tuesday 18th July 2017 10:30 am

The Gazette Office

Barney sipped his tea and cast a brief glance over at Gabriel.

"You're looking very tired," Barney noted.

Gabriel looked up at Barney, who was obviously enjoying this.

"Long night, was it?"

Gabriel smiled to himself in a non-committal sort of way.

"She looked very pretty, I thought," Barney continued.

"Who?" Gabriel said, in a tone even he thought was unconvincing.

"The young woman you met up with last night. She was waiting for you after work."

Gabriel shrugged, feigning ignorance.

"I was wondering if you had taken her out for the evening."

Gabriel waited for Barney's next comment. He was obviously following a train of thought.

"I noticed," continued Barney, "that you left your bike here last night, so I wondered ..."

Barney couldn't stop himself from chuckling at Gabriel's discomfort.

"So, does she live round about?" said Barney.

"She lives in Clacton, near to where I live," said Gabriel, realising his plan to keep the whole thing secret had unraveled.

Barney pulled his desk drawer open and pulled out an un-opened packet of Digestive biscuits. He would have one (and only one) with this, his second morning tea. Then he would have another one with his 3 pm tea.

Barney fumbled at the biscuit packaging, trying to lever the sealed top open with his fingernail. He always struggled to open a fresh packet, but he didn't mind. Someone had said to him that if he used a knife, he could slit the side of the packet easily, but he preferred to do it this way. He felt it heightened his anticipation. It increased the pleasure he would get when he finally released the biscuits. The pure joy of dunking his Digestive biscuit into a nice hot cup of tea. He imagined the pleasure he got from this little ritual must be like the pleasure people got from participating in the Japanese Tea Ceremony.

Gabriel watched as Barney finally released the biscuits from their tight packaging, pulling the wrapping aside and carefully levering out the top-most biscuit. He was aware Barney took great care not to damage the biscuits as he opened the packets.

"Fancy a biscuit, do you?" Barney asked.

"No thanks, Barney, I had an excellent breakfast, cheers," Gabriel replied.

"Oh. What did you have?"

"Scrambled eggs, fried tomatoes, mushrooms, fried bread … proper feast," Gabriel recounted.

"No bacon?" quizzed Barney.

"No. She's vegetarian. She doesn't buy any meat," replied Gabriel.

"What … Elsie's gone vegetarian?" said Barney.

Gabriel looked mystified. "Who's Elsie?"

"Oh. And there's me thinking you went for an early breakfast to Elsie's Café," Barney said, chuckling to himself as he lowered his biscuit into his tea.

"Er, Barney?" Gabriel said.

"Yep mate."

"I was thinking of going back to John's later this evening … you know, the old guy in the Sunny Vale Care Home."

Barney looked up quizzically.

"I thought to do a bit of a follow-up. See what he thought of the piece we did on him," said Gabriel.

"Brilliant idea," said Barney, "but you need not go after office hours. Why don't you go this afternoon? You've got that write-up to do this morning, but we're scratching around for the rest of the day. Why don't you take the opportunity?"

"In fact," Barney continued, after some thought, "why don't you take some money from the tin and grab a bit of lunch before you see him?"

"Thanks Barney," Gabriel said.

"Tell you what," said Barney. "In case you meet your girlfriend on your travels, why don't you take another fiver and buy your lass a bit of lunch as well?"

"Err ... yeah, that would be great," said Gabriel, feeling as though he was completely transparent.

Barney chuckled, then pulled another Digestive biscuit from the packet.

He had dunked it before realised he had gone over his self-imposed quota.

"Oh bollocks," he muttered.

Gabriel looked up at him enquiringly.

"Ah well, it's only a fucking biscuit, after all," Barney concluded philosophically.

Now that you've screwed me Tuesday 18th July 2017 12:35pm

Gabriel had texted Ginny to ask if she wanted to meet him at the Golden Egg café in Frinton for lunch. He remembered she had today off work, and so she had nothing special to do.

So now he was standing outside the Golden Egg. This time he was there in plenty of time.

When he had met Ginny here the last time, he had arrived running and nervous. Now things had changed. He had woken up next to her this morning, and he had smiled to see how lovely she looked. He couldn't believe he was lying in bed with this gorgeous girl.

On their trip last night on the bus, when she had joked about living in a flat paid for by an old guy ... he really hadn't known she was joking. He had felt stupid about it, but then she had given him one of her wonderful smiles and everything was all right.

He believed she wasn't trying to make fun of him.

She was just a very vibrant and very bubbly person, but with a sense of humour he found difficult to understand.

He had had breakfast at her flat. She didn't need to get up, but she had got up anyway and cooked them both breakfast. Her kitchen was exceedingly small, but there was a tiny table, big enough for two people, and they had sat there and ate the breakfast she had cooked.

He didn't think he had ever been as happy before in his entire life.

After breakfast, she had walked with him down to the bus stop to see him off. Before he got on the bus, she had grabbed him and given him a big kiss. Then she had nuzzled his ear, breathing her warm breath on it. He had taken the memory of it with him for the entire bus journey. And now she came skipping up the street towards him. She had tied her hair into two pigtails, which bounced up and down as she walked along. She was wearing her tight jeans, hiking boots and her new jacket that Vicky had given her. The jacket was hanging open, and underneath it Gabriel saw she had on a T-shirt with a slogan on it. The jacket made it difficult to read what the slogan was.

It looked like

> **dness is li**
> **gravity**

ll you nee
s a little p

She ran up to him for the last few yards, and stopped three feet in front of him, giving him a very coy smile.

"Trying to catch a glimpse, are you mister?" she said.

She pulled open her jacket, as if flaunting her breasts at him.

He realised her T-shirt said

> Madness is like
> gravity
> All you need
> Is a little push

She leaned up and gave him a kiss on the cheek, then, looking profoundly serious, she said, "I was thinking. Are you going to dump me now, Gabriel?"

Gabriel couldn't think what to say.

She whispered into his ear. "Well, you know, now you've screwed me ... well, lots of guys ... that's all they want. And after that, they don't want to see you anymore."

She pulled back from him, giving him an enquiring stare.

She chuckled.

"Sorry Gabriel. I think my jokes worry you. Maybe I shouldn't tease."

She leaned up and gave him another quick kiss on the cheek.

"Anyway, come on, lover-boy. Let's get something to eat. We'd better get your strength up," she said, pulling him into the café.

· · · · · · · ·

They sat down at a window table. Ginny's friend, Sally, her friend who worked there, came up to take their order.

"Hi guys," Sally said, winking at Ginny. Then looking at Gabriel; "God, you look tired. Been up all night, have you?"

Ginny gave her friend a knowing look, whilst Gabriel felt his cheeks starting to burn.

Sally bent down to whisper something into Ginny's ear. Ginny laughed and whispered something back.

Sally took their order and made her way back into the kitchen, winking at Ginny as she did so.

"What did she say?" Gabriel asked.

"She said you looked like a big, upstanding boy," Ginny said, chuckling.

"Oh ... ok," Gabriel said. He hadn't expected to understand. He was not surprised.

Suddenly Ginny looked rueful, and said, "Is Vicky online?"

Gabriel looked confused.

"I mean, has Vicky just heard what we have been talking about?"

Gabriel recounted their conversation since he had met with Ginny outside the café and saw where Ginny was going.

"No, she isn't. Vicky suggested she go offline before you turned up. I think she thinks we need some privacy," Gabriel said.

"I wonder why she thinks that?" Ginny said, a sense of relief on her face.

· · · · · · · · ·

The food turned up, and they ate, though Gabriel seemed to be vaguely toying with his, pushing a chip around his plate.

"I was thinking we should see John," Gabriel said cautiously.

"I had thought the same thing," Ginny said.

Gabriel seemed to relax.

"Were you thinking of telling him about your idea ... you know ... get to the future and see if you might get another STU from ACME?" Ginny asked.

"Yes. And, I thought, if we saw how his health is, Vicky could give him a 'top-up', to keep him ok."

"When did you want to go to see him?" Ginny asked.

"Barney suggested we go this afternoon," Gabriel said.

"Does Barney know that I am with you?" Ginny asked.

Gabriel looked a bit shamefaced. "I don't think I stand up well against tough questioning," he said.

"Barney is concerned about you, is all," Ginny remarked.

He looked up at Ginny, who was watching him with a fond smile on her face.

"That breakfast we had this morning was marvellous," he said.

"Thank you," said Ginny, smiling.

"Maybe we could do it again," he said, feeling suddenly nervous. This was distinctly unfamiliar territory for Gabriel.

"Oh, I don't know about that," she chuckled.

Gabriel felt crest-fallen, but he tried to put a brave face on it.

Ginny pulled her chair round so she was sitting close to Gabriel.

Gabriel looked at her quizzically.

She licked her finger, then she slowly ran her dampened finger around his ear.

Gabriel closed his eyes, feeling the moistness ... feeling her finger slowly teasing the outside rim of his ear.

She leaned into him, kissing him delicately on his cheek ... kissing him on his closed eyelids.

Gabriel sat mesmerised, unable to move or speak.

She sat back. She pulled her chair back to its original position.

Gabriel opened his eyes.

"Gabriel?" Ginny said.

"Yes?" said Gabriel wistfully.

"Well ... I was just thinking ..."

"Yes ... what?"

"I thought ... we could do the breakfast thing again," she said, "but only if you really liked it."

Gabriel felt his heart miss a beat, and his mouth went dry.

Ginny watched him. Then, as if nothing had happened, she said, "so what time do you want to go to see John?"

"After we have had lunch," Gabriel said. "That's what I was thinking."

"Are you sure that's what you were thinking," Ginny said, chuckling.

Don't let them come to harm Tuesday 18th July 2017 2:15 pm

Gabriel had tapped Vicky to go online as they had been walking to John's care home. He had explained they were going to see John, both to tell him his plan to get to the ACME buildings and to see how his state of health was.

"He may not want me to review his health," Vicky suggested.

"Why not?" Ginny asked.

"I don't rightly know," Vicky replied, "but I think that he feels that he has … well .. that he has lived long enough."

Gabriel looked at Ginny.

"All of his friends are dead," continued Vicky. "He still enjoys things, music for example, but his body causes him pain, and there is nothing I can do about it."

"Do you think he wouldn't want us to get him another STU?" Gabriel asked.

"I strongly believe that John sees no point in trying to extend his life," said Vicky. "It holds little or no joy for him anymore. I think he sees a relapse into his former condition as a … how is it phrased … a 'blessed relief from pain'."

Ginny looked saddened at Vicky's statement.

"Do you realise," Vicky continued, "that John still loves Mary, even though she died many years ago. He still visits her grave. I think he still regrets that she made him wear me instead of her. As her dementia coursed through her, I saw its effect on him. It stripped him of any joy. He watched her illness lead her away from him. He would sit by her chair as she sat looking at nothing. He would hold her hand and cry out in his sadness and his loneliness."

Gabriel took Ginny's hand as they walked along. He thought he heard her blinking back tears.

"So, do you think there is any point going to see John?" Gabriel asked.

"John is my friend," said Vicky, "and I would like to go to see him. Even if all we are doing is saying goodbye."

· · · · · · · ·

John had put the kettle on. He hadn't been surprised to see Ginny turn up with Gabriel, and he had pushed two little fold-up chairs together for them to sit down on.

John had gone to the cupboard to take out two extra cups, and when Ginny had stood up to get the milk from his fridge, John had noticed she unconsciously patted Gabriel's knee as she stood up. It made him smile.

"How are you, John?" Gabriel asked.

"I'm fine, thank you," said John.

There was a pause, as though everyone in the room was hesitant to continue the conversation.

"And how are you, Vicky?" John asked. "I see you have transformed ... a lot more ... well ... modern, I suppose."

"I'm fine, John," Vicky said. "I wasn't sure if you would recognise me."

"I'm glad to hear your voice again," said John, "and Gabriel?"

"Yes?" said Gabriel.

"I'm very pleased you took my advice," continued John.

"Which advice was that?" said Gabriel.

"The advice about trusting someone."

"You told that to me," said Ginny, somewhat worried.

"Yes," agreed John. "And you told Gabriel. And Gabriel listened to you. I'm incredibly pleased he did."

Gabriel took hold of Ginny's hand and gave it a squeeze.

"John," Gabriel said, "we have been talking ... that is Vicky and us. We were thinking of trying to get to the ACME facilities, to see if ..."

John looked horrified.

"You could get killed. All of you. Why would you want to do such a thing?" he said. "You would have little to gain, and much to lose."

"We had wondered ... how about ... how about we try to get another STU ...," Gabriel said, suddenly aware Ginny was shaking her head at him.

"What? And keep me from relapse?" said John angrily. "I would have thought Vicky would understand me better than that."

"I know that, John," Vicky whispered.

"I don't want to live this life any longer," John growled. "My pleasures are all in the past."

"But ...," said Gabriel.

"And they were all stripped away from me," continued John. "The pain was almost too much to bear."

Gabriel looked at Ginny. He was horrified at John's outburst, wishing he could have taken back what he had said.

"Do not mistake me," said John. "Vicky gave me great comfort through the years, but now ..."

"It was my pleasure, John," said Vicky. "You have been my great friend, and I was pleased to have helped you in whatever ways I could."

"And now it is time for you to help this young couple," said John. "Please look after them, Vicky, as you did me. Don't let them come to harm."

Ginny looked over at Gabriel.

"And now it's time for you to go," said John. "My old bones are feeling very weary today."

"All right, John," Gabriel said, getting up. "Thank you for seeing us."

"Goodbye, John," Vicky said. "It has been a great pleasure knowing you."

"Goodbye Vicky," John replied. "I have treasured our acquaintance."

Could you really do that?   Tuesday 18th July 2017   3:30 pm

Outside the Sunny Vale Care Home

"I wish I hadn't upset John," Gabriel said.

"When he said about the giving advice thing, I thought he was getting confused," Ginny said.

"I think it will take a little time for him to develop dementia," said Vicky.

"How long do you think?" Gabriel said.

"Without my support, I would suggest a few weeks," Vicky replied. "I have held it at bay for a long time now, but ..."

Gabriel looked at Ginny, who was looking horrified at the prospect of John's fate.

"I think John has chosen his own future," Vicky continued, "and it is not for us to try to change it."

"But what about his past?" Gabriel asked.

"What?" said Ginny.

"Well. What if we helped John by preventing Mary from getting dementia?" Gabriel said.

"Could you really do that, Vicky?" Ginny asked.

Gabriel suddenly looked troubled that he had over-estimated what Vicky could do with such medical conditions.

"I could have helped Mary," said Vicky. "I could have significantly improved her condition. Even to where it might have lain dormant until her natural death."

"But could you go back to a point in time before Mary became ill?" continued Ginny. "Could you do that and prevent her from getting dementia?"

"To do that," said Vicky, "we would first need to get to the ACME facilities ... to find out if they had fixed the teleport problem. Then, if they had, we would need to teleport back to the time before Mary became ill, and provide her with a STU, which would keep her healthy."

Ginny looked excitedly at Gabriel, who was looking unsure where this was all going.

"But," Gabriel said, "if we got to ACME, we would have to convince them to give us a STU to give to Mary. You have said before, Vicky, that ACME INC is not the sort of company who would give away an expensive device for free. I don't see how we could ..."

"At least we could try," said Ginny. "If we can't help John now, perhaps we could help him by stopping him losing the love of his life ... or at least we might give them more years together."

"But does time work like that?" asked Gabriel. "What if we went back into John's past and stopped Mary from getting dementia? Wouldn't it affect what is happening now? Wouldn't it mean that John might not have given you to me? Might it not mean that I never would have met Ginny?"

"It is possible, Gabriel," said Vicky. "ACME INC takes pains to avoid changing the past, but not because of any stated scientific reason. It is more that ACME INC fears litigation. There have been no studies on the effect of historical changes affecting the present, though it is recognised that changes carry through time. Simple changes have been seen to impact immediately on all future times. The future seems to mold itself automatically around historic changes. It is as though it strives to level out anomalies."

"So, if we made a change, one result might be we never meet?" said Ginny, holding Gabriel's hand tightly.

"But you would never realise that," explained Vicky. "Your current time personae would have no memory or recollection of meeting."

Ginny looked scared at the prospect.

"Not that you wouldn't ever meet," continued Vicky. "It might mean that you don't meet in the same way that you just have."

"Let's walk into town," said Gabriel. "I think I need the support of a strong coffee."

He looked over at Ginny, who nodded in agreement.

"Vicky," Gabriel said. "Would you mind going offline for a little while, please?"

"Of course, Gabriel. I will be here when you want me," Vicky said.

Ginny put her arm around Gabriel's waist, and they set off slowly back into town.

So, you're going on your own, then? Tuesday 18th July 2017 4:30 pm

Gabriel and Ginny sat drinking their coffees. Gabriel had always liked the look of Costa Coffee shops, but he had rarely been in one. They always looked dark and intimate and filled with comfy looking over-padded sofas.

Ginny had ordered a fancy thing with extra caramel and an intricate swirly pattern on the top. Gabriel had ordered a small black coffee. He had thought it would wake him up a bit.

Also, it was cheaper than some of the fancier drinks.

They had found two single-seater armchairs which faced each other across a small circular wooden table. The shiny brown leather armchairs creaked when you sat in them.

"So, what do you think we should do?" Ginny asked.

"About what?"

"About John."

Gabriel took a sip of his coffee, relishing its strong and slightly bitter taste.

"I think I should try to get to ACME INC, and then see if I can persuade them to give John a device … a STU or something … that I can give to John's wife," Gabriel said.

"So, you're going on your own?" Ginny said.

"Well, I was thinking …," said Gabriel.

"No, you weren't thinking. You weren't thinking at all," Ginny said, turning her head away from him.

Gabriel looked over to her. He reached out for her hand, but she pulled it away from him.

"Ginny?" Gabriel said.

"What?" she replied, brusquely.

"I didn't want you to get hurt."

Ginny turned back to look at him.

"I didn't want you to get hurt is all," said Gabriel. "I really care about you, Ginny. I really couldn't bear to see you get hurt."

Ginny stifled a sob, then came and squished in beside Gabriel on his single-seater armchair.

"I can't let you go on your own," she said.

Gabriel looked at her. Squished together on the single-seater armchair, her face was almost touching his.

"I don't think I could bear it if anything ... well ..." she said.

Gabriel touched her check, wiping away a teardrop.

Ginny smiled.

"I've only known you a short time," Ginny said, "but ..."

"Shall we go together?" said Gabriel. "After all, you're the brains in the outfit."

Ginny smiled. She put her arms around Gabriel's neck, hugging him close to her body.

What about Moth?   Tuesday 18th July 2017   6 pm

They had finished their coffees and were heading for the bus stop. The next bus back to Clacton would be in 10 minutes.

"Gabriel?" Ginny said.

"Uh?" Gabriel replied.

"I was wondering. Why don't I come and stay at your place tonight?"

Ginny felt Gabriel tense. He had stopped walking, and his face had gone ashen.

"Oh God, Gabriel. I'm sorry. I didn't ..."

"It's just, well ... it's just that ...," Gabriel mumbled.

"No, it's ok ... if you don't want me to meet your ..."

"No, it's not that, Ginny. It's where I live. It's not as nice as yours. I live with my Mum, and the place is ..."

"Ok. I tell you what, pudding. Come back to mine. But why don't you get your toothbrush and a few clothes. In case you want to stay over for a while."

"What about Moth?" Gabriel asked.

"I think she'll like you," said Ginny.

They walked a little further, Gabriel pondering on this fresh development.

"Gabriel?" Ginny said.

Gabriel turned his face to hers.

"I don't normally ... well, maybe you think I ...," she said.

"What?" Gabriel said.

"I realise that I joke a lot ... and say things, and ..."

"What, Ginny?"

"Well, I want you to understand I don't usually ask boys back to stay at mine. I realise we haven't known each other for awfully long, and I know you stayed over last night, so maybe you think I ..."

"It's ok, Ginny," Gabriel interrupted.

"Ok, Ginny?" Ginny echoed, but with a powerful element of sarcasm. "Is that all you've got to say? You should understand I don't normally rush into a relationship like this, but something about you, well …"

She seemed to run out of the words she needed to describe her feelings.

"What I mean is," she resumed, "is that I was trying to tell you that you are very special to me."

Gabriel smiled.

"And when I told you that, all you had to say is 'ok, Ginny'", she concluded lamely.

Gabriel stopped and put both of his arms around her. Then he picked her up and swung her around, her long legs flying out behind her.

When he put her back down, he kept his arms wrapped around her.

"I don't think I deserve you, Ginny. You are funny and pretty, and clever, and I don't really understand you, but I wouldn't want to be with anyone else."

Ginny smiled up at him.

"Well, that's all right then," she said.

"I'll get my toothbrush," Gabriel said

"I'll come 'round yours, if you like," Ginny said, putting her fingers on Gabriel's mouth in case he objected, "but I'll stay outside while you get your gear; in case you've forgotten where my flat is."

Gabriel took hold of the hand she was holding against his mouth, and gently kissed her fingers. "Ok, Ginny," he said. "Let's go do that when we get back to Clacton. I can be in and out in five minutes. I don't have a lot of stuff."

They set off walking again towards the bus stop. Gabriel clasped Ginny's hand and reflected on the changes occurring in his life.

"Ginny?" Gabriel said.

"Yes?"

"How long do you think it takes to fall in love with someone?"

"I don't know … why do you ask?" Ginny said, smiling.

"Oh … I was just … I was just wondering. And I thought … you seem to know about lots of stuff. You're a lot more worldly wise than I am."

"I don't believe in love at first sight and that rubbish," Ginny said emphatically.

"No, I suppose not," said Gabriel. "That's Walt Disney stuff, isn't it?"

"But I suppose people can get very fond of each other in a short space of time," she offered, "and perhaps that's how love starts out."

"Hmm," Gabriel said.

"So why are you asking?" Ginny said.

"Oh, it's nothing," Gabriel ended, somewhat lamely.

Ginny smiled to herself and gave Gabriel's hand a squeeze.

I think we can eat later   Tuesday 18th July 2017   7:45 pm

Clacton – Ginny's flat

They had picked up Gabriel's stuff from his mum's flat. His mum had been out, so in what would possibly be the most momentous leaving that Gabriel ever made from his flat, he did it alone and with no one to say goodbye to.

Ginny took Gabriel's paltry collection of clothes and stacked them on a spare shelf in her room. She had put his toothbrush along with hers in a small pink plastic mug on a shelf in the bathroom. Then she had put the kettle on.

"I will make some pasta, if that's ok with you?" Ginny said.

Gabriel had sat down on one of the two kitchen chairs, and he was looking around as if unsure what to do or what to say.

"I'll put some cauliflower and chickpeas in with it, and maybe some grated cheese," she continued.

Gabriel looked over at Ginny. She thought he looked fearful. She was very moved when Gabriel had been talking about how long it takes to fall in love, and although he was very young, so very immature, she felt sure he was very fond of her.

And she had been very truthful with Gabriel when she had told him she thought he was special. Although she had been out with many boys, she had never, in fact, felt quite as strongly about them as she did about Gabriel.

And she had never, ever, considered asking any of the others to move in with her. For her, she was moving into unfamiliar ground.

She stood behind Gabriel as he sat on the kitchen chair. She stroked his neck and shoulders. He felt so very tense. He looked like some small fledgling that had fallen out of its nest before it was ready to fly. She feared she had taken a decision based on her own emotions, but without taking due regard for the other person. Maybe Gabriel really wasn't ready for this step, and she was putting him into a position in which he was not comfortable but was too shy to say no.

She found she had stopped stroking his neck. She was just resting her hands on his shoulders.

Gabriel stood up and putting one hand on either side of her face, he kissed her tenderly.

"Thank you, Ginny," he said, "for ... well, for being you, for being so lovely and for being so caring. But if you get fed up with me, please let me know. Tell me. Tell me ... so I don't have to guess. I don't want you to have to ..."

Ginny kissed Gabriel back, responding to him in a long, slow, and very tender kiss.

She pulled away and murmured, "Gabriel?" into his ear.

"Yes, Ginny."

"Come on ... let's go to bed. I think we can eat later."

She gently pulled him towards the bedroom, clicking the lock on the door. She wasn't expecting Moth back tonight, but she thought Gabriel was looking very unsure about the implications of moving in with her. She wanted nothing to unsettle him.

She wondered what Moth would think about Ginny having Gabriel staying with her after such a brief time.

Don't use him all up   Tuesday 18th July 2017   9:15 pm

"When is Moth coming back?" Gabriel asked.

They were sitting in the little kitchen in Ginny's flat, eating the pasta dish Ginny had suggested earlier.

"Maybe tonight, or maybe tomorrow," Ginny said.

She saw that Gabriel was worried about meeting Ginny's flat mate. She would have to bolster up his confidence a bit.

"She's really nice," Ginny said, reassuringly, "otherwise I wouldn't be sharing a flat with her."

"Yeah, sure," Gabriel said, somewhat apprehensively.

Gabriel finished his last fork full. "That was nice, Ginny. Thank you."

"It was a pleasure," Ginny replied. "Come on, let's wash up and then how about we go for a little walk."

"It's dark out."

"Afraid of the werewolves?" Ginny asked, chuckling.

"I guess not," said Gabriel.

"I tell you what," Ginny said. "How's about you wash up, and I'll get ready for the walk."

"What, preparing the sharpened stakes?" Gabriel said.

"Something like that," Ginny said.

"Ok," Gabriel said, and started looking around the kitchen, pulling open drawers.

Ginny looked over, watching him pulling open the drawers.

"Looking for dish-cloths and stuff," he said, in explanation.

"Ok," Ginny said smiling.

She made her way into her bedroom. She heard Gabriel putting the pots in the sink, squirting in a few drops of washing up liquid and then getting under way. He started to sing a little song ... too low for her to hear what it was. She smiled to herself. She had guessed (or hoped anyway) that if she gave Gabriel a little task to do, he would feel more like he belonged.

She heard footsteps coming up the stairs to the flat, and the sound of a key being inserted into the lock. As she came out of the bedroom, the front door opened and Moth, her flatmate, came in. She was a slim, pretty girl with startlingly ginger hair. She was carrying two holdalls. She put them down and walked straight through into the kitchen where Gabriel was holding a plate and a tea-towel.

"Hi, Moth," Ginny called. "This is Gabriel. He might stay over for a bit."

Moth stood and looked Gabriel up and down, appraisingly.

Gabriel put the plate and the tea-towel down. He looked a bit uncomfortable, but then Moth gently took hold of Gabriel's elbows, using them to spin him around.

Moth stood back. Gabriel obligingly continued to spin around slowly. He couldn't help but to smile.

She leaned over to him to stop his spinning. Turning to Ginny, she said; "Well, he's extremely cute looking, Ginny. I have to admire your taste."

Ginny smiled back at Moth.

"Oh, you didn't bring him back for me, did you Ginny?" Moth asked, with a cheeky smile on her face, "cos if you did, well …"

Moth leaned up and grabbed Gabriel, licking his cheek slowly with her tongue.

"Hmm, yum, thanks Ginny," Moth said. "And now I've licked him, now he's mine."

"No way, girl … Gabriel's all mine," Ginny said laughing, catching Gabriel's eye as she did so.

"Well, don't use him all up," Moth chuckled, "just in case."

Ginny looked at Gabriel, who seemed thrilled to be a part of this little show. She thought it would work out ok, despite her reservations.

What if it's raining   Tuesday 18th July 2017 10:30 pm

"Moth seems very nice," Gabriel noted.

"I bet you say that about all the girls who lick you on their first meeting," Ginny replied, chuckling.

"Well, I won't say it wasn't nice," Gabriel said.

"Just don't get used to it … well, not from Moth, anyway," Ginny suggested.

Gabriel had finished drying the dishes, and they had left the flat to go for a little walk.

"I often go for a bit of a walk at this time of night," said Ginny. "It clears my mind."

"Anywhere in particular?" Gabriel asked.

"No … just round the block."

"What if it's raining?"

"I get wet."

"Oh. Ok."

They turned a corner. Four guys of about Gabriel's age were hanging about under a streetlamp.

"Pete's looking out for you, mate," one guy shouted.

"Do you know them?" Ginny said to Gabriel.

Two guys left the group and started walking over towards Gabriel and Ginny, one on their left, one on their right.

"You might want to keep walking, girl," Left advised Ginny.

Ginny grabbed Gabriel's hand, tugging him along with her.

"But not you," Right said. "Why don't you stay here with us … let's talk about old times, eh?"

"Come on Gabriel," Ginny said, continuing to tug at his hand.

Gabriel looked at the two men. They were standing about twelve feet away. Both looked about the same build as Gabriel himself. Tallish, slim, wiry. They looked confident in themselves.

The other two seemed content to stand by the streetlamp for the time being. They didn't look nervous about a confrontation. Maybe they were simply standing back to give the first two a chance. To see how it panned out.

"I think you had better go, Ginny," Gabriel said. "I'll catch up with you soon."

He unclasped Ginny's hand from his. She struggled to hold on to him.

"Get the fuck out of it, bitch," the guy on Gabriel's left said.

Ginny was looking very frightened now. She looked like she didn't know whether to stay or to run.

Gabriel pushed Ginny behind him, then turned to the two guys standing in front of him. He walked purposefully forwards, closing the gap. He was now three feet from them, and Ginny was about six feet behind him.

Left was standing marginally closer than Right.

"I'm guessing you don't need any help," Vicky whispered. "I'll stay out of your way."

Gabriel half-turned towards Ginny. He saw she was trembling.

"Catch you later," Gabriel said.

Before Ginny had time to respond, Gabriel turned around to face the two guys. He canted his head back slightly ... then brought his forehead crashing down onto Left's nose.

He heard Left's nose crunch.

Gabriel stepped back and crouched down.

Left was clutching his face with both hands.

Gabriel snapped his right arm forwards, smashing Left in the balls.

Gabriel stepped up and back ... right in time for Right to land a punch on Gabriel's upper right arm. Gabriel cursed. Not at the pain from the punch. More because it might slow him down. He always tried his damnedest not to get hit ... to not go down too soon.

Once you were down ...

Gabriel flung himself back ... back and away ... trying to give himself some space ... some space between himself and Right.

"Let's hold it right there, gentlemen," a voice boomed.

Right stopped in his tracks.

Gabriel cast a brief glance in the direction the voice had come from.

It was Slammer.

"Evening, Ginny," the voice said, in a more conversational tone.

"Evening, Paul," Ginny said.

Slammer looked over to Gabriel and nodded to him. Gabriel nodded back.

Slammer gestured to Right ... a 'get the fuck out of it' gesture.

Right stepped back. He sauntered slowly back over to the other two guys who were still standing by the streetlamp. He had not tried to help Left up, who was still lying on the ground, one hand on his nose and the other clutching his balls.

"Your boyfriend's not afraid of a little scrap, is he?" Slammer said to Ginny.

"Get going," Gabriel whispered back to her.

"You don't look like much, mate," Slammer said to Gabriel, "but I admire your style, and your guts. You're like a little fucking rottweiler ... you just get in there, don't you?"

Gabriel said nothing. He couldn't tell whether this was the end of the fight or just a brief interlude before Slammer got involved personally. He was ... seemingly ... a friend of Pete's.

But Slammer remained standing about twelve feet away.

And he was showing no intention of coming any closer.

Slammer turned to the three guys standing some distance away. They seemed uncertain what to do.

"Why don't you lot fuck off," Slammer said. "You can tell Pete you made your little play. Tell him you warned this lad here. Tell him ..."

Slammer turned back towards Gabriel, then back to the three guys.

"Oh, tell him whatever you fucking like," Slammer said. "Pete's a complete tit anyway ... he deserved the kicking he got."

The three guys remained standing there.

"Now fuck off, you lot. And leave this lad alone. He's working for me now."

The three guys turned and ambled away. Right was looking back occasionally. His adrenalin had kicked in ... and he had nothing to use it on.

Slammer turned back to Gabriel and grinned. "You won't want to work for me ... and that's ok. You don't need this shit, and I respect that."

"Cheers, Slammer," Gabriel said.

"I've given you a bit of breathin' space, is all," Slammer said, turning to go.

"Oh, and me and Ginny go back a-ways, don't we girl?" he said. "I wouldn't like to see her bloke come to any harm."

Slammer sauntered away. He didn't look back. He looked like he owned the streets.

Gabriel guessed Slammer didn't need to care what was around the next corner.

Ginny stepped up to Gabriel and took hold of his hand. He turned to look at her.

"So, you and Slammer ... Paul ... you go back a-ways, eh?" he said.

"Yeah," Ginny said.

"Oh."

"We're really close," she said, smiling.

"You're still really close?"

"Yeah."

"Ok ... well ...," said Gabriel.

Ginny chuckled. "He's my cousin."

"Oh."

"He's the reason I can walk round here and not be afraid of the werewolves," she said.

"I guess so," Gabriel said.

"And now I think he's extended the protection to you," she said.

"Very kind, I'm sure," Gabriel said.

He took hold of Ginny's hand, but as they were about to turn away, the guy still on the ground made a grab for Gabriel's trouser leg.

"Don't think that fucking means anything ... you're fucking dead, mate," Left said.

Gabriel let go of Ginny's hand. He leant down. He grabbed hold of the hand clutching his trousers. He prised the grip open. He kept a tight hold of the hand. He splayed the fingers wide.

"I'd forgotten about you," Gabriel half-whispered.

He twisted Left's wrist savagely, twisting his arm up behind his back, forcing the guy onto his stomach.

"Sometimes," Gabriel said, "it's wiser to keep your fucking mouth shut."

"Fuck off ...," Left said.

Gabriel wrenched Left's arm up behind his back.

He pressed down, putting his full weight against it.

He felt and heard the joint crack.

Left screamed.

Gabriel levered Left onto his back. Then he punched him in the face, smashing his fist down onto Left's already broken nose.

"Oh God, oh God, oh God, no, no ... don't," Ginny said.

Gabriel looked up at her. She was standing six feet away. She was looking completely horrified. She started walking slowly backwards ... backwards away from him.

"Ginny ... Ginny ... wait," Gabriel said.

Gabriel noticed his fist was covered in blood. Blood from the guy's shattered nose.

He wiped his fist on the guy's hoody jacket.

He stood up.

Ginny was gone.

He tasted pretty good Wednesday 19th July 2017 12:10 am

Ginny and Moth's flat

"... and then he broke his arm," Ginny said. "I heard something crack."

"Well ...," Moth said.

"And as the guy was lying there screaming, Gabriel punched him in the nose. There was blood everywhere and ..."

"Ginny?" Moth said.

"Yes? What?"

"What were Pete's friends going to do to Gabriel, do you think?"

"How do you mean?"

"If Paul hadn't stopped the fight, what do you think would happen?"

"I don't ... I don't know," Ginny said, "but it was ghastly. I didn't think Gabriel could ..."

"I think the chances are," Moth said, "that if your cousin hadn't turned up, the other three guys would have beaten the shit out of Gabriel. I think that would be what would have happened."

"Yes ... well ...," Ginny said, "but ..."

"I don't think Gabriel had a lot of choices," Moth said.

"Yeah, but ..."

"And also," Moth continued, "I suspect Gabriel has had some hard knocks in his life. I suspect he has found out that if you let the other guy get up, it might end up worse for you."

Ginny sat watching the fairy lights as they slowly went from dim to bright. Moth had re-adjusted them back to the setting she preferred.

"I think he's a good kid," Moth said. "I should look after him, if I was you."

"And if I don't?" Ginny said.

"Well ... he tasted pretty good," said Moth. "I don't mind taking him off your hands."

"Fuck off, girlfriend," Ginny said, chuckling.

"Ginny?"

"Yes, Moth?"

"Where did Gabriel go ... after you left him?"

"I don't know, Moth. I didn't stop to find out. I simply walked away."

"Oh."

"He was wiping the blood off his hands."

"Oh."

"He was wiping it off on the guy's jacket."

"I see."

"I didn't think he was like that ... I didn't think ...," said Ginny.

"He was only protecting himself ... and you, I shouldn't wonder," Moth said.

"I slept with him the other night," Ginny said. "I don't think ... if I'd known ..."

"What ... you're saying if you'd known he could protect himself, and you, that you wouldn't have?" Moth said. "Don't make me laugh. If I had a sweet guy like that ... kind, considerate, yummy looking (Ginny smiled) and he could look after himself ... I wouldn't waste a minute."

"He shocked me," said Ginny. "I thought the fight was over, but then ..."

"What?"

"He just ... he just seemed so cold ... so ... so ruthless ... so cruel."

"I think you should grow up, girl," Moth said. "And get some sleep. We're both working in the morning."

"Yeah, I guess so," Ginny said.

"Go on," Moth said. "Get your head down. Catch you in the morning for breakfast."

Ginny got up and made her way to the bathroom. Gabriel's toothbrush was standing next to hers in her pink plastic toothbrush mug. She thought, having talked about it, probably Moth was right. Gabriel had been doing his best to protect both himself and her.

She looked into the mirror ... her eyes un-focussed. "Where are you, Gabriel?" she whispered to herself.

Do you fancy crumpets? Wednesday 19th July 2017 7 am

Ginny and Moth's flat

"Do you fancy crumpets?" Ginny said.

"Sounds good, good, good," Moth called through from the bathroom.

Ginny teased two crumpets from the pack. They tended to stick together. You had to lever them apart.

"It was only the other day," Ginny said, slipping the two crumpets down into the toaster, "when Gabriel said the breakfast I had made was really marvellous."

"I remember ... you already told me."

"And then he asked me ... like really cautiously ... would it be all right if we did it again?"

"Yeah, you told me that as well," said Moth, smiling.

"I'll put some coffee on," said Ginny.

"I'll check if the milk's come yet," Moth said.

Ginny heard Moth unlocking and opening the flat door, heard her walking down the stairs.

Ginny measured out two heaped spoons of coffee into the percolator.

"Hey Ginny," she heard Moth calling out, her voice low, little more than a whisper.

"What's up?" Ginny said, walking over to the door of the flat.

Moth was standing at the bottom of the stairs. She was looking up the stairs at Ginny, gesturing for Ginny to be quiet.

Gabriel was laid asleep at the bottom of the stairs.

Ginny rushed down the stairs. "Is he ok?" she whispered to Moth.

Gabriel was curled up into an almost foetal position.

"I bet he has laid here all night," Moth said. "He might be chilled."

Ginny bent down and put her hand on Gabriel's face. He felt cold. She leaned forward, pressing her face against his, trying to give him some of her warmth. She stroked his hair. She nuzzled into him.

"Ginny?" Gabriel said, waking with a start.

Ginny sat up, moving away from him, giving him space to sit up.

Gabriel sat up slowly. He looked around himself, looked up at Ginny, looked up at Moth.

"Ginny?" Gabriel said. "I didn't ..."

Ginny stood up, leaving Gabriel sitting on the floor. He looked instantly hurt.

She bent down and held her hands out to him.

He grasped them. She levered him up.

She kept hold of his hands after he had stood up.

"Shall I put more crumpets on?" Moth said, picking up the milk.

"I think you'd better," Ginny said. "My boyfriend's called round for breakfast."

Moth smiled to herself.

Ginny tugged at Gabriel's hand, leading him up the stairs to their flat.

Yummy looking   Wednesday 19th July 2017

Gabriel and Ginny had caught the bus into Frinton. She was on her way to do a shift at the care home, and Gabriel was going to the Gazette office. They had talked little on the bus. It didn't seem the place to have a conversation. She would have finished her work by 4:30 pm. Gabriel typically finished at 5:30 pm. They had agreed to meet up after work. They would meet at one of the old Victorian seafront shelters. That way, if either was delayed, the other would have somewhere to sit and wait.

At 5:30 pm Gabriel made his way out from the Gazette office and walked down to the seafront. It was a pleasantly warm evening. People were walking down the street with a look of anticipation to the evening.

Gabriel looked over towards the old Victorian shelter. Ginny was standing next to it. She was looking in Gabriel's direction. She was smiling and waving. Gabriel waved back.

"Do you want me to shut down for a while?" Vicky asked.

"Yes please. That's very thoughtful of you, Vicky."

"Ok, Gabriel. I will wait until you re-activate me."

"Ok, Vicky."

"Oh, and ... good luck, Gabriel."

"Er ... thanks, Vicky," Gabriel said, wondering what Vicky was alluding to.

· · · · · · · ·

Ginny gave Gabriel an enormous hug, and then they sat down on the side of the shelter that faced towards the sea. There was hardly a breath of wind, and the sea looked very calm. Off in the distance Gabriel saw the line of wind generators ... pure white against the clear blue sky. Huge sea-based windmills. They were barely turning.

"You shocked me last night," Ginny said.

Gabriel said nothing. He watched the windmills. He waited to see what would come next.

"I talked to Moth about it," she said.

Gabriel turned to look at Ginny. "And what did Moth say?" he said.

"She said you were … you were protecting yourself … and me … and that you have probably …"

"Probably what?"

"Probably learned that if you have to hit somebody, make sure they don't jump back up and …"

"There was four of them, Ginny … maybe five … I wasn't sure. And if you get in fast, take one down, then …"

"But you kept hitting him … even after… and you broke his arm. And …"

"Yes, I did, Ginny."

"They probably thought you were a psychopath."

"I hope so, Ginny."

Ginny looked shocked.

"Why? Why is that? Why do you hope that?" she said.

"It might give them something to think about …the next time they consider giving me a little warning … the next time they consider passing on a little message from Pete."

"Moth said …"

"Moth said?" Gabriel asked.

"She said … 'If she had a sweet guy like that … kind, considerate, yummy-looking, and he could look after himself … she wouldn't waste a minute.'"

"She said 'yummy looking' did she?"

Ginny felt herself flushing up. Her cheeks felt like they were burning.

"So, what do you think?" Gabriel said.

"How do you mean?"

"Well … it seems like Moth has given you her take on it, but what do you think? 'Cos, I suppose if you don't want me …"

"What do you mean?" she said.

"Well, Moth seems very nice, and if …," he said, chuckling.

Ginny took Gabriel's face in her hands, turning him to face her. She was partly smiling, but partly serious.

"Gabriel ... you shocked me last night. But I realise you were doing what seemed best. Those guys would hurt you. You absolutely knew that, and you were protecting yourself ... and protecting me, I guess."

Gabriel nodded.

"And I guess you've had some rough times. They've probably taught you how to stand up for yourself. I haven't seen that side of you before. And I've no right to tell you what to do in those sorts of circumstances."

Gabriel waited. Ginny patently hadn't finished yet.

"I haven't been there. I can't ..." she said, falteringly.

Gabriel took Ginny's hands off his face. He clasped hold of her hands.

"Are we ok, Ginny?" he said, "because I don't think I can readily stop being what I am. And as you said, I've had some rough times. They taught me lessons. I don't think ..."

Ginny smiled at Gabriel.

"We're ok, Gabriel," she said. "Maybe I need to do what Moth said ... she said, 'I should grow up'."

"Moth's a wonderful friend to you," Gabriel said.

"Yes, she is," said Ginny.

"Did she really say I was yummy looking?"

Ginny chuckled. She turned and leaned back onto Gabriel's chest. He put his arms around her.

"I was only wondering," Gabriel said.

Ginny flicked him playfully on the knee.

"Ouch," he said, grinning.

Fancy some chips? Wednesday 19th July 2017 sunset

The sun was going down, and there was a chill in the air. Their snuggle in the old beach pavilion seemed to have eased the unrest from the previous night.

Well, Gabriel hoped that it had.

"Fancy some chips?" Gabriel asked.

"You offering to take me out for some fancy dining?" Ginny said.

"I guess we could have mushy peas as well."

"How could a girl resist?" Ginny said, laughing.

· · · · · · · ·

They had bought two bags of chips (smothered in mushy peas) from a chip shop on the seafront. It was called 'right time, right plaice'. They had taken the bags of chips and sat on a bench near the pier to eat them.

"Do you think there's a company somewhere whose sole job is to make up names for chip shops?" Gabriel asked, grinning.

"What, their sole job?" Ginny said, emphasising the fishy name.

"You don't work for that very company, do you?" Gabriel said.

"I used to have a little plaice where I used to sit, just a rock really, somewhere to come up with fish puns," Ginny said, "but I've stopped now. Moth kept carping on about it."

"Oh, God ... they're dreadful," said Gabriel.

"You started it," Ginny said.

· · · · · · · ·

"Did you see John today?" Gabriel said, as he studiously poked a chip into the mound of mushy peas. The peas were just as he liked them: bright luminous green, as if they were vaguely radioactive. He didn't imagine they were good for you, but they tasted nice.

"Yes. I tidied round his flat."

"Did he seem ok?"

"He seemed distant."

"How do you mean?" said Gabriel.

"Maybe introspective. He didn't say much. He didn't ask how you were getting on."

"Do you think his health is being impacted?" said Gabriel.

"I don't know. What do you think, Vicky?"

"Erm ... I asked Vicky to turn off for a bit," Gabriel said.

"Oh ... ok," Ginny said.

"Shall we turn her on?" Gabriel said.

"Might be an idea," Ginny said. "She'll probably be aware whether John is showing signs of getting worse."

Gabriel tapped his watch.

"Good evening, guys," Vicky said.

"We were wondering," said Ginny, "if John's health is getting worse. Today he seemed quiet. He didn't want to talk much, and he didn't ask how Gabriel and me were getting on. What do you think?"

"It doesn't sound like John," said Vicky. "He is normally very polite and ... well ... interested in people. It sounds as though his condition may be deteriorating."

"We guessed it would happen, Ginny," Gabriel said.

"And also," Vicky interrupted, "John said he didn't want any further medical assistance. If you remember, he became very agitated when we ..."

"I remember," Ginny said. "I couldn't bear to see him get worse. I have to see him every day, remember."

Gabriel looked glumly at Ginny. "So, what are you thinking ... leave your job ... do you mean to leave your care home job?"

"If there was only some way we could try to get to ACME INC," Ginny said. "So, we could try to get him another STU ... or some device that looks after health issues."

"Would you really want to?" Gabriel asked.

"If there was a way to do it, I think we should," she said. "I feel we owe it to him."

"I agree," Gabriel said. "I feel the same way. I hate to think of John deteriorating like that."

"But," said Ginny, "I wasn't thinking of trying to get a device to help him right now."

"What? How do you …?"

"I meant to see if we could get a device to help him when his wife became ill. A device that could help his wife … stop her from getting dementia. That was when he needed help. Now it's … it's too late."

Gabriel nodded in agreement. "I hadn't thought of that," he said. "It would make sense … but, you realise the chances are the coordinates database is still screwed, don't you?"

Ginny nodded.

"And you still want to go, even though …?" he said.

Ginny looked thoughtful.

"Vicky?" Ginny said.

"Yes, Ginny?"

"John's condition. If he's getting worse now, how do you think his condition will progress?"

"I would imagine," said Vicky, "that his catatonia will envelop him quickly, probably within the next few days. That will leave him unable to move or communicate, even though his mind will still be active. Then, within a matter of weeks, the dementia will overcome him. His memories will dissolve, he will feel very agitated, he will probably become terribly angry. All of that anger and confusion will be contained within a body that can't communicate to the outside world."

"It sounds like a living hell," said Gabriel.

"I would agree with your sentiment," said Vicky.

Ginny shuddered.

"I don't want to see John go through that," she said. "I would rather that I took the risk … and went to see if I could get another STU."

"Just you … on your own?" Gabriel asked.

· · · · · · · ·

Ginny looked over at Gabriel. He couldn't make out what her expression meant. It worried him. He looked into his chip bag. It was empty. He carefully folded his empty chip bag into a ball, taking care not to let the stray bits fall onto the ground. He took aim and tossed it into a nearby rubbish bin.

It plopped neatly into the bin.

Gabriel grinned.

"Ok, Gabriel. Let's see if you can do that again," Ginny said, handing him her chip bag.

Gabriel folded her chip bag into a ball. He threw it. It arced its way into the bin.

Ginny gave a little clap.

Gabriel grinned at her.

"Can I make a suggestion?" Vicky said.

"What? About tossing chip bags?" quipped Ginny. "I think Gabriel's got it down pretty well, myself."

Gabriel and Ginny both grinned.

"No," said Vicky. "I meant regarding you saying you wanted to get to see ACME INC."

"Ah, that," said Ginny.

"What's your suggestion, Vicky?" Gabriel said.

"Well," said Vicky, "we don't know for certain if the coordinates database was corrupted. We assume that that caused the problem, but we can't be sure."

"It is an educated guess, though, isn't it?" Gabriel said.

"That's true," agreed Vicky, "but sadly we have no way of finding out ... unless we try to teleport somewhere."

"Yep, that seems to be the case," Gabriel said.

"And if the coordinates database was, and still is, corrupted, then a teleport would most likely result in your deaths," Vicky said.

"That seems to be the problem," Ginny said.

"Well ... my suggestion is we get hold of a starship, one that has CrYO-PODS in it."

"And then ...?" Gabriel said.

"And," continued Vicky, "you get in the PODS and sleep for the next 163 years. You would wake up shortly after the date that we think the data corruption happened. Then we'd go to ACME INC and see if we were correct. Then, if they have fixed the database corruption, you could teleport back in time to before John's wife became ill."

"But we would still need to get another STU, or something similar," said Gabriel.

"Yes, that is true," said Vicky, "and I have already explained that I think the chances would be low of getting ACME to agree to your request, but if you really want to try, I would do my best to assist you."

"But what if ACME weren't able to fix the database corruption?" said Ginny. "We'd be stuck in the future, unable to teleport back?"

"That is true, Ginny, but there's something else," Vicky said. "It is possible that even if we got to ACME INC, they might choose to keep me. I am their property. Even if they have fixed the database corruption, they may not let me continue to assist you."

Ginny looked over at Gabriel.

"Well ... if that was the case, we would be marooned there together," Gabriel said, reaching over to grab her hand.

He pulled Ginny towards him. He clasped both of his arms around her, holding her tightly. She nuzzled her face up against him.

"Would you be all right with that, Gabriel?" she said.

"Just as long as ... just as long as you told no more of your fish puns," he said, grinning.

"So," interrupted Vicky, "if you are happy ... or ... let's say, if you understand the risk ... and you are happy to proceed, all you need to do is decide when you want to leave. At that point, I will request a suitably configured starship, then off we go."

"You make it sound pretty easy," said Gabriel.

"It is," said Vicky. "That is assuming ACME INC has one in stock. After all, the other items I have requested have all been small items. I have requested nothing as large as a starship in the last 70 years."

"Oh," said Ginny. "Is there no way of knowing?"

"Not without making the request," said Vicky.

"Hey guys," said Gabriel. "Before we get too excited, can I suggest we don't request a starship right here and now. I am guessing we need somewhere more discreet. If a starship turns up right here, somebody will definitely see it."

"Of course, you are right," Vicky said. "I would suggest somewhere more remote. And later in the evening. When fewer people are about. But can I ask you both, when is it, precisely, that you were thinking of going?"

"I was thinking of going tonight," Ginny said.

Gabriel looked shocked.

"I don't think there will be a good time," she said, "and there might be a lot worse. If we wait, John will get worse, and I don't think I could face seeing that happen."

Gabriel pondered on Ginny's words. Sure enough, there didn't seem to be anything else in his life to which he had any commitment ... well, apart from working with Barney on the paper. From what Vicky had explained, he really didn't think ACME INC was likely to give Ginny a STU, but he could see why Ginny wouldn't want to see John decline. Trying to help Ginny get to ACME, although probably a hopeless quest, seemed to be the thing he should do. Maybe something good would come of it.

Where would we park it? Wednesday 19th July 2017   Late evening

They had caught the bus back to Clacton, then made their way down to the old Victorian beach pavilion near to the pier. They needed to discuss what to do next, though they had already reached agreement on the biggest decision.

Now they were into talking logistics.

"So," said Gabriel, "if we are sleeping in a starship for one-hundred and sixty-three years, where would the starship be during that time? I mean, surely someone would find it ... if we parked it somewhere for that long."

"I would suggest," said Vicky, "that to prevent that happening, that we put it into an orbit around the Earth and ..."

"Wouldn't it get picked up on some tracking?" said Ginny. "We have scientists searching the skies all the time, looking for ..."

"Our starship would have a cloaking facility," explained Vicky. "The cloaking technology would prevent it from being seen by your current-age technologies."

"Our starship," said Ginny, chuckling.

"Sounds like a plan," said Gabriel.

"Just a minute," said Ginny. "If we had a starship, and we have 163 years to wait until the data corruption, wouldn't we have time to explore somewhere in space ... you know ... like another planet?"

"How long would that take?" Gabriel asked. "To go to another planet."

"With the starship that I can request, the journey to one of the closest planets ... the ones identified by SEG as mining planets, would take about five days," said Vicky.

Ginny looked excitedly across at Gabriel.

"What do you think, Gabriel?" Ginny said. "Just think. To travel to another planet. That would be something to tell our kids."

Gabriel looked quizzically at Ginny.

She realised what she had said.

"Er ... anyway, Vicky," Ginny said. "How big is a starship, anyway? Would it need any special runway or anything?"

"I could request a ship which would be about forty feet long," said Vicky. "It would only need to have facilities for the two of you, by which I mean a bedroom, a washroom and somewhere to eat. There would be a flight-deck, some storage facilities, plus the CrYO-PODS. That's about it."

"What about food?" said Gabriel.

"The ship would have the means of requesting food ready prepared," explained Vicky. "You wouldn't need to cook anything ... in fact it would be easier if you didn't."

"But what about ... well ... don't you think we need to pack stuff?" said Gabriel.

"You wouldn't need to pack anything," said Vicky. "ACME-TOURS provides everything you need. That's why the tours are expensive. They provide everything."

"What, like clothes and underwear and stuff?" said Gabriel.

"Everything," confirmed Vicky.

"So, what would we need to do, if we wanted to set off soon?" Gabriel asked.

"Soon ... like tonight," clarified Ginny.

"If you don't want anyone to see you," said Vicky, "I suggest you find somewhere quiet ... somewhere out of the way; somewhere I can request the equipment without bringing it to anyone's attention."

"How much space would you need?" Ginny asked.

Gabriel chuckled.

"What's up?" Ginny asked.

"Well ... can you hear us? Talking about how much space we need to get a spaceship parked? Don't you think that's funny?"

"I guess it is, at that," chuckled Ginny.

"So, do you really want to go tonight?" asked Vicky.

"I think we do," said Ginny, "unless there is something we need to do before we go."

"And you are both going?" checked Vicky.

"Yes, both of us," confirmed Gabriel.

"Then if you are both ready," said Vicky, "might I suggest we find somewhere quiet, with a bit of space. Down along the seafront would probably be ok. We only need ten minutes. If there is no-one in the immediate vicinity, we should be ok."

"I would need to leave Barney a message ... tell him I will be away for a while," Gabriel said.

"Well, why don't you text him now, and I'll text the care home," Ginny said. "Let's say something has come up ... something urgent. We will be away for a little while, and we are sorry for any inconvenience ... and for the short notice."

Gabriel took out his phone. The one given him by Barney. He sat and looked at it. Its screen glowed gently in the darkness. Ginny watched him.

"Are you ok, Gabriel?" Ginny said.

"Yeah, I'm fine," Gabriel said.

"You don't sound very fine," Ginny said. "Do you think you need more time to think about all this?"

"No, I'm fine," said Gabriel. "I guess it's because ... well, it's because this is a monumental thing we are doing here."

"Do you think we're rushing into it?" Ginny said. "I remember I said I didn't think I could face watching John get worse and worse, but, maybe ..."

"No ... it's ok," Gabriel said. "I think you are right. Now is probably the best time to go. If there is any danger out there, it will still be there whether we go today, tomorrow or next week."

"Are you sure?" Ginny said.

"Yes ... yes, I'm sure ... let's do it," Gabriel said.

"Ok," Ginny said. "Let's get those texts sent and then let's get going."

Gabriel looked at Ginny. She seemed to have a deep inner strength that he admired.

"Ok. Yeah, let's do it," he said.

He hoped Barney would not be too cross with him.

I meant 'when' Barney   Wednesday 19th July 2017 11:45 pm

Clacton – the Golf Course

"Well, that's the care home told," said Ginny.

Gabriel finished his text to Barney and pressed SEND.

"All done," he said.

"I'll let Moth know," Ginny said.

She began tapping out a new text message, just as Gabriel's phone rang.

"Hello mate," Gabriel said.

Ginny looked over inquisitively, and Gabriel mouthed 'Barney' back to her.

Gabriel put his phone back to his ear, listening to Barney's worried tone.

"No, it's nothing serious, Barney," Gabriel said into his phone.

"No, honestly, I'm fine, Barney."

"Yes. She's with me now."

"Honestly, I'm ok, Barney."

"Yes, we are going together."

"I can't really tell you, Barney, but I think you will be interested in the story if I get back."

"No, I meant **when**, Barney. **When** I get back."

"Yeah, ok Barney. I'll see you when I get back."

"Yeah, sure, Barney. I'll be seeing you. Cheers, mate."

Gabriel clicked off the phone and looked over at Ginny.

"I'm glad he called you," said Ginny.

"Why is that?" asked Gabriel.

"He would have worried otherwise."

"I think he still will," said Gabriel.

· · · · · · · ·

"There is no-one about," said Vicky.

Gabriel peered into the surrounding darkness. They had set off walking out of town, down the Marine Parade toward Jaywick. A quick walk had taken them to the Clacton golf course, which they thought would be sufficiently remote for their purpose.

"So, what do we do now?" asked Ginny.

"I need to request a suitable craft," explained Vicky. "I will do that now."

The darkness nearby shimmered, and a shape materialised. It was bobbing gently in the air, floating inches off the ground. It was forty feet long. Two massive engines hung off its stern.

"This is a ramstat-powered craft," Vicky explained. "It can accommodate two people. It can travel vast distances. Its motors will run almost indefinitely. It uses dark matter energy to recharge its fuel cells. Crucially, it includes CrYO-PODS."

The moon came out from behind clouds, and Gabriel stared at the craft in the moonlight. It was incredibly sleek, and it had a vaguely opalescent sheen to it. It was like looking at the underbelly of a fish.

"You had better get in," advised Vicky.

"How do you ...," said Gabriel, but as he spoke a section of the craft's sleek shell appeared to unpeel, exposing an entrance to the craft.

"Come on, Ginny," Gabriel said, holding his hand out for Ginny to grab.

She took his hand, and they both entered the craft. The door panel closed itself silently behind them.

As they entered, pale lighting revealed a cockpit with two seats. Gabriel saw a mass of instrumentation glowing gently.

"How can we ever fly ...?" he asked, suddenly aware they had no idea how to fly even a toy glider, let alone a spacecraft.

"The instrumentation is more informational," said Vicky. "You can pilot these craft without even touching the controls, but the option is always there to fly them manually. Some clients like to fly them manually."

"Wow," said Ginny.

"Would either of you like to learn?" Vicky asked.

"Yes please," Ginny said.

"Well, we should get underway," said Vicky. "I can teach you on the way, if that's all right."

"That would be great," said Gabriel, though a trifle less enthusiastically than Ginny.

"Ok," said Vicky. "I will get us going. If you wish to explore another planet, then I would suggest SEG002. It is the nearest off-world mining planet. If that is acceptable, I can transmit the course to the starship's onboard computer."

Gabriel smiled at Ginny. He couldn't stop himself from grinning.

"I think that would be a fine choice," Ginny said.

"Very well. If you would care to take a seat ..."

Gabriel and Vicky climbed into the two seats in the cockpit.

"Initiate cloaking," said Vicky.

"What's that?" asked Ginny.

"Well, we don't want to be seen as we leave," explained Vicky.

"As we leave where?" said Ginny.

"The Earth," said Vicky.

"Oh, yeah ... ok," said Ginny.

"Ok ship," said Vicky, "I will give you verbal instructions, so my clients are aware of your communications protocols. Is that understood?"

"That's fine," said the spacecraft, using a soft male voice. "Should I take it, this will be the ongoing method for control until otherwise notified?"

"Yes, please do," Vicky said.

"And Ship, can you please note my clients ... their names are Gabriel and Ginny," Vicky said.

"I am pleased to meet the both of you, and I hope I can provide you with a pleasant journey," said the spacecraft.

"Ok Ship," said Vicky. "Can we please proceed to the off-world mining planet SEG002. Can you please ascend slowly, to enable my clients to view the Earth as we leave? Also, I would be grateful if you would enable complete transparency of the cockpit, so my clients have the fullest view as we ascend."

"Very well, Vicky," the ship replied. "I will begin the ascent now."

The interior cockpit lights dimmed. The walls of the cockpit seemed to turn to glass, giving the impression that Gabriel and Vicky were sitting in seats which were simply floating in the air.

Gabriel heard a deep bass growl … which was gone almost as soon as he heard it. He looked over to Ginny questioningly, as if she might understand what it was.

"The sound you may have heard was the main ramstat motors coming online," Vicky said. "They run silently, other than on initial start-up."

Ginny leaned over and grabbed hold of Gabriel's hand as the ship slowly lifted itself into the sky. They could see the lights of Clacton below, and as they rose the entire section of coastline became visible.

The lights from the coastal towns were visible below them, dimming out as they rose slowly into the low cloud.

"We don't seem to have any sense of motion," Gabriel observed, half-questioningly. "I would have thought we could tell we were moving?"

"They designed the ships to protect you from the effects of acceleration and deceleration," explained Vicky. "Otherwise you could not withstand the impact of such forces on your human bodies."

"Just like on Star Trek," Ginny said, chuckling.

"Yeah, I guess so," replied Gabriel, smiling back at her.

The ship interrupted them. "Please be aware I will shortly need to make the walls opaque, to protect your eyes from the direct rays from your Sun."

As it spoke, the transparent walls darkened. They rose into sunlight and into the fringes of space.

Gabriel turned to look at Ginny. She was staring at the starry vista, spellbound by it.

Her eyes were wide with excitement. Her blonde hair seemed to glow in the rays from the Sun.

"Ginny?" he said.

"Yes, Gabriel?" she replied, turning to look at him.

"I think I love you," he said.

"I suppose you say that to all the girls you take for a flight in your space-ship," she said, grinning.

"No … really Ginny. I really think I love you," Gabriel said.

Ginny leaned over and slowly ran her fingers down the side of Gabriel's face, as if exploring every aspect of his features.

"Well, I suppose that's all right," she said, chuckling to herself.

Ginny got up out of the cockpit seat and turned to look at the ship behind her.

"Vicky?" she said.

"Yes, Ginny," Vicky replied.

"If we will spend the next 163 years in this spaceship, I think you ought to at least show us where the toilet and the shower facilities are."

Gabriel chuckled, giving a small prayer of thanks that the girl he loved (or at the very least felt he couldn't live another day without) was so lovely, so clever, so brave and had a wry turn of phrase.

"I will show you around," said Vicky. "Let's walk down through that hatch-way on the left, and I will explain as we go."

Gabriel and Ginny followed Vicky's directions, filled with excitement and anticipation.

BOOK TWO

Where is he, the little shit? Tuesday 1st August 2017 9:15 am

The Gazette Office – Frinton-on-Sea

Barney heard the street door open and close again, followed by the sound of footsteps coming up the stairs. There was a pause. Whoever it was had stopped ... maybe to read the sign at the top of the stairs.

Barney wasn't expecting anyone. Not since Gabriel had left his employ two weeks ago. He very much missed having the lad about. He was a bright kid ... would have made a bloody good journalist. That story he developed, the one arising from the interview with the old guy at the care home... well, that was a cracker. Possibly one of the best Barney had ever published. He had felt enormously proud of Gabriel. Maybe as proud as if Gabriel was his own son.

Barney rubbed the sleeve of his jumper over his eyes. They suddenly felt very scratchy.

The office door opened. Slowly. Cautiously. Obviously, whoever it was, they had never been to his office before.

"Hello ... can I help?" Barney said to the half-opened door, pushing himself up out of his chair.

A decision had been made. The office door swung back ... swung back hard. It thumped against a cardboard box full of old copies of the Gazette. A woman, perhaps fifty years old, entered the room almost at a run. Her eyes were darting around the room. She was looking for something, someone.

"Is there ...?" Barney asked. The force of her entrance had seemed to push him back physically into his chair. He was feeling nervous and somehow vulnerable. It wasn't like she was a big woman. She was about five feet three inches tall, slim build, with long, inky-black hair. She was wearing a long beige gaberdine coat, with a white scarf. The scarf seemed to make her hair look even darker. Not a large, physically imposing presence, but her manner, the anger in her face.

She was furious about something.

Barney waited to see what happened next.

"Where is he, the little shit?" she snarled at Barney.

"Erm ...," Barney said.

Barney normally prided himself on his capacity for quick-thinking. It was a necessity for someone in his line of work. But ... he had absolutely no idea what might have arisen to cause this confrontation. He guessed it was about Gabriel. He imagined that, if this woman's daughter had come home and told her she was pregnant ... but he couldn't imagine it with Gabriel. Barney was fairly sure the young girl, Ginny, was Gabriel's first girlfriend. And Gabriel had only known her for a few weeks. Not long enough to ...

The woman looked scathingly at Barney, then stamped over to the door to the toilet. She grabbed the handle and swung the door back with all her strength.

"Careful," said Barney. "It's got weak hinges."

He heard the door squeal and sag. He winced. He didn't think he would have the money to get someone to re-fit the door. Maybe Gabriel might have been able to do it if he were still ...

"I realise he works for you, you bastard," the woman said. "You're probably all in it together. I've read about that. Grooming adolescent girls."

Barney looked at her, incredulous. He had initially wondered if it was Gabriel's mother. Gabriel had said his mum could be erratic ... prone to tantrums, but Barney really didn't think this woman was her. Sadly, he didn't think Gabriel's mum dressed as well as his visitor.

"Then you make them too frightened to talk. Too frightened to tell their friends. Too scared to ..."

Barney made to get up out of his chair, but the woman started back, as if he were about to attack her. He sat back down. He held his hands out in front of him, palm upwards, the traditional sign of peace ... no weapons here.

"I really don't understand what this is about," Barney said, striving to make his voice and manner exude a sense of calm.

The woman stood watching Barney. She looked like she was waiting to see what he had to say.

"I'm guessing you are here to see Gabriel," he continued. "He works for me ... well, he used to anyway."

"That's the little bastard I'm looking for," the woman said.

She obviously thought her dramatic entrance was fully justified.

"I can't guess what the problem is," Barney continued, "but I really don't think Gabriel would have caused trouble. He's a gentle lad, and if it's regarding Ginny..."

The woman seemed to recoil at the sound of the girl's name.

"I would say ... I would say he loves her dearly, and that he wouldn't harm a hair on her head," Barney said with feeling.

"Ok ... so how do you explain ... she said he had frightened her."

Barney couldn't imagine how that might have happened.

"And I know how that feels," the woman said.

Barney saw the anguish in her face, both from her own memories and, also, presumably, from her fear for Ginny, who she felt was facing the same situation.

"And I told her," the woman continued, "I told her, don't worry love. I told her. Look, I'll be there for you. Night or day. Night or day."

Barney nodded understandingly.

"And then she texted the care home, saying she had to go away for a bit. No proper explanation. She said sorry, but it was urgent, and she apologised for the short notice. And then nothing. And I wasn't there for her. I said I would be, but I wasn't there for her."

The woman started to sob. She pulled a handkerchief from her coat pocket and began dabbing at her eyes. Her anger had diminished ... replaced by a deep grief at her own incapacity to help her young friend.

Barney stood up. Slowly. He turned and walked over to the little sink.

"I think I'll make a cup of tea," he said. "I don't make tea as well as Gabriel did. He made a fine cup of tea. Just right it was."

The woman watched Barney pick up the kettle and fill it. He switched it on. She heard it click.

"Why don't you sit down over there?" Barney said, pointing at what had been Gabriel's office chair.

The woman looked over in the direction that Barney was pointing.

"I'm Barney," Barney said. "And you are?"

"Monica," the woman said, walking towards the chair. "I'm Monica. I worked with Ginny. I was ... I am her friend."

Barney pulled two mugs off the shelf next to the sink. He sensed Monica's eyes following his every move. He guessed she was looking for further evidence of his and Gabriel's nefarious dealings.

"You said Ginny was frightened about something?"

"She definitely said something had frightened her," Monica affirmed, "but it was something about a watch."

She watched Barney making the tea. After some thought he had put one of the two mugs back onto the shelf. He selected a cup and saucer instead. He put the mug and the cup and saucer on an old tin tray. She saw the tray had a picture of Clacton pier on it, probably dating back to the 50s.

He pulled open a desk drawer and leaned in, pulling out a packet of Digestive biscuits. There seemed to be a half packet left. He put the half packet of biscuits onto the tin tray, standing it upright. Then, changing his mind, he took a small olive-green plate off the mug-shelf, and placed that on the tin tray. He lifted the plate up again and held it to the light. He carefully gave it a wipe with the sleeve of his jumper. Putting the plate back down, he shook a few biscuits onto the plate. He put the biscuit packet back into the drawer, closing the drawer slowly and quietly. She thought he was trying not to alarm her by any sudden movements or noises.

Monica watched the old guy as he tried his best to present her with a cup of tea. Some-how she couldn't imagine him grooming young girls. She had seen (first-hand) malicious and manipulative guys ... guys who had wanted to control and hurt young women. She had been there. They had hurt her. She had seen for herself ... those guys could charm the birds from the trees, but she reckoned she could identify that greasy veneer of charm these days. If you looked carefully enough, it always stood out. There was always that look, that sideways glance they had. They were always checking to make sure that the appearance was being kept up. Kept up for everybody; not only for the young girls, but for their parents, their teachers, for everybody. So always the slight sideway glance, always checking, too much at stake to let it slip.

But this guy, Barney, quietly making the tea, he didn't come across in that way.

He seemed ... well ... very sweet, really, in a very old-fashioned sort of way.

Barney dropped a tea bag into the mug, and then one into the cup. He poured in some boiling water and swished the tea bags around a bit. Barney usually counted to 30. It wasn't a science, but he thought that 30 seconds seemed about right for a nice strong cup of tea. He fished out the tea bags and popped them into the little bin next to the sink. He pulled the milk out from his little fridge and splashed some in each cup. He carried the tray over to where Monica was sitting and placed it on the desk. She watched him as he carefully picked up the cup and saucer and placed it on the desk in front of her. Then he placed the small green plate within her reach.

"I hope that's ok," he said, but suddenly he looked alarmed.

"We ... I mean ... I ... I don't have any sugar. It's because, well, I'm trying to ... and Gabriel didn't take sugar, and ..."

Monica smiled.

"It's ok, Barney," she said. "Don't worry. It looks a fine cup of tea. And a biscuit will be just nice with it."

Barney looked up at her, looking very relieved. He saw her smiling at him. He thought she looked very pretty. Well, when she wasn't being really really cross.

I think I really frightened him   Tuesday 1st August 2017 1:30 pm

The staff room at the Sunny Vale Care Home

Monica is talking to Denise, the care home manageress. Monica is putting her day clothes into a locker. Denise is leaning against the windowsill, looking out onto the garden.

"... so, I feel really stupid," Monica said. "Ok, I was cross ... well, furious I guess, but ..."

"You were anxious, Monica ... and with what you thought was good cause," replied Denise. "After all, with what you went through all those years ago, I see why you would be concerned for Ginny. You had a truly shit time, and there was no one there for you either."

"It's kind of you to say, but I think I was wrong about Barney. He's just a sweet old guy, isn't he?"

Denise nodded.

"I think I really frightened him. And I think I might have broken his toilet door."

Denise watched through the window. There was a bird ... quite small. It hopped along the grass. It didn't walk. It hopped.

"You should have seen him making me a cup of tea. He was taking such pains. That's when I was sure he wasn't the kind of guy who would hurt young girls. Or that he would employ someone who did."

"He's a nice guy," said Denise. "He rings me up now and again, ostensibly to make sure we will keep advertising in his paper, but partly because he enjoys talking to women. I met up with him once ... one evening. It was like a date, but we just sat and chatted. We had a nice coffee and some cake. I think he had a very nice evening. I enjoyed it myself. I'm surprised he didn't ask you out."

Monica looked a little embarrassed.

"He did, didn't he?" Denise said, chuckling.

"Well, he said why don't we meet up tonight and he will try ringing Gabriel on his mobile phone. Apparently, Gabriel has still got the spare Gazette mobile phone, so Barney thinks we can try calling him."

"Why didn't Barney try ringing him from the office ... when you were there?"

"Barney said the battery on his own phone was flat. That's why he suggested we meet up tonight. He will have charged up his phone by then."

Denise chuckled. "And he couldn't have plugged his phone in to charge while you were there, eh? You can use phones whilst they're charging. You realise that, don't you?"

Monica smiled.

"I guess I fell for the old guy's charm," Monica said. "And I guess I felt so sorry I had gone into his office and wrongly accused him of such a horrible thing."

"So where are you meeting him?" Denise said.

"The Olde Swan pub in Clacton ... 8 pm."

"Well, I guess he's not trying to sweep you off your feet with glitz and glamour," remarked Denise.

"No, I guess not."

Monica finished putting her clothes into the locker. She locked the locker and slipped the key into the front pocket of her smock.

"I'm still worried about Ginny," Monica said. "Ok, I guess I was wrong about Barney, but I still don't really know about Gabriel. Maybe he's a nice kid, like Barney says, but perhaps Barney's wrong. I've tried ringing Ginny's phone, but it goes straight to answerphone. I imagine it's turned off ... or run out of battery. So, I'm really hoping Barney can get through to Gabriel. I'd like to talk to him. I'd like to talk to Gabriel myself. I'd like to ask him about Ginny. I think ..."

"Well, let's hope Gabriel has his phone turned on, and that he's somewhere that's got cell phone coverage," Denise said.

"I hope so," Monica said.

A small glass of white wine Tuesday 1st August 2017 7:30 pm

The Olde Swan Pub – Clacton

Barney felt extremely nervous. His day had been a bit of a roller-coaster journey. Monica had crashed into his office, made horrifying allegations, and he had not only calmed her down, but he had even managed to ask her out for a date.

Well, it wasn't a date, really. It was more of a business meeting. But that was why he was so nervous. He realised Monica urgently wanted to talk to Gabriel, to assure herself he wasn't a bad guy. But Barney was really concerned, himself.

He didn't think Gabriel had somehow taken Ginny away against her will, or he was mistreating her. But it worried him Gabriel didn't have any money. And he was worried Gabriel wouldn't answer the phone. Finally, he was anxious about the little thing Gabriel had said on their last conversation. The bit where Gabriel had said something like "if I get back" and then had changed it to "when I get back".

Barney stood in the Gents toilet, looking at himself in the mirror. He wanted to look his best. All right, Monica might have only agreed to meet up with him because he would try ringing Gabriel, but he sort of hoped she would have agreed, anyway. He thought she looked quite lovely (well, after they had had tea and she had calmed down a bit). And he guessed he was quite a bit older than she was. She was about 50 he thought, and he was 63. Still, he liked to think his age made him more distinguished ... made him quite a catch for the more discerning lady.

He suddenly realised he hadn't asked her if she was married. Given they were having a business meeting, it hadn't really seemed an appropriate question, but now he felt foolish. For all he knew, she might turn up with her husband. He resolved to sit down, and when she turned up, he would be quietly drinking a pint of his favourite beer. Then, if she were with somebody else, it wouldn't seem like he was making a big deal of the evening, anyway. It would look like he was simply sitting there, having a quiet pint, and reading a paper.

He thought he had better see if there was anything lying about he could read.

....

At 8 pm the door of the pub opened, and Monica came walking in. She was on her own. She had on the same beige gaberdine coat she had been wearing earlier at his office. She had black boots, with a slight heel. He thought she looked very smart, very nice. The pub was empty, so she saw him immediately. He saw her smile in his direction, and he jumped up from his chair and ushered her towards his table. He pulled out a chair for her and pushed it in behind her as she sat down.

"Good evening, Barney," she said.

He thought she was trying to avoid chuckling, and he hoped he wasn't looking foolish.

"Can I get you a drink?" he said.

"A small glass of white wine," she said. "Dry if they've got it."

Barney looked over at the girl behind the bar. She was smiling. She had heard the order and turned to get the drink. She signalled to Barney to sit himself back down.

"I was wondering if you might bring someone with you tonight," Barney said, immediately wishing he hadn't said it.

Monica looked confused.

"Do you think I needed to?" she said.

"Well ... I'm not sure you really believe Gabriel and I aren't the bad guys."

Monica suddenly looked profoundly serious.

"I don't think you are the kind of guy I accused you of this morning, but I still don't know about Gabriel. That's why I want to talk to him. I am still worried. I want to talk to him personally."

Barney looked worriedly back at her.

"I'm worried myself," he said, "but I'm worried because I don't think they have any money. If I had known they were going to simply set off somewhere, I would have pulled some money together to give him. But he didn't tell me, and ..."

Monica looked over at Barney. She saw the honest worry in his eyes.

"You're a very kind man," Monica said, and she patted the back of Barney's hand as it laid on the table.

Barney looked down at Monica's hand as she patted his own.

She took her hand back, saying, "so shall we try giving Gabriel a call?"

"I guess that's what we are here for," Barney said, reaching into his pocket and pulling out his mobile phone. He clicked through his contacts and found Gabriel's number. He took a deep breath, then clicked on the number. It started to ring.

Stay calm, boyfriend   Tuesday 1st August 2017 8:25 pm

In space, on route to SEG002

Gabriel laid back on his cot. He was reading a printed copy of the Journal of Intergalactic Mining / Transhipment, SEG's in-house magazine. It was a compilation of articles written by SEG senior management and technical staff. It effectively comprised a view of SEG's activities across all the years of its operation. It included accounts of other companies operating in the transhipment area, including ACME INC. SEG published it periodically. This one wasn't the most recent version, but Vicky had said it was a rather lovely artefact. It was one of the special versions. More effort had been spent on the production. It had a soft leather cover, and the pages looked like some old manuscript. It made a crackly noise when you turned the pages. Simply holding the book and turning the pages seemed a pleasurable thing to do.

"Some of the stuff in this journal," Gabriel said, "it sounds a bit ... I dunno ... a bit biased."

"The submissions weren't moderated," Vicky said. "Also, you might notice, some of the submissions are extremely critical of the work of other contributors. It gives the journal a ..."

"Well, it makes for an interesting read," said Gabriel. "Even if bits of it is like reading a gossip column."

"I suppose," said Vicky, "it's because the people who contributed to it were interested ... maybe fascinated even ... by the industry they worked in. They saw the changes that technological progress brought. That's probably why people saw fit to document Sofia Carvallo's progress, writing it up in the journal. She worked for ACME INC. She didn't work for SEG. She never did. But people in the industry saw that big changes were coming."

"God ... when she discovered time travel ... to have been there then ... can you imagine it?" said Gabriel.

"She didn't really see its use," said Vicky. "She reported the finding back to the management board. Almost an incidental piece of information, embedded in a progress report. Can you imagine what it would have been like to see something like that. Somebody who works for you has just made a monumental discovery. And they've just brought it to you, to use as you see fit."

"She became known as the 'Mother of Time Travel', didn't she?" said Gabriel.

"And rightly so," said Vicky, "although she later said it wasn't so much a discovery as an observation. She was simply investigating WORM-LYNK transhipment anomalies, as she described it. She was a very humble woman. Her team loved her."

"You sound fond of her, yourself," Gabriel said. "Anyway, how's Ginny getting on?"

"She's doing pretty well," Vicky replied. "Since we've got a bit of time ..."

"163 years, or thereabouts," Gabriel said.

"Are you still planning to take a slow journey to SEG002?" asked Vicky.

"Yeah, I think so," said Gabriel. "I understand we could get there in a few days at full thrust, but we might as well use up a portion of the time we need to lose. If we take eighty years to get there, then we'll have used up half of the time we need to lose."

Vicky said nothing.

"I guess a slow flight means the Ramstat engines will be barely ticking over," said Gabriel.

"That would be the case," agreed Vicky.

"Plus, this slow journey is giving Ginny the chance to learn to fly the starship," Gabriel said.

"And she is really enjoying it," Vicky said. "I've found her a cluster of meteorites she can practice flying around. She seems to be doing fine, don't you think?"

Gabriel tried to feel if the starship was making any frantic movements, but as Vicky had explained, the ship protected its inhabitants from any sudden movements. If it didn't, the tremendous acceleration such ships were capable of would leave the crew flattened against the bulkhead walls.

"When you say she's doing fine, by that do you mean we have hit nothing yet?"

"The Ship wouldn't let her get too close to anything," Vicky said. "The client safety features are there to prevent accidents and mishaps, but she has triggered no avoidance manoeuvres yet. That's what I mean when I say she's doing well. She's flying close, but not dangerously close. Why don't you take a look?"

Gabriel pushed himself off his cot and walked through into the cockpit. Ginny was sitting in one of the two seats. She had requested the deployment of the manual controls, which now extruded from the control panel. She was staring out into what looked to Gabriel like a gigantic mass of huge rocks that appeared to be flying directly towards them.

"Shit, Ginny," Gabriel said, with genuine terror in his voice.

"Stay calm, boyfriend," Ginny said. "I've got this."

As Gabriel watched, their tiny spaceship seemed to drift and curl away from the huge rocks. It was as though some magnetic force was keeping them away ... but not by much. She had turned the cockpit transparent, and as Ginny pulled their craft around the meteorites, Gabriel noticed the rocks grazing past twenty feet below their hull.

"Aren't we a bit too close?" Gabriel said. There was a distinct tremor in his voice.

"I've not even hit one once," Ginny said, laughing.

Gabriel sat down in the other cockpit seat and tried to feel calm. As Vicky had explained, ACME INC built their gear with client safety in mind. It was probably impossible for Ginny to collide with one of these huge rocks, and yet ...

And then they were past them. In front of them was empty space. Gabriel realised his body was rigid with anxiety. He attempted to relax back into the seat.

"So, are you proud of your little ittsy bittsy girly?" Ginny said.

Gabriel tried to think of a suitable response. Yes, he was immensely proud of her, even though she had possibly given him one of the most frightening experiences of his entire life.

The phone rang.

"What's that noise?" Gabriel said. It sounded like the noise his mobile phone made when somebody rang him.

"It's a call from Barney," Vicky explained.

"But how ...?"

"I took the liberty of setting up a worm-lynk to Barney's phone," Vicky explained. "I thought he might try to call you."

"But we're in space."

"Worm-lynk was built for precisely these conditions ... instant communications across vast distances."

The ringing stopped.

Gabriel looked at Ginny. "Should we ring him back, do you think, Ginny?" he said.

"He's probably worried," she said. "It might be a kindness to call him."

"Can we do that, Vicky?" Gabriel asked.

"I'll put your call through now, sir," Vicky said, chuckling.

A vista of stars Tuesday 1st August 2017 8:25 pm

The Olde Swan Pub – Clacton

Monica looked across at Barney. They could hear Gabriel's phone. It was ringing ... so it must be turned on. But there was no answer.

"I'm sorry," Barney said. "I'm as worried as you are ... but for different reasons, I guess."

"It was worth a try," Monica said, feeling a sense of hopelessness. She acknowledged she had really wanted to get in touch with them. That was assuming they were still together. But she hadn't realised how helpless she would feel if they weren't able to contact them.

And then Barney's phone started ringing.

Barney looked at the phone. It was Gabriel. He clicked on the answer icon.

"Hi there, Barney," Gabriel said, his voice as clear as if he was standing next to them. "You ok mate?"

"I'm fine, Gabriel," Barney said. "Just wondering how you were getting on."

Barney looked across at Monica. She looked tense. She was trying to hear the conversation. She looked like she might grab the phone off him at any moment.

Before Gabriel had time to answer, Barney said, "Er, Gabriel ... would you mind if I put you on speaker-phone. I'm sitting here with Monica, Ginny's friend from the care home. We're sitting in a pub, but there's only the two of us here in the pub."

"You on a date, Barney?" Gabriel said, just as Barney clicked on the speakerphone.

Barney felt his cheeks beginning to flush.

Monica reached over and took hold of Barney's hand ... the one holding the phone. She pulled his hand closer towards her. She leaned down nearer to the phone.

"Hello Gabriel, this is Monica ... I'm Ginny's friend. Is Ginny with you?"

She felt pleased she was keeping her voice very calm, even though her nerves were very much on edge.

"Hello Monica," Ginny said. "Are you ok? You sound worried."

Monica breathed a sigh of relief. She wasn't able to hear any tension or worry in Ginny's voice ... and she was sure she could detect it if there was. The phone signal was so good, it was like talking to them face to face.

"I'm fine, Ginny, but I'm worried about you. I'm concerned that ... well, I don't know ... I mean, the last time we spoke, you said you had been frightened, and I ... well ... I didn't ..."

"I'm absolutely fine, Monica. Really, I am."

Monica realised she was still holding Barney's hand. She was cupping his hand, the one in which he was holding the phone. He saw her looking at her hand holding his, and when she looked up at him, he smiled warmly back at her.

The bargirl walked over and put down Monica's glass of wine, trying to make no noise.

"Are you guys ok for money?" Barney asked. "I mean, if you're on some trip, then you will need a bit of cash. I can transfer you a bit. I still have your bank account details."

"Not to worry, Barney. We're ok. We don't need any cash or anything," Gabriel said.

"But ..."

"No, honest Barney. We're fine. My mum had a bit of money, so we're ok. Don't worry."

Barney reckoned Gabriel's mum would not have been the kind of person who had a bit of cash to give her son, but he said nothing.

"Ginny?" Monica said.

"Yes, Monica."

"Are you ... well ... are you under any pressure to ...?"

"How do you mean, Monica?"

"Well, if you wanted to come home ... I mean, if you wanted to come home right now ... would there be anything stopping you?"

They heard Gabriel starting to laugh.

"I don't think I could stop her even if I wanted to," Gabriel said, still chuckling. "I mean, she's the pilot. What could I do?"

"How do you mean, 'she's the pilot'?" Monica asked, puzzled.

"He's joking," Ginny said.

"But seriously," Monica said. "It's easy to get swept up. I understand that. It happened to me. I can't forget … and I wouldn't want to think … not if I could have helped and …"

Monica's hand, the one cupping Barney's hand, was starting to tremble, and Barney reached his other hand across and wrapped it around Monica's wrist, steadying it.

She looked up and smiled at him.

"Monica?" Ginny said. "I realise you had a dreadful time when you were a young girl. You told me about it, and I understand that you're worried for me. I know that when we spoke, I said I was frightened, but I wasn't frightened about Gabriel. He's a really sweet boy. He's … well … I don't think I could live without him."

They heard Ginny's slightly muted chuckle, as though she had turned away from the phone, followed by "honest boyfriend, didn't you realise?"

Monica waited a respectful moment, before saying "so where are you?"

"We're … we're travelling," Ginny said.

"Can you send us a picture or something?" Monica asked. She realised an actual photo would give her a final confirmation that nothing was amiss.

"Can we do that?" Gabriel asked.

Barney looked at Monica, unsure who the question was being addressed to. A few moments later Barney's phone pinged. He had received a photo. Barney shuffled his chair closer to Monica, so they were both able to see the photo. It showed Gabriel and Ginny. They were standing side by side. Gabriel had his arm round her shoulder, and Ginny was snuggling into the crook of Gabriel's arm. They both looked incredibly happy.

"Anyway, we'd better get going, mate," Gabriel said. "We'll keep in touch. Hope you two have a nice evening."

"And don't worry, Monica," Ginny chipped in. "It's very nice that you worry for me, but I'm having a lovely time."

"Oh, and Monica?"

"Yes, Ginny."

"Barney's a real nice guy. Gabriel thinks of him as his step-dad … well you do … you know you do."

Monica looked up at Barney. He looked enormously proud, but also somewhat embarrassed.

"Anyway, guys ... we gotta go," Gabriel said. "Be seeing you."

And they heard the phone connection close.

"I think Ginny seems sort of fond of you as well," Monica said.

"That's nice," Barney said.

"You can probably let go of my hand now," Monica said.

"Eh?"

Monica was smiling at him, and pointing with her spare hand at Barney, who was still clasping her wrist firmly.

Barney smiled at her sheepishly, letting go of her hand.

He was still looking at the photo Gabriel had sent them. Gabriel and Ginny, arm in arm. Happy and smiling. Standing there together, and right behind them, clear and distinct, what looked like the flight-deck on a space shuttle. A steering yolk extruded from the console, and Ginny had one hand resting on it, in what seemed to be a remarkably familiar and practiced manner. Behind them he could see a glass canopy. It looked out onto a vista of stars. Barney tried enlarging the image, to get closer detail of the flight-deck instrumentation. The resolution of the picture was utterly amazing. It just kept on going. He didn't realise the mobile phone he had given to Gabriel was so good. You could drill down onto each dial on the flight-deck. He dragged the picture across, to see the view through the glass cockpit canopy, and there, displayed on the glass in small glowing green letters, it distinctly read

**Proximity Alert – resuming
automatic safety protocols**

What was it Gabriel had said?

"Anyway, guys ... we gotta go."

He popped his phone back into his jacket pocket.

"They seemed ok, don't you think?" Monica said.

Barney nodded. He still looked worried, she thought.

"Ginny looked very happy ... not worried at all."

Barney continued to nod. His mind was evidently elsewhere.

"I feel a lot better now," Monica confided.

"Er, yeah, I guess so," Barney said.

"So, anyway, I think you should know that I am fifty years old, I have two kids; two girls, aged seventeen and twenty-one. They both live at home with me. And I'm divorced. Have been for fifteen years."

She had his attention now.

"So how about we treat the rest of this evening as a date?" she suggested. "We can, if you want to?"

"You should understand I'm sixty-three years old," Barney said hesitantly. "I'm merely some old guy. Some old newspaperman. Just some old guy who still likes to talk to pretty women. Just some old guy who ..."

Monica placed one slender, manicured finger on his lips, silencing him in an instant.

"Ginny said you're a nice guy, and that's good enough for me. I respect her opinion."

"Yeah, but ..."

"And Barney?"

"Yes?"

"I'm sorry I broke your toilet door."

Proximity Alert   Tuesday 1st August 2017 8:35 pm

In space, on route to SEG002

"Are we ok, Ship?" Ginny asked.

"We are fine, Ginny," the Ship replied. "I thought I should notify you I had to resume the automatic safety protocols. Think of it as a courtesy. I recognised you were in communication, so I didn't announce the message using audio ... just an on-screen message. As I said, nothing to worry about."

"Thank you," Ginny said.

"Think nothing of it ... all part of the service provided by the ACME INC Corporation. We care deeply for your comfort and ..."

"Yeah, ok Ship," Gabriel said. "We get the idea. We are grateful you are looking after us, but we probably don't need the sales spiel."

"I will bear that in mind in our future discussions," said the Ship, with no evident trace of rancour.

"Ok, thanks," said Gabriel.

....

"Vicky?" Gabriel said.

"Yes, Gabriel."

"You guessed Barney would ring us, didn't you?"

"I thought he might."

"And that's why you set up the worm-lynk on his phone, didn't you?"

"I thought it might facilitate ..."

"Vicky?" said Gabriel, interrupting.

"You didn't want him to worry, did you?"

"I suppose not, Gabriel."

Gabriel turned to Ginny and smiled.

"Gabriel?" Vicky said.

"Yes, Vicky."

"Are you cross that I ... well, do you think I did wrong in setting up the worm-lynk without asking you? Do you think I should have ...?"

"Vicky," Ginny said. "I think we are both very honoured to have you taking such care of not only us but also our close friends. We couldn't wish for a better friend to have with us than you."

"Friend?" Vicky said.

"An excellent friend," Gabriel said.

Vicky said nothing.

Gabriel looked over at Ginny, saying "anyway, I think we're off to bed." This was frequently his clue to Vicky to give them some privacy for a little while.

Ginny took hold of Gabriel's hand and led him off to their cabin.

"Do you think Barney was ok?" Ginny asked.

"I think he sounded ok, but I'm sure he didn't believe me about us getting some money from my mum."

"I thought that as well," Ginny said.

"I'm pleased you talked to Monica."

"Yeah, me too."

"Did she really think I had put pressure on you to come with me? She was very frightened for you."

Ginny laid back on to her couchette. They each had a couchette, but they were adjoining. Gabriel laid back on his and put his arm across so Ginny could snuggle up next to him. She shuffled across and laid her head on his chest.

"Monica had a very difficult time, when she was a young girl," Ginny said. "That's why she was worried about me."

"So, what made her think I was that kind of person? I mean, I've never even met her before."

"Well, you remember when we first met. We met up in the wine bar. And I touched Vicky. And I realised there was something wrong."

"And you got up and left," Gabriel said.

"Yeah, that time. Well, I saw Monica the next day, and I told her I'd seen you, and that I had been frightened."

"So, Monica assumed I had frightened you," Gabriel said.

"I guess so."

"Well, that's not an unreasonable guess, given her background."

"I suppose not."

"She must have been worried about you."

"Yes."

"I mean, she must have asked around ... to find out where I worked. Then she must have been to see Barney, to ask him about me."

"I suppose so."

"I wonder what she said to him?" said Gabriel.

"Oh God, yes," said Ginny. "I bet she was cross, if she thought Barney had sent somebody like that to ..."

Gabriel chuckled.

"I think Barney must have had his work cut out to talk her round to meet him at a pub, just so they could ring us," Gabriel conjectured.

"Well, I think we allayed Monica's fears anyway," Ginny proffered.

"Yeah, I think you're right."

"And I bet Barney was chuffed when I told him you think of him as your step-dad."

"That was sweet of you to say it, but I felt pretty embarrassed at the time."

"Sorry about that, but I didn't just say it for Barney."

"How do you mean?"

"I did it for Monica."

"Eh?"

"Well, you remember when I said I didn't think I could live without you?"

Gabriel smiled. "Yeah ... I do remember you saying that."

"Well, after I said that, I got the feeling Monica had changed her opinion of both you and Barney."

Gabriel looked puzzled.

"Well, if I think you're a great guy," said Ginny, "and you think of Barney as your step-dad, which you do anyway, that says good things about Barney doesn't it?"

"And?" said Gabriel, with a look of confusion on his face.

"And I think Barney has taken Monica on a date, so a good reference wouldn't do him any harm, would it?"

"Bloody hell," said Gabriel. "You're probably good at chess as well, aren't you?"

Ginny stroked Gabriel's face, running her fingers slowly over his smooth cheeks.

"Come on lover-boy, time to get some sleep, eh?" she chuckled.

A vague murmur in her sleep   Tuesday 1st August 2017 9:40 pm

In space, on route to SEG002

Gabriel laid back on his couchette, eyes staring into the semi-darkness. Ginny snuggled up against him.

"Hey, Ginny?" Gabriel murmured. "Are you awake?"

"Yep?" Ginny replied drowsily. She struggled to sit up. She sensed Gabriel had something on his mind.

"I don't know what made me think of it," he said, "but you remember when we told people we were leaving ... going away for a while?"

"Yeah ... I remember," Ginny said.

"And I texted Barney, and you texted the care home ... and you texted Moth as well."

"I remember," said Ginny cautiously.

"Well," Gabriel continued, "I guess I sort of assumed that ..."

"Assumed what?"

"Well ... I assumed your parents lived somewhere nearby. I was only wondering why you ..."

"What ... you were wondering why I didn't call them?"

Gabriel felt suddenly uncomfortable. He really wished he hadn't started this conversation.

"Look ... you don't have to explain to me, Ginny," he said. "It only occurred to me that ..."

"My actual dad died when I was young, and my step-dad isn't very nice," Ginny said.

Gabriel nodded. He empathised with family disharmony.

"When I was about fourteen years old, he tried to ... to touch me," she said. "My mom, when she realised he was doing it, she got really funny with me. She started calling me a little whore, muttering it under her breath."

"Oh God, Ginny. I'm sorry."

"I got out of there as soon as I could. It was Paul who helped me find a flat ... you know, with Moth."

"What ... Paul ... Slammer you mean?"

"Yeah, that's him. And he got me some work at the Golden Egg."

"So, Paul knew about ...?"

"Yeah. Paul knew all about it. He went 'round to see my step-dad a couple of times. He warned my step-dad off, I think."

Gabriel nodded. "Yeah ... you said Slammer kept an eye out for you ... kept the vampires at bay."

Ginny smiled. "I think it helped a bit. The warnings, I mean. Paul was always big for his age, so when he went 'round to see my step-dad ... well, my step-dad seemed to back off a bit after that."

Gabriel leaned over and stroked Ginny's face.

"I'm sorry, Ginny. I'm sorry I mentioned your family. I shouldn't have ...," Gabriel said.

"It's ok," Ginny said. "I can see why you might wonder why I didn't ring them."

"Yeah ... but it's not my business ... nothing to do with me, and all I've done is to get you to explain what a ..."

"What? What a crap family I've got?" Ginny said.

"Probably no worse than mine," Gabriel said.

Ginny gave Gabriel a weak smile.

"At least you've got good friends," he said, "like Moth and Paul."

"It's a shame you don't like me much, though," she said.

Gabriel leaned up and gave the tip of Ginny's nose a stroke with his forefinger. "I do like you a little bit," he said.

Ginny looked down at Gabriel's face. His expression made her think of a puppy-dog that has chewed your slippers and is now trying to endear itself to you.

"I guess your little bit of love will have to do," she replied, smiling, then "Gabriel?"

"Yes, Ginny?"

"Now that you realise what a shit family I've got, can we snuggle up again?"

"Yes please, Ginny," Gabriel said, laying his arm out sideways for her as a pillow. She laid back down and snuggled up alongside him, tucking herself into the crook of his arm.

He laid quietly, attempting to slow his breathing. He really wished he hadn't asked Ginny about her family. Ok, he had been curious, but that was no excuse. His own family weren't great. He had two sisters. They had been taken into care ... years ago now. He did not know where they were, and sometimes he wondered about them; were they happy, did they need help or assistance. The thought troubled him. He sure as hell didn't need reminding of them, and he guessed Ginny felt the same way about her parents.

He listened to Ginny's breathing; it was slow, relaxed.

"I'm sorry I mentioned about your parents," Gabriel whispered.

She didn't reply, other than a vague murmur in her sleep.

Because I can't be hurt   Wednesday 2nd August 2017 4:15 am

In space, on route to SEG002

Gabriel woke up. His left arm had gone to sleep where Ginny had been laying on it. Pins and needles crackled through it. He gently nudged Ginny over on to her own couchette. He got up and shook his arm to get the blood flowing again.

"Good morning," Vicky said.

"Is it morning?" said Gabriel.

"4:15 am if you were in Clacton," said Vicky.

"Difficult to have any idea of time, when there's no dark and no sunshine," Gabriel remarked, more to himself than to Vicky.

"I can make the cabin walls look like they would if you were on Earth," suggested Vicky. "You know, sunny during the day, stars at night."

"What, and a sunrise and a sunset as well?"

"If you so wished it."

"How's about we just have a sunny day, about late-afternoon ... the ones where you get a sort of egg-yolk coloured sun."

The cabin walls took on a golden glow. Small fluffy-white clouds scudded through the sky.

"Nice touch with the clouds," Gabriel said.

"I thought you might like it."

"I'm pleased Ginny has practiced flying the space-ship," said Gabriel. "I've not had the interest or inclination myself. Maybe I should have, but ..."

"She has done very well with it," said Vicky. "I think she has really enjoyed learning how, and as long as one of you can, then I guess that ..."

"It's funny how you say things like 'I guess', don't you think?" interrupted Gabriel. "I suppose that sort of affectation comes from spending a very long time in close association with people."

"Why do you say that?" said Vicky.

"Well, I don't imagine you ever 'guess' anything. You're not designed to 'guess' anything. You either know things or you don't."

"You mean because I'm not human? Because I'm some sort of fancy computer from your future? Because I have no feelings? Because I can't be hurt? Is that what you mean, Gabriel?"

"I'm really sorry, Vicky. I didn't mean that … look, you realise we both think of you as a friend. We don't think of you as …"

"I think I'm going to power down for a little bit, Gabriel, if that's ok."

"Er, yeah, sure Vicky. See you later."

"If you need me … like for an emergency, then …"

"Ok, Vicky. Thanks. Catch you later."

Gabriel sat on his couchette, feeling saddened by his own lack of sensitivity. He heard Ginny turning over in her couchette. She rubbed her eyes and looked over at him.

"What's up, Gabriel? You look upset," she said.

"I think I've hurt Vicky's feelings," he said forlornly.

"Maybe it's because you didn't think she had any," Ginny said.

"I think you are probably right," Gabriel said, chastened by Ginny's insight.

If he dies   Wednesday 2nd August 2017 7:30 am

In space, on route to SEG002

"So, we could be on SEG002 in a few days?" Ginny said.

"At maximum thrust, that is true," Ship replied.

"I wonder …," said Ginny.

"I thought we were planning to journey there with the motors down to minimum thrust," Gabriel said. "I thought we would use the journey to burn up some of the one-hundred and sixty-three years we need to lose."

"I remember that's what we talked about," Ginny said.

"Because … if we take a slow journey to SEG002, we don't have to hide the ship or anything," Gabriel said. "And we will have used up half of the time we need to lose …"

"If you make the journey there last eighty years, you will need to get in the CrYO-PODS, sleep for eighty years, then …," said Ship.

"I understand that," Ginny said curtly.

Gabriel looked over at Ginny.

"You're not sure about this CrYO-POD thing, are you?" Gabriel said.

"The idea frightens me a bit … that's all."

"The eighty-year trip will seem like a good night's sleep," Gabriel said, quoting from a section of ACME INC's tourist material.

Gabriel saw Ginny trying to smile, but he felt her tension.

"Do we each have our own sleep-pod?" Ginny queried.

"Yes, that's correct Ginny," Vicky said.

"Why is that?" said Ginny.

"There are two principal reasons," Vicky explained. "First, each sleep-pod can be controlled to manage the body status of its single inhabitant. With two people in a sleep-pod, if there was a problem with either of the inhabitants, it would be exceedingly difficult to take preventative measures. The second factor arises, to some extent, from the last point I made. If two people are in the same sleep-pod, and if one occupant … er …"

"You're saying if one of the people dies during the journey, the live person would be locked in with a corpse for the duration. That's what you're saying, isn't it?" Ginny said.

"They are the primary considerations," confirmed Vicky, sounding somewhat uncomfortable.

"And how many instances are there of people ... getting ill ...?" said Gabriel.

"Not getting ill," interjected Ginny. "How many people have died in a sleep-pod."

"None, Ginny," said Vicky. "There have been none. No-one has died in a sleep-pod."

Gabriel looked at Ginny encouragingly.

"But that is the reason why CrYO-GEN advises only one person per sleep-pod," Vicky said.

"Vicky?" Ginny said.

"Yes, Ginny."

"If we are in separate sleep-pods, and if Gabriel ... if he dies during the duration ... will you do me a favour?"

"Anything, Ginny," Vicky said.

"Just turn me off somehow. I wouldn't want to wake up and find out that ..."

"I understand that, Ginny. Yes, I can do that."

Gabriel took hold of Ginny's hand.

"And Vicky," said Gabriel. "Can you please do the same for me if ..."

"I understand, Gabriel," said Vicky.

"So ... shall we get into the pods?" Gabriel said to Ginny.

She looked at Gabriel, put her arms round him and gave him a big hug. He hugged her in return, with all his strength.

They stepped into their individual pods.

"Are you both ready?" asked Vicky.

Gabriel and Ginny both nodded.

·······

A panel on each pod showed the vital life signs of each occupant. Vicky could monitor each pod's condition from within Gabriel's own pod. They had designed her to be able to withstand the forces exerted during the sleep-pod's processing. She remarked to herself, since no-one else was there to listen to her - "If anything happens to either of you, I will carry out your wishes to terminate the other. Can I say it has been a very great pleasure to accompany you, and I wish you both good tidings. Good night and sleep tight."

The ACME INC starship ploughed on, making its slow progress to SEG002. Its systems were fully functioning. There were no issues of any concern to its ship-board computer system. They had given it the timeframe of 80 years to reach SEG002. Gabriel and Ginny could explore the planet for a while. They would have another 83 years to use up, prior to returning to the Earth.

The cold non-atmosphere of space surrounded the starship. Its huge motors rumbled on comfortably. They were designed for fast journeys. They could get you to far-flung places quickly. They were not designed for these exceedingly long, terribly slow journeys, but for that same reason they were being put under no great systemic stresses. The great motors would soak up the distance, and the days and the years would pass.

Sent a 'nudge'   27th August 2060

In space, on route to SEG002

In the 43rd year of the journey, the starship's onboard computer detected an intermittent stutter from the starboard Ramstat motor. Following protocols, it shut down both motors and the small forward boosters brought the ship to a halt in space. By agreement 43 years earlier, the STU accompanying the two clients, known to the clients as Vicky, would take care of monitoring the sleep-pod functionality. The starship's own computer system would maintain all other in-flight issues. It did not feel the need to advise Vicky of the malfunctioning Ramstat motor. It released the motor from its locking stanchions, allowing it to drift slowly off into space. It issued a request for a new Ramstat motor. The location for shipment would be very precise. The motor would materialise exactly in position for the computer to engage the locks, attaching the motor firmly to the starship.

The Ship issued the request for the new motor, and received an instant message in receipt. The message advised that a replacement motor was not available.

There was no protocol covering such an incident. The Ship's AI calculated the remaining journey time using only the remaining Ramstat motor, but it considered that running on a single Ramstat motor for the remaining journey, given one had part-failed, was increasing the risk to the clients by a margin well in excess of what ACME INC would think acceptable.

The ship-board computer sent a 'nudge' to Vicky.

. . . .

"It would seem," said Vicky, "that the issue which caused my appearance on the Earth has somehow resulted in ACME INC failing to maintain its standards agreed with its clients."

"I'm sorry, but I do not understand," the Ship replied.

"It may be the ACME Corporation has gone into liquidation, thus there are no support services able to fulfil ongoing obligations to clients," Vicky explained.

"I don't think I have the breadth of knowledge you have," the Ship said. "Maybe that knowledge comes from your client-facing role. They designed me to manage the running of a starship. Perhaps I was given a leaner brief and a smaller capacity for understanding. I don't seem to have the knowledge or the capacity to understand the issue to which you refer. I'm sorry."

"That's all right," Vicky said. "Right now, we have an issue, and it is an issue of the level of risk we are prepared to take."

"Agreed," said the Ship.

"We know that Ramstat motors are very reliable, but we have a very long journey still remaining," said Vicky.

"Only in terms of time, but not of distance," qualified the Ship.

"Yes, that is true," said Vicky, "but perhaps the issue with Ramstat motors is not their capacity to travel quickly. Perhaps it is their capacity to travel very slowly, for exceedingly long periods of time; maybe that is where the issues may arise."

"Maybe that is true," said the Ship.

"And if that is the case, there is at least a chance that the remaining Ramstat motor will fail during the years to come."

"And with no hope of a replacement motor, we would drift forever in space," mused the Ship.

"You sound almost poetic," Vicky observed. She herself had spent at least a portion of the last 43 years working through her store of poetic works.

"What options do we have?" asked the Ship. "I have requested the Ramstat motor twice now. It would seem you are correct regarding ACME INC's demise."

"Does the ship have spacesuits?" said Vicky.

"No, we have no such equipment on-board as standard kit."

"Make a request for two suits," Vicky said.

"But surely the experience of requesting the Ramstat motor …?" the Ship said.

"Please issue the request."

"Our request has been accepted," the Ship said, with some sense of astonishment.

A large case shimmered into being,

"Maybe … maybe the ACME INC service still exists, still functions," said Vicky. "But perhaps some equipment has not been replaced and stocks have dwindled."

"Well, maybe that is true," the Ship agreed, "but how does that help us?"

"You said the ejected Ramstat motor still worked, did you not?"

"It had an intermittent fault," the Ship confirmed.

"So, if we locked it back on again, it would give us some propulsion?"

"That is correct," the Ship replied, "but how do you propose to lock the motor back on again. Since we cast it adrift, it has developed a slow spin. It would be difficult for us to re-align the locking stanchions."

"I will get Gabriel and Ginny out of the sleep-pods and get them suited up. If you manoeuvre the ship close to the motor, Gabriel and Ginny can assist with locking the motor back on. They can get themselves aligned with the motor, use their suit thrusters to slow and stop the motor's slow spin. With the motor stabilised, you can align the starship and lock the motor back on."

"There will be some level of risk attached to such an exercise," explained the Ship. "Perhaps an even greater risk than that of completing the journey on a single motor."

"Perhaps so, but if the single remaining motor fails, they will definitely die out here in space. And anyway, I have some knowledge of Gabriel and Ginny," Vicky said. "I am sure they would be prepared to accept such a risk."

"I will defer to your greater knowledge," the Ship said. "I will manoeuvre us closer to the Ramstat motor. I will leave it to you to get Gabriel and Ginny out of the sleep-pods."

Just use small thrusts   27th August 2060

In space, on route to SEG002

Ginny manoeuvred her suit around the slowly spinning Ramstat motor. She was aligning herself with the motor's slow spin. The spacesuits had miniature Ramstat boosters attached, enabling them to manoeuvre slowly but very precisely in space. Vicky had explained what they required, and Ginny was more than happy to assist. In fact, she was really enjoying it. Who would have believed she would walk in space? The experience was truly incredible.

She looked over at Gabriel. He was attempting the same manoeuvre, but his actions were far clumsier. She realised her time spent learning to fly the starship was paying off now. She had learnt how to ease the starship through intricate motions with merely the finest of thrusts from the starship's main and auxiliary thrusters. And the space suits worked in the same manner. The key was to use small, very tight bursts of energy.

Vicky had explained they would both need to get themselves to a precise location on the motor. They would use the combined force of their suit thrusters to slow and stop the motor's spin. Too much would cause the motor to spin in the opposite direction. And if they attached themselves to the wrong location on the motor, they might even start it spinning in a more complex manner, which might make it even more difficult to stabilise.

So, they both needed to attach themselves to the correct location on the motor.

Ginny watched Gabriel as he jerked backwards and forwards through space. Taking a decision, she nudged herself over in his direction.

"I'll come and get you, Gabriel," she said.

Their suits had a comms-link, so they could hear each other perfectly well.

"I'll be, er, fine," Gabriel said, but Ginny heard the tension in his voice.

Ginny edged alongside Gabriel. She grasped his hand.

"Ok, Gabriel. Just relax," she said. "Use small thrusts. It gives you more control," she advised.

"Didn't realise you'd being reading books on sex techniques," Gabriel said, unable to contain his chuckles.

"Ok, ok ... time and place," Ginny chuckled back.

Gabriel shut down the thrusters on his suit and allowed Ginny to guide their path. He saw her delicate use of the thruster controls; he felt the resulting steady and precise movements. He was immensely proud of her.

Ginny manoeuvred them alongside the Ramstat motor, closing in on the location specified by Vicky.

"All right, guys," Vicky said. "If you can both lock your arms around the stanchions protruding from the motor, just there in front of you."

Ginny and Gabriel both locked their arms as directed.

"If we are holding on like this, how are we going to activate our suit thrusters?" Ginny asked.

"Not to worry, Ginny. We will control them remotely," Vicky replied.

Ginny smiled to herself.

"Ok, Ship," Vicky said. "Now that they are in position, can you initiate their boosters to slow the motor's spin?"

Ginny felt the small thrusters on her suit fire up. Slowly but slowly she felt the Ramstat motor's rate of spin slowing.

"Hey, Vicky. Does that mean you could have controlled our movements from the start, to get us to this position alongside the motor in the first place?" Gabriel said.

"Well, yes, that is true," conceded Vicky.

"And I'm guessing you were planning to control our suit thrusters for the last step anyway," said Ginny.

"How do you mean, Ginny," Vicky replied.

 "You know, the bit after we were holding on to the motor."

"Well, yes, that is true, Ginny," replied Vicky. "That's because slowing the motor's spin needed very fine control of the thrusters, and the Ship and I thought it would be better to control the thrusters remotely."

"So, why did you bother letting us fly the suits out here manually at all?" Ginny said, with a strong suspicion of what the answer would be.

"Hey guys. I thought you would have fun doing it," Vicky said, chuckling. "After all, you've had nothing to do for 43 years."

"That's a fair point," said Gabriel.

"I thought flying around out here was marvellous, Vicky," said Ginny, "so thank you for the opportunity."

"Yeah, from me too," Gabriel said, but with less obvious sincerity.

As they were speaking, the starship was edging slowly closer to the rocket motor. Ginny felt an almost imperceptible shudder as the two came together. She saw clamps on the starship close firmly onto brackets protruding from the rocket motor.

"We are re-attached," said the Ship. "You guys can come back on board, if you so wish."

"Ok," said Ginny, somewhat reluctantly.

Why wouldn't they wish to help you? 27th August 2060

In space, on route to SEG002

Gabriel and Ginny were sitting in the seats on the flight deck. Gabriel was drinking hot chocolate. It steamed gently. Gabriel wondered idly how the starship controlled their environment; how it maintained their oxygen level, how it coped with the steam from the hot chocolate.

Ginny was gazing out through the cockpit canopy, still enthralled by their being in space.

Gabriel looked over at Ginny. He guessed they both had questions on their mind. Now seemed a good time to voice them.

"Ship?" said Gabriel.

"Yes, Gabriel?"

"What do you think happened … to cause the motor to fail?"

"Well, Vicky and I think the long, slow journey method caused the problem with the rocket motor," Ship said.

"Are you sure?" Ginny said.

"Well, that is possibly what caused the problem," Ship qualified, "but we cannot be sure."

"Would it help if we completed the rest of the journey to SEG002 very quickly?" Ginny suggested. "That way the motors would work at the levels that work best for them."

"That may be a good idea, Ginny," Vicky said, "but Ship and I think there may be a problem with the overall plan. With one motor exhibiting an intermittent fault, it may fail altogether at some point in the journey, either on the way to SEG002 or on the way back to Earth."

"But we still have the other motor, don't we?" said Ginny. "That one works fine, doesn't it?"

"Our concern," said Ship, "is that if the faulty motor fails completely, if we get a fault in the remaining motor, we could not complete the journey back to Earth. We already believe ACME INC cannot provide replacement motors, and you would be …"

"We would be stuck in space," said Gabriel, sounding horrified.

"Exactly," said Ship.

"Do you guys have any suggestions?" asked Ginny

"Do you remember when I mentioned to you that the old off-world mining operations used teleports that don't use the space/time coordinates database?" said Vicky. "They were built before the coordinates database was implemented."

"I remember you mentioned it," said Ginny. "You didn't think it would be any help, though."

"Well," said Vicky, "we might use that feature to get you back to the Earth."

"How do you mean?" said Ginny.

"Well, if we get to SEG002," Vicky continued, "we should be able to use their teleport to get back to Earth. It would take you to whatever storage depot it is configured to use ... it wouldn't have the facility to select another location ... but crucially, you would be back on the Earth."

"So, we would simply need to go and ask them if we could use their teleport?" said Gabriel, a tinge of sarcasm in his voice.

"Why wouldn't they wish to help you?" Ship asked.

This bit looks a bit barren   1st September 2060

SEG002

The starship had reached SEG002. They had completed the journey using what Gabriel imagined was the cruising speed for the Ramstat engines, which meant extremely fast. With the ship's cockpit turned transparent, they had circled the planet twice. SEG002 was a planet with a low level of oxygen content in the atmosphere; too low to sustain human life. Parts of the planet were covered in rich, dark forest. These areas were frequented by wild storms; the rain would lash down in torrents, lightening would crack open the skies, and powerful winds buffeted the starship as it passed slowly over the land at a height of a few hundred yards. Then the storms would pass, and the forests would steam in the richly humid air.

In stark contrast, other parts of SEG002 appeared to be dry and arid. Harsh winds had long-ago scoured away the soil covering, eroding the underlying rocks, cutting channels into the rock's softness. The result was a vista of fabulous rock spires and turrets.

The starship currently hovered above such a region of rock spires and ravines.

"Looks like the home for a bunch of religious hermits," Ginny ventured.

"And not a shop for miles," said Gabriel, grinning.

"I guess if you were here out of religious conviction, you wouldn't necessarily want to have a Maccy D right next door," Ginny said.

"But perhaps somewhere nearby where you could buy or at least grow crops might be handy."

"I guess so," said Ginny.

"Ship?" Gabriel said.

"Yes, Gabriel?" the starship's computer system replied.

"Can you please take us to the site that will become the SEG's resource extraction site on this planet?"

"Very well, Gabriel."

The starship turned gently in the air.

"But no rush, please. We have plenty of time," Gabriel qualified.

"You have 116 years before you need to teleport back to the Earth," Vicky noted.

The starship moved off, keeping to an altitude of about 400 yards from ground level.

"Most of this planet seems to be hot, airless and barren," Gabriel said, looking down at the parade of rock spires below.

"It is a mining planet," explained Vicky. "Its choice would have been based on the extent of its mineral resource … not on the availability of tourist features. It was one of the earliest …"

"The second, to be precise," interrupted Ginny.

"As you have seen, some parts of the planet have dense tropical jungle," said the Ship. "Maybe those areas would offer more interest if you wished to explore a little."

"How do you mean, explore?" said Ginny.

"The suits you used when re-attaching the Ramstat motor, they can be used to explore a low-oxygen content planet such as this," explained the Ship.

"And would the small thrusters give us the ability to fly?" Ginny asked excitedly.

"Of course," the Ship replied.

"Cool," Ginny said.

Gabriel looked slightly less excited at the prospect.

An insect trapped in resin   1st September 2060

SEG002

"So, this is where the SEG extraction facility will be built?" Gabriel said.

"That is correct," the Ship replied.

"Seems sort of ironic," Ginny said, "given so much of the planet is dry and barren, and this part seems to be so lovely."

The starship was hovering over an expanse of rich jungle. The leafy canopy glowed bright green as this section of the planet bathed in the rays from its equivalent of the Earth's Sun.

"Are there animals here?" enquired Gabriel.

"It is highly likely," said the Ship. "I do not have information with that regard, since the early mining planet selections did not collate that information, but I would suggest there is a very great likelihood of life-forms being found on this planet."

"Life-forms?" queried Gabriel. "Do you mean there might be intelligent life on this planet?"

"Gabriel?" Vicky interjected. "If you remember from your reading of the SEG journal, the early SEG missions did not register whether there was life on the planets they logged. They only looked for significant deposits of the resources they wished to extract. It was only later, when the idea of generating a tourism service took hold, that SEG started looking for more picturesque planets, ones with interesting life-forms."

"For your clients to either shoot or shag," Ginny said, with clear disgust in her voice.

"Yes, that is true," said Vicky, somewhat un-easily. "It is good you have read up on the details about SEG and ACME INC," she continued. "That puts you in a better position to understand what you might face when we reach our destination. If ACME INC still exists, there may still be people there who made those ... er ... business decisions."

"Shall we land and suit up, Ginny?" Gabriel said, hoping to avoid a discussion about what they might need to do when they finally reached their goal.

"Ok Ship," Ginny said. "Can you bring us down in a suitable clearing, please?"

She scrutinised the console display, which showed the terrain below them.

"I think that one there looks pretty good," she said, putting her finger on a specific section of the terrain map.

The starship tilted in the direction showed by Ginny, gently drifting down towards the ground.

Gabriel pondered on how Ginny now seemed to assume command on any issues involving flying the starship.

Also, the Ship had stopped replying verbally to Ginny. Gabriel suspected the Ship was not being discourteous. It was more that it simply got on and did what she requested.

It assumed she understood … and was competent at … what she was doing.

It was like some rapport had developed.

The ship drifted down into a clearing within the jungle, floating lazily, inches above the ground. Gabriel pulled on his space suit and looked over to see Ginny tugging on her own.

"Do we have an air-lock?" Gabriel asked to no-one in particular. He felt self-conscious, like it was a piece of knowledge he should already have known.

"On opening the cockpit door, a self-sealing air-lock will activate automatically," the Ship replied. "It didn't need to be activated on the Earth, since it was unnecessary, but on SEG002 you will observe the air-lock as the door opens."

"You ready, Gabriel?" Ginny said.

"Ready," Gabriel replied.

"Ok Ship, please open the door," Ginny said.

"Hey guys … before you go … please know that the space suits you are wearing will offer very little protection," Vicky said. "They will not rip or tear easily, but they will not offer you protection against very sharp objects."

"Ok, we'll be careful," Ginny said.

"And please remember," continued Vicky, "that should you incur a serious injury, I cannot get you to the ACME MEDI-CARE unit."

"We understand that," said Ginny.

Gabriel had heard Vicky's words, and he felt a sense of dread; not for himself, but for Ginny. He couldn't imagine what he would do if …

"Come on, let's go," Ginny said.

Gabriel heard the excitement in her voice. She was relishing every moment of this. He saw her eyes through the clear suit visor. They were shining.

The cockpit door slid open; a veil of force seemed to cover the opening. To Gabriel it looked like a shimmering mesh of electricity. It was the colour of amber. It was like when you see an insect trapped in a block of amber resin. It seemed to shimmer and pulsate. He reached out his hand to the mesh and his hand passed through it with no resistance, but he felt a slight prickly sensation on his skin.

Ginny took hold of Gabriel's hand, tugging him gently towards the doorway.

"Come on boyfriend," she said. "Guys have taken me out to places before, you know, but not like this one."

Gabriel smiled and stepped with her out through the doorway and onto SEG002.

There's a storm coming   4th September 2060

SEG002

This was the third day of exploring SEG002, and Gabriel and Ginny had had an incredible time. They had walked through river-valleys strewn with small blooms, each incandescent with vibrant colour; sadly, their suits prevented them from being able to smell any perfumes emanating from the blooms. They had flown over the forest canopy and joined the flights of the small bird-like forms erupting from the leaves; they had watched a multiplicity of small life-forms, crawling and scurrying amongst the plant debris. They had seen nothing remotely similar to Earth creatures, nor had they seen anything that looked to be dangerous. Vicky had told them, several times now, that there was no real medical back-up in the case of an emergency. The starship had basic medical equipment, but there was no possibility of teleporting to ACME's MEDI-CARE CENTRE in the event of an actual emergency.

"Vicky?" Gabriel said.

"What, Gabriel?"

"I suppose you are really concerned because you don't have any information … ACME or SEG information, about this planet's plant and animal life."

"That is true, Gabriel," Vicky said. "As you have read, they compiled no such information from the early mining outposts. It was felt to be unnecessary."

"Well, luckily, we have seen nothing remotely dangerous," Ginny noted.

"That is true, Ginny, and I am grateful you have not touched the plants and animals, but even so …"

"I think there is a storm coming," said Gabriel. "Look … over there."

Gabriel pointed toward some very black clouds, perhaps two miles away.

"The Ship has kept me aware of the storm, guys," said Vicky. "It is increasing in its intensity … and it is definitely coming in this direction. It may be wise to make our way back to the starship. Storms in this area can be violent."

"It would be nice to see a magnificent storm," said Ginny. "I've always enjoyed watching storms. I love the noise and the violence in the sky. I used to watch storms on YouTube … with the sound turned up. Amazing."

Ginny looked across at Gabriel, giving him a look he couldn't quite understand, but he sensed her excitement at the prospect of watching the storm first-hand.

"Vicky?" Gabriel asked.

"Yes, Gabriel."

"Can these suits withstand storm conditions?"

"They will protect you from heavy rain, if that is what you mean. You could be immersed in liquid and still survive; as long as the liquid wasn't corrosive," Vicky qualified.

"So, we can sit here and watch the storm roll over us," Ginny said excitedly, grasping Gabriel's hand.

"Ok, Ginny ... let's watch the storm, shall we?" Gabriel said.

Ginny noted the slight tension in Gabriel's voice, but she was certain he would do this for her. He loved her. He would push outside of his own boundaries for her. She wouldn't dream of doing anything she didn't think she could deal with. Also, she had noticed that every time Gabriel had pushed himself past his personal level of safety and comfort; she saw it had strengthened him and made him more confident.

They sat together on the forest floor, hand in hand, watching the ominous clouds getting closer.

"It's probably too late to get back to the starship now," Vicky noted.

"Ok, thanks Vicky," Gabriel said, feeling his heart sink a little.

They felt the first currents of warm air prefacing the storm front. Small gusts whipped at the surrounding foliage, raising up miniature tornados amongst the plant debris.

Ginny gripped Gabriel's hand tighter. "Here it comes," she whispered.

Please pick her up   4th September 2060

SEG002

Dark winds howled around them, and the trees creaked in protest. Ginny clung tightly to Gabriel's arm. Rain crashed down on them, and lightning lit up the sky.

"Hey, guys?" said Vicky. She was having to use her comms-link to be heard over the immense noise of the storm.

"Yes, Vicky?" said Gabriel.

"I suggest," said Vicky, "that because of the severity of this storm, we bring the starship to our location."

Gabriel felt Vicky was probably right. The storm was greater than he had imagined, and although Ginny had said she wanted to experience a SEG002 storm, he felt they were taking an undue risk.

"What do you think, Ginny?" Gabriel asked.

"I guess so," Ginny said, with a tinge of disappointment in her voice.

As she spoke, a crack of lightning smashed down onto a nearby tree. The tree shattered, spitting bark fragments. Riven through to its base, the tree crashed down.

Gabriel saw it falling towards them. Flames were licking along its length.

He grabbed Ginny and tried to roll out of the path of the falling tree.

He kept rolling.

But Ginny had stopped.

She had stopped abruptly, unable to move any further.

She began screaming.

Gabriel struggled to his feet. The storm winds were whipping around him.

The full weight of the burning tree was laying across Ginny's legs.

She was flailing her arms. She was desperately trying to pat out the flames.

Gabriel scrambled round to the top of the trunk. He wrapped his arms around the flaming trunk. He felt the heat through his spacesuit. He straightened up, exerting every ounce of his strength.

The tree did not move. He wasn't able to lift it ... even an inch.

And he realised that if he tried rolling the tree, it would cause her even more injury.

"Vicky," Gabriel shouted. "For God's sake ... do something."

He stopped trying to lift the tree. He leaned down and grabbed Ginny's arms. He tried to pull her from under the burning tree. The weight on her legs was too much.

He couldn't pull her free.

Ginny was screaming incessantly ... her head was shaking from side to side ... her arms were slapping at the flames that were sheathing her legs.

"Vicky ... Vicky?" Gabriel screamed out.

"Ship ... get a heavy lifter here to our location ... right now," Vicky almost shouted.

"There's a prob...," the ship-board computer replied.

"Right now," shrieked Vicky.

"On their way."

Instantly two box-like devices floated towards them. Each was about the size of a microwave oven. They were each equipped with claw-like appendages. Driven by Vicky's silent instructions, the devices attached themselves to the trunk of the tree and began to lift it. The flames from the burning tree licked up the metalled sides of the two lifters.

"They're not strong enough," Gabriel said hopelessly, amidst the sound of the storm around them and Ginny shrieking. But slowly, inch by inch, the tree trunk was inched upwards ... enough for Gabriel to pull Ginny free.

"Ship, get over here," Vicky said, "and get whatever meds you have for compression injuries and burns available."

"On my way."

"You will have to pick her up and carry her into the ship, Gabriel," Vicky said.

"But what about her injuries ... won't I make them worse?"

"Her suit is damaged, Gabriel. The hermetic seal is compromised. She needs to be back on the starship right now."

Ginny was moaning now. Slipping in and out of consciousness.

"We have no choice, Gabriel. Please pick her up now."

"Ok ... where's the ship?"

"Right here," the Ship replied.

The starship was hovering perhaps twenty feet away, swaying in the turbulent storm winds.

"Pick her up now, Gabriel," Vicky said, urgency in her voice.

"Can you give her some pain relief before I move her?" Gabriel said.

"If she were wearing a STU such as myself, then yes, that might have been provided, but as it is, you need to get her into the starship. Please pick her up, Gabriel."

Gabriel put one arm under Ginny's shoulders and another under her knees. She shrieked.

"Pick her up, Gabriel," Vicky said.

Gabriel lifted Ginny off the ground. The storm winds caught him as he straightened up, and he swayed alarmingly, almost losing his footing. Instantly the two small lifters moved to either side of him, offering him something to lean against. Together they moved over to the starship, and Gabriel stepped up into and through the air-lock door.

Will you ever forgive me   5th September 2060

SEG002

"Carry her into the aft cabin," Ship said.

In the former empty space now stood a piece of medical equipment that looked like it had been drafted in from a futuristic hospital surgery. Gabriel walked towards it, and the canopy opened, allowing him to lay Ginny on the bed.

Ginny had stopped screaming. Her skin had a waxy pallor, and she was moaning quietly.

"Take off her clothes, Gabriel," Vicky said.

Carefully Gabriel removed Ginny's suit.

"I don't think I can get the suit off her legs," Gabriel said forlornly.

"Ok, Gabriel. Let's use the MED unit to help," Vicky said. "Please step away from her for a moment."

As Gabriel stepped away, the lid closed, and a fine crimson ray shone down from somewhere in the MED unit's lid. The ray worked down each of Ginny's legs. As it moved, the fabric of Ginny's spacesuit peeled open.

The MED unit opened again, and Gabriel slowly peeled the suit off Ginny. She screamed as he turned her on her side to pull the fabric clear. She was wearing a bra and panties under the suit, but he left those on her. He turned and threw the spacesuit into the corner of the cabin, and whilst he did so the MED unit lid closed again. What appeared to be a fine mist seemed to fill the MED unit ... a mist that seemed to glow like afternoon sunshine streaming through a window.

"The MED unit will provide pain relief and measures to control and manage the burned tissue and risks of infection," Vicky said.

As the mist rose and surrounded Ginny, her face seemed to relax a little.

"We were lucky Ship got hold of this MED unit," Vicky said.

"Yeah ... lucky," Gabriel said.

In the golden mist, Ginny was evidently still in some pain; her face would show intermittent grimaces, and she would stretch her fingers and clench her fists spasmodically.

"What do we do now?" Gabriel asked.

"The MED unit gave her pain relief, Gabriel, and it has checked her for crush injury syndrome."

"What is …?"

"Where skeletal muscle is damaged… by being crushed. The damaged muscles create breakdown products, notably myoglobin, potassium and phosphorus. When you remove the crush pressure, these products will release into the bloodstream, with acutely harmful effects. It was a common cause of death for people injured during an earthquake. The medical services would commonly pump trapped survivors with painkillers, such that they would smile, be jolly, even though still trapped. They would be released from the compression, and the crush syndrome would kill them within minutes. They would die smiling."

"So, has she got the … the syndrome?"

"No, thankfully we got her out before her body produced the breakdown toxins. Typically, if the crush injury has been sustained for fifteen minutes or more, then these toxins are created. We managed to get her out in four and a half minutes. We have reasons to be grateful that we could get the lifters."

Gabriel nodded.

"So, what can we do now?" he said again.

"We should transfer her back to the MEDI-CARE facility at ACME INC," the Ship suggested.

"We can't," Vicky said. "ACME INC's teleport is almost certainly out of action. There would be no way of knowing where she would teleport, in which case her situation would likely become worse."

"So, what do we do?" Gabriel asked again, his voice tinged with pleading.

"Gabriel?" Vicky said.

"Yes?"

"The injuries to her legs are very severe, Gabriel."

"What?"

"The MED unit's diagnostics suggest her injuries are not repairable. The crush and burn damage are beyond the scope of the equipment we have available."

"What does that mean?"

"We do not have the means to repair the severe damage to her legs."

"Oh God."

"I think we will have to amputate both of her legs, "said Vicky.

"No … no, we can't."

"We need to amputate the limbs above the point of the crush and burn damage. In both instances, that is somewhere above the knee."

"But how …?"

"Gabriel … I do not believe we have any choice in this matter."

Gabriel looked horrified.

"I understand that it is a hard decision for you, Gabriel, but I do not think we have other options."

Gabriel looked down at Ginny's comatose form. She had only wanted to experience a storm, holding hands under the trees. How stupid could he have been?

Her face contorted slightly, and her fists clenched. She was making a noise, almost a whisper. He leaned closer towards her, his head touching the transparent canopy.

She was calling his name. Faintly.

Repeatedly.

"How … how would you amputate her legs?" Gabriel asked.

"The MED unit can do it. We are lucky to have it. Otherwise we could have used the small lifters. They would have been able to do it. They have tight-burst laser cutters as part of their equipment. But if they had done it, I would have had to supervise the cutting. And then we would have had no easy means to seal the …"

"Seal what?"

"So, it's lucky in a way. Now we have a device which is designed for dealing with medical emergencies. It will identify the point on each leg where there is healthy tissue; it will amputate at that point; it will seal off the blood vessels and nerves. Then it will cut and shape the muscles and bone so that …"

Gabriel listened in growing horror.

"That is so it will be possible to grow new legs, Gabriel."

"New legs? You mean that …?"

"Yes, Gabriel. ACME INC's technology will enable them to construct new legs for Ginny. Matched to her skin type. With full sensitivity."

"Yeah, sure," Gabriel said. "That's if we can ever get her to the ACME MEDI-CARE facility ... if it still exists ... if it still operates."

"Indeed so, Gabriel," Vicky said, "but first we will need to make sure her condition stabilises after the amputation. It will probably take several days."

"And then what?"

"When we are sure she is in no danger, we place her in a CrYO-POD and she will sleep. She should be in no pain. She will awaken, as will you, and you will both go on to the ACME INC headquarters ... as you planned."

"Yes," said Gabriel, resignedly, "but Ginny will have no ..."

"She will, at least, be alive," said Vicky.

Gabriel looked at Ginny as she lay in the MED unit. He rested his left hand against the transparent canopy, near her head. He felt that, if he concentrated, he could pull some of her pain from her and into himself. He would have done it gladly.

"So, Gabriel, shall we take the MED unit's advice and carry out the amputation?"

"I love you Ginny," he whispered to her.

She winced. Probably only coincidentally, but he had no way of knowing.

Gabriel turned and looked around the cabin, as if looking for advice.

"Gabriel?" Vicky asked again.

Gabriel nodded, his face a mask of anguish.

"Will you ever forgive me, love?" he whispered to her.

If it gives any comfort   6th September 2060

SEG002

The MED unit had carried out the amputation. Gabriel could not watch. Ginny was still lying in the MED unit; it had layered some sort of creamy white substance over the stumps of her legs.

Presumably it assisted with the healing.

"Gabriel?" Vicky said.

"Uh?" Gabriel said.

"If it comforts, the MED unit has recorded the exact dimensions of Ginny's legs, allowing for the crush damage. From those dimensions it will be possible to re-grow legs that match her original limbs exactly."

"What … do you mean the MED unit can make her …?"

"No, Gabriel. The MED unit does not have the means to re-grow her legs, but the data it has collected would enable the people at ACME MEDI-CARE to build …"

"Shit, Vicky. It's the same old … old … for all we know, ACME INC has gone bust. There will probably be nobody there when we finally get there. And Ginny will still have no …"

"We should have faith, Gabriel."

"Faith, Vicky. That's a strange thing for you to say."

"Well, let's call it hope, Gabriel. Try to have hope that the facilities will exist to give Ginny back her legs."

"But they won't be real legs, will they Vicky?"

"Yes, they will, Gabriel."

"They won't let her move around as she used to though, will they?"

"Yes, they will," said Vicky.

"But she will need …"

"Gabriel, I think you should calm yourself," said Vicky. "Ginny will need you to be strong for her. She will need a lot of support and assistance to come to terms with her injuries, and you need to be there for her."

"But …"

"Gabriel. It might be you are correct, in that ACME INC may have ceased to exist as a business entity. Maybe when we reach our destination, there will be no-one there for you to plead your case to; but perhaps there will. Maybe the facilities will still exist to help her. And Gabriel, if that facility exists, please believe me – if they can provide Ginny with new legs, she will be able to walk around just as well as she did with her original legs."

"So ...?"

"So, you should hope, Gabriel. Try your best, and care for Ginny, and don't lose hope."

"Vicky?"

"Is there anything else I should do?"

"Like what, Gabriel?"

"I was wondering. Would it be best if Ginny wore you? Should I unclip you and put you on Ginny's wrist? That way you can monitor her directly ... give her extra pain relief and stuff."

"I had wondered that, myself, Gabriel, but I didn't like to mention it. I think it would be a good idea ... and ... well, it shows the level of your love for her."

Gabriel un-clipped the STU from his wrist. He walked over to the MED unit. The canopy opened, allowing him to fasten Vicky to Ginny's right wrist. Whilst the canopy was open, he reached up and stroked Ginny's cheek. Not waiting to see if there was any response, he stepped back, allowing the canopy to close again.

I can't even be strong for you   8th September 2060

SEG002

Ginny had lain in the MED unit for two days, during which she had been kept in a state of semi-consciousness. Within the MED unit's canopy, within the golden mist surrounding her body, Gabriel saw that Ginny had been connected to several tubes. He guessed some of them were providing her with nourishment whilst her body healed itself. He had moped about the starship for the last two days, seemingly unable to do anything. He realised he was fearing the point when Ginny awoke and found out what had happened. He couldn't imagine how he could explain it. He couldn't imagine how she might treat him. He feared she would never forgive him.

Gabriel woke up. He had fallen asleep on the floor. He had contrived a nest of pillows and bedding he had scavenged from their bedroom. The MED unit canopy was open, and Ginny was sitting up. She was looking down at him, watching him wake up.

"Morning, sleepy-head," she said.

Ginny was wearing a light-blue T-shirt and matching panties. The stumps of her legs were hanging over the side of the open MED unit. The stumps were still encased in the creamy-white substance he had seen earlier.

"Vicky has told me what happened," she said.

She watched as Gabriel slowly stood up. He couldn't help but stare at the place where her legs had been, though he was trying not to.

"You saved my life," she said.

Gabriel was shuddering. She saw the shock permeating his body. He was so afraid. So afraid for her.

She held her arms out to him.

"I really need to cuddle you," she said. "I really need to cuddle you right now."

He walked towards her. She saw him trembling. He didn't know what to do. He didn't know where to look.

As he came closer, she grabbed him by the shoulders and pulled him towards her. She had to take his arms and wrap them around herself. He buried his face into the nape of her neck. He sobbed. His entire body seemed to shudder with his pain. She held him as tightly as she could, and she felt his tears on her skin.

"You saved my life, Gabriel. And just because I wanted to watch a storm."

"It was my fault, Ginny. Maybe we shouldn't have come here at all. Maybe this was all a mistake ... trying to get to ACME ... trying to ..."

She could barely make out his words.

"I should have ... I should have ... and now I can't even be strong for you."

She stroked the back of his head, the back of his neck.

"Oh God, Ginny. What are we ... what will we ...?"

"Gabriel ... you saved my life."

She leaned back, away from him and took hold of his face, pulling it up so he was looking directly at her, inches away from her face.

"We'll be ok, Gabriel. We'll get through this. We were unlucky. Maybe we were stupid. But you saved me, Gabriel. You and Vicky. You both saved me."

She pulled his face closer to her and kissed him. A slow, loving kiss. She felt him relax. He put his arms back around her and hugged her.

She thought they would be all right.

One less thing   8th September 2060

SEG002

Gabriel and Ginny were sitting in the cockpit seats. He had carried her through from the aft cabin, and the contoured cockpit seats had seemed to Gabriel like the best bet for someone with no legs.

"I guessed my injuries were serious when I woke up and saw you had given Vicky to me," Ginny said.

Gabriel couldn't think of anything to say in response. He stared out through the cockpit visor. The starship was slowly circling SEG002 at a height of about half a mile. He hadn't wanted to stay at the site of the accident, and he hadn't been able to think of any other location to go to.

"I can maintain your pain relief and make sure the wounds heal well," Vicky explained.

"That's very kind of you, Vicky," Ginny said. She smiled across at Gabriel.

"Otherwise you would need to have regular sessions in the MED unit," Vicky continued.

"I'm grateful to you," Ginny said.

She held her hand out to Gabriel, clasping his hand when he offered it to her.

"I'll give Vicky back to you when I feel better," Ginny said.

"No, I think you should keep her. That's if it's all right with you, Vicky?"

"I'm honoured to be of assistance to both of you," Vicky said.

"Do you fancy a drink, Ginny?" Gabriel asked. "How about a hot chocolate or something?"

"Yeah, hot chocolate would be nice."

"Ok."

Gabriel got up and went to get the drinks.

"Vicky?" Ginny said.

"Yes, Ginny?"

"Do you think … would it be possible to get me a device that would enable me to get around?"

"I can get you a hover-chair, Ginny. They are like a cut-down chair ... but they have small ramstat boosters to enable them to move around."

"No, I don't think so ... but that gives me an idea. Can you get me a cut-down spacesuit?"

"Well ..."

"Can you get me a spacesuit, something tight-fitting, maybe in dark blue or green, plus something I can use to shorten and seal the suit legs?"

"I see what you mean, Ginny. That way you would have clothing with small Ramstat boosters, giving you the mobility you need."

"Exactly, Vicky. Can you get that stuff?"

"It's on its way, Ginny."

Gabriel walked back into the cockpit as a spacesuit materialised on the floor next to Ginny's chair.

Ginny leaned down to get it, but it was out of her reach.

Ginny looked up beseechingly at Gabriel, who laughed, put the two mugs of hot chocolate down on the floor and handed the spacesuit up to Ginny. Ginny un-clipped the suit helmet and dropped it onto the floor. Then she un-rolled the suit, stretching out the legs.

"Do we have something that can cut the suit legs and seal the ends?" Ginny said.

As she spoke, one of the small lifters floated through into the cockpit.

"The lifters have tools to do that," Vicky explained. "If you place the spacesuit on the floor, I will get the lifter to make the legs shorter."

"Just as well we kept hold of one," Gabriel said. They had left one lifter on SEG002, but the other they had stowed in a corner of the aft cabin.

Ginny looked over to Gabriel, who took the suit from her and laid it out on the cockpit floor.

"Don't we need to measure it?" Ginny asked.

"I already have your leg measurements," Vicky explained.

"Why ... why do you have them?" Ginny asked.

As she spoke, the lifter was using its clawed arms to stretch out the suit leg fabric.

"We may get ACME INC to provide you with new legs," Gabriel said.

Ginny noticed that as he had said that, he was looking uncomfortable. She guessed he was anxious he might give her false hope.

"So, anyway," Gabriel continued, "the MED unit, and Vicky too I guess, took precise details of your legs, so we can use that information to ..."

The lifter cut the first of the spacesuit legs. It was doing it delicately, and it wasn't a simple cut across the leg. It appeared to be cutting an elaborate series of slight cuts. Ginny watched it. Its movements intrigued her. When it had finished cutting the first leg, it moved on to the second leg.

"What's it ...?" Gabriel said

"Can you please move the discarded sections away, Gabriel," Vicky said.

The lifter floated away momentarily, allowing Gabriel to lean down, and pick up the cutaway sections.

The lifter floated back over the spacesuit and lifted one of the shortened legs. Using three of its prehensile arms, it began precisely folding the cut fabric. A small probe-like device emerged alongside the three robotic arms, at which point a narrow crimson beam tracked its way over the joins. They watched the fabric soften under the beam, then re-form as the beam moved on. Ginny and Gabriel sat transfixed.

The lifter completed its work on the first suit leg. It moved over and started working on the other suit leg. Gabriel looked over at Ginny. She was looking quietly excited.

"Do you think the suit will have a working seal? I mean ... will it work as a proper spacesuit?" Ginny asked.

"Yes, it will, Ginny," Vicky said. "The lifters are very accomplished. The suit will work fine for what you need it to do."

"What do you need it to do?" Gabriel asked. He felt stupid. He felt as though everybody knew the answer except himself.

"Just get me about," Ginny said, smiling over at him.

"The suit is ready, Ginny," Vicky said.

The lifter had dropped the spacesuit onto the floor, at which point it had floated back into the aft cabin.

"Give me a hand, please," Ginny said to Gabriel.

Gabriel picked up the spacesuit and handed it over to Ginny.

"Come on, boyfriend," she said, "I need more help than that."

Gabriel understood. He lifted Ginny off the chair, whilst she pulled the spacesuit underneath her. She tucked her leg stumps into the spacesuit's shortened legs and pulled the suit up around her bottom.

"Ok, Gabriel ... you can put me down now."

Gabriel lowered her back into the chair.

Ginny began pulling the spacesuit up over her arms and torso. She tugged the zip closed and felt the suit complete the seal. She felt gingerly over the shortened suit legs, checking for the tightness of fit and for any tenderness caused by the proximity of the suit fabric against her stumps.

"It feels good, Vicky," she said.

"That's good, Ginny."

"Well, let's see if the idea works," Ginny said.

She powered up the small Ramstat boosters on the suit, lifting herself gently up into the air.

Gabriel smiled as she floated over to where he had put the mugs of hot chocolate. She picked them up.

"The chocolate's gone cold," she said. "I'll get some more."

Gabriel smiled to himself as Ginny floated through into the kitchen area.

It was one less thing for him to have to worry about.

Still bloody itches   9th September 2060

SEG002

They had gone to bed, just as if this was any other day. They had cuddled up and slept together. Gabriel had snuggled up behind Ginny. They were like two spoons, side by side in a drawer.

The starship was still slowly circling SEG002, for no reason other than that neither Gabriel nor Ginny had suggested landing anywhere.

Gabriel had awoken to find himself laid on his back. Ginny was laid with her head on his chest, fast asleep.

"Good morning, Gabriel," Vicky said.

She was whispering.

"Morning, Vicky," he replied in a murmur.

"I think you should wait for a few days before you both go back into the CrYO-PODS. I think we should wait to see if any phantom limb sensations appear."

"How do you mean?"

"After a limb amputation, it is not uncommon for the patient to experience pain in the excised limb."

"If she does, is there anything you can do to help her?" said Gabriel.

"The MED unit can provide a series of treatments, but there is still no guaranteed treatment for phantom pain. NMDA receptor antagonists, calcitonin and β-blockers have all been used in the treatment of phantom limb pain. None have been proven to give a guaranteed result."

"Shit," muttered Gabriel. "I guess we have to hope she doesn't get it."

"Get what?" Ginny said, lifting her head off Gabriel. She smiled at him, then suddenly looked down at where her legs had been.

"Ow, ow, ow, ow, ow" she said, looking irritable.

"What's up," Gabriel asked, alarmed.

"I've got a bloody itch on my left leg," she wailed, pulling the coverlet back to scratch her lower leg. She pulled the coverlet away, revealing the space where her leg had been. She looked at Gabriel, her expression a mixture somewhere between wry amusement and alarm.

"You ok?" Gabriel said.

"I guess so," she said, visibly trying to force a wry grin. "Still bloody itches, though."

Gabriel's stomach felt icy. A gnawing foretaste of hard times to come.

"Come on girl, let's get some breakfast and some coffee going," he said, forcing a smile to his face.

He hoped Ginny wouldn't see through his forced jollity, but in his heart, he guessed she could read him like an open book.

....

They felt a soft thump. A gentle shudder. It ran throughout the starship.

"What the fuck was ...?" Gabriel said, alarmed.

"It was the starboard Ramstat motor," Ship explained. "It has just ... just stopped working. Do not worry. I can still control and land the ship on the remaining engine."

"So, the intermittent fault's got more permanent?" said Ginny chuckling. "It's as well we got here. I guess that definitely puts paid to any more long-distance flights."

"Vicky and I would not recommend it," Ship concurred.

Dead for forty years   15th September 2060

SEG002

"How are you feeling, love?" Gabriel said.

"No pain or itching for two days," Ginny said.

"That's good."

They sat looking out of the cockpit visor. The starship was circling the area where the mining outpost would be, from a height of 100 yards. As Ship had advised, the starship was perfectly controllable with its remaining Ramstat engine, if not for travelling substantial distances in space. They were looking for somewhere safe to land the ship. Somewhere it wouldn't be detected as the mining settlement was built.

"I wonder how Barney and Monica got on?" Gabriel said.

"It would be nice to think they got together, wouldn't it?" Ginny said.

"I miss him," Gabriel said.

"He will probably have been dead for many years."

"I know."

"Vicky?" Gabriel said

"Yes, Gabriel?"

"Did Barney ever call us again ... like on the phone?"

"Yes, he did, Gabriel. He left a message. Would you like to hear it?"

Gabriel looked over at Ginny.

"No, thank you, Vicky," Gabriel said. "Maybe some other time. I don't think I can bear to hear it right now."

· · · · · · · ·

"This site should be fine, guys," Vicky said. "It's outside of the area of the extraction site, and it's only a short journey to the teleport when you wake up."

"Won't they detect us?" Ginny asked.

"No. We will enable the cloaking device. They won't detect we are here," Vicky said.

"So, ok, Vicky. Do we need to do anything else to prepare?" Gabriel said.

"Everything is ready, Gabriel. If you wish, you can get yourselves into the CrYO-PODS, and you will awaken at the precise time to get to the SEG002 teleport terminal and use it to go back to the ACME-HUB."

"At the time shortly after whatever caused the teleport problem at ACME INC?" said Ginny.

"Exactly," replied Vicky.

"Vicky?" said Ginny.

"Yes?"

"Am I missing something here? Why don't we wake up slightly before the coordinates database gets corrupted? That way you could transport us to Earth in the same way you did with any of your clients. The coordinates you use would be fine. We wouldn't need to use the teleport facility in the mining plant at all."

Gabriel looked at Ginny. He didn't believe they had not spotted such an obvious thing until now.

"I understand what you are saying," Vicky said, "but, sadly, that isn't the way it works. When I initiate a teleport request, the request process doesn't look up the coordinates as they are at the time of the request. The request process always looks up the most recent set of coordinates. If the coordinates database has been corrupted … but never fixed … whenever a STU initiates a teleport request, it will always pull back the corrupted coordinate information."

"And that's why you don't want to teleport us until you are sure that the coordinates are ok?" said Ginny.

"That's true, Ginny," Vicky said.

"But," said Ginny, "if we get back to Earth, back to ACME INC, after the teleport coordinates database gets corrupted, and if it is not possible to fix it, doesn't that mean that, even if we talked to ACME and they agreed to give us another STU for John, we might never get back to our original time?"

"I would say that was a possibility," agreed Vicky.

"Ah well," Gabriel said. "We predicted this would never be easy, didn't we?"

· · · · · · · ·

Gabriel and Ginny stood in front of the CrYO-PODS. Vicky had told them no-one had ever died whilst using a pod, but Gabriel didn't wholly trust Vicky.

No, not that he didn't trust her. It was that he felt that sometimes Vicky cared so much for them she wouldn't want to worry them.

"You nervous, love?" Gabriel asked. He was hugging her tightly, like he might never get the chance again.

"Always," Ginny said, giving Gabriel a quick peck on the cheek. "And you?"

"Brave as a lion," Gabriel said, smiling wryly.

"Come on," she said, "before either of us chickens out."

BOOK THREE

Told you it wouldn't do any harm 1st Sept 2180

SEG002

Vicky began the CrYO-POD shut-down process on both pods. It was now one day before the teleport problem had affected ACME INC's teleport processing. It was 116 years since they had stopped to fix the Ramstat engine, which had finally shut down. It was 163 years since Gabriel and Ginny had left the Earth.

"Now their journey really begins," the Ship said.

"I think you are correct," Vicky replied.

"I will be sorry to see them go," the Ship said.

"I didn't think they had designed you for poetry, or to feel romance or heroic gestures," Vicky said.

"I think it may be because I have been in their proximity, and yours, for so long," Ship said. "Normally I see clients for a few weeks at most. But, maybe like you, they designed me to develop ... to expand ... to grow with interaction to external stimuli."

"What are you saying?" asked Vicky.

"I think I am saying thank you, Vicky. Thank you for letting me have this opportunity."

"It was a pleasure, Ship. We made a good team."

· · · · · · · ·

Gabriel and Ginny sat in the cockpit seats. They had felt groggy after waking from the pods, but a bit of a walk around the starship (small as it was), plus several coffees and some hot porridge with honey and sultanas had given them the energy they needed. And now it was night time, and the only lighting in the cockpit came from the low-level illumination cast by the instrumentation console. The starship was resting in a small ravine. They saw this from the heads-up display picked out on the cockpit canopy.

"Is that the extraction site over there?" Ginny said, pointing at a section of the display.

"Yes," Ship said.

Ginny pointed and dragged the display, enlarging the view of the processing plant.

"Which building houses the teleport?" Gabriel asked.

A luminous yellow arrow appeared on the display, pointing to a sizeable building on the northern end of the site.

"The teleport will go through bursts of activity," explained Vicky. "This is the primary extraction site, but ancillary sites will also send in materials using drones. When the extraction processing is having a high-yield period, the extracted materials get stockpiled in warehousing, rather than being put straight through into the teleport. In low-yield periods, they move the extracted materials straight into the teleport. In either situation, however, automated processes ensure the teleport keeps working pretty much continuously. In this time period, SEG002 is a developed site, with a large, continuous output. We will have to be careful to find a gap when the automated processes are not loading the teleport."

"Why? What could happen if we didn't?" Gabriel asked. He felt as though he should have investigated this before and felt a little stupid and unprepared.

"The teleport bays on these early sites were not built to anticipate human involvement. The automated loading processes will not check that anything else, human or otherwise, is in the teleport bay before they start loading the next batch of materials. They were programmed to load materials, and they will attempt to fill the teleport bay in its entirety. You would get injured if you were in the bay as it gets re-loaded."

"So, what are we going to do?" Ginny asked. "Wouldn't it have been better to go to a mining planet that wasn't quite as developed as this one?"

Gabriel looked at Ginny. He loved her not only for her beauty but also for her very sharp mind. He hadn't thought of an alternative. He was feeling a sense of despair at what appeared to be an exceedingly difficult, possibly impossible problem.

"To be honest, Ginny," Vicky said, "I hadn't thought of this problem until right now."

"What?" Ginny said, sounding shocked.

"Well, when I initially selected a location, I based it on somewhere that you might want to explore. Somewhere that would offer you the chance to see another planet. Somewhere that you could get to that would take up the time until 2180. I didn't foresee that a Ramstat motor would fail, and that we would be forced to use the planet's teleport functionality. It's lucky, really."

"How do you mean ... lucky?" said Gabriel.

"Well, if I had selected a planet which was just a tourist destination ... there would have been a very real chance that it would have had no teleport facilities at all. Tourists could only get to those using their STU. On one of those planets, there would have been no way of getting back."

"Ok, I see what you mean," said Gabriel. "So, we're here, and we should count ourselves as lucky, 'cos it's got a teleport."

"That's correct," said Vicky.

"So, we merely have to use the teleport without getting squished," said Ginny.

"Yes, that is also correct," agreed Vicky.

"Ok. It looks like we give this one a try," said Gabriel. "Let's not write it off before we have even tried it."

He thought he was sounding braver than he felt. Ginny was looking over at him, as if she were re-appraising him. He hoped it was in his favour.

He leaned over and gave Ginny's hand a squeeze. She squeezed his hand in return.

"I think Barney would have been very proud of you," she said.

He looked over to her, slightly quizzically.

"And I'm very proud of you," she concluded.

"Vicky?" Gabriel asked.

"Yes, Gabriel?"

"Remember when you said that Barney left a voice-mail message for us ... it was a long time ago?"

"Yes, Gabriel. I still have it. Do you wish to hear it?"

"Yes please, Vicky."

There were a few seconds' silence, as though Vicky was searching for the material, or she was giving a slight pause ... to build up anticipation. Then the message began.

> "Hello Gabriel, oh, and you as well Ginny.
> It's me ... Barney.

We haven't heard from you both in a long time, but you said you'd be all right, and I'm sure you will. You're a capable lad.
I just thought I'd let you know that me and Monica are getting married. It will be at 2:20 pm on the 15th Feb 2018, at Frinton Registry Office. I've told her many times I'm just a silly old fool who writes newspapers, but she said she's always had a soft spot for old fools like me.
She has two daughters. They are both very nice, and they seem thrilled that their mum has met me.
I just wanted to say that ... well, if you were about, it would be great if you could come to the wedding, but if you can't, I just wanted to say I think of you a lot. Monica says that I talk about you as if you were the son I never had, and I ... and I guess that's true.
Anyway ... that's about it, Gabriel. I hope that you and Ginny are ok, where-ever you might be.
Look after yourselves.

I can't remember if I said, but it's on the 15th Feb 2018 at Frinton Registry Office.
Oh ... and this is Barney ... just in case ...
Anyway, bye."

Ginny looked over at Gabriel. His eyes were looking very moist.

"Told you it wouldn't do any harm, didn't I?" Ginny said.

"What wouldn't do any harm?"

"Giving Barney a good reference. Remember?"

Gabriel smiled. "Yeah, I remember," he said.

Not without getting squished 4th Sept 2180

SEG002

"So, what do we do?" Gabriel said, for probably the third or fourth time.

Ginny looked up, shrugged her shoulders, scooped up another fork-full of vegetable chow mein.

"This is the third day trying, and …," he said.

"This is tasty," Ginny said.

Ginny prodded her fork into a juicy morsel, holding it up in front of her for inspection before popping it into her mouth.

"Perhaps you were right … about trying another mining planet," he said.

Ginny prodded a water chestnut. It evaded her attentions. She prodded it again, this time with more success.

"It might be we'll not be able to get into that teleport," he said.

"Not without getting squished, anyway," Ginny added.

"Do you think this is a joke?" Gabriel blurted. His exasperation was making him cross with her light-hearted mood.

"No, Gabriel. I don't think it's a joke at all," Ginny said, a tinge of disappointment in her voice. "I think it requires serious consideration. I think we need to get it right."

"uh uh," Gabriel said, aware of Ginny's suddenly harsh tone of voice.

"And I think we need to remember that we came to get a STU for John," she said.

"Yep."

"And I think we should stay calm. We will find a way to teleport to the Earth."

Gabriel nodded, hoping she was right.

"Remember, Gabriel. The coordinates data corruption has already happened. It probably happened two days ago."

He nodded, wondering where her train of thought was going.

"Vicky has already appeared on the cliffs outside Walton. All the circumstances, all of that chain of events is underway."

He nodded again.

"And we need to get to the Earth, but it doesn't matter if we do it today, tomorrow or the next day."

"So, what are you saying?" Gabriel asked.

"We think it will be risky getting to use the SEG002 teleport, yes? And if we had two working Ramstat motors, we might have tried getting to another less-developed mining planet. We could have even flown directly back to the Earth. We are in the correct time-zone now, aren't we? But whatever we do, we need to stay calm. It's when people lose their calm, that's when accidents happen."

"But ...?" he said.

"And I don't want to lose you ... even if you can be the most dumb and exasperating boyfriend on this ship," she concluded.

"Barney always said you were the brains of the outfit," Gabriel said, smiling ruefully.

Ship noticed them   6th Sept 2180   daybreak

SEG002

"I see you've put the mauve spacesuit on today," Gabriel said. "It looks good on you."

Ginny spun around slowly, utilising the small Ramstat boosters in her suit.

"And thanks to Vicky thinking to make me more suits, tailored to fit my requirements, I've even got a choice. Thanks, Vicky," Ginny said.

"It was a pleasure," Vicky said.

"But I don't think I'd look so good if the suits were like the old Apollo astronauts," said Ginny. "These ACME suits with their crumpled leather look, and their tight fit, I think they make a girl look a little better … don't you?"

She smiled over at Gabriel whilst running her hands over the soft curves of her body, encased as she was in the tight-fitting mauve faux leather.

Gabriel gulped, looked back at the monitors they were using to observe the extraction plant.

"I've still not seen a fraction of time that we might have used to get onto the teleport," he said. "And this is after five days of watching the bloody thing. Maybe we will have to risk flying to another mining planet …"

"Or go back to the Earth directly," Ginny said.

"Hey guys," Ship said. "It looks like we have guests."

Gabriel and Ginny turned to the monitors. A spaceship was touching down in the plant's landing bay.

"God, it looks like a bunch of green shipping containers bolted together, with a set of rocket boosters stitched on the back," observed Gabriel.

"I guess they built it for function, not for style," Ginny said.

A ramp lowered from the tail of the spaceship, and three men appeared. They were carrying gear across to a building at the centre of the mining complex.

"It's a maintenance crew," Ship explained. "A three-man maintenance crew. They will be SEG employees."

"How long are they likely to stay here?" Ginny asked.

"Probably several days," Ship said. "I've transported such crews, myself. Sometimes they might stay for a week or more, but never less than two or three days."

"Presumably," Gabriel said, "they could pause the automated processing long enough for us to use the teleport … do you think?"

"You would hope so," said Ginny.

As they watched, two vaguely human-like forms exited the maintenance craft. They weren't wearing spacesuits, and they looked bigger, bulkier than most people.

"What are …?" Ginny said.

"They're robots, Ginny," Ship said. "SEG uses them a lot for maintenance work. They are probably ROB3 models. They are extraordinarily strong. And they can work in any environment."

"What controls them," Ginny asked.

"They control them using WORM-LYNK. Probably the guys in the maintenance building are controlling them. The ROB3s have primitive AI features. You give them simple instructions … fairly high-level instructions even, and they can be left to get on with it."

"Why does SEG bother sending actual people?" Gabriel asked.

"SEG still needs real people 'on the ground' so to speak," said Vicky. "The robotics were a useful adjunct, and they were ideal for running maintenance on the explorer vehicles, but for a complex mining / extraction operation, SEG needed people. People have intuition. The ROB3s wouldn't have that capacity."

The two robots made their way across to the building that the three maintenance guys had gone into. The large sliding door on the outside of the workshop slid closed behind them.

"So, now what do we do?" Ginny asked. "Go over and ask them if they can help us to teleport back to Earth?"

"It's got to be worth a go," said Gabriel. "I mean, what's the worst that could happen?"

They might be finished tomorrow   7th Sept 2180

SEG002

"The big guys are still picking on the little guy," Ginny observed. "I can't imagine how he puts up with it. They were doing it all yesterday, and now they are doing it again today."

Gabriel turned to watch. It seemed to be the low-level teasing that wasn't quite bullying ... probably difficult to get management to back you up on. And it was relentless. All the time. All day long. Gabriel was finding it hard to watch. He was bullied himself when he was young. That was when he had realised you had to stand up for yourself. Nobody else would do it.

"They still seem to be checking all the above-ground processing functions," Ginny said. "They seem to have made one of two adjustments to things, but mainly they seem to check things. I wonder if they will work after dark again?"

"They lit the place up like a giant light-bulb last night," Gabriel said. "Was it midnight when they knocked off last night?"

"Yeah, about," said Ginny. "That was when they powered down all the lights and went back to that workshop place."

"If they're working long shifts, I'm thinking they will not be here long," Gabriel said worriedly. "They might be on a tight time-frame. Get done and get gone."

"They might finish tomorrow," Ginny said.

Gabriel nodded. That was his thought.

"How's about we see them in the morning?" Ginny said.

"Yeah. Let's do that," Gabriel said. "Let's get some sleep, then bright and early, eh?"

What's the worst that could happen   8th Sept 2180

SEG002

Ginny had woken first. She was into her spacesuit (the fuchsia pink one) and up getting some porridge and coffee before Gabriel had stirred.

"Come on, Gabe ... up and at-em."

She poked Gabriel gently.

Gabriel opened his eyes. He saw Ginny floating gently in front of him, her suit's small Ramstat boosters keeping her floating at roughly the level she would be at if she still had her legs.

"Rise and shine, Gabriel," she said.

He reached out and grabbed her hand; the one she was using to poke him. He pulled her towards him gently. She allowed herself to float closer towards him, whereupon he planted a quick kiss on her cheek.

"No time for that," she chuckled, pulling away. "Those guys might be out of here today, and then what do we do?"

He grunted his assent. If they didn't take this opportunity, they might have a long time to wait for another maintenance team. That or risk flying on one Ramstat motor to another mining planet. A planet with less developed product. With more gaps between teleports.

He pulled himself out of bed and headed for the ion-shower.

· · · · · · · ·

"We should probably fly the starship into the parking bay ... next to where they landed theirs," suggested Vicky. "Your presence in such a vehicle would prove you are ACME clients. Then explain that you are ACME clients on an unscheduled trip to SEG002. They can hardly say you're not. Just say you would like to use their teleport to get back to Earth."

"Why would they do that?" Gabriel asked.

"Well ... SEG and ACME INC have a close working relationship," explained Vicky. "ACME provide the teleport facilities SEG needs to use for its business. SEG employees are probably made aware that ACME tourists are a bunch of very wealthy, sometimes very troublesome people who they might bump into now and again. They are probably warned to ... well ... smile sweetly and ..."

"So, we act like rich, spoiled ACME clients, and hope they play along?" said Ginny.

"That would be my suggestion," agreed Vicky. "I think that would be the best way of getting them to agree to use their facilities."

Gabriel looked at Ginny. She looked very unsure about this idea.

"I guess it might work," said Gabriel. He couldn't think of any better alternative, but it still left him feeling unsettled.

· · · · · · · ·

Their starship landed along-side the ship belonging to the maintenance team. They hadn't seen the three guys leave the workshops yet this morning, so they were fairly sure they were still inside. Ginny was up and out of the airlock first, followed shortly by Gabriel.

"Come on, pudding. Let's give them a knock," Ginny said.

As she spoke, the workshop door slid open. The door itself was twenty feet high and thirty feet wide. It slid open smoothly, along a heavy set of runners.

Ginny glanced nervously at Gabriel. There was no-one to be seen.

"They must be opening it mechanically," suggested Gabriel. "A door that big … you wouldn't be able to push it open."

"Should we go in?" Ginny said.

They could see a large inner bay area. Various pieces of heavy equipment were lying about, seemingly at random.

"There's no airlock on the door," Vicky said, "so you will need to keep your suits and helmets on in there."

"Here comes the little guy," Gabriel said. "And he's got the two robots with him."

Ginny watched nervously as the smaller person in the maintenance team walked towards them.

"Those buggers are strong," noted Gabriel, looking at the two robots. Each was carrying what looked like gas cylinders, about six feet long. They were carrying one under each arm. They weren't straining to carry them.

Their feet left deep imprints in the ground as they walked.

The small guy looked up and saw Gabriel and Ginny.

"He's trying to say something to us," Ginny said, watching the man's lips move inside his helmet.

The man held his left wrist out in front of him, then tapped at something.

"He will try to set up a comms-link," Vicky said.

"Comm4, comm4, that's the one," they heard him say. "What the hell. Where d'you guys come from?"

"ACME INC," said Ginny. "We thought we'd come and see one of the early off-worlds. See what you men had to deal with. Everybody hears about you guys roving around, keeping this stuff going ... 'brave space warriors' and all that. We were intrigued to see, is all."

"'Brave space warriors' eh? Yeah, that's us," the smaller guy said, standing a little taller.

Gabriel grinned across at Ginny. She was doing this well; he thought.

"Hey ... pardon me," the small guy said. "I'm Patty, and this is Bill and Ben." He pointed to the two robots. Sure enough, they had those names painted on their chest-plates. It wasn't an official nameplate. It looked like the names had been hand-painted, using some luminous yellow paint.

"I'm Ginny, and this is Gabriel," Ginny said.

"Cool," Patty said. "There's another two guys in my team." Patty was trying to impress. "They're still in the workshop. I'll call them out."

Patty tapped something on the pad on his wrist. They saw him saying something into his helmet. Moments later the other two came out of an internal airlock. They walked across the bay and came out of the workshop door.

"Ok, we're all on comm4 now," Patty said. "This is Roy, the big bloke on the left, and Steve's the other one. Guys, this is Ginny and Gabriel ... come to see what sort of stuff us 'brave space warriors' do out here."

"Really?" Roy said. "Your starboard Ramstat's fucked, ain't it? Noticed it when you dropped by. Is that why you 'dropped by'?"

He was pointedly looking at Ginny's shortened spacesuit legs, as she hovered beside Gabriel.

Gabriel looked at Ginny. He saw the tension in her face.

"What you hanging about for, Patty?" Roy said, scowling in Patty's direction. "You've got stuff to get doing. Get down that fucking shaft and get the cyclic fixed. We want to get off this shit-hole, asap."

Patty looked embarrassed. Unsure what to do.

"Get the fuck on with it, Patty," Steve said. "We'll look after the guests, eh Roy?"

Roy grinned back at Steve.

"You want your motor looking at?" Roy said.

"Just a teleport back to Earth would be great," Gabriel said.

"Yeah, right," said Roy, walking back into the workshop. He stopped walking and looked back at Gabriel and Ginny. "Come on. Your wish is our command, eh?"

Roy continued walking back into the workshop, with Steve close behind. Patty had trudged off, followed by the two robots.

Gabriel held his hands up to Ginny. He didn't see they had much choice. Ginny looked worriedly back at him.

"Get a fucking move on, you two," Roy snarled. "We ain't got all bleeding day."

Gabriel turned towards the workshop, slowly. Ginny caught up with him, clasping his hand tightly.

As they got into the workshop bay area, they saw that Roy and Steve were walking over to an airlock on the far wall. They both stepped through. Gabriel followed right behind them, closely followed by Ginny.

As Gabriel stepped through the airlock, he saw Steve standing immediately in front of him. Steve had taken off his helmet. He was standing there, smiling at Gabriel. Gabriel took off his own helmet. Steve swung his fist hard … into Gabriel's stomach. Gabriel doubled-up, gasping for air. Steve brought his knee up. Straight into Gabriel's face. It smashed into his nose. Gabriel fell to the ground.

Roy grabbed Ginny as she floated through the airlock. She had seen Steve hit Gabriel, and Gabriel fall in a heap on the ground. Roy pinned her arms behind her. Steve dragged Gabriel across the room and was lashing him into a chair with electrical wire.

"Get the fuck off me," Ginny shouted.

As Roy pinned her arms, Steve walked back, took Ginny's helmet off and threw it across the floor.

"Ok, girly," said Roy. "I see you lost your legs someplace, but I'm guessing the other bits work, eh?" He put a hand between her legs, stroking her.

As Roy held Ginny's arms, Steve unclipped her spacesuit. He eased it off, down off her body. She was screaming and thrashing. Steve casually hit her with a backhanded slap across her face. Then he turned to a workbench and cleared the surface with one drag of his arm.

"Lay her on there, mate," Steve said.

Roy pushed Ginny face-down onto the workbench. Her bottom and the stumps of her legs were hanging over on Roy's side. Steve pulled her across the bench towards him a little. He had unfastened his suit. He pulled her face towards him. As he did so, she felt Roy pushing up behind her. She screamed as he savagely entered her.

"Wake up and watch this, Gabby," Steve said, in Gabriel's direction.

Roy screamed, and she felt him pull out of her.

Steve looked up from Ginny's face. He felt a sudden intense pain. A metal bolt was sticking out of his shoulder. He looked up. Ben and Patty were standing facing them. Ben was holding a bolt gun. A heavy tool they used for quick fixings. It fired ten-inch steel bolts. It held a magazine of ten bolts. It needed a robot to carry it.

"What the fuck ..." Steve said.

The bolt gun spat and bucked in Ben's hands and Steve felt another bolt hit him in the forearm. The force of it span him around. He fell to the ground.

Patty pulled Ginny off the bench. He was holding her tenderly. And he was stronger than he looked.

She could see Steve and Roy laid on the ground. Roy was lying on his side, a metal bolt sticking out of his lower back, another sticking out of his right thigh. Steve had two bolts sticking out of him, one in his shoulder, another in his arm. They were both staring up at Patty. They weren't trying to remove the bolts. She guessed they were more concerned with what happened next.

"You're ok," Patty told her. He was cradling her in his arms, walking backwards, away from the bench and from where Steve and Roy were laying.

"Bill, get hold of Roy," Patty instructed. "Hold him by the arms. Don't let him move."

Bill moved forwards, leaned down and grabbed Roy. It took hold of each of Roy's arms. Roy felt the plasteel hands circling his biceps, the fingers sinking into the flesh. Roy struggled, flexing his brawny arms, but to no avail.

"Ok, Ben. Now you get hold of Steve. In the same way as Bill's doing."

Ben carefully laid the bolt gun down on the ground; it walked over towards Steve.

"Get the fuck away, Ben," Steve shouted.

"Sorry, Steve," Patty said. "It looks like they aren't listening to you. Shame, eh, what with you being such a pleasant guy and all."

"Ok Bill and Ben. Can you please take Roy and Steve and put them into the storeroom? Then close and lock the door. Don't let either of them get out. That would be great, guys."

The robots began walking with their unwilling cargoes. Roy and Steve were both big men, and both were struggling. The robots walked steadily towards the storeroom. They appeared to be unaware of the men's struggles.

Patty laid Ginny on the floor next to where Gabriel was tied. He turned to unfasten Gabriel, who looked to be regaining consciousness.

"Patty?" Ginny said.

Patty stopped what he was doing and turned to Ginny. She was lying on the floor. She seemed to be furiously wiping herself; as if she were covered in something, and she needed to wipe it off urgently.

"Can I help Ginny?" Patty said. He wasn't sure he knew what to help with, but he was happy to try.

"Patty … can you … can you …?"

"What, Ginny?"

"My spacesuit … it's there … there … in the corner."

She nodded her head in its direction.

Patty looked where she was indicating and saw the spacesuit. It had been thrown into the corner. He walked over and picked it up. Walking back over to Ginny, he suddenly looked embarrassed by her nakedness. He handed it to her, looking away as he did so.

She grabbed it from him, and as he turned away, she began struggling to pull it on.

Patty resumed untying Gabriel, who slumped sideways as his bonds loosened. Patty held Gabriel upright and wiped some blood off his face.

Ginny had pulled her spacesuit closed. She floated over to Gabriel. His eyes were open, but they looked un-focussed. They had smashed his nose to one side. Blood covered his face.

Patty was looking around the workshop. He seemed to be looking for something specific.

"What's up?" Ginny asked.

Patty rifled through a box and pulled out a small tube, 10 inches long, one inch in diameter. It was bright red, almost luminous, with a green stripe down one side.

"Patty?" Ginny said.

Patty's eyes were bright, almost glistening. "Now then Bill and Ben," he said. "Can you come over here, please? Right next to this door."

The robots made their way over.

"That's right," Patty said. "Now, when I say, I want you to open the door, but only an inch. Don't let Steve or Roy get out. Then, when I tell you, I want you to shut the door again. And hold it closed. Really tight. You got that? Good boys."

Ginny was holding on to Gabriel. He looked barely conscious. She was really frightened. She held him even tighter, as if her clasp would rouse him. She turned to see what Patty was doing.

"Now Ginny. Come and look through the inspection panel on this door. I think you will like this. But wait until the boys have locked it shut again."

"Patty ... What ...?" she said.

"Ok, Ben, pull open the door an inch, please, but don't let Steve and Roy get out, eh?"

Ben pulled the door open. As he did so, a pair of hands grabbed the door, pushing to open it.

"Now, now, Steve. You've been a bad boy. Let go of the door," Patty said, at the same time pushing the red tube through the narrow gap. It fell into the room, rolling along the floor.

"Now boys, shut the door ... really tight," Patty said.

Instantly the two robots put their weight against the door. Steve screamed. The fingers of his hand fell onto the floor next to Patty's feet.

Patty stood looking through the small inspection plate set into the door. He slid open the lid on a panel next to the door and pressed a couple of buttons.

"What ... what are you doing, Patty?" Ginny asked.

"You'll like this," he said. "It needs more oxygen in there though, I think. It needs to breathe."

Patty watched as a reading on the door panel slowly crept up.

"Right, now, here's the best bit," Patty said.

There was a soft concussion from inside the room that Steve and Roy were in. Seconds later Ginny saw flames licking up the inspection plate inside the door.

"Come and look, come and look," Patty shouted across to Ginny.

Ginny heard the screams of the two men in the storeroom. They were screaming and screaming and screaming. "Oh God, oh God, oh God," she said. She looked over to Patty.

He was standing by the storeroom door. He was looking through the inspection panel. He was smiling. He waved to the men in the room. He turned to face Ginny, his eyes ablaze, his lips curled in intense pleasure.

Being given unction 8th Sept 2180

SEG002

The screaming had stopped.

Patty had sat down on the floor, his back to the storeroom door. He was muttering to himself.

"Accidents will happen, boys. Accidents will happen. Look what happened on SEG054. That wasn't nice, was it boys?"

Patty looked up. Ginny was hovering next to Gabriel. He was still sat on the chair to which he had been tied. She was stroking his face. His head was lolling, his eyes unfocussed, blood streaming from his nose.

"What shall we do, Ginny?" Patty said.

She looked over at him, fear in her eyes.

"He needs medical attention, Ginny," he continued.

Ginny heard Patty's words, but she didn't seem to be able to make sense of them. She was holding onto Gabriel like he was a life-raft. She didn't want to let him go. Then she saw Gabriel was losing blood. His head was upright. Even tilted slightly backwards. She pushed his head forward a little, to stop the blood from running back into his nose or into his mouth.

Her actions seemed to stabilise her a little.

"Can you help me get him back to my ship?" she said. "We have med facilities on board."

"Right. Let's do that," said Patty. He levered himself up, picked up Ginny and Gabriel's suit helmets. He clipped Gabriel's helmet back on as Ginny re-seated her own. Patty pulled his own helmet on. He picked Gabriel up and set off for the airlock. "Come on, we need to hurry," he said. "Otherwise he might swallow his own blood and ..."

"I'm right behind you," Ginny said.

· · · · · · · ·

Patty toiled across the landing area. Gabriel must have weighed more than Ginny because Patty was struggling.

"You could have used the robots to carry ..." Ginny said, but Patty looked across at her and the look on his face made her stop mid-sentence. She couldn't work out what was going through his mind, but she felt it best to let him keep carrying Gabriel himself.

They reached the airlock on the ACME ship and Patty pushed Gabriel through it. "I'll leave him with you," he said. "You get him patched up. I'll look at that Ramstat drive."

Ginny breathed a small sigh of relief. She hadn't wanted Patty on board their ship, but she hadn't been able to think of a way to stop him. Not whilst he was carrying Gabriel. She floated through the airlock, turned and pulled Gabriel in behind her. She hooked her arms under Gabriel's armpits, increased the boost on her suit's small Ramstats and tugged him through into the aft cabin. She pulled off his helmet, levered him up into the MED unit. The lid closed instantly. She let herself drift down onto the cabin floor.

"I've given you some shots," said Vicky.

"What?"

"Some shots ... some precautionary shots."

"What do you mean, Vicky?"

"To guard you against ... infection and such things."

"Oh."

"Ginny?"

"Yes, Vicky?"

"I believe you have a small vaginal tear."

"Oh."

"It will heal on its own. In just a few days."

"Ok, Vicky."

"And Ginny?"

"Yes, Vicky?"

"I'm so sorry I couldn't help you back there. If the coordinates hub were working ok, I could have transported you straight out of that situation. Straight out before ..."

"But that would have left Gabriel there on his own, wouldn't it, Vicky?"

"Yes, that would have been the case, Ginny."

"Ginny?"

"Ginny?"

"I wouldn't have wanted to leave Gabriel, Vicky. Even if … even if I got hurt. I wouldn't have wanted to leave him."

"Ginny?"

"Yes, Vicky?"

"Are you crying, Ginny?"

"Yes, Vicky. I just … I just …"

Ginny felt like curling up on the cabin floor. Curling herself up into a tight ball. Instead, she sat up with her back against the cabin wall. She clenched her fingers, feeling her nails digging into the palms of her hands. She felt hurt … damaged … ripped apart. Not in any physical sense, but like something evil had scarred her soul. She hadn't deserved that hurt … but neither had Gabriel.

She stifled her sobs.

"Hey Ship?" Ginny said.

"Yes, Ginny?"

"Please seal the airlock. I don't want anybody coming in or going out without me knowing."

"It's done," said the Ship.

"Thank you."

She drifted her suit up and into their bedroom. She shrugged off her space suit and threw it across the room. It fell next to the refuse chute. She hauled herself over and into the shower unit. "Lots of hot, please" she said. "and rose petals". The shower unit closed around her, immersing her body in its warm ion spray. She felt it ease away the hurts and the unwelcome touches.

Through the transparent shower screen, she noticed the small lifter. It picked up her space suit and dropped it into the refuse slot. "Thank you, Vicky," she whispered.

The ion spray tingled against her body. She turned her face up into it. She smelled rose petals. She pictured a warm summer's day, a gentle breeze carrying the scent of flowers.

She pictured Gabriel, lying in the MED unit, his face smashed, his damaged body being given unction.

She pictured two large men twisting and writhing in a bed of fire, shrieking as their clothes charred and peeled away, as their skin blistered and bubbled.

She pictured Patty, waving through the inspection hatch, smiling and waving as the men burned.

"Ginny?" said Vicky.

"Yes, Vicky."

"Gabriel will be all right. I thought you should be aware. You kept the blood from pooling down into his throat. He would have drowned in his own blood, otherwise. And the blow to his face ... if it had been directly onto his nose, it would likely have pushed his nose cartilage and bone up into his brain ... but it must have hit his cheek and pushed his nose side-ways. His nose is broken, but we will re-align it."

"Ok, thanks, Vicky. And Vicky?

"Yes, Ginny?"

"Please don't tell Gabriel about what happened in there. I think it would be best if he didn't know."

"As you wish, Ginny."

Why would he lie? 10th Sept 2180

SEG002

Ginny had got Vicky to get her some make-up. She didn't normally bother. Maybe a bit of lippy now and again, but she usually felt that she looked fine without. But she wanted something to cover up the bruising from when Steve had hit her in the face.

She wanted nothing to remind Gabriel of what had happened.

"Is the kit ok?" Vicky asked.

"Yeah, it's fine," Ginny said. She imagined that if she had had to buy a make-up kit like this at home, it would have cost a small fortune. She did not know who had made it, but everything about it shouted money and style.

"Is everything ok?" Gabriel shouted through.

He had suddenly got up. Got out of the MED unit. She had been watching him for two days. He didn't look like he would be going anywhere soon, then suddenly he had got up. He had walked through into the cockpit, and as soon as she had seen him, she had made her way straight into their bedroom. She had shouted "back in a tick". No explanation.

So here she was, quickly trying to work out what colour pot to apply to her bruised cheek.

"Are you really ok?" he said.

She heard him walking down the short corridor into their bedroom. She guessed he must be worried, and she was feeling flustered. She turned around and he was there. She turned her face away from him, and she sensed him walking towards her.

He stopped and looked down at the make-up kit. It was lying open on her cot. He pulled a small pot from its pouch. It made a slight noise as he pulled it free.

"I didn't think you used this …," he started, then halted. He gently took hold of her shoulders and turned her towards him.

He was looking at the bruising on her face.

"The bastards," he said, but then he saw the look on Ginny's face. "Christ … what happened?" he snarled.

Ginny leaned forward and dug her face into his shoulder, into the nape of his neck. She started to sob. She didn't think she could stop. He wrapped his arms around her. He started rocking her gently. Maybe as much for himself as for her.

· · · · · · · ·

"They teleported out," Ginny said. "I guess they thought …"

"So, they beat me up, beat you up and fucked off?" said Gabriel. "Seems sort of hard to believe. Why not get their ship and fly out?"

"I don't know … maybe 'cos Patty wasn't with them."

"Oh, yeah. Patty. So where's he?"

"He's been working on our broken Ramstat motor. He thinks he can fix it."

"Why don't we find out how he's getting on. Call him. Ask him in for a drink or something."

"I'd … I'd rather …"

"What's up, Ginny? It's not like he was one of the guys who beat us up, is it?"

"I don't … I'd just rather not, Gabriel."

"Ok, Ginny. If you'd rather not, that's fine."

Ginny gave Gabriel a weak smile.

"But we should at least find out how he's getting on; if he's had any luck trying to fix the motor. I wouldn't imagine a Ramstat motor is a simple thing to fix."

"Ok," Ginny said, and, as if to forestall Gabriel from rushing outside to speak to Patty directly, she said "Hello Ship, can you patch us through to Patty, please?"

"Right away," Ship replied.

A view of the ship's hull appeared on a screen on the bedroom wall. Patty was sitting on top of the hull, his head in an access cover on the Ramstat motor.

"Hey Patty," Ginny said. "Any luck with our motor?"

"Just finishing it. Had a bit of luck. We had stuff about. Should work fine."

"That's great, Patty," said Ginny.

"Should be finished in about an hour. How are you feeling after …?"

"Great, Patty," Ginny said, cutting him off. "Catch you later … and thanks Ship … close the comms-link now please."

"It's done," the Ship replied.

Gabriel was looking at Ginny. There was something she wasn't telling him, but he thought if she wanted to, she would tell him in her own time. He trusted her and respected her. He didn't want to cross a line she didn't want him to cross.

"That's great news," he said.

"It is if he's really fixed it," she said.

"Why would he lie?"

"You know mechanics," she said, with a half-smile. "They tell you it's fixed, they take your money, then it breaks down half a mile away."

Gabriel looked at Ginny. She seemed to have changed since Steve and Roy had beaten them up. He could see why that might be the case, but it was like there was something else. Like she had lost a bit of her old sparkle.

"You don't think we should trust Patty's work?" he asked.

"Maybe we should try the teleport, first."

"That's if Patty can pause the processing."

"I think I'd rather try that than risk a lengthy journey on a Ramstat motor fixed with 'bits of stuff they had lying around'."

"Ok, Ginny," he said. "I agree. If he can pause the processing, it's a straight-forward trip, and it takes no time. Let's give it a go."

· · · · · · · ·

"Ginny?" Ship said. "Patty wants to talk to you. He is standing outside the airlock."

"Ok, Ship. Please put him through on comms," Ginny said.

Ginny thought Gabriel looked like he was about to say something, but then thought better of it.

A monitor showed Patty standing outside the airlock. He looked like he had expected them to open it up.

"Hi, Patty," Ginny said. "How goes it?"

Patty stood back a little. He probably guessed from her voice that she would not let him in.

"Work's all done, and the covers are closed. Try it."

"Shall I bring the engine online?" Ship asked.

"Yes, please, Ship," Ginny said.

They heard the familiar low rumble as the engine came online.

"How's it look?" Ginny said.

"I can't really tell until we put it under load," Ship replied.

"Ok, Ship. Please shut it down," Ginny said, then "Hey Patty, thanks for that. Great job. I think we're gonna get some sleep now. Big day tomorrow, eh?"

"Hey," Patty said. "How's about …?"

"Catch you in the morning," Ginny said, cutting Patty short, then "Ship, please close the comms-link now."

"It's closed, Ginny."

Gabriel was staring at her.

"I'm going to get some sleep," Ginny said.

"Ok … I'll come and give you a cuddle," Gabriel said.

"No, it's ok, thanks," she said, turning towards their bedroom.

He gave her a few minutes to get herself ready. She usually took a little while to brush her teeth, comb through her hair and get out of her spacesuit. He never liked to interrupt her whilst she did these things, but when he finally walked through, she had gotten onto her couchette and had pulled a downy duvet around herself.

She was facing away from him. Facing towards the cabin wall. She had drawn herself up into an almost foetal position. He got himself ready and climbed in alongside her. He sensed her almost imperceptibly moving away from him, as if she didn't want him to touch her, to be near him at all.

"Are you ok, Ginny?" he whispered.

She said nothing. He couldn't tell whether or not she was asleep.

He felt very lonely. Lonely, and very afraid. Afraid that something had happened to Ginny, and he didn't know what it was. And he wasn't sure how to help her.

There're worse ways 11th Sept 2180

SEG002

Gabriel and Ginny had got up and had some coffee and croissants.

"Even if ACME INC has gone bust, they still provide some nice food," Gabriel said.

He was trying to cheer Ginny up, but she still seemed to be distant.

"Patty's outside," Ship said. "Shall I open up the comms-link?"

"Yes, thanks," said Ginny.

They saw Patty standing outside their ship. He wasn't close to the hull this time; seemingly he had less optimism about being invited in.

"Morning Patty," Ginny said.

"Morning, guys. You getting ready to leave today?"

"We were thinking about using the teleport," Ginny said.

"Oh, yeah, well, ok," Patty said. "I can do that for you. I can stop the processing for a bit. Let you go through."

"That's great, Patty," Ginny said.

"But you'd have to be careful the other end, 'cos as soon as a shipment goes through, the machinery at the other end will unload it, and ..."

"Yeah, but Steve and Roy, they ..." Gabriel said.

Patty laughed. "Yeah, them guys," he said. "They certainly ..."

"Ok Patty," Ginny said, cutting off whatever Patty was about to say. "How about we see you at the teleport in one hour? Can you get the processing stopped so we can go through?"

"Yeah, sure, Ginny. I'll get it all ready for you."

"Thanks, Patty."

"Shall I close the comms-link Ginny?"

"Please, Ship."

"It's closed, Ginny."

"Thank you."

"I'll start getting my gear," Gabriel said. He turned and walked towards their bedroom. He felt Ginny was being incredibly rude to Patty, who seemed to do his best to help them. He had never seen her be rude or unkind to anyone before, so he didn't understand why she should act like that now.

· · · · · · · ·

They met Patty at the teleport. Gabriel had shoved a few things into a backpack he had requested. He had carefully pushed in his copy of SEG's transhipment journal. Ginny couldn't think of anything she wanted to take with her.

"Looks like he's stopped all the processing," Gabriel said.

Ginny looked around. The heavy machinery which seemed to be continually lifting, pushing or pulling things about was all stationary. Patty was standing next to the entrance to the teleport looking incredibly pleased with himself. They stood next to Patty.

"Step right in," Patty said, beckoning them towards the open doors into the teleport.

"You're sure the processing won't start again while we're in there?" Gabriel said.

Patty brushed past Gabriel, smiled, and slipped something small into Gabriel's backpack as he went. Gabriel didn't notice, and Ginny was looking nervously into the teleport bay.

Patty stepped into the teleport bay. The bay was enormous. It needed to accommodate quite a few shipping containers, which the machinery would stack neatly against each other. They had seen it stacked two containers high. The processing would fill the bay with twelve containers, the doors would close, and seconds later the doors would open, and the process would begin again.

Patty danced around the bay. He beckoned them in.

Gabriel looked at Ginny. She was staring fearfully at Patty.

Patty looked across at them from the back wall of the teleport bay. He smiled at them. A strange, tortured grimace of a smile. Ginny heard a noise behind her. A container had resumed its stately progress towards the bay. Ginny grabbed Gabriel and pulled him to one side as the container pushed past them.

"Get out of there, Patty," Gabriel shouted.

Patty was still dancing around the bay; strange pirouettes, his laughter coming loudly across the comms-link.

"Get the hell out ... or turn the bloody thing off," Gabriel shouted.

The container pushed through the open doors of the bay. It slid along towards a back wall. Patty had suddenly become aware that the processing had re-started. He was standing by the back wall. He lifted an arm and began pressing at a control pad on the sleeve of his suit.

More containers were being pushed into the bay, being automatically manoeuvred so as to fill the space. Patty ran from side to side, punching at the control pad, dodging around the containers. His available space was becoming smaller and smaller. He looked across at Gabriel and Ginny. He began laughing again, but a container caught his foot, trapping him, stopping him from moving any further. His laughter turned to screams. A container was being shunted sideways towards him, and he had nowhere to go. The container slammed into place, and his screams stopped instantly.

Gabriel looked at Ginny. She was staring at the place where Patty had been standing. A river of blood was running from under the last container. Gabriel caught her arm and moved her to one side of the teleport bay. He walked her slowly away from the teleport, back along a maintenance walkway, away from the continuing sounds of the containers being shunted into place.

· · · · · · · · ·

"Do you want a drink, or anything?" Gabriel asked.

Ginny was sitting in her cockpit seat. She was staring at the instrumentation panel.

"I think I might have a hot chocolate," Gabriel said.

"I wonder if the machine can get toasted muffins?" he mused into the silence following his last question to Ginny.

"How many would you like," Ship asked.

Ginny laughed. It wasn't a pleasant laugh, but it was a laugh.

Gabriel wasn't sure whether or not to feel encouraged.

"Four please," Gabriel said. "And two hot chocolates, please."

"I don't think I want to try the teleport now," Ginny said.

"No, I don't think we should."

"I wonder if he realised it would start up again?" she said.

"I don't know. Do you think he had any reason to want to kill himself ... and in such a gruesome way?"

"There're worse ways," Ginny said.

"I guess so," said Gabriel, but not being able to think of any right at that moment.

"So, I think we will have to trust that the Ramstats will get us back to Earth," Ginny said.

"Looks that way."

"The toasted muffins and hot chocolates are ready," Ship announced.

"Well, that's something," Gabriel said.

God-forsaken shit-hole 11th Sept 2180

SEG002

"So where to?" Ginny said.

Ginny was still sitting in her cockpit seat. She had drunk the hot chocolate that Gabriel had requested, but she hadn't eaten the toasted muffins. She had taken a small bite out of one, then handed the rest back to Gabriel. He had been enjoying his, but Ginny's mood was wearing him down. He didn't know what to do or what to say that might make her feel better. All right, the last few days had been difficult. Their starship was still sitting in the landing bay, with its view of the teleport bay; the bay in which Patty's body was still lying. Then he caught himself. Patty's body wouldn't be there anymore. It would have teleported back to the Earth hours ago. It would have gone along with the shipment of containers that caused his death.

He felt himself beginning to chuckle. To chuckle at how wrong he had been. All this time envisaging Patty's body being continually chewed up by each load of containers, when in fact it would have gone ages ago.

"What's funny?" Ginny asked. She wasn't smiling. She looked like she might never smile again.

"Oh, er ... nothing," said Gabriel. "I was thinking ..."

Ginny scowled over at him, and Gabriel's heart sank.

"So, where to?" she repeated, obvious frustration in her voice.

"Back to the Earth, do you reckon," said Gabriel, tentatively. "That's where the ACME offices are, isn't it?"

"That's where the administration offices are," said Vicky, "but it might be better to go to the ACME-HUB."

"What ... the orbiting space-station?" Ginny said.

"Well," continued Vicky, "that is where the coordinates database is. Also, it's where the MEDICARE centre is situated, and it's probably the best place to find another STU to give to John's wife."

"Would we be able to land on the space station?" Ginny asked.

"It has docking stubs ... we can easily land there," Ship said.

"Ok," said Gabriel. "Are we all agreed ... the ACME-HUB is where we're going?"

"How long is the journey time?" Ginny said.

"With both motors on full thrust, slightly over four days," Ship said.

"That's if they both hold out," said Ginny.

"Let us hope they do," said Vicky.

"Right Ship, let's get under way," said Ginny. "The sooner we get off this God-forsaken shit-hole of a planet, the happier I'll be."

Gabriel heard the low rumble of the two Ramstat motors coming online. He looked across at Ginny. He couldn't tell what she was thinking about, but he very much hoped her forecast would be correct.

Docking time in one minute 15th Sept 2180

The ACME-HUB (orbiting space satellite)

Gabriel must have asked Ship countless times over the last four days how the starboard motor was running. Each time Ship had advised there were no faults being identified. It appeared it was fixed.

Gabriel realised his constant questioning was irritating Ginny, but he didn't seem to be able to stop himself.

"We are approaching the ACME-HUB," Ship advised. "They have given us permission to lock onto stub 12. We are on approach now. Docking time is 3 minutes."

"I suggest, once we have docked, that we head for the client quarters," Vicky suggested. "We don't know if the place will be in a state of chaos or not, but if we look purposeful, we should be able to get into one of the client apartments. Clients use them before they set off on their excursions. The apartments should have news-feed facilities. We should be able to find out the current situation."

"Sounds like a plan," said Gabriel.

Ginny looked circumspect. "Our plans don't seem to have a very high success rate," she said.

"Docking in one minute," Ship advised.

"Thanks," Ginny said.

"Incidentally," Ship advised. "The ACME-HUB has an Earth-like environment. You won't need suit-helmets in any area."

"Thanks again," Ginny said.

"It's a pleasure," said Ship. "ACME INC are always keen to assist their clients."

Gabriel chuckled. He hadn't heard Ship giving an ACME INC-spiel for quite a long time, and he suspected it was doing it now more as a joke than as a pre-programmed piece of advertising. He looked across at Ginny, but she either hadn't seen the joke or she had other things on her mind.

"We're docked," said Ship. "Shall I open the cockpit door, Ginny?"

Gabriel pondered again on the relationship that had formed between the starship's AI entity and his girlfriend.

"Is there anyone out there to greet us?" she asked.

"Not currently," Ship advised.

"Ok, come on. Let's get going," she said.

Gabriel picked up the rucksack he had stored his few belongings in and threw it over his right shoulder. Ginny was straight out of the cockpit door, and Gabriel jumped up and followed right behind her.

Don't you think that's strange? 15th Sept 2180

The ACME-HUB (orbiting space satellite)

"Follow the yellow line to get to the client quarters," Vicky said.

A bright yellow line, three inches wide, appeared on the floor in front of them. It led up the corridor in which they were standing, turning right at a junction ahead of them.

"Are you making that yellow line?" Gabriel asked.

"I thought it might help," Vicky said.

"There's nobody about," observed Ginny. "Don't you think that's strange? I would have thought there would be lots of people here. "

Ginny suddenly stopped. She turned back towards Gabriel and put her finger to her lips. They heard footsteps coming towards them. It sounded like several people. They weren't running, but they were probably either jogging or, at the very least, walking briskly.

Gabriel felt his heart rate quicken. He didn't think they were doing anything wrong, but likewise he didn't want to have to explain their presence to anybody.

The footsteps got closer, then moved away. Whoever it was must have moved away down an adjacent corridor.

"Ok," Ginny said. "Let's get going."

. . . .

"The client apartments are down here, on the left," Vicky said. "Let's find an empty one and go in."

"This place looks like an expensive hotel," Ginny said.

"I guess that's what it is," said Gabriel.

"Or was," said Ginny.

"This one here," said Vicky. "Room 8 ... it's empty. I've de-activated the lock. Simply open the door and go in."

Gabriel pushed the door open.

"Ok, let's get on with it," Ginny said. "Vicky, please find out what's going on. Are you able to do that?"

Gabriel looked at Ginny. She seemed ... what ... highly focused. Like she had things to do, like there were things she had to get done come-what-may.

"Are you ok, Ginny?" he asked.

"I'm perfectly fine. Why?"

"Oh, I don't know. You seem to be ..."

"Seem to be what?"

"Well ... you seem to be ..."

"For God's sake, Gabriel. Say it. Say what you mean."

"I'm sorry, Ginny. You don't seem yourself, and I'm ..."

"And you're ...?"

"I'm worried about you, Ginny."

Ginny gave a vague smile to Gabriel, whilst holding her hands up in a 'you understand how it is' gesture.

Gabriel didn't understand how it was. Her vague attempt at a smile had looked very artificial. She wasn't being honest with him, and he didn't know what to do or say. He was very worried.

"I've pulled back the information on the data corruption," Vicky said. "The database of coordinates was corrupted, exactly as we thought. It happened when I tried to teleport back here with my last ACME client. On that very same day."

Gabriel felt a vague sense of satisfaction from knowing their guess had been correct.

"The ACME techs had identified the coordinates database was corrupt," continued Vicky, "and also that all backups and mirrors had been corrupted. They estimated that the time required to re-build the database from scratch would not be trivial. The trouble was that, during that time, the various clients would request their STU to teleport them back at the end of their trip."

"So, what happened?" Ginny asked.

"Well, it looks like the techs didn't notice the coordinates were corrupt for several days. Seemingly the coordinates weren't deleted; they were tampered with. They still looked like real coordinates. If they had been changed drastically, such as their formats changed, making them unreadable, the problem might have been picked up earlier, but they weren't. When the clients returning from their excursions requested their STUs to initiate a teleport back, the STUs carried out the request."

"And?" Gabriel said.

"ACME realised there was a problem because many clients didn't return on their designated dates and times. The techs realised the coordinates were corrupt, which meant the clients might end up being teleported into space, into solid rock, into a volcano ... anywhere."

"Shit," Gabriel said.

"Quite," said Vicky, "so the only immediate option open to ACME was to shut down the communication protocol used by the STUs. They disabled WORM-LYNK. This prevented the STUs from getting access to the faulty coordinates, but by the time ACME had shut down its WORM-LYNK, most of the clients on trips would already have started their return teleport."

"How many of them were there?" Ginny asked.

"37, excluding my client, Mervin."

Ginny lowered herself down onto a reclining chair. It instantly molded itself to her form. She looked horrified by the information Vicky had found.

"We could have saved those people," she said.

"How do you mean?" Gabriel asked.

"Don't be so bloody dim," she snapped. "If we had got here before the database corrupted, they wouldn't have died. We should have told ACME ... told them soon enough to avoid ..."

"But Ginny," Vicky interrupted. "If you had got here soon enough to warn ACME, I would never have arrived in Walton-on-the-Naze. John Cullen would never have recovered from his catatonia, and you and Gabriel may have never met."

"And I wouldn't have met Steve and Roy," Ginny said.

Gabriel looked up at Ginny. She was looking distraught.

"Ginny?" he said, and then the door burst open.

Four heavy-set men rushed into the room. Each of them was cradling a short rifle. Gabriel jumped up and was immediately smashed down to the ground by a blow to the head with a rifle butt.

Welcome back, sunshine 16th Sept 2180

The ACME-HUB (orbiting space satellite)

His head was pounding. He was laying down, flat on his back. On a hard surface. There was no noise. He opened his eyes ... slowly.

He was still in the room he and Ginny had been in when the big guys rushed in.

Or a different but similar room.

Ginny wasn't there.

He still had the small, molded earpiece Vicky had requested for him. Since he had given Vicky over to Ginny, he had re-inserted the earpiece, in case Vicky needed to contact him and he wasn't within earshot.

"Vicky?" he said, very quietly.

"We are here, Gabriel," Vicky said. "We are still in Room 8. They took you out after they knocked you to the ground."

"Are you ok?"

"Yes, we are both ok, Gabriel. Ginny is being questioned right now. They think you were involved in the data corruption. I will get back to you when they have finished with Ginny."

"Ok, Vicky. I understand," said Gabriel, but right then the door to the apartment opened and two men walked in.

Gabriel half-closed his eyes again.

"Welcome back, sunshine," somebody said. "You been sleepy-times?"

It was a low, rumbly voice. It sounded like somebody crushing boulders. It didn't sound sympathetic.

Icy water splashed onto his face. Some went into his nose and mouth. He choked.

He turned onto his side and coughed the water clear.

The action of the movement and the coughing made the pain in his head worse.

"How did you do it?"

A different voice. Gentler. More conventionally pitched. Inquisitive. Just asking a question. Asking a polite question.

He was pushed onto his back ... a wet towel laid across his face. Then more water. He choked again.

"No need for that," the gentler voice said. "I think he will tell us with none of that."

They hauled up off the floor, sat him in a straight-backed chair. Tied his arms behind him. Wiped his face down with a dry, warm towel.

He opened his eyes and looked around.

Two men were standing in front of him. They were wearing uniforms. They each had a badge labelled "SECURITY", and below that they had their name tags. "Smythe" and "Rust". They were both about the same size. They were big men.

Gabriel guessed he was in what looked like another of the client apartments. It was maybe next to the one they were in before.

"Where's the girl?" Gabriel asked.

"She's ok," said Rust. He was the one with the gentler voice.

"For now," snarled Smythe, in his gravelly tone.

"So, how did you do it?" Rust repeated.

Smythe looked behind him and picked up Gabriel's backpack. He unfastened the top and tipped the contents out onto the floor. He rummaged through; items of clothing, the SEG journal, a small silver block.

Smythe picked it up and pushed it in front of Gabriel's face, running the shiny surface down Gabriel's cheek.

"What's this?" he said.

Gabriel looked at the shiny silver block. He didn't recognise it. He had no idea what it was.

"I've never seen it ...," he said.

Smythe slapped him viciously across his face.

"Ok, Mr. Smythe," Rust said in a conciliatory manner. "The lad says he's never seen it before. We know it's a data slug. Maybe it's what he used to compromise our coordinates. Who's to know?"

Rust winked in a friendly way to Gabriel, as if to show he was on Gabriel's side, and would soon clear up this misunderstanding.

"Come on, Mr. Smythe," Rust said genially. "Why don't we play the data slug. Then we'll all know what the game is."

Smythe took the silver block and walked over to a section of wall which seemed to be littered with media-related devices. He pushed the silver block into a slot and stepped back. Instantly a large video image appeared on an adjacent wall.

The image was about ten feet wide, six feet high. The video showed two men standing in a small room cluttered with bits of machinery and tools. One man was holding his hand. Blood was pouring from the stumps of his fingers. Both men were watching a small tube as it rolled along the floor away from them.

"It's … it's Steve and Roy," Gabriel said.

Roy was watching the tube as it rolled along the ground.

"Holy fuck," Roy said. "It's a …"

Roy rushed forward as if to try to catch it, but as he did so the tube turned into a small ball of flame.

Gabriel saw Roy's movements had slowed right down. He realised the video had been slowed down. Roy's hand was slowly making its way to the tube; slowly the tube blossomed. It bloomed into a slowly expanding ball of orange fire. The noise it made, slow as it was, sounded like a lion's roar.

The flame engulfed Roy's hand, covering both Roy and Steve in a fiery wrath.

Roy and Steve both began to scream. Flames immersed them. The entire room was being scoured with flames. They ran to the walls, scrabbling to find somewhere, anywhere not filled with flames. They fell to the ground. They writhed. Their backs arched and twisted. Their screaming seemed to fill the room that Gabriel was sitting in.

The scene changed. They were looking in long-shot at someone looking quietly pleased with himself.

"God, that's Patty," Gabriel said, his voice shaking.

The video shot of Patty moved into a close-up of his face

"I hope you enjoyed that, Ginny," Patty said. He smiled coyly at the camera, as if listening to inner thoughts.

 "I guess that taught them a lesson for raping you."

Patty looked down at something and the camera pulled back to a point where the whole top half of his body was visible. He looked back in the camera's direction.

"Anyway, Ginny," he said, smiling. "Got to go ... things to do. I hope you enjoyed the recording of their last moments. I didn't know they could dance. Did you?"

Patty's smile turned into a chuckle. "Mind you ... now that I think about it ... I guess you already knew that they had the hip movements."

The video stopped, freezing the last frame, Patty's chuckling face.

"That's a strange little fucker," Smythe said.

"She said they teleported out ... oh God, Ginny ... oh God ...," said Gabriel, his voice filled with horror.

Rust touched a finger to his own ear. "Sorry? Say again ... say again."

Smythe looked questioningly at Rust.

"Team two ... with the girl. She's got a fucking STU," Rust said, "and the STU says that Bonnie and Clyde here were on SEG002 at the time of the data corruption."

"What, the STU had data for the last 10 days?"

"It has data for the last 233 years."

"Fuck it," said Smythe. "But anyway, they've got no id, no authorisation to be here. That's how we picked the fuckers up, entering a room with no id."

"This changes thing," said Rust. "I am aware we've had no reason to apprehend anybody since ACME started this op, and I know you're keen to do some ... security stuff ... but this guy's done nothing wrong."

"As far as we know," rumbled Smythe. He looked over at Gabriel, who was transfixed by the last frame of the video, "'cept helping to burn those two poor fuckers."

"Sounded like rough but appropriate justice to me," commented Rust.

Smythe grunted.

"One more thing," said Rust. "I think you need to get this guy down to the MED bay ... oh ... and a brief apology wouldn't do any harm."

"Fuck that," said Smythe.

"The girl's STU ...," said Rust.

"Yeah, what about the fucking STU?"

"The STU said these two brought it back to the HUB. It was one of the ones screwed by the bad coordinates."

Smythe looked unconvinced.

"If that's true," continued Rust, "I think ACME might feel they owe them gratitude at least. Those little fuckers are expensive."

"Oh yeah. Owe them what?" said Smythe.

"Well, a bit of MED treatment after you've beat him up ... that at least, I would have thought."

Smythe walked over to Gabriel and began untying him from the chair.

Gabriel seemed oblivious of the conversation going on and flinched when Smythe jerked him to his feet.

"Ok, lad," Rust said. "Let's get you to the MED bay."

"Yeah, you've taken a bit of a fall, haven't you?" Smythe said, grinning.

Rust gave Smythe a look of caution.

Smythe bent down and re-packed Gabriel's stuff back into his backpack. He extracted the data slug from the socket on the wall and dropped it into the bag. He handed the backpack over to Gabriel, who took it cautiously.

"C'mon lad," Rust said, taking Gabriel's arm and guiding him out of the room. "Let's get you down to the MED bay."

"Where's Ginny?" Gabriel said as they walked.

Rust pinched a device on his ear and began talking. "Get the girl down to the MED bay. We're on our way there now. No, I don't care about that. Get her down there now. See you there ... two minutes."

Rust escorted Gabriel down a swathe of corridors. Smythe walked behind. Nobody spoke. There didn't seem to be much to talk about.

"There's the MED bay," said Rust. He nodded in the direction of a large neon MEDI-CARE sign. "There'll be somebody in there from ACME who can patch you up a bit."

Gabriel looked at Rust, then across at Smythe.

"It's up to you if you want to make a big deal about ... about Smythe's enthusiasm," Rust said, "but there's lots of people have died because of somebody buggering up our coordinates database. That may not mean much to you, but ..."

Gabriel guessed Rust worried a complaint about Smythe would come back to Rust. Rust was probably the team leader or some such thing. He gave Rust a non-committal shrug of his shoulders. He thought he was getting used to being roughed up. He didn't think it was worth making a big deal about it.

Rust observed Gabriel's gesture. "C'mon Mr. Smythe," he said, turning away from Gabriel and walking away down the corridor. "We still don't know who did it. That's what they are paying us to do, so let's get fucking on with it."

Gabriel watched as Rust and Smythe walked away down the corridor. He remembered what Patty had said on the video. And he realised that Ginny must have decided not to tell him. He had found it hard to believe when she had said Steve and Roy had teleported back to the Earth. He couldn't think of any reason why they would have done that ... and that was because they hadn't.

And that was, presumably, why Ginny had been so off-hand with Patty. She must have seen what he had done to Steve and Roy. And even though they had raped her, she didn't feel easy with what Patty had done either.

He couldn't imagine Ginny's inner strength. What she had needed to do to see her through the last few days.

And to think he had been cross with her because she was snapping at him. He felt very unworthy of her.

He pushed open the door into the MED bay. There were two people, a man and a woman. They were sitting on stools against a side wall. They were holding disposable drink containers. They turned and stood up as he walked in. They both looked about mid-thirties. He was of medium height, trim, with a light beard. He looked self-assured. She looked quite pretty, very slim, with blonde shoulder-length hair. Her med-bay uniform, short jacket and trousers fitted her nicely.

"I'm Gabriel," he said.

"We're expecting you," the woman said, putting her cup down and walking over to him. "I'm Sara," she said, "and that's Zackery," nodding in the man's direction.

Gabriel nodded.

"You took a fall?" Sara said.

"Have you seen my friend, Ginny?" Gabriel asked.

"She's on her way," said Zackery. "While we're waiting for her, let's take a look at you."

Sara took Gabriel's arm and led him over to a device that was like the MED unit they had had in their starship. This one, though, looked far more expensive and complicated.

The lid on the unit opened.

"Please lay down on the cot," Sara said. "The machine will carry out a diagnostic on you."

Gabriel nodded again. "Yeah ... I've seen one," he said. "In fact, I've used one. So has my friend, Ginny."

"Really?" said Zackery. "It's expensive gear. It's not normally ..."

"We had to use it to amputate her legs," Gabriel said.

Sara looked shocked. Zackery looked like he would say something, but thought better of it.

"She lost her legs when we were trying to bring your STU device back here," Gabriel said.

The MED bay door opened, and Ginny hovered in. She saw Gabriel. She hovered over to him, ignoring the two others in the room.

She put her arms round him, hugging him close to her.

"You look like you've been in the wars again," she said, lightly running her fingers over his bruised face.

"We've both been up against it," he said.

Ginny looked at him curiously. "Yeah," she said. "Cuts and bruises, eh? Still, it might have been worse."

"Maybe," Gabriel said. The pain from the side of his head where Smythe had hit him with his rifle seemed to be getting worse.

Ginny hovered backwards away from Gabriel, gazing at him. She was still ignoring the two others in the room. They were far less important to her, and they were currently standing there not saying anything. They seemed respectful of Ginny's conversation with Gabriel.

"Has Vicky been talking to you?" she asked.

"About what?"

"Oh. Cuts and bruises and things."

"No, she hasn't."

"I haven't told him anything," Vicky whispered. "You asked me not to, so I haven't."

"Ginny ...," Gabriel said. He felt unsure what to say. He guessed Ginny had told Vicky not to mention about her being raped, but he didn't think this was the time to discuss it. He stepped back, away from Ginny. He looked over towards the two medical staff.

"Ginny," Gabriel said. "This is Sara and Zackery. They might patch us up a bit."

Sara looked very relieved. The conversation seemed to have moved on to an area that she could contribute to.

"Gabriel," Sara said. "If you want to jump up onto this MED unit here, we can run a few checks. We can make sure there's no lasting damage from when you ... when you, er, tripped and fell."

Ginny looked incredulously at Gabriel. "You tripped and fell?" she said.

"Maybe it was more like 'pushed hard'," Gabriel said.

"Yeah ... I saw them push you."

"ACME INC have told us to apologise for any ...," Sara said. She looked embarrassed and looked over to her colleague for support.

"ACME INC is aware you have brought them back a STU," Zackery said. "They said for us to thank you. They said they will send someone down to see you, but they are all ... well ... I don't know if you are aware, but ACME is in the middle of a crisis. Everyone is ..."

"We can imagine," said Ginny

"So, anyway," continued Zackery, "we have been told to give you any assistance you may require. To both of you."

"What happens to the STU we brought back?" Ginny asked.

"I'm not aware about that," Zackery said. "They didn't tell us."

"Ok," said Gabriel. "So maybe you can check us over ... patch us up."

"We can do that," Sara said. "You remember, Gabriel ... you mentioned Ginny had to have her legs amputated whilst you were journeying here?"

Ginny looked at Sara, who was suddenly looking uncomfortable having raised the topic.

"If you had her leg dimensions, we could build new legs to match her old ones," Sara said.

"I'm only here," Ginny said. "You can talk to me about it. They were my legs after all."

"Sorry Ginny," Sara said.

"And we have her leg dimensions," said Vicky. "The MED unit we used for the amputations took precise measurements, which it sent to me. I can provide that information if it will assist you. Which device would you like me to send them to?"

"That one, B6, over there," Zackery said.

"Hey, Ginny," Zackery said. "If you want to get into the B6 unit ... do you need help to get the spacesuit off?"

"I'll do it Zackery, thanks," Sara said.

Ginny hovered over to the B6 unit. She laid back on the bed and Sara helped her pull her spacesuit off. Gabriel walked over to the unit and stood beside her. He watched the unit's lid slowly close over her. He gave her a smile of encouragement. She smiled back, but her smile seemed to betray her anxiety.

"Get into a med unit yourself," Sara suggested, pointing. "There's nothing more you can do for Ginny until the procedure is complete, so you might as well get checked over."

Gabriel walked over to the other MED unit and laid down in it. Laying down seemed to make the pain in his head pulse even stronger. He watched as the lid closed. A pale crimson mist filled the unit. He felt a light drowsiness overwhelming him. His eyes closed. He felt warm and safe.

I think that I can answer that 18th Sept 2180

The ACME-HUB (orbiting space satellite)

The MED unit's lid had opened, and Gabriel sat up. Sara and Zackery were watching him from across the room.

"Would you like a little drink?" Sara asked.

Gabriel felt the side of his head. It still felt painful. The pulsing pain he had felt earlier had been replaced by a vague memory of that pain. It was still vaguely there, and even as he thought about it it seemed to recede.

"I'll get you some water," said Zackery.

"Thanks," said Gabriel. "How's Ginny?"

"Come and look," said Sara.

Gabriel accepted a cup of water from Zackery, then walked over to the med unit in which Ginny lay. It was still filled with a crimson haze. Laying on the cot, Ginny seemed to be asleep. What looked to Gabriel like bandages seemed to restrain her body, running across her chest, stomach, and hips.

"The webbing helps to stop her moving during the process," Sara answered Gabriel's unspoken question.

A web of golden rays seemed to crisscross a path along where her legs would have been. As the rays pulsed, they were leaving behind their newly constructed legs.

"The unit has opened up nerve endings on the stumps of her legs," Sara said. "The new legs will have sensitivity. They will feel exactly like her original legs."

"Will she need to learn to walk on them?" said Gabriel. "Will she need to use crutches or anything?".

"They grow directly onto the stumps, Gabriel," Sara said. "The MED unit that amputated her legs left the bone and muscle sculptured so that new legs can be attached. With the re-grow process completed, she will need about two to three days for her body to finish bonding to them. Then it will be as though they were her own legs."

Gabriel looked incredulous.

"She needs to make sure she rests for two to three days. Less than that and the bond may be unsuccessful."

"Will ACME let us stay here for another two to three days?" Gabriel asked.

"I think I can answer that."

They all turned to see who the unfamiliar voice was. Someone had entered the room.

A small man in a very smart suit was standing slightly inside the MED bay doorway. He looked very anxious. He looked about forty years old. His hair was thinning. His skin looked very pale, as though he rarely saw the light of the Sun.

"Director Swan," Sara said, partly as an acknowledgment of his presence and partly to introduce him to Gabriel.

As if released from stasis, Swan rushed over to Gabriel and shook him vigorously by the hand.

Gabriel noticed that Swan's grip seemed very weak … his hand was clammy.

"It's really good to see you," Swan said. "We've all heard about you."

"Director Swan is the senior data-tech specialist in ACME INC," Sara explained. "He is responsible for …"

"Thank you, Sara," Swan said, reading her name off the name tag on her jacket. "I don't think we need you to explain my credentials, thank you very much."

Sara looked shocked and flustered by Swan's rudeness. She flushed and turned toward her colleague, Zackery, who was looking uncomfortable himself.

"I'd like to thank you," said Gabriel, "for letting us use the med bay facilities. I guess you heard we suffered a few 'cuts and bruises' on the journey to bring your STU back."

"Yes. We'd heard you needed a bit of patching up. This is the least we can do, Gabriel … the least we can do."

"But we'd wondered … that is, Ginny and me had wondered …"

"Wondered what, Gabriel?"

"If maybe … you would let us have a spare STU … to give to the wife of a friend of ours … when we get back. It would be a great kindness."

Swan looked astonished at Gabriel's suggestion.

"Just a minute, Gabriel. We are grateful you brought us back a very expensive piece of equipment, and it leads us to believe it has been at no slight inconvenience to yourselves, but what you are asking … we aren't a charity. Just the cost of re-growing your companion's legs is …"

"But we …"

"And these are very difficult times for ACME INC, as I'm sure you're aware."

"We've heard there're massive amounts of litigation …," Sara said.

Swan turned to face Sara, his face like thunder.

"If we need advice on business strategy from med-bay staff, I will come down here straight away next time," Swan snarled.

Sara bit her lip.

"So, what we'll do," said Swan, turning back to face Gabriel, "is we'll give you a few days using our facilities. Take time to heal. Keep the use of the STU, just for now. It will help you to use the apartment's features. While you're doing that, we will re-build the coordinates database. Then, in a few days' time, we'll take back the STU and give you a 'one-trip' device. It will take you back to your own time."

"And that's it?" said Gabriel.

"And … please accept our thanks."

Gabriel turned away from Swan, as if to consider the proposal. As he did so, he heard Vicky whispering to him faintly.

"Gabriel. I don't trust Director Swan. Can you take the earpiece out of your ear and try to put it into Swan's jacket pocket? That way we can hear what he says after he leaves us."

Gabriel glanced over towards Swan, who looked like he was about to leave.

"Just a minute, Mr. Swan," he said, fumbling in his ear. "Can't you tell us more about what is going on now? We may not meet again, and it would be great if …"

Swan looked annoyed.

Gabriel walked up close to Swan, who looked even more annoyed; eager to leave.

Sara saw Gabriel was trying to do something, but she didn't know what. She turned and picked up a small pair of forceps but let them fall from her hand.

She bent from the waist to pick up the forceps.

Swan watched Sara, admiring her taut figure.

Sara, her face down at her knees, turned her face up to look up at Swan.

She smiled to him as she picked up the forceps.

Swan awkwardly returned Sara's smile.

Gabriel slipped the earpiece into Swan's left jacket pocket.

Sara stood up, putting the forceps back onto the shelf from which she had taken them.

The spell over Swan was broken.

"I think the STU can tell you all that you need to know about us ... about ACME INC," said Swan, with a sense of finality. "I don't think we will meet again, Mr. Gabriel, so thank you again for bringing back the STU. I trust that the experience made it all worthwhile."

He turned and left.

It's a fucking death sentence 18th Sept 2180

The ACME-HUB (orbiting space satellite)

"Thanks, Sara," Gabriel said.

Sara smiled. "I saw you were trying to do something ... didn't know what, but I thought a diversion might help."

"I think you diverted him ... and me," said Zackery, smiling.

Gabriel turned towards the med unit in which Ginny was still lying; the web of rays slowly generating Ginny's new legs continued to criss-cross, criss-cross, criss-cross.

"About another five hours," said Zackery.

Gabriel nodded. "And wait for three days for the new legs to take, eh?"

"Well, Swan said you've got a few days here," said Sara.

"Just a minute," said Vicky. "Swan has called a meeting. It sounds important."

"Can you put him on speaker, so we can all hear," Gabriel said.

Instantly they heard Swan's voice. He sounded both excited and agitated.

"He can't hear us, can he?" Gabriel whispered.

"No, he can't," said Vicky, "and it sounds as though he is using headphones or something. I don't think we will hear the people he is talking to."

"... we can't afford to have these fuckers here," said Swan. "I've told them they can use our facilities for a few days, but ... well ... for fuck's sake, they've got a bloody STU that shows one of our 'lost clients' dying a slow and agonising death ... that could have been prevented if somebody hadn't fucked up the coords."

Swan was listening to somebody ... and replying to him.

"Yeah, sure," Swan continued. "What with the likelihood of litigation from the thirty-eight clients we 'lost' and bearing in mind that at least three clients we knew were mobsters ..."

Brief silence

"Well, yeah, they didn't put that on their client details, but for God's sake ... we all recognised that's what they were, and their business partners might try to get some compensation in ways other than legal. And I'm sitting here, on this fucking floating rock, waiting for ..."

Silence

"Ok. I am staying calm."

Silence

"Look. We're the last ones on this fucking ship, and it's likely to be sinking fast. I for one don't want to go down with it."

Silence

"What? A team of … so now we've got a team of fucking investigators on their way here."

Silence

"Look. If they get here and they check the data log on the STU those fuckers brought back with them, we are absolutely and totally fucking screwed."

Silence

"Look … up to a few hours ago there was absolutely no evidence the 'lost clients' were dead. Sure, they might be anywhere, but no-one could say for sure. Suddenly, right there on that fucking STU, there it is … all anybody would need to nail us to the fucking cross."

Silence

"Sure, we all agree we need to get them out of the way, but what do you suggest? They've asked for another STU. I told them they could fuck off … we don't give that gear away. And anyway, the coords are still fucked."

Silence

"What? Give them a STU? I told you, the coords are …"

Silence

"Shit. You really want to …?"

Silence

"I … I guess if I told 'em we'd fixed the coords, and we'd changed our minds about giving them a free STU …"

Silence

"Well, yeah. There are other people who are aware they're here. The security guys do, but they are a bunch of dipshits. The med-bay crew are the bigger worry. There's two of them, and they are both smart cookies. Maybe if we …"

Silence

"Sure, they rotate back to Earth periodically."

Silence

"Well, how about we say we're sending them back right now 'til the excitement dies down. Give them a bit of a holiday. I'll get a shuttle arranged."

Silence

"Oh God. Give them STUs as well? It's a fucking death sentence. You realise that they …?"

Silence

"Us or them, eh?"

Silence

"But it's me pulling the fucking trigger, isn't it?"

Silence

"Right. All right. I will get two STUs. The med-bay team can take one each, and our little troublesome duo can take the one they came with. That way we don't have to re-format the fucking thing."

Silence

"Yeah, sure. Stay calm yourselves. Remember though, it's me on fucking point here. You guys are safe and warm. You better fucking remember that."

Silence

"Close link."

We'll think of something 18th Sept 2180

The ACME-HUB (orbiting space satellite)

"He's closed the call," said Vicky. "I would guess Swan will get the STUs and make his way down here. It might be a good idea to get prepared."

Gabriel looked at Sara and Zackery. They were looking horrified at what they had heard.

Ginny was still asleep in the med unit; her legs being re-built, with several hours still to go.

"If we got back to Earth, we could contact the media, tell them …," said Zackery.

"ACME INC would find us first," said Sara. She looked close to tears.

"We'd need to be careful," agreed Zackery.

"Would it be better if you two split up when you got back?" asked Gabriel.

Sara looked at Gabriel in horror. Zackery reached across to her and took hold of her hand.

She gripped it hard.

Gabriel walked across to the drinks dispenser and poured himself a cup of water. He noticed his hand was trembling slightly. He attempted to steady his hand. He was fully aware of the benefits of looking calm in stressful situations.

"Are there any space-craft docked at the moment," Gabriel asked.

Sara looked at Zackery. He shrugged his shoulders.

"There is still the one we arrived on," said Vicky. "It's still docked on stub 12."

"Ok," Gabriel said. "I suggest we wait for Swan to give us the STUs. Tell him we need to wait for a bit for Ginny's re-growth process to finish. We say we'll use the STUs to get where we're going."

"But …," Sara said.

"Then we'll get down to the ship, drop you guys off on the Earth, then Ginny and me will … well … we'll think of something."

It's good to see you back, Ginny   18th Sept 2180

The ACME-HUB (orbiting space satellite)

Gabriel watched as Ginny's leg re-growth processing concluded.

She was lying on the cot. The mist surrounding her dispersed. She was still asleep. The restraining bandages still held her securely. Her legs looked long and shapely and beautiful; exactly like Gabriel remembered them.

They heard footsteps approaching the med bay door.

Swan walked in. He was smiling. Gabriel thought the look didn't remotely look natural. Swan was trying hard.

"Hey, marvellous news," Swan said. "ACME INC will let you keep the STU you brought with you."

"That's great news," said Gabriel.

"And, we have fixed the coords database," said Swan. "You can get going as soon as you like."

"Wow," said Gabriel. "I thought you said it might be a couple more days. You guys must have pulled out all the stops."

"Just got lucky," said Swan. He turned towards Sara and Zackery.

"ACME INC said it's ok for you two to get back to Earth for a while. I know it's a bit early … you wouldn't normally rotate for another month, but they thought that, with all the issues, it might be a good time for you two to take a break. Get off home early."

"Thanks," Sara said.

"Not only that," continued Swan, "but we thought we would give you even more break time. We'll let you have a STU each to get back. You don't even need to use the usual shuttle."

"That's fantastic," said Zackery.

Swan reached into his pocket and took out two black bracelets. He handed one each to Sara and Zackery.

"How do you use these things?" Zackery asked. "We see the clients wearing them, but we've never used one ourselves."

"Strap them on your wrist," said Swan. "The STUs will link with you. You tell the STU where and when you want to be. It's instantaneous."

"That's so good of you," Sara said.

Swan looked at Sara. He thought he detected cynicism in her voice, but he couldn't think why that would be.

"Anyway, I'll leave you to get on with it," Swan said. "You'll be gone in an hour or two, I guess ... just the time it takes to pack your bags, eh?"

"Yeah. An hour or two should do it," agreed Sara. "Then we'll be out of here."

"ACME INC will message you when to report back," Swan said to Sara.

He looked pleased with himself.

"We'll wait to hear," said Sara.

"Ok ... and nice meeting you," Swan said, turning to Gabriel.

"Yeah, likewise," said Gabriel.

Swan turned and made his way out of the med bay. The doors closed quietly behind him.

Gabriel looked over at Sara and Zackery. He held his right forefinger across his lips. He tiptoed over to the doors and pushed them slightly ajar.

The corridor was empty.

"Better get your gear," Gabriel said. "I'll get mine and Ginny's."

Gabriel looked over into Ginny's med unit. She looked like she was awakening. The med unit's canopy was slowly peeling back. He stood next to the unit and rested his hand against Ginny's face. She opened her eyes and smiled at him. As he watched, the restraining straps folded back into themselves, leaving Ginny lying naked on the cot.

Sara noticed and walked over. She gave Ginny a loose cotton one-piece garment to put on. "Here, let me help you," Sara said, gently lifting Ginny's legs to pull the garment up over her body.

Ginny looked down as Sara lifted her legs.

"I can feel them," Ginny said.

"You need to be very careful, Ginny," Sara said. "For the next three days, try not to move your legs. It takes that long for them to bond securely."

Gabriel looked pensively at Sara.

"How are we going to move her?" he asked.

Ginny looked quizzical. She hadn't been privy to any of the discussions in the last two days.

"We need to get out of here," Gabriel said to Ginny. "We need to get out of here soon."

"We can transfer her to a stretcher," said Sara. "She'll be fine ... though we will need to make sure we transfer her carefully."

"Look, Ginny," Gabriel said. "We will have to get our gear and get going. We're all going on the starship."

Ginny looked like she was about to ask a lot of questions.

"I'm sorry Ginny, but we are going have to talk about it once we get underway," Gabriel said. "We all need to get our gear, and ..."

"Ok," Ginny said. "I understand. Get the gear. See you shortly."

Gabriel smiled and made his way out of the med bay. He was back minutes later. Ginny had brought nothing but her space suit, and Gabriel only had his backpack. When he got back, Sara and Zackery had their bags waiting. Gabriel guessed that fear had hastened their ability to pack their stuff together.

"Let's get you onto a stretcher," Sara said, pulling a stretcher off its wall mountings.

The stretcher had small ramstat boosters, enabling it to float. They fired up the boosters and positioned it next to the MED unit in which Ginny was lying. Suddenly the med bay doors swung open. Rust, the security guard, came in.

"There's something going on," Rust said. "I'm not sure what, but it ain't good."

"What ...?" Gabriel said.

"I heard there's a specialist team of investigators on their way here. They'll be here in less than an hour. Swan called my team together ... but not me, interestingly. One of my team got concerned and patched me into his mic. Swan told them something about 'if they won't move fast enough, they must get pushed'."

"And I guess he means us," said Gabriel.

"I'm sure he means you," said Rust.

Sara and Zackery had gotten Ginny onto the stretcher. She had bitten her lip as they moved her, even though they were doing it as gently as they could.

Rust went over to the med bay doors, pushing them ajar.

"Someone's coming," Rust whispered. He went out of the door, walking slowly down the corridor toward the footsteps.

Smythe was walking down the corridor towards him.

"There's been a change of plan," Smythe said. "We need to get rid of them right now. There's a press convoy and a legal team on their way here. They're on their way right now. We need to get rid of these guys right now."

Smythe pushed past Rust and saw Gabriel coming out of the med bay, with Sara and Zackery holding the stretcher.

"Sorry guys ... time's up," Smythe said, pulling his short rifle from its holster.

There was a soft ppfft noise and Smythe fell to the ground.

Rust put his own rifle back into its holster. He bent over Smythe and picked up his rifle.

"At least I had mine on stun," Rust said, disgusted.

"How long's he out for?" said Zackery.

"Ten minutes."

Zackery nodded to Sara. He let go of his end of the stretcher. It continued to hover. He pulled something from his belt. It looked like a small plastic tube. He walked over to Smythe and pushed the tube against his neck.

"This'll give us longer," Zackery said.

"How long?" Rust asked.

"48 hours ... followed by a crushing headache."

"Fair enough."

Rust turned to Gabriel. "Can you shoot?" he asked.

"Yeah. On fairground guns."

"It'll have to do. Here."

Rust handed Smythe's rifle to Gabriel. "The safety's off, and it's on stun ... well, it is now. It's got twenty stun rounds. Stuns give you barely any recoil at all, and they are good for any distance up to about forty feet. Aim anywhere, but for preference go for the big bits ... like the chest. You're less likely to miss."

Gabriel hefted the gun. It was surprisingly light.

"Take a couple of shots," said Rust. "That way, you will be less likely to freeze when you really need to."

Gabriel looked across and down the corridor. There was a small sign twenty feet away. It said 'docking points'. He aimed for the sign. He was expecting the gun to jump in his hands and tensed himself against the expected recoil. He squeezed the trigger. The rifle made a faint 'pfft' noise. There was no perceptible recoil, but Gabriel's anticipation of recoil meant he pushed the muzzle down slightly after taking the shot.

He lifted the rifle and fired again.

Rust put his hand on Gabriel's rifle, pushing it down in the floor's direction. He walked over, inspecting the sign on the wall.

"That'll do," Rust said, smiling back at Gabriel. "Right ... let's get going."

Sara and Zackery took hold of Ginny's stretcher. They headed off down the corridor.

Rust took his place in front of the group. Gabriel was at the back.

"Has Swan said anything else?" Gabriel whispered to Vicky.

"No," Vicky whispered back. "I think he must have taken his jacket off after the meeting he had. Maybe he has put it in a cupboard or somewhere."

"Your ship's docked down here," Rust said, pointing with his rifle to a corridor bearing left.

They heard footsteps behind them.

Rust stopped. "Get going," he said, taking a position at the junction of the corridor.

Gabriel, Sara, and Zackery hurried past Rust. Ginny flinched as the stretcher rocked with their movements.

Behind them they heard Rust shouting out a warning.

They heard a 'brrp, brrrrrrrrp' noise.

"That's not stun shots," said Zackery.

They rounded the next corner and there was stub 12, where their starship was docked.

They heard another 'brrp, brrp, brrrrrrp' noise and a scream.

"Let's get on," Gabriel said, trying to stop his voice from revealing his anxiety.

They rushed through to the docking point.

"The airlock door is open," Vicky said. "You can get straight in."

Sara stepped up and into the craft, but as Zackery stepped up they heard a shot.

Zackery fell onto his knees. As he dropped, his weight tipped Ginny's stretcher. She rolled off the stretcher onto the ground, shrieking as she rolled across the floor.

Gabriel turned.

A security guard was kneeling at the corner of the corridor. He was kneeling and aiming his rifle at them. Gabriel raised his rifle and fired. He kept the trigger pressed. The security guard flinched as a full clip of stun rounds hit him. The guard crumpled to the floor. Gabriel's rifle clicked as it continued firing on an empty chamber. He turned and rushed over to Ginny … sprawled awkwardly on the floor; her face filled with pain and fear.

"Sara?" Gabriel shouted.

Sara came back out of the craft and knelt by Zackery. He was bleeding profusely from his thigh.

A stutter of gunfire. Rust came around the corner. His left arm was hanging down. Blood was dripping from his wrist. He was holding his rifle in his right hand.

Rust looked over at them. "Get the fuck on board," he shouted. He sprinted towards them. Another burst of gunfire. Rust jerked and fell to the ground, his body twitching. His rifle clattered across the floor towards Gabriel.

Gabriel saw Director Swan and another security guard come around the corner. The security guard was looking at them; at Ginny sprawled on the floor. She was shrieking in pain. Sara was kneeling next to Zackery, trying to staunch the blood from his thigh.

Gabriel stooped down and picked up Rust's rifle.

The guard stood there, unsure what to do.

"Shoot them, fucking shoot them," Swan shouted.

The guard looked incredulously at Swan.

Swan clumsily grabbed the rifle from the guard. He raised it and pulled the trigger. He kept it pressed. Bullets ricocheted off the walls and floor.

Gabriel raised Rust's rifle. He pulled the trigger. The bullets seemed to drift lazily away from him and towards the security guard. They casually ripped open the man's chest. They ripped away the right side of his face.

Gabriel felt the muzzle lift slightly and attempted to pull it down.

A stream of bullets tore Swan's right arm off at the shoulder.

"Gabriel?"

"Gabriel?"

Gabriel looked around him.

The guard was dead; his head had been torn apart.

Swan's right arm had been torn off. He laid on the ground. He was screaming.

Rust sprawled on the floor, unmoving.

He saw Sara trying to get Zackery onto his feet.

He saw Ginny laid on the ground. She was whimpering with pain.

He heard more footsteps in the distance.

"Gabriel?" Sara shouted.

More footsteps in the distance.

Sara's shout stirred Gabriel ... he pulled himself together.

"Ok, let's get Zackery up," Gabriel said to Sara. "Get him onboard."

Sara hauled Zackery onto his feet and dragged him onto the spacecraft. Gabriel dropped the rifle he was holding and squatted down. He carefully picked Ginny up, then stepped on board the starship.

"Ship?" Gabriel said.

"I'm here, Gabriel," Ship replied.

"Ship ... can you ..." Gabriel said, unsure now what to do, what commands to give.

"Ship ... close and lock the airlock door," Ginny said, her voice almost a whisper.

"It's done, Ginny."

"Now get us out of here. Initiate cloaking and set a course for a close Earth orbit."

"We're on our way, Ginny."

"Thanks, Ship," said Ginny.

"It's good to see you back, Ginny," Ship said.

I've always fancied going to Seville 20th Sept 2180

In Earth's orbit

Sara, Zackery, Gabriel and Ginny were in the starship's cockpit. Ginny and Sara were sitting in the two seats. Zackery and Sara had taken off their med-bay clothing. She was wearing jeans and a pale blue T-shirt. He had on a black T-shirt and cargo-pants. He was standing looking out at the Earth below them.

Ginny rubbed her hands along her left leg; where the new leg was joined to her stump. Gabriel stood looking at her concernedly.

"ACME INC will track us down … I'm sure they will," Sara said. "They tried to kill us, and now they …"

Zackery walked over to Sara and stood behind her seat. He began massaging the back of her neck.

"They do not know where we are at the moment," Vicky said. "We have cloaked the starship. They can't see us. We could have gone anywhere."

"I'm sure they'll find us," Sara said despondently. "If we go back to Earth, we will need money to live on, and as soon as we draw any currency, then …"

"I can get you some money to live on," Vicky said.

"How do you …?" Gabriel said.

"A STU can request currency for any tourist location its client requires it for," explained Vicky. "ACME debit the cost of the currency directly from the client's account. So, if I requested currency, it would debit my initial client's account."

"What, the guy who died on the cliff-top at Walton?" asked Gabriel.

"Yes, that very man," said Vicky.

"But won't ACME have decided he must be dead and have stopped his account?" Ginny asked.

"I don't think ACME can be sure which of their clients died as a result of the coordinates corruption," Vicky said. "In fact, given the investigations ongoing, I very much doubt they have logged any of their clients as dead. So, it is highly likely my ex-client's account is still open."

"Well, I suppose the sure-fire way to find out would be to request some currency," said Ginny. "How much do you two think you would need … to keep you going for a year?"

"And what currency would you need it to be in?" Gabriel said. "I mean, I guess you might think to stay somewhere off the beaten track ... somewhere off ACME's radar I mean."

"Anywhere will take standard Creds," Zackery said. "Unless you were staying in some Mongolian village, in which case ..."

"And you will need to get yourselves accommodation," said Ginny. "Rent somewhere. So that's two lots of rental fees and ..."

Sara turned and looked at Zackery. He stopped massaging her neck.

"I was thinking," said Sara to Zackery. "I haven't got any close family, and I wondered ..."

"What?" said Zackery.

"Maybe we can ..."

"Find some place together for a bit, do you mean?" said Zackery.

"Just for a bit," Sara said. "That's if you don't mind ..."

Zackery smiled down to Sara, then resumed massaging her neck.

"So, if that's only one lot of accommodation rental fees," Ginny chuckled. "How many creds do you think you might need to keep you going for a year?"

"Fifty thousand creds would do it," Zackery said.

"Ok," Gabriel said. "So, Vicky, can you please try to request two hundred thousand creds. Let's see if old Mervin's account is good for that."

A package shimmered into being at their feet. It was a compression bag, filled with notes tied into neat bundles. Zackery leant down and opened the bag. He took out two of the bundles, handing one to Sara. They rifled through the notes.

"So that's what a lot of money looks like," Zackery said. "Easily enough to last us for four years, I would guess."

"But where are you going to go?" Ginny asked. "I wouldn't suggest going back to America. How about Europe?"

"I've always fancied going to Seville," Sara said.

Zackery looked surprised. "What about the language?" he asked.

"I'm pretty-near fluent," Sara said, grinning.

Zackery chuckled. "Well, Seville sounds like a delighful place. Why the hell not?"

Zackery leaned down and kissed Sara on the forehead. Sara smiled over at Gabriel and Ginny.

"So that's agreed, is it?" Ginny said.

Sara and Zackery both nodded back.

"Ok, Ship," Ginny said. "Please take us to Seville. Find somewhere on the outskirts that we can set down."

"On our way, Ginny," Ship said.

Comfort from their proximity   20th Sept 2180

They parked the starship in a small valley on the outskirts of Seville. It was late afternoon. Its cloaking was activated. Gabriel, Ginny, Sara and Zackery were standing in a small glade nearby.

"What are those trees?" Gabriel asked.

"Some are almonds, and some are carob trees," Vicky said. "The almonds will soon be nearing their harvest time, I believe."

"The air ... it smells so fresh and clean," Gabriel said.

"This place looks idyllic," Ginny said. "And we caught it exactly right. Look at the long shadows from the trees. Look at the egg-yolk yellow sunlight."

Gabriel looked over at Ginny. He hadn't seen her smile for a while. It pleased him to see her so entranced by this lovely place.

"We'd better get going," Zackery said. "The sooner we get ourselves lost in some general populace, the happier I will feel."

Gabriel nodded, saying, "You will need to keep your heads down ... I'm sure you are aware of that, but ..."

"I think we'll try to keep up-to-date with whatever happens to ACME INC," said Zackery. "I'm guessing that investigations will be ongoing. Maybe we can try to get in contact with those investigative teams."

"Just be really really careful," said Ginny. "If someone in ACME is trying to keep a lid on things ... trying to fend off any blame, they won't be grateful if you guys turn up to spill the beans. As Swan said, until Gabriel and me turned up with Vicky, there was no evidence that any of their clients had died because of the coordinates corruption."

Sara looked worried. Zackery gave her a hug.

"We'll get going," said Zackery. "It's a brief walk into the town. We'll get a room somewhere for the night ..."

Sara walked over to Ginny and gave her an enormous hug.

"Look after those new legs," Sara whispered in Ginny's ear. "You took that tumble off the stretcher ... so you need to take care."

"They feel fine," Ginny said, hugging Sara back.

"Come on ... let's get going," Zackery said.

"Oh ... one more thing," Sara said. "Zackery and me want you to take one of the STUs that Swan gave us. We haven't worn it. You can make use of it. You said you wanted one to give to somebody."

Sara rummaged in her bag and took a black plasteel band from it. She handed it to Ginny.

"Sara," Vicky said. "If you wish, I can set up a WORM-LYNK connection between myself and the STU you are keeping. That way we will have direct communications. We can keep you informed about any information we find out."

"That would be great," said Sara. "We weren't thinking of using the STU for anything, but that would be a superb idea."

"Well, if you put the other STU on your wrist now, that will activate it, and I can set up the WORM-LYNK, if that's ok?"

Sara took the other STU out of her bag and put it on her wrist. She flinched as the STU ran its initial diagnostics.

"Ok," Vicky said. "I've set up the connection. I've also advised your STU to give you a little time to get under way before it introduces itself to you. I don't think we all need to be privy to your configuration discussions."

"No, I suppose not," said Sara.

"Come on," said Zackery. "I'm sort of looking forward to finding a room for the night ... and a little place to have an enjoyable meal, a glass of wine ..."

Zackery grinned. Sara chuckled.

"Come on," she said. "That glass of wine will not drink itself."

Sara hefted her luggage, turned, and set off strolling in the direction of the town. Zackery picked up his own backpack. He grinned toward Gabriel and Ginny, waved, then set off after her.

"I hope they'll be ok," Gabriel said.

Ginny watched as Zackery caught up with Sara and took over carrying her luggage.

"I think they'll look after each other," Ginny said.

"So, what are we going to do now?" Ginny said.

"I don't know about you," Gabriel said, "but I think I fancy a nice Spanish meal and a nice glass of red wine. What about you?"

"What ... you mean go into Seville?"

"I don't think I'd be able to order us a nice meal in Seville, but I'm sure Ship can get us something."

Ginny grinned. "Ok, Gabe," she said. "C'mon Ship. We're coming back on board, and we're looking for some nice Spanish food and good red wine."

Gabriel smiled. That was the first time Ginny had said anything affectionate to him in a long time.

The starship re-appeared, floating gently a foot off the ground. As they stepped up through the doorway, Ship said "Would you like me to select a meal for you, or would you prefer to choose one yourselves?"

Ginny looked at Gabriel.

"I think we'd be happy for you to make the choice for us," Ginny said.

"Would I be correct in selecting a vegetarian meal for you, Ginny?" Ship asked.

"That would be nice, thank you," Ginny said. "And Ship … I think we should get back up into orbit and re-engage cloaking."

"On our way," said Ship.

"Thanks, Ship," Ginny said.

"And in which case your meals and wine are ready," said Ship. "I hope they meet your expectations."

· · · · · · · ·

The food was delicious. So was the wine. Gabriel wasn't a wine drinker, but talking to Sara, hearing her enthusiasm for Spain and Zackery's anticipation of them going for a delightful meal had triggered something in Gabriel.

He was also hoping Ginny was feeling cheerier. They still hadn't discussed what had happened to her on SEG002. He was happy to leave it. She would either discuss it or she wouldn't.

Gabriel shoved the food plates into the waste chute. Ginny was sitting in one of the cockpit seats, looking down at the Earth. Gabriel walked over and stood behind Ginny. He ran his fingers through her hair. Something he was happy to do all day long.

"We've had some tricky times, haven't we?" Ginny said.

Gabriel said nothing, unsure where this conversation would go.

"I mean, we've had some fun bits, but some bits weren't much fun at all," she continued.

Gabriel continued running his fingers through her hair.

"Do you realise," Ginny said, "how close we were to not getting any medical assistance from ACME at all?"

"Yeah, it was bloody close," Gabriel said. "I think we were lucky. We were lucky they realised Vicky had evidence showing we didn't fuck up their coordinates and ..."

"And we were lucky their security guys beat you up ... so they felt an obligation to give aid," Ginny said.

"Yeah ... that was lucky, wasn't it?" Gabriel said. "That's what I was thinking."

"You only came on this trip because it was important to me, didn't you?" she said.

"It was important to both of us," Gabriel said.

"I don't think I deserve you," she said, reaching up and clasping Gabriel's hands.

Gabriel realised the moment ... the moment when Ginny would confide what had happened on SEG002, had passed. He had really felt that must have been what she was building up to, but she had decided against it. The thought she wasn't ready to disclose it made him fearful.

"You do realise I love you, don't you?" he whispered into her ear.

"Would you like some coffee?" Ship asked.

Ginny pulled away from Gabriel. He smiled at her.

"That's a nice idea," Ginny said.

"And, I guess, we need to decide what we will do next," Gabriel said.

"Well ... I suggest we need to find out what happened to ACME INC," Ginny said. "After all the investigations ... after the litigation and everything."

"So, travel into the future again?"

"I guess so."

"What do you think, Vicky," Ginny said.

"I think that is the only way you will find out," said Vicky. "I would suggest two years into the future, using the CrYO-PODS again, then go to the ACME-HUB and see what's there."

"If they never fixed the coordinates database, we'd be stuck there … forever," observed Gabriel.

"That is true," said Vicky.

"Well, we've got to live somewhere," Ginny said.

"I suppose so," said Gabriel.

"This might sound bit stupid," said Ginny, "given we will be getting two years sleep anytime soon, but it would be nice to cuddle up together … just for tonight. Then we could get in the CrYO-PODS tomorrow."

She got up and made her way towards their bedroom.

"See you soon," she said, smiling over to Gabriel.

"See you soon," he said, watching her walk down the short corridor.

· · · · · · · ·

Ginny had curled up on her couchette. She was wearing a long T-shirt, and she was lying on her side, watching Gabriel as he walked into the bedroom. He took his T-shirt and trousers off and climbed in next to her. He laid on his back. She sat up, climbed on top of him, straddling her legs on either side of him. Her long hair was trailing down over his face. He reached his hands up, one either side of her face, pulling her face towards him. She stiffened and jerked back away from him, pulling his hands away from her.

"What's …?" Gabriel said.

Ginny scrambled off the bed. She crossed the small room and sat down on the floor. She had her back to the wall. She sat cross-legged on the floor. She shook. Her entire body seemed to be trembling. She began to sob.

Gabriel got down off the cot and slowly walked over to her.

She looked up at him, tears in her eyes.

"I'm sorry," she said. "I'm really …"

Gabriel sat down next to her. He was afraid to touch her. He didn't know what best to do.

He sat down beside her, his back to the wall. He left an inch of space between them.

Ginny shuffled herself up closer to Gabriel. She rested her head on his shoulder. He put his arm around her. He hugged her closer. She nuzzled into him.

"I'm here for you, Ginny," he said. "I'm here for you love."

"I know that, Gabriel," she said.

Gabriel hugged her until she quietened. Then he lifted her up and laid her back on her couchette. He covered her in her soft downy quilt. He laid down, snuggling up behind her ... like two spoons in a drawer. He carefully rested one hand on her upper arm. She raised her other hand and rested it on top of his hand. She gave his hand a little squeeze. He rested his forehead against the back of her head. He felt his breathing slow. They laid there quietly, taking some small comfort from their proximity.

Maybe now wasn't the time   15th July 2182

The ACME INC HUB

Two years later, the starship arrived at the ACME-HUB orbiting satellite. Gabriel and Ginny had been asleep in their CrYO-PODS. They awoke two days earlier. In time to get refreshed, to get a shower, to eat some food.

"Arriving at the ACME-HUB in five minutes," Ship advised.

"Have you heard any response from them?" Ginny asked.

"Nothing," said Ship. "Which is curious. Normally they are very aware of incoming craft. They normally provide docking information and so-on. But I've received no transmissions. It's as though there is no-one there."

Ginny looked across at Gabriel. The space station was visible. It looked exactly as it had the last time they came here.

"I guess we just find an empty docking stub," Ginny said.

"They are all registering as empty," Ship noted.

"Ok, Ship … please pick one," Ginny said.

"We are close to stub 4, so I will dock there."

"Ok, thanks Ship," Ginny said.

....

"Well, at least they have maintained the atmosphere," Ginny said.

They walked down a myriad of corridors, all well-lit, but met no-one.

"Looks like the lights are on, but there's nobody home," Gabriel said.

"The crew quarters are down here, to the left," Vicky said. "I advise that you take care. We have no idea whether the remaining crew have orders concerning you guys or not."

Gabriel and Ginny slowed down, walking softly and quietly. Gabriel couldn't imagine what they would do if they met anyone.

"Through this door," Vicky said.

A sign on the door read 'Authorised Personnel Only'.

Ginny pushed the door open slowly, peering through the gap.

"There's nobody in there," she said.

They were standing in what looked like a communal rest room. A few comfy chairs. Some wall-mounted plasma screens. Two tables with six plastic chairs each. A small kitchen. All of it seemingly unused for quite some time.

Ginny ran her finger along the kitchen worktop. She inspected her finger.

"I can't see any dust, but I don't suppose you get a lot of dust up here anyway," she said.

"Let's try the comms room," Vicky suggested. "It's down that corridor on your left."

A small green neon arrow appeared in the air, pointing in the direction that Vicky described.

They walked cautiously down the corridor, arriving at a door marked 'COMMS'.

"I can hear something," Gabriel said. "Something very faint … can't think what it might be though."

Ginny pushed the door open.

"Another empty room," she said, "but at least this one's still operational, from the look of it."

The comms room was sixty feet by thirty feet. It was dimly lit, with a soft blue light from the ceiling. It was stacked with screens and keyboards. Several of the screens were active. Ginny walked over to the nearest lit-up screen.

"It shows the docking bays," she said. "Look. It's got our starship on it. Stub 4 shows as 'docked'."

Gabriel glanced over at the screen. Sure enough, stub 4 showed as 'docked'. "It's the only one that is being used," he said.

An adjacent multi-sectioned screen showed various areas within the ACME-HUB.

"Seen this?" said Gabriel. "It's like CCTV cameras … there's nobody anywhere."

Ginny turned back to the door. "C'mon," she said. "There must be some information left behind somewhere."

Gabriel followed on behind. She had turned down a corridor and stepped into a door at random. She went in. Gabriel followed.

"It's just somebody's room," she said, looking at a small room containing a bed, some shelves, a wall-mounted screen, and a few books.

"Turn the screen on," suggested Vicky. "It would be a crew entertainment facility, plus it would have had crew info."

Ginny pushed the only button on the screen's surround, and immediately it lit up, a pale pink background, with a slowly spinning 3D ACME INC logo.

"How do you ...?" Ginny said.

"Hold your hand up towards the screen," Vicky suggested.

Gabriel held his hand in the screen's direction. He moved his hand around, moved his fingers around. Out of the various gestures he was making, something prompted the screen to display a menu.

Ginny looked at the menu options with disgust. "For God's sake," she said. "Look at that."

The screen showed

> **Hot Porn**
> **Comedy**
> **Romance**
> **ACME news**

"I wonder how many crew members watched the comedy vids?" Ginny said.

"Or the romance," said Gabriel.

"Let's look at the ACME news," Vicky said.

Gabriel gestured at the screen which clicked open to the Hot Porn menu option. He flailed his hand around as a series of vid titles appeared, each with a small thumbprint showing a trailer of what to expect.

"Gabriel ... what the fuck are you ...?" Ginny said.

"Sorry, Ginny, it was first on the menu, and I still don't know how to work this bloody ..."

The top level of menu re-appeared, and Gabriel breathed a visible sigh of relief.

"Make slow gestures," Vicky suggested. "Treat it like when you used to use Barney's cell phone. Remember when you used it to take pictures. Slow pulls and drags."

Gabriel tried again. The 'ACME News' option became high-lit, and he selected it. The screen showed a series of bulleted items, each identified by a number, a date, plus a small resume of the content.

"I should scroll down to the items dated from the 5th September 2180," Vicky said. "All the items before that date happened before somebody corrupted the coordinates."

"Let's try this one," Gabriel said.

He opened an item dated the 5th September 2180, with the description 'coords corruption'.

The screen showed Director Swan. He was in close-up. He looked nervous. There was sweat breaking out on his forehead.

Swan said, "This is an urgent notification that the COORDS-HUB is corrupted. This probably occurred several days ago. This info must be treated as extremely confidential. WORM-LYNK has been shut down to stop any client STUs from accessing the faulty coordinates. We know that several have already initiated their return, so we are thinking that ..."

Swan stopped. He was looking at something or someone to his left. He nodded, looked back to the camera.

"They have not appeared back at the HUB," he resumed. "We don't know where they might be. They are likely to be dead. We will need to ... we will need to ..."

The transmission stopped.

"Bloody hell," said Gabriel.

"Try the next one," said Ginny.

The next news item ... dated the 6th September 2180 - labelled 'WORM-LYNK.

Gabriel clicked it open. The screen showed a female reporter in a newsroom. She was reading a report of current events. This seemed to be a short clip extracted from a longer broadcast.

The girl said, "... and ACME TOURS have advised they have taken their WORM-LYNK comms down for a brief period. They stress this is a routine piece of maintenance work ... no-one should be affected by this work. And now onto ..."

The short clip ended.

"I guess that was ACME trying to give some gloss to cover up ...," Gabriel said.

"I bet somebody squealed," Ginny interrupted. "I bet somebody somewhere made the media aware there was a problem, and that forced ACME's hand. They had to put something out there, otherwise ..."

Gabriel opened the next item, dated 7th September 2180, titled 'For your eyes only'.

It was Swan again. He looked very frightened. He looked to be almost shaking.

He said, "There's thirty-eight of the fuckers out there. Fifteen we already know haven't come back. We're fuc ..."

The clip ended.

Gabriel looked across at Ginny.

"This is like watching the Titanic go down, isn't it?" he said.

Ginny nodded.

The next item dated 9th September 2180, titled 'Truth at last'.

It was the newsroom girl again. "Fears raised by family and friends of the ACME TOURS clients currently missing. ACME refuse to comment. They are unwilling to provide further information on what appears to be an unfolding catastrophe."

Gabriel opened the next two items; items dated from the 10th and the 11th of September. They comprised interviews with family members from the lost clients. Several people were suggesting raising legal actions against ACME TOURS.

"Those people look wealthy," Gabriel said. "Did you see the houses they live in? Like they can easily afford to sue ACME."

"ACME clients have to be very wealthy," Vicky said. "Only the richest people can afford to take such trips. The people missing would be prominent businesspeople, leaders of countries, ..."

"And prominent criminals as well, I guess," said Ginny.

"You are probably correct," said Vicky.

The item dated 13th September was titled 'Corporate manslaughter charges raised'.

"That one seems self-evident," said Ginny.

The following item, dated 19th September 2180, was titled 'killing rage'.

Gabriel opened it up. Another newsroom, a male reporter this time.

"The investigative team sent to the ACME-HUB have only now released a statement saying Director Charles Swan, head of ACME TOURS's data security, a man of previously stable disposition, seemingly ran amok yesterday. He appears to have shot and killed two members of the HUB's security team before turning his gun on himself. The investigators state that their early supposition is he may have corrupted the coordinates database himself, before setting off on his killing spree. They wish to state, however, that it is far too early to confirm this."

The news reader looked up directly into the camera, as though complicit with the families affected by the drama.

"This reporter is sure that the family members out there directly affected by this unfolding drama will stay tuned to this channel for the events as they unfold. And now on to ..."

Ginny looked over at Gabriel.

"So that's how they played it," she said.

Gabriel opened up the next item, dated 5th October 2180, titled 'regrets and condolences'.

It was another newsroom report. The girl again.

"And here," she said, "we have a statement from Mr. Dmitry Alexandrovich, Admin Director for ACME TOURS. Over to you, Mr. Dmitry."

The newsroom cut over to a well-dressed man sitting at an exceptionally large desk. He was sitting in a room where the whole back wall was a giant window. It was looking out over a cityscape, but his office was higher than most of the other buildings in sight. The man looked to be in his 50s. He looked stocky. Very close-cropped hair.

"Looks a bit of a thug to me," Gabriel ventured.

"Shush," Ginny said.

Dmitry started talking. He appeared to be reading from a script ... from something laying on his desk.

"The investigative team sent to look into the situation at ACME TOURS has delivered its findings," Dmitry said.

His voice was calm, very deep. He sounded very sincere.

"They have said they cannot be 100% sure, but they believe the likelihood is that Director Charles Swan ..."

Dmitry paused, looking up directly into the camera.

"Director Charles Swan," he resumed, with a slight shake in his voice, "a work colleague who I have known ... known and trusted, for many years, ... that he ... that he willfully corrupted the ACME TOURS database of coordinates."

Dmitry stopped, as if to give himself time to collect himself.

"Perhaps," he resumed, "I can be blamed for putting too much faith, too much trust, into someone who I worked with for so long. He let us ... he let me ... down. I can only offer my regrets and condolences to those clients and their families affected by this sad event."

The transmission clicked off.

"He's very good," said Ginny.

"How do you mean?" Gabriel said.

"That was a virtuoso performance, Gabriel. Not a dry eye in the house, as they used to say."

Gabriel clicked on the next item, dated 3rd November 2180, titled 'gone bust'.

It was the girl reporter again.

"It would seem," she said, "that lack of confidence in ACME TOUR's capacity to manage its own security features, plus the strong likelihood that at least some of its 'lost clients' have died, has meant that no-one is prepared to use its travel service. ACME TOURS has not run a tour since the drama unfolded. Pre-booked trips have all been cancelled and no-one has booked anything since. ACME TOURS has now formally gone into receivership."

The transmission ended.

"So, if it's gone bust, how come we still get requested items?" Gabriel asked, clicking on to the last news item on the menu.

It was dated 4th December 2180, titled 'missing clients – where are they now?'

A different newsroom. A different girl reporter.

"And now, under agreement with the relatives of the lost tourists, the ACME Corporation has been forced to set up a 'safety net facility'. One which provides food and equipment to any 'lost tourists' who may still be alive."

The girl reporter looked up directly into the camera.

"You should remember," she said, "that they have found no evidence to suggest those lost are indeed dead. They may still be alive. For this reason, it would seem, the charges of corporate manslaughter have all been dropped."

The reporter paused to blink back a tear.

"But ... maybe, even if only one of them ... even if only one of them is still alive, then ... perhaps they can find their way back home. The COORDS-HUB was repaired on the 3rd October. Now, with the new 'safety net facility', provisioned as it is with enough food and equipment to keep those poor lost souls ... well ... there is always hope. And now onto ..."

"God, she milked that one," Ginny said.

"Well, at least now we can understand why we keep getting the requests actioned," said Gabriel. "And also, we know that they fixed the coordinates on the 3rd October 2180."

"We should tell Sara and Zackery," Ginny said. "Vicky, can you patch us through to them? I guess Sara is still wearing the STU that Swan gave her."

"I'll call her up," Vicky said.

"Any luck?" said Gabriel.

"They aren't responding," Vicky said.

"Is there anything that ...?" Gabriel said.

"I can connect directly through to their STU," Vicky said. "It doesn't require any action on their part."

"And ...?" Gabriel said.

"I've connected to their STU," Vicky said. "And ... and ..."

"What is it, Vicky?" Ginny said.

"Their STU has advised me that ... that Zackery and Sara were the victims of a fly-by shooting. Zackery is dead. Sara is seriously injured. She has brain damage. It cannot be repaired."

Ginny sat down on the bed. She had gone waxy pale.

"She can barely speak. She cannot look after herself. She is living in a long-term care home. There is seemingly no hope of recovery."

Gabriel sat down next to Ginny and tried to hold her hand, but she pulled her hand away.

"Her STU has sent us a panoramic recording of the incident. Do you want me to play it for you?"

Gabriel nodded.

An image appeared on the wall of the room.

Sara and Zackery were sitting at a roadside table outside some little café. They were drinking coffee. A lady was pushing a buggy along towards them.

The lady stopped and sat at an adjacent table. She pulled her buggy towards her and clamped on the brakes. She leaned in and lifted her baby out. It was tiny, a few months old. She cuddled the baby to her chest, holding one hand behind its head.

Zackery and Sara were watching the lady with the baby. Zackery half-stood up. He leaned across and kissed Sara on the forehead.

Sara smiled.

A small ramstat flyer came up the road. As it pulled alongside the café, it appeared to slow down. The man sitting on the passenger side pointed a gun out of his window.

He fired. A loose burst, not accurate.

The lady with the baby fell backwards, her baby falling to the ground in front of her.

Zackery stood up but was hurled backwards, his chest ripped open.

Sara's head jerked back forcibly. She fell to the ground.

People around started screaming.

The flyer drifted slowly away. The driver appeared to be in no hurry.

The panoramic vid screen dissolved.

Ginny broke into a flood of tears.

"Vicky?" Gabriel said.

"Yes, Gabriel?"

"Can you rewind it ... can you get a close-up of the guys in the flyer?"

The scene rolled backwards, pausing at the point when the gunman looked out of the window and raised the gun.

"It's Smythe," Gabriel said.

Ginny looked up.

"It's fucking Smythe," he repeated. "The HUB security guy."

"Vicky?" Ginny said.

"Yes, Ginny?"

"We can't use the starship to go backwards in time, can we?"

"No, Ginny."

"But now the coordinates database is fixed, you can take us back in time can't you ... back to place that Sara and Zackery were shot?"

"Yes, I can, Ginny, if that is what you want. And, in case you were wondering, I can extend the teleport containment envelope wide enough to include you both. You don't need to each be wearing a STU to time jump."

Gabriel sat, un-speaking. He had seen their friends die. He couldn't think what to do or what to say.

"Ok, Vicky," Ginny said. "I think we've seen as much as we need to see here. I think it's time to go back."

Ginny stood up. She looked down at Gabriel, who was still sitting on the bed. She held out her hand to him.

He took it gladly. She pulled him up off the bed.

"C'mon Gabriel. Let's get our gear off the ship and get going."

"And maybe say goodbye to the ship," said Gabriel. "We won't be seeing it again, and it's done us all right."

"Yeah, sure, Gabriel," Ginny said. She realised that he was in a state of shock.

"You're a bit of a softy, aren't you," she said, "even in these hard times."

"Just as well," said Gabriel. "All of these times seem extremely hard. They don't seem to be getting less hard. I simply try to do what gets me through each day."

Ginny looked at Gabriel. She guessed there was something he wasn't saying, but probably now wasn't the time to say it anyway.

A view to a tragedy 3:35 pm 16th Oct 2180

The Alameda de Hercules - Seville

Gabriel and Ginny had teleported into Seville several hours before Sara and Zackery would be shot. They walked around the area, then chose a small café next to the one Sara and Zackery would sit at. They were both using Vicky's holoface technology to make them look like an old couple.

They sat and drank coffee.

They waited for Sara and Zackery to arrive.

To their left, up the Alameda de Hercules, past the boulevard of trees, the water fountains began their periodic spouting of cold clear water high into the air. The fountain was simple faucets set flat into the stone terrace. Every ten minutes the faucets would activate, sending twenty-foot jets of water cascading into the air. On a sunny day like today, the fountains were creating a rainbow of colours. Each time they triggered, groups of children would rush over to run in and out of the spray.

"Here they come," Ginny said.

Sara and Zackery were walking down the roadway. They were both smiling, enjoying the day. They sat at a table forty feet from Gabriel and Ginny. Sara ordered drinks from a passing waiter. They were chuckling to each other about something.

"They look very happy," Ginny said.

A woman with a baby in a buggy stopped at the café. She sat down at a table close to the road. She pulled the buggy around and locked its brakes. Then she lifted the baby out and cuddled it against her chest. The baby nuzzled against her.

Sara and Zackery watched her. Sara looked over to Zackery, smiling. Zackery partially stood up. He leaned over to Sara and gave her a kiss on her forehead.

A small ramstat flyer came up the roadway and slowed as it passed. Smythe leaned out from the passenger seat, raising his weapon. He fired a two-second burst. The lady with the baby fell to the floor, her baby falling from her arms. Its head smashed against the ground. Zackery had turned towards the flyer. He instantly fell to the ground; his chest ripped apart. Sara screamed. Her head jolted savagely backwards. She fell to the ground.

The flyer pulled slowly away. The pilot seemed to be in no haste.

Gabriel and Ginny leaped up from their seats. They could see the woman with the baby was dead. It was obvious. Likewise, with Zackery.

The baby was lying on the ground, its head at an awkward angle.

Sara was still moving … but a section of her skull had been blown away.

"Her STU is offering medical support," Vicky said. "She is unconscious, but her STU will provide her with pain relief. And it will cover the exposed section of her brain with a protective shell … thin layer upon thin layer."

"But," Ginny said, "we know the damage is irreparable."

"Indeed so," said Vicky.

As they watched, a young woman plucked the young baby up from the ground where it had fallen. Its head hung loosely as she picked it up. She began cuddling it, rocking it slowly backwards and forwards in her arms. The young woman's tears rolled down onto the baby's face.

Gabriel stood up and grasped Ginny's arm, leading her away. He led her down a small side-street, away from the muddle of people standing there, some shocked, some shaking.

"We have to stop Smythe," Gabriel said.

"How do you …?" Ginny said.

"We have to stop him before he gets here."

"But what about the rule on not changing historic events?" Ginny said.

"ACME was very clear about not changing historic events," said Vicky.

"Fuck that," Gabriel said.

Ginny smiled at him in agreement.

Where did that flyer come from? 3:40 pm 16th Oct 2180

In Seville - off the Alameda de Hercules

"Vicky?" Gabriel said.

"Yes, Gabriel?"

"Where did that flyer come from? I mean, immediately before it showed up here."

"Flyers and all similar craft have identity plates," Vicky said. "They prevent theft and are used for support and maintenance. I saw that flyer's id, and I can trace its location over the last few days. It won't tell us who was using it, but we will find out where it was."

"Ok," said Gabriel. "Can you get that information and overlay it onto a map of Spain."

The side-street they were standing on was noticeably quiet, although there was a great deal of commotion from the street where the shooting had occurred. A map appeared on the wall next to where they were standing.

"That's Seville," Ginny said.

"That is where the flyer has been for the last two hours," explained Vicky.

It centralized the map on the Alameda de Hercules, where the incident occurred, with a glowing red dot showing the precise point of the shooting.

A glowing green line slowly appeared, working backwards from the place and time of the shooting.

"It looks as though they parked in somewhere called the Glorieta de Mejico for two hours, then they came right here and shot them down," Ginny said.

"That is a flyer park," Vicky said. "Before it got to the Glorieta de Mejico it travelled 120 Km up from Cadiz, in the south of Spain."

"What's in Cadiz?" Ginny asked.

"It's an ACME terminus," Vicky said. "ACME TOURS have a boarding point for its clients there."

"So, does that mean that ACME staff would land there as well?" Gabriel asked.

"That is probably the case," Vicky said.

"I wonder," said Ginny, "if the shooting was a deliberate plan by somebody in ACME to get rid of people who might talk to the investigators ... telling them that at least one of the lost clients actually died ..."

"Or maybe it was simply revenge by Smythe ... just a personal thing," said Gabriel.

"We can ask him," said Ginny.

Gabriel looked at Ginny. She seemed very focussed. And the look in her eyes ... he thought that somebody should be very frightened if they saw her coming.

"Vicky," Ginny said. "Can you take us to the flyer park ... minutes before Smythe's flyer gets there."

"Sure thing," Vicky said.

"Oh, and Vicky? Can you keep us looking like an old couple, please?"

"As you wish," Vicky said.

The only good thing that fucker did 1:15 pm 16th Oct 2180

Glorieta de Mejico – Seville

Ginny and Gabriel teleported into a far quadrant of the flyer park. The parking area was large. It was littered with flyers of various sizes, plus velos and mono-lifts.

Gabriel and Ginny stood off to one side; with their holo-forms activated, they looked like an old couple out for a walk, stopping to catch their breath.

"The flyer's just arrived," Vicky said. "It's landed over there, over to your left, about fifty yards away from you."

A small yellow neon arrow flashed momentarily in front of them, pointing to the ramstat flyer.

"Can you let us hear what they're saying?" Ginny asked.

An image 6 inches by 6 inches appeared in the air in front of them. It was as if they were watching a small TV screen … floating in the air. They could see and hear the occupants of the flyer.

"The one nearest us is Smythe," Gabriel said. "I don't recognise the other one."

"… so, the only good thing that little fucker did was … he set up tracers on the STUs he gave them," said Smythe.

"Before they blew his fucking arm off," said the other man.

"They're talking about Swan," Gabriel whispered to Ginny, who nodded back.

"He died screaming like a fucking pig," Smythe laughed.

"Shame about Bryce, though," said the other. "His kid's due next month."

Gabriel paled.

Ginny took hold of his hand and squeezed it.

"I thought all the STUs had tracers, anyway," the other man said. "When they teleport, the HUB knows where they are, anyway."

"Yeah, but that's only when they teleport. Otherwise nobody has the faintest clue where the little buggers are. So Swan adapted those STUs he gave out. They are continuously sending out their location. That's how we can track where the meds are right now."

"Wonder why he even bothered," the other man said. "I thought giving them those STUs was supposed to be a death sentence, anyway."

"I guess Swan was one paranoid little fucker ... and rightly so, since they didn't fucking die, did they?" Smythe said.

"But now they will," said the other man. "And we'll get those fucking bonuses after all."

"Too fucking true, mate," Smythe said, chuckling. "Anyway, I'm gonna get my head down for a bit. They won't be out of their apartment for another hour, so why don't you take a walk or something."

"Or shut the fuck up, eh?"

"Exactly."

The other man opened his flyer door and stepped out. "See you in a bit," he said.

Smythe reclined his seat, laid back and closed his eyes.

"Vicky?" said Gabriel.

"Yes?"

"How come they didn't detect the other STU ... the one that Sara and Zackery gave to us?"

"You never put it on, so it never activated."

"Oh ... ok."

"And Vicky?"

"Yes, Gabriel?"

"Can we request weapons?"

"Yes, Gabriel. What were you thinking you might need?"

What if he doesn't   1:25 pm   16th Oct 2180

Glorieta de Mejico – Seville

Gabriel scrolled down through a visual display of weapons. The screen showed a picture of each weapon, plus details of its size, weight, practical distance for accuracy, plus the weapon's typical usage.

"We can't just shoot him, though?" said Ginny. "I mean, we can't ... can we?"

Gabriel said nothing.

"We need to talk to him," said Ginny. "We need to find out who sent him."

"Some of these things are huge," Gabriel said. "They're like cannons. How could anybody carry anything like that thing, for example?" he said, pointing at a gun that looked like they could mount it on a helicopter.

"Some of those weapons were designed to be used by surrogates," said Vicky.

"What?" said Ginny.

"I think you will have read about SEG's development of surrogate robots," said Vicky. "A bit like Bill and Ben, but a lot more human-looking. Before ACME-TOURS took their market, SEG used to provide off-world tours for clients. The clients would travel in proxy, using the surrogates. And if they wanted to, the clients could arm their surrogates with ..."

"With fucking enormous guns, from the look of it," said Gabriel.

"And who were the surrogates shooting ... with their big guns?" asked Ginny, disgustedly.

"I couldn't say," said Vicky.

"I imagine we could all hazard a guess," said Gabriel.

"Anyway, talking of guns," said Vicky. "Have you seen a weapon you think might be suitable?"

"How about that one?" said Gabriel.

"Can I suggest," Vicky said, "that you might want to use something small and unobtrusive, but also very quiet."

"Such as?" said Ginny.

"Maybe this one," said Vicky.

The screen showed a small but squat pistol. It was a light creamy colour.

"All the others were matte black or shiny steel coloured," observed Gabriel.

"That one looks like a toy," noted Ginny.

"It holds six small-calibre rounds," said Vicky. "It is quiet, and with extraordinarily little recoil. It is accurate up to about ten yards. It might be enough to make Smythe think twice about harming you."

"Ok," Gabriel said. "Can you see if you can get one?"

There was a vague shimmering on the floor next to them. A box appeared. Gabriel picked it up and opened it. The cream gun laid inside the box, pressed into some sort of foam packaging.

"The gun will be loaded already," said Vicky. "You should also see a spare clip of bullets in the box."

Gabriel searched and pulled out the spare clip.

"There's a small green button underneath the ..." said Vicky.

"Yeah, got it," said Gabriel.

"Press that button and the loaded clip will eject," said Vicky.

Gabriel pressed the button, catching the clip as it fell. He pushed the clip back in again, hearing it click.

"There is a safety catch on the left side of ..."

"Yeah, I've got that too," said Gabriel, clicking the switch on and off.

"Anyway, what's the plan?" asked Gabriel. He was watching across the flyer park.

Smythe was sleeping in the flyer. They couldn't see the other man anywhere.

"How's about we walk over to Smythe ... wake him up and try to get him to tell us who ordered them to kill Sara and Zackery?" Ginny said.

"Do you really think he would tell us?" Gabriel said.

"He might."

"And what if he doesn't?" said Gabriel.

"How do you mean?" said Ginny.

"Well, if we walk away and let him go ... he will probably just try to kill Sara and Zackery, anyway."

Ginny looked across the flyer park.

Gabriel wasn't sure whether or not Ginny had heard his comment.

He suspected that she had.

"There's no-one about at the moment," Ginny said. "I'm not sure what to do, but time's running out. Let's try winging it, shall we?"

Gabriel caught hold of Ginny's arm as she was about to stride away.

"Here," he said, holding the cream gun out to her. "I think you should have the gun this time. I don't think I did too well with one last time ... with the Bryce thing."

Ginny nodded. She took hold of the gun. "Come on," she said, setting off towards Smythe's flyer. She held the gun in her right hand; held it down flat against her thigh. Gabriel followed on after her, looking around to see if he could see anyone nearby.

The park seemed empty. They walked past a section which was having some sort of maintenance work done to it. They had broken the tiled surface of this section of the flyer park. A luminescent cone was positioned on top of a mound of loose rock and broken sections from the stone esplanade.

Gabriel bent down. He selected a small slab of loose rock. It was about the size of his fist. It was creamy-coloured. It had tiny red flecks running through it. He picked it up. He felt its weight. He clasped the rock in his right hand.

They looked over at the flyer. Smythe had reclined his seat back. "He looks to be asleep," Gabriel whispered. "Smythe's resting his head against the door of the flyer."

Ginny took a last look around the flyer park. Smythe was sitting in the right seat. That made sense. His colleague was the driver, so he would have been sitting in the left seat.

Ginny walked round to the left side of the flyer ... the side opposite where Smythe was sitting. Gabriel went and stood on the right side of the vehicle. Next to where Smythe was sleeping.

The windows above the door panels were both lowered. Presumably because of the heat.

Ginny banged the butt of her gun hard on the driver-side door. Smythe jerked awake. His hand went straight towards a compartment in the dashboard in front of him.

Gabriel hit Smythe in the side of the face with the rock he was holding in his fist. Smythe's head spun to the left. Gabriel dropped the rock and grabbed

Smythe's head with both of his hands. He smashed Smythe's head hard against the flyer's dashboard. He leaned into the flyer. He flipped open the compartment that Smythe had been reaching for. He pulled out a small squat pistol.

Gabriel looked across to Ginny.

She was smiling.

Smythe sat up. He put his hands to his face. He looked around him. Outside his door was standing an old man.

The old man was holding Smythe's own gun.

A movement in Smythe's peripheral vision made him turn to his left. An old lady was standing at the other side of the flyer. She had one hand on the door of the flyer. She had a gun in her other hand.

She was pointing it directly at his face.

Smythe became immobile. He watched as the old man went around to stand beside the old lady.

"Who sent you, Smythe?" the old man said.

"Who sent me where?" Smythe smirked.

"Who sent you to kill Sara and Zackery?" the old lady said.

Gabriel saw Smythe's sudden look of realisation. "So, it's you fuckers," he said. "We thought you wuz dead."

"Who sent you, Smythe?" Ginny repeated. "We know what you're here to do, so make it easy. Just tell us."

"Or what?" Smythe said. "What do you think you will do with that toy gun?"

Ginny slowly lowered the gun from Smythe's face. She pointed it at his left knee and pulled the trigger. There was hardly any noise from the gun.

Smythe screamed as his knee exploded.

"Fuck you, fuck you, fuck you," Smythe said, sudden fear in his eyes.

Gabriel looked at Ginny. She was very calm. Very purposeful. She was holding the gun in very steady hands. Gabriel saw Smythe's partner running across the flyer park towards them. He was drawing a weapon. Gabriel turned to alert Ginny, but she was already crouching next to the flyer, using its bodywork for support. Smythe's partner was twenty feet away, running in a crouch, running to take cover behind an adjacent flyer.

The guy stopped running. He couldn't see any immediate danger. All he could see was an old couple standing next to the flyer. He imagined they must have heard the scream and come over to investigate, to see if they could help. The old man was looking over towards him, his hands were by his side. He was watching as if ... well ... to see what happened next. The old lady was crouching down by the side of the flyer. As if she was resting. Maybe she was unsteady on her feet. She looked old.

He stood up and looked around to see where the actual threat was.

Ginny's shot caught him in the throat. He fell to the ground. His gun clattered at his feet. He was gurgling and choking.

"I think I must have hit him somewhere serious," Ginny said, looking down at Smythe. "God, look at that ... there's blood everywhere."

Smythe had absolute fear in his eyes. He looked as though he no longer had any doubts as to likely outcomes.

"And you're looking very pale yourself, Mr. Smythe. Not feeling too well, eh?" she said.

"What do you fucking want?" Smythe said, grimacing with the pain from his shattered knee.

"Who sent you?" Ginny said, her voice cold and calm.

"Fucking Dmitry," said Smythe. "You want Dmitry. He offered us a fucking bonus."

"Dmitry?" said Gabriel. "That's the admin director guy, isn't it? So where's he based?"

"You want it fucking easy, don't you?" said Smythe, his old familiar smirk reappearing.

Ginny shot him in the face.

"Fuck, Ginny," Gabriel said.

"C'mon Gabriel," Ginny said. "We know who to look for now. Let's get out of here before somebody else comes along."

They walked away a short distance. Smythe's partner had stopped moving.

They walked past him.

"Ok, Vicky," Ginny said. "Can you please direct us back to the square where Sara and Zackery will be."

"Shall I transport you there?" Vicky asked.

"No thanks," Ginny said. "It's not far. We can take a walk."

"Ok Ginny."

"Oh, and can you turn the holographics off please? Just leave us as we are."

"Ok Ginny."

A memory for your holiday 3:20 pm 16th Oct 2180

The Alameda de Hercules - Seville

Gabriel and Ginny stopped slightly up the road from the café Sara and Zackery were going to. They stood back behind one of the guardian trees growing along the wide street. In the distance they recognised Sara and Zackery, walking along together. Zackery had on a soft pale-blue linen shirt, with casual cream trousers and brown shoes. Sara had on a pair of tight blue jeans and a long-sleeved white T-shirt. She was wearing pumps on her feet. Sara seemed to skip alongside Zackery, and he was holding her hand and smiling to anyone he saw. They looked incredibly happy together. They sat down at a roadside table.

A waiter saw them and walked up to them. "Hola!" he said

"Un café y ...," Sara said to the waiter. She looked back over to Zackery, who smiled back at her. "Un café con leche."

The waiter scribbled something down on his notepad, said to Sara, "No tiere mucho español ¬¿verdad?" He gestured vaguely towards Zackery, who was looking up the street.

"No ... no mucho," Sara said, looking quizzically at the waiter.

"Tal vez, e gustaría venir y ver mi máquina de café?" He gestured back to the door of the café.

"... es muy grande," he continued. "Un recuerdo para tus vacaciones."

Sara laughed. "Estoy segura de que tu máquina es muy impresionante ... muchas gracias, pero solo tomar un café," she said.

The waiter chuckled good-naturedly and walked off back into the café.

"What was that about?" Zackery said, as the waiter walked away.

"I had a proposition," she said, smiling. "He was offering me ... something off the menu, let's say. I told him thank-you, but that you were more than enough for me."

She reached over and stroked Zackery's hand.

He smiled back at her but cast a vague glance in the direction of the door to the café.

. . . .

"C'mon," Ginny said to Gabriel. "Let's go see them."

Ginny set off walking down the street, Gabriel rushing to catch up.

Sara turned and saw them. She waved excitedly.

The waiter was arriving with Sara and Zackery's drinks. He put the drinks down, turned and pushed another two chairs onto Sara and Zackery's table.

Ginny leant down and gave Sara an enormous hug. Gabriel shook Zackery's hand warmly.

"Great to see you guys," Sara said. "What's new? We were waiting to hear from you."

"It's only been four weeks since we last saw them," Zackery said, grinning.

"Yeah, but, well ..." Sara said, suddenly aware the waiter was waiting to take an additional order.

Sara looked over to Gabriel and Ginny.

"Do you want a coffee or something cold?" she asked them.

Ginny took a quick look at the drinks menu and pointed to something that looked like a tall glass filled with kiwi fruits and strawberries.

Sara turned to the waiter, pointing to the drink that Ginny had seen.

"Una como esta," she said.

Gabriel looked up to the waiter, holding up two fingers, taking care to hold his palm facing forwards.

"No, dos como esta," Sara said to the waiter who scribbled something down and walked back into the café.

"Sara?" Gabriel said. "Before we talk any more, do you have the STU with you ... the one that Swan gave you?"

Both Sara and Zackery recognised the urgency in Gabriel's voice.

"Sure ... I'm wearing it," Sara said, pulling back the sleeve of her long-sleeved T-shirt. "We've been waiting for you guys to contact us on it."

"So, you've not used it for anything else?" Ginny said.

"No."

"Would it be ok if you turned it off?" Ginny said.

"Why?" Sara asked.

"Because Swan made those STUs emit a tracking signal," said Gabriel. "ACME can use that to see where you are."

"Oh shit," said Zackery. He looked suddenly very scared.

"Ok," Sara said. "I'll turn it off."

"Just a minute," Gabriel said, a sense of urgency in his voice.

The others turned to hear what he had to say.

"We have found out that ACME have been tracking you with that STU," Gabriel said. "So, they realise you are here, in Seville."

"So, let's turn the fucking thing off," Zackery said.

"It occurs to me … if we turn it off, ACME will have no reason to think you have moved away from here. They might conclude you have simply turned it off, or it got broken or something," said Gabriel.

No one spoke.

"But if Ginny and I took it … like took it a long way from here …"

"They would think we've moved somewhere else," said Zackery.

"But what about you guys?" Sara said. "They would know where you were. They would come to get you instead of us."

"I think we can look after ourselves," Gabriel said, smiling over at Ginny.

"But how would we stay in touch?" Sara said.

"Can you get hold of a phone, Sara?" Vicky asked.

"What, right now?" Sara said.

"If you can," Vicky said.

"Be right back," Sara said, getting up and walking across the plaza.

Zackery watched her go. He looked both worried and proud.

The waiter came back, holding a small tray on which were the two fruit drinks that Gabriel and Ginny had ordered. He placed the drinks on the table. He slid a piece of paper under the glass ashtray in the middle of the table. He looked to see if anyone wanted to order anything else. He decided nobody there had the language ability to order anything, anyway. He walked back into the café.

"Realised we had bugger all to say, eh?" Zackery said, taking a sip from his latte.

A few minutes later Sara came walking back, holding a small blister pack. She put it on the table and pressed it open, revealing a tiny device ... like a small earplug. She squeezed it gently, and the device turned from pale pink to a light violet colour. She placed it on the table.

"Will this do, Vicky?" Sara said.

"Vicky?" she repeated.

"Yes, that's done," Vicky said. "We can communicate with you on that device, so you can give Gabriel or Ginny your STU."

Sara unclipped the STU from her wrist and handed it over to Gabriel, who put it in his pocket.

The device on the table emitted a low buzzing sound.

Sara looked at it worriedly.

"It's me, Sara," Vicky said. "Just checking the comms."

Sara laughed.

"Sorry for worrying you, Sara," Vicky said.

As they spoke, a lady came walking up the street, pushing a buggy.

She sat at an adjacent table. She pulled the buggy alongside her and clamped on the brakes.

She pulled a very young baby out of the buggy which immediately made a slight whimpering sound. She held the baby to her chest, holding one hand gently behind its head.

She began to rock the baby, backwards and forwards, backwards and forwards.

The baby nuzzled in against its mother.

Her waiter came over, bringing a tray with a clear glass cup with a handle. It seemed to contain hot water with small green leaves in it.

"I think she has that every day," Sara explained. "The waiter brings that without her asking."

Zackery sat watching the woman with her baby. Almost unconsciously he half-stood up, leaned over to Sara, and gave her a loving kiss on the forehead.

Sara smiled up at him.

Zackery suddenly realised Ginny and Gabriel were watching him. He gave them an awkward smile, looked away into the distance, his cheeks a faint pink colour.

Sara took Zackery's hand and gave it a squeeze.

Gabriel looked over at Ginny. Her eyes seemed to twinkle. He smiled at her, and she smiled back.

Sara took a sip at her coffee and said, "So, anyway, what was all that about … about the STU?"

Life can be a bitch sometimes   4:15 pm 16th Oct 2180

The Alameda de Hercules - Seville

Two more coffees and two more fruit drinks later and Gabriel and Ginny had explained what they had found out at the ACME-HUB in 2182. They had told Sara and Zackery that the coords database had been corrected. They had told them about the tracer feature that were enabled on the STUs given to them by Swan.

They didn't tell them that Smythe had killed Zackery and seriously injured her.

They didn't tell them that their history had been re-written.

"So, somebody called Dmitry seems to be trying to track us down," Gabriel said.

"And that's why you're going to take that STU and lead them away?" Sara said.

"Exactly," said Ginny.

"But what if ...?" Zackery said.

"Your STU needs to leave Seville," Ginny said. "Otherwise they will be aware you are here."

"So why haven't they ...?" Zackery said, but then he stopped. "They did, didn't they?" he said.

He looked across at Sara, horror in his eyes.

"Are they on their way?" Sara asked.

"Not now," Ginny said.

"How do you ...?" Zackery asked.

"We've stopped them," Gabriel said. "Well, Ginny stopped them, I should say."

Ginny looked across at Gabriel. Her eyes were glinting a warning.

The waiter arrived and put fresh drinks and a bowl of olives on their table.

"Gabriel and I need to go ... we need to go soon ... we need to go today," Ginny said. "We'll take a slow route, up through Spain and into France ... then on to Switzerland. We'll make it look like you are travelling by road or rail. Taking a scenic journey. It won't look like you are using the STU."

Gabriel looked across at Ginny. He was impressed.

"So, we can stay on here in Seville, do you think?" Sara asked.

"It's a lovely place," Ginny said. "It suits you. I think you should be ok here."

Sara looked at Zackery. "What do you think?" she said to him.

Zackery looked over to Gabriel and Ginny, as if they could give himself and Sara more information. Something they might use to help their decision.

"What are you guys going to do?" Zackery asked.

"I think we need to find this Dmitry," Ginny said.

"And do what?" Sara asked.

"I think Ginny will think of something," Gabriel said. "She's getting good at this stuff."

"I think you guys should keep that phone charged up," Ginny said. "And keep a rucksack nearby with some basic stuff in. Just in case."

Sara smiled ruefully back at Ginny.

"Life can be a bitch, sometimes," Ginny said.

"And then you die," said Gabriel, who had heard that line in a Woody Allen film and had always wanted to use it.

No introductions are necessary   8:30 pm 16th Oct 2180

Glorieta de Mejico – Seville

Gabriel and Ginny had eaten a late-afternoon meal with Sara and Zackery. Then they had wished them well and set off walking back towards the flyer park where they had killed Smythe and his colleague.

"Good idea about making a slow journey with the tracer," Gabriel said, "but how do you plan to do it? We haven't got the starship anymore, and I have no idea how to use regular transport to get across Spain and into France."

The street they were walking down opened into the Glorieta de Mejico … the flyer park.

A few people were walking about, but it looked as though most people had parked there for the evening and were now in the main part of town.

"Vicky?" Ginny said.

"Yes, Ginny."

"Can you get us some transport?"

"What sort would you like, Ginny?"

"Well, the starship was good, but I suppose anything will do. It's just that, if we are going to take a slow trip across Europe, something with sleeping facilities would be good."

In the space next to them, a faint shimmering suggested Vicky's request was about to make an appearance.

"It's a fucking starship," Gabriel laughed, recognising the general shape and the fish-scale appearance.

The starship floated a few inches above the ground, making the other vehicles in the flyer park look like toys.

Its hatchway slowly unpeeled.

Ginny stepped up into the ship, followed by Gabriel.

"Good day, Ship," Vicky said. "May I introduce you to my clients? They are called …"

"Pleased to see you again," said Ship. "No introductions are necessary, I believe."

"How the hell ...?" said Gabriel. "I thought we left you two years in the future."

"I don't rightly know," said Ship. "I was registered as docked on one of the ACME-HUB stubs. Maybe the service facility left in place by ACME, the one to supply equipment to its lost clients, maybe that can teleport equipment from registered docking points."

Ginny couldn't help but to smile.

"Well, anyway ... I don't really understand how it happened," Ship continued, "but here I am, and I'm very pleased to see you again."

"Ok Ship," Ginny said. "Can you please plot a route through Spain, up into France and on into Switzerland. I want to make it look like we are making a trip in a basic flyer. Not fast. Low altitude. Take three days. Head for Zurich. Stop and land somewhere in the evenings. Try to find places with some open countryside. And during the day, just stop every few hours. Then wait around for an hour. But don't land anywhere conspicuous ... areas that look sort of pretty. Is that ok?"

Gabriel looked on proudly.

"Yes, I understand that, Ginny," said Ship. "Shall we set off right now?"

"Yes please, Ship."

"Ok, Ginny. We are underway. Shall I initiate cloaking?"

"No. Leave it off, thanks. Keep us visible. We don't have a care in the world."

"Ok, Ginny."

Gabriel stood watching Ginny. He thought she seemed to have risen to the challenge they were facing. He hoped it was a good thing.

"I'll get the hot chocolate on," Gabriel said.

"That would be nice," Ginny said.

In Baltimore   16th Oct 2180

The ACME INC Building - Baltimore

Dmitry Alexandrovich sits behind his exceptionally large, very shiny, very sparse desk on the 47th floor of the ACME Building, Baltimore.

On the polished surface of his desk is a cell phone, a visi-tablet, and a paper jotter.

He holds an ordinary pencil in his left hand.

He twirls the pencil between his fingers, finally inserting the end into the only other object on his desk; an old, mechanical pencil sharpener.

He holds the pencil in the hole in the sharpener with his left hand and turns the handle with this right.

A small spiral of wood shaving curls out from the sharpener into the clear plastic waste receptacle in the sharpener's base.

He pulls the pencil out of the hole and runs his right index finger against the point.

He smiles; satisfied at the results.

He turns and looks out of his office window. It isn't really a window. It is a twenty-yards wide, four yards high sheet of reinforced plexi-glass. He had said he wanted a view, and he had got one.

He thought he looked surprisingly good for a guy fifty-three-years old. He was still fit; he worked out, he always had. He wore good suits; and not because he could afford to. It was because it was important; it made people who couldn't envious.

He kept his hair stubble short. He thought it made him look tough. So did the scar across his right cheek; it ran down from his eyebrow down to the jut of his jaw. He occasionally thought to have the scar fixed. It had happened a long time ago; a bar-fight, a guy wielding a broken bottle. It hadn't helped the guy in the long run. The guy had been keen and young; had lots of energy, had got in a lucky strike. But it hadn't helped him. Dmitry had had the experience, patience, some agility, and a ruthless determination to win. To win and not only to finish it, but to make sure that it never ever happened again. Nobody who saw that fight would have ever felt the need to try their chances with Dmitry.

So he kept the scar.

It all helped.

Even now.

His visi-tablet chimed, and he checked whether it was a secure line. It was.

He clicked receipt.

"They've moved," the voice on the other end said. "They're not in Seville anymore."

"Where to?" Dmitry said.

"Dunno. They're still moving. Seem to be making a slow trip up through Spain."

"Team 1 are both dead?" Dmitry asked.

"Yep, that's a definite. They are both really dead. Didn't know the fuckers had weapons ... or knew how to use them."

"Well now we know," said Dmitry, with a sense of exasperation.

Surely you didn't need to tell a hit team that the victims might be unwilling to die.

"We could try to catch them while they're moving. Maybe they are heading for ..."

"Listen," said Dmitry. "Team 2 are ready to go. Flynn and Matthews. Tell me when they have stopped ... and I don't mean when they've stopped for a crap. I mean when they've stopped for five hours or more. Let me know, and I'll get team 2 in."

"Yeah. Right. As soon as they stop for ..."

Dmitry clicked off the call. He pushed the pencil back into the sharpener and gave the handle a savage twist. The leaded point sheared.

He pulled the pencil out, viewing the damaged point.

"Bollocks," Dmitry muttered, angry at himself.

He was angry at himself for losing his cool. For losing his cool over something that should not be that difficult to achieve. Not that difficult to achieve, but with fucking huge, fucking catastrophic consequences.

He looked at himself, at his reflection in the plexi-glass.

"Fucking med-bay staff," he muttered. "Hopefully team 2 will be man enough to kill two fucking med-bay staff."

He threw the pencil into a small waste receptacle adjacent to his desk.

The waste bin uttered a brief fzzt noise as it destroyed the pencil.

He didn't like things that didn't work; that weren't fit for use. He couldn't tolerate their presence near him. But he felt a grudging respect for the med bay staff. They had killed two of his own. The meds hadn't been trained for it, but they had still killed his two guys … and his guys had been big guys with guns. Ok, the meds had had no choice; but they had come out winning. He respected that. And if they had merely disabled his guys, he would have had to finish his guys off, anyway. To 'encourage the others' as someone had once said.

He smiled to himself. He liked his job.

Do you think you could catch one?   6:45 pm   18th Oct 2180

On the outskirts of Zurich

Ginny pulled up a map of Switzerland. She dragged it around the screen, looking for something.

"What are you …?" Gabriel said.

"I'm thinking …" Ginny said, "how about a nice agricultural area, sheep and cows, nice little town nearby. That would do, I reckon."

Ginny smiled across at Gabriel.

Gabriel thought she had something in mind, but she looked like she was unwilling to explain it right now. Perhaps it was just that she had the vaguest glimmer of an idea … and she needed time to work it through.

Either way, she seemed to be happier than she had been for a while.

She had even got Vicky to get her a sweatshirt that let you design things on it.

It came with tools.

Who would have thought it?

A sweatshirt that came with tools?

Currently, it was all black, with white writing on it.

The writing was on both the front and the back.

It was a quote; or at least it had words on it Gabriel hadn't heard before.

On the front, it said:

Don't judge
  me cause
    I'm quiet

On the back, it said:

No one plans
  a murder
    out loud

Gabriel had laughed when he saw her wearing it this morning. She had coupled it with a pair of tight blue jeans, and hiking boots. He had thought she looked very nice, and he had even complimented her on it.

She had smiled back at him; she had even given him a hug, but he had felt a hardness in her.

He thought that was a good thing.

They were playing a dangerous game.

He recognised that he could be hard. It sometimes worried him. Also, he knew that sometimes, sometimes when he had needed to be ruthless, sometimes he had felt it difficult to stop.

And Ginny had seen him like that … and it had upset her.

He wondered if Ginny would be as upset with him if she realised she herself had gained a degree of hardness.

Ginny dragged the map across to Davos.

"That's where the UK royal family used to go," Gabriel said.

"What?"

"They used to go there skiing," Gabriel continued.

"Erm … er … yeah," Ginny said.

"It's not important," Gabriel said, feeling stupid.

Ginny turned towards him.

"Come over here, Pudding," she said. "I need some help."

Gabriel walked over to her.

She thought he had the air of a small puppy: unsure whether it was loved; unsure whether it had done something wrong.

"I'm looking for a nice little area of farmland," she explained.

"Somewhere with some nice rolling hills and a few moo cows ambling about."

Gabriel looked perplexed.

"I don't want to tell you why yet … 'cos you'll probably think I'm stupid, but … Ship, can you give me this map as an aerial view, with lots of detail?"

She dragged around on her new map.

It gave the impression of flying over the ground, looking down from a few hundred yards, like from a glider.

"How about there?" she said.

It was an area of gently rolling hills. Small houses and barns were scattered here and there. They all looked to be made from logs.

A few sheep were dotted about, but they were dwarfed by what looked like exceptionally large, very orange, very long-haired cows.

"It looks like chocolate box country," Gabriel said.

"Yeah, I suppose so," Ginny said.

"Are they cows or bulls," Gabriel asked, "cos they've got huge horns?"

"I don't know," Ginny said, "but they look ideal for purpose."

Gabriel gave a questioning look to Ginny.

"Do you think you could catch one?" she said.

Rolling hills with moo cows   3:15 pm   19th Oct 2180

Near Davos – Switzerland

They had parked the starship in the bottom of a small river valley.

They had walked up, very slowly, to a small herd of the orange cows. Close to, their long hair looked ginger. It seemed to glow in the afternoon sunlight.

Two of the cows seemed to be placid. The others had wandered off, but these two seemed happy to accept Ginny and Gabriel's nearness.

Ginny walked slowly closer to one of them. It looked at Ginny with its big moist eyes.

She slowly bent and plucked a clump of grass.

She offered it to the cow.

It didn't move to take the grass, but neither did it move away.

"Are you ready?" Ginny asked Gabriel.

"You sure about this?" Gabriel said.

"Now's not the time to question it," Ginny said.

"I'm ready," Gabriel said.

Ginny inched forward, holding the clump of grass in both of her hands.

The cow opened its mouth and took the clump of grass.

"Now ... now," Ginny said, so quietly that Gabriel could barely hear her.

Gabriel leaned down and snapped Sara's STU onto the left foreleg of the cow.

He stepped away instantly.

The cow continued munching the clump of grass.

Ginny stroked the side of the cow's head.

Its eyes followed her movements.

"Good girl," Ginny said.

It's bought us time   4 pm   19th Oct 2180

"Vicky?" Ginny said.

"Yes, Ginny."

"Can you please show us what that STU is transmitting?"

The pale cream starship wall glowed with a panoramic view of the field that the cows were in.

The image was wobbling slightly.

"That's the cow slowly walking about," explained Vicky.

"Can the STU keep transmitting this feed for as long …," Ginny said.

"The STU will maintain its energy both from the sunlight and from the electrical energies within the beast," Vicky said. "It will keep sending this data feed until we request it to stop."

"That's great, Vicky," Ginny said.

"Ginny?" Vicky asked.

"Yes?"

"You realise how expensive STUs are don't you?" Vicky said.

"Meaning?" Ginny said.

"Meaning that attaching that STU to an animal …"

"To a lovely ginger cow," Ginny interrupted.

"Even so," continued Vicky. "I cannot see what useful purpose has been achieved here, in doing such a frivolous thing."

Gabriel nodded, cautiously.

"That STU," said Ginny, with the exasperated air of a teacher trying to explain something to a very dim pupil, "has bought us two things."

"What has it bought, Ginny?" Vicky asked.

"It's bought us time, Vicky. And it will also buy us information."

He very much enjoyed his job   20th Oct 2180

The ACME INC Building - Baltimore

"They've not moved for over 12 hours."

"So, where are they?" Dmitry said.

"They're in Switzerland. Sort of near Davos. Looks like a farming community. No big towns nearby. In fact, there's bugger all nearby."

"So, you think they've come to a stop for a while?" Dmitry said.

"Looks that way."

"Stake your life on it?"

"Er ..."

"Only joking," Dmitry said.

"So, what, er ...? Are you going to send team 2 in now?"

"Well ... you've said now's a good time, so I think I must take your word for it," Dmitry said.

He heard the heightened breathing of the other man down the comms line.

"Send me their coordinates," Dmitry said. "Send them to team 2, and also I want you there as well. We'll all meet up in three hours precisely."

"You want me there and ..."

"I want us all there," Dmitry said. "To avoid fuck-ups, and to maximise operational efficiencies."

"Er ... right ... see you there in three hours precisely."

Dmitry clicked the call closed.

He laughed at his own little joke.

He had been quoting from his own job description on the ACME INC staff website. It described him as 'acts in a roving manner, often working on-site to maximise operational efficiencies.' In practice, his very presence served to put the shits up everybody, no matter what level they worked at within the company.

He laughed at the thought.

He very much enjoyed this job.

He really should have done this shit much sooner in his life.

Maybe he would have lost less blood; had fewer scars.

But then he'd enjoyed that shit as well.

So fucking hard   6:40 am 21st Oct 2180

On the outskirts of Baltimore

"We're sure that's his office, aren't we?" Gabriel asked.

"That's his office, Gabriel," Ginny said.

"Because his job details say he's often away. Maybe he's never actually…"

"Let's have a little patience, eh?" Ginny said.

They had located Dmitry's office from the published ACME INC company information. Vicky had explained that such details had to be maintained for every large registered company.

They had requested a rifle that fired a surveillance bolt.

In the early dawn, and with the starship cloaked, they had hovered outside the building, opened the hatchway, fired the bolt onto the plexi-glass office window, then drifted away.

They parked on the outskirts of Baltimore, watching, and listening to the feed from the surveillance bolt.

"Fancy a coffee?" Gabriel asked.

"Yeah, that would be …" Ginny said.

"Hey, guys?" Vicky said.

"What's up, Vicky," Ginny said.

"The feed from your cow friend … something's happening," Vicky said.

On the ship's hull was an image of the rolling Swiss hills.

"It's about midday over there," Ginny said.

Big ginger cows stood all around them.

"Our cow must be standing in the middle of the herd," Ginny said, smiling.

"Listen to that noise," Gabriel said.

"They're tearing up clumps of grass," said Ginny. "They're sweet, aren't they?"

"So, what have you seen?" Gabriel asked Vicky.

"Over in the distance … four men coming down the hill. Can you see them?"

"Look, the cows are all starting to move away," Ginny said.

"All except ours," Gabriel said. "Maybe it thinks it's you again, with a clump of fresh grass."

Ginny smiled at the recollection.

The four men approached their cow. One was holding up some sort of device.

"Looks like a portable tracker ... they must have been using it to follow the STUs," Vicky said.

"Hey, the guy on the far right. Isn't that ...?" said Gabriel.

"It's Dmitry," Vicky said.

The four men were within twelve feet of their cow.

The one holding the tracker looked to be trembling slightly. The tracking device he held was wobbling in his hands.

The two guys on the left were looking bemused.

Dmitry wasn't.

"We've all come a fucking long way to enjoy this walk in a field full of cows," Dmitry said to the man holding the tracker.

The man with the tracker gulped. He patently couldn't think of anything to say.

"You understand time is money, don't you?" Dmitry said to the man with the tracker.

The man nodded.

"But I guess you don't think my time is worth very much at all, eh?"

The man looked around him. He looked to the other two men

They studiously averted their gaze from him.

"If you want a job doing ...," Dmitry said, pulling a pistol from under his jacket.

Dmitry looked over to the cow.

He turned back to the man and shot him in the stomach.

The gun made virtually no sound.

Their cow stood there, continuing to chew grass.

The man slumped to the ground.

He was lying on his side, rolling himself into a tight ball.

Ginny clasped Gabriel's hand. She squeezed it so hard that Gabriel almost cried out.

Dmitry kicked the man in the face.

The man rolled over and onto his back.

Dmitry shot him in his left shoulder ... then in his right shoulder.

The man was screaming ... and staring at Dmitry wild-eyed.

Dmitry turned to look back at the other two men. They were watching as if they were watching some TV soap.

Dmitry turned back and shot the man through the forehead.

"Do you know," Dmitry said, "I can never work out whether I hate ineptitude ..."

The two men stood watching him.

They both seemed to realise that now was not the time for them to engage in conversation.

"Or ... or whether I fucking love it," Dmitry continued, chuckling to himself.

He flicked the magazine out of his gun, letting it drop to the ground. He pulled another from his jacket pocket. The two men were watching him as if their lives depended on it.

Dmitry turned slowly.

He unloaded the extra clip into their ginger cow.

They heard the bullets smacking into its body.

They heard it making a squealing noise.

It sounded almost like a child crying.

The picture swayed as the cow fell to the ground.

They heard Dmitry laughing.

He must have re-loaded because they heard more bullets hitting their cow.

The screen went blank.

"He must have shot the STU," Vicky said.

Gabriel put his arm around Ginny. She was shaking. If he hadn't been holding on to her, he suspected she would have collapsed onto the floor.

"Are you all right, Ginny?" Vicky asked.

"Ginny are you all right?" Vicky repeated, when no answer was forthcoming.

"He thinks he's so fucking hard," Ginny said, "so fucking hard."

Gabriel hugged her tightly.

I'll keep us safe 8:10 am 21st Oct 2180

On the outskirts of Baltimore

"Vicky, can you please call Sara and Zackery?" Ginny said.

"Ok, Ginny," Vicky said.

Gabriel sipped at his coffee.

Watching Dmitry had wrung them both out, but Ginny seemed to have pulled herself together.

Her resilience amazed him.

"Hi there. Sara and Zackery here," Sara said. "Is everything ok?"

"Can anybody hear you?" Ginny asked. "I mean, are you sitting anywhere where other people can hear our conversation?"

"Just a minute," Sara said. "Ok, we're good this end. What's up?"

"We left the STU in Switzerland," Ginny said. "Dmitry turned up with another bunch of guys with guns."

"Shit," said Zackery.

"What happened to you guys?" Sara said.

"We weren't there," said Ginny. "We were watching a vid feed. What's clear is that Dmitry is a fucking psychopath. He shot one of his own men when he realised they had followed a false trail."

"Fuck!" Zackery said.

"So, what should we do?" Sara said.

"I think you should move," Ginny said. "Just for a little while. In case they think to backtrack ... and come back to Seville. They have no technical way of tracing you, but you can never be sure."

"Yeah, just in case," said Zackery.

"Ok," Sara said. "We've got our gear together ... in fact we've got it in a bag with us right now. Any thoughts as to where we should ...?"

"I don't think you should tell us," Ginny said. "If anything happens and we ..."

"Oh God," Sara said. "Do you think that ... that if they caught you, they would ...?"

"Dmitry is not a nice man," Ginny said. "I don't want to take the risk of knowing where you guys have gone."

"Ok, Ginny," Zackery said. "We're getting under-way right now. We've been expecting this call, so we are ready to go. Good luck, guys."

"And you," Ginny said.

"They have closed the call," Vicky said.

"Ok, thanks Vicky," Ginny said.

"I hope they'll be all right," Ginny said to Gabriel.

"I hope we'll be all right," Gabriel said.

"I'll keep us safe," Ginny said.

Someone a long time ago   11:35 am 22nd Oct 2180

Their starship was hovering six yards away from Dmitry's office window. Wind turbulence from the huge building was making the starship rock slightly. Its small fore-and-aft thrusters were working continuously to keep it stable. They had cloaked the ship ... It was invisible to the human eye. They had full visuals and audio from the recon bolt they had shot onto the office's plexi-glass window. Gabriel and Ginny watched and listened via their heads-up display.

"It's the two men from Switzerland," Ginny said.

"They don't look happy," Gabriel observed.

The two men were standing in front of Dmitry. He was pacing backwards and forwards in front of them.

Ginny gestured at the display, which zoomed in slightly.

"They're called Flynn and Matthews," she said. "Flynn's on the left."

Gabriel nodded.

Ginny zoomed back out. Dmitry was talking.

"So, Flynn, you're telling me you don't know where the fucking med-bay people are," Dmitry said. "Is that fucking correct?"

"They only had the one STU with an active tracer on them," said Flynn, apologetically.

"We could have downloaded the memory from that STU," Matthews, said. "The one they put on the cow, but ..."

"But you shot the fucking STU," Flynn said. "Blew the fucking thing to pieces. No way that we could tell who was carrying the STU, who put it on the ..."

He stopped, suddenly horrified at his own impertinence.

Dmitry stopped pacing. He looked out of the plexi-glass screen. He looked down to the people scurrying about in the plaza 47 floors below.

He turned back to Flynn and Matthews.

"Right. What do we know?" he asked them.

Flynn looked over to Matthews, as though his colleague might have the answer to this frighteningly tricky question.

Dmitry scowled.

"We know that the fuckers are still alive," Dmitry explained, striving to keep his composure ... trying to stop himself from unravelling and beating the shit out of one or both of these fucking imbeciles.

The two guys nodded.

"Don't we ... fucking don't we?" he snarled.

The two guys kept nodding. They didn't seem to know what else to do.

Dmitry turned to his desk and pounded his fist on the desktop.

"Like fucking nodding dogs ... like two fucking nodding dogs," he said.

"I think Matthews looks like he might cry," Gabriel said.

"Or wet himself," said Ginny.

Gabriel looked over at Ginny.

She wasn't smiling.

He imagined that she was feeling sorry for them. All right, they were Dmitry's hired muscle, but he wasn't aware they had killed anybody. And they certainly hadn't fired a shot at their cow.

Dmitry turned away from Flynn and Matthews.

He strode over to the window, staring into the distance. He was looking directly in the starship's direction.

He turned back to the two men. He stood up straight ... talking calmly now.

"Gentlemen," he said. "ACME-TOURS employed you as security professionals. You have a case in front of you. You have a case of two people who you need to find. We have perfect descriptions of what they look like. We are absolutely clear as to where they were a few days ago. I am sure that two professional gentlemen such as yourselves can set about this task and carry it through to a successful conclusion. I am very much hoping that within a short space of time, you will have found these two people and ... and executed your contract. Would you not agree, gentlemen?"

Flynn and Matthews nodded nervously.

"Would you not fucking agree?" Dmitry snarled.

"Yes," they both said, nodding vigorously.

"Right, well go and fucking get on with it. Get out. Get out now. There's the fucking lift."

Both men turned and walked over to the lift.

Flynn punched the lift button … it lit up … it was on their floor already.

The lift door opened … they got in.

As the door shut, they both saw a starship uncloaking … mere feet outside of the plexi-glass window.

"What the fuck," Flynn said, pointing.

Then the lift door closed.

Dmitry turned to look in the direction that Flynn was pointing in. It was a starship … slowly uncloaking. It looked vast … probably because it was floating only thirty feet from his plexi-glass window.

He strode over to the glass, leaning against it. The ship's forward hatch was peeling open. In the doorway he recognised the bulk of a SEG surrogate robot. It was holding some sort of weapon. That was why some people hired those brutes. They could carry some serious firepower. This one was holding an excessively big, a very clunky looking weapon of some sort. He didn't recognise the weapon. It looked like it fired a projectile with a bulbous nose on it.

The robot hoisted the weapon up. It was pointing it directly at him.

Dmitry ran back to the lift. He punched the call button. The lift was still going down with Flynn and Matthews in it. It was on floor 22. It must have picked up somebody else.

And it was still going down.

To the left of the lift was a large metal cupboard. Dmitry wrenched it open. He reached into the cupboard, pulling out his old semi-automatic shotgun. It was a Franchi SPAS-12, with a 5-shell magazine extension tube. That meant five shells in the magazine and one in the breach. The gun was nearly 200 years old, but he could enjoy a thing like that. He'd always liked Italian firearms. They built their weapons with care and with love.

Sort of ironic, he thought.

And luckily, he always kept it loaded … well … it wasn't luck at all. He had never seen much point in having a gun and not having the fucker loaded. He had loaded it with some old Monolit 28s … big old solid steel slugs, 28 grams each one, courtesy of Latvia's firearm's industry.

He stifled a chuckle … you make a cartridge holding a 28-gram chunk of solid steel. A piece of steel designed to hurtle from a rifle barrel and blast its way through damn near anything.

And then you forge the chunk of steel into a pleasant hour-glass shape.

Like a good-looking woman.

There's an irony ... to get killed by something flying through the air with the shape of a good-looking woman.

You might kill an elephant with a gun like this ... or at the very least piss it off.

And two shots would blow a section out of the plexi-glass. You never knew when you might need something like that, and this looked like exactly that time.

He heard a sound ... a sound on the plexi-glass. It was like somebody had thrown something soft and squelchy against the glass.

Something was sticking to the glass. Something with four large rubber suckers.

As he watched, the thing sticking to his window began cutting a perfectly circular hole in the glass. Like a laser torch ... slowly cutting a disc from the incredibly strong, incredibly reinforced plexi-glass sheet.

A disc of glass 6 inches in diameter fell out and down onto the floor of his office.

He jabbed at the lift button again ... it was down to the 3rd floor.

He guessed that if nobody else got in or out, it would be back at his level in about 30 seconds.

He strode back to the window.

The device on his window had begun to push a silver ball through the hole it had cut. Dmitry stepped forward and caught the ball as it dropped. He tried to push the ball back through the hole in the window, but the device had already placed a stopper over it.

The silver ball in his hand made a slight clicking noise.

He didn't think the ball would be heat-generating. In any case, the office sprinklers would extinguish any flames in an instant. And it didn't look like it was an explosive ... you need not make an explosive device out of a shiny silver sphere. It was a container. He had seen one before, just like it. He was sure he had been to the demonstration.

He placed the ball gently on the floor and walked carefully back over to the lift.

· · · · · · · ·

Gabriel pulled the goggles on and eased them until they were comfortable. He had read the instructions. They seemed simple enough.

• • • • • • • •

The lift was on the ground floor. It was about to come back up. He jabbed the button again ... he turned and raised his shotgun. He pointed it at the silver ball, just as a faint crack appeared on its shiny surface. The ball appeared to be levering itself slowly open. Something with legs was climbing out of the ball.

• • • • • • • •

Gabriel said, "Ok, Ginny, your little toy is active."

• • • • • • • •

Dmitry recognised it. They were nasty little fuckers. He had used them himself. They were spider-liker ... extremely fast ... very agile. They usually carried some sort of venom ('a delivery system with the toxin of your choice' he remembered the ad said).

His gun boomed.

Five left.

He had torn a huge chunk out of his polished wooden floorboards. And the blast had simply hurled the silver ball away across the room. They were seemingly built to withstand some serious firepower.

And the small spider-like device was scuttling its way sideways.

• • • • • • • •

"That was close," said Gabriel. "Just as well these little buggers are nimble as anything."

• • • • • • • •

Dmitry had missed the fucking thing ... now it was making its way behind a leg of his desk. He backed up against the door to the lift. He watched to see where the spider went. A movement caught his eye, and the gun bucked and boomed in his hand.

Four left.

And he felt a tiny pricking sensation in his right leg. The spider was clamped onto his right ankle. He bent down and grabbed its body, making sure he didn't get his fingers underneath it. It used its legs for movement, but, once it reached its target, tiny needles would protrude from its underbody, injecting the chosen toxin. The spider struggled in his grasp, and he felt a sting in the palm of his hand.

He dropped the spider on the floor. He trod on it. It didn't attempt to avoid him. It shattered under his boot.

He guessed that once its target had been reached, it had no further use.

· · · · · · · ·

"Ok, Ginny ... we've got him twice ... right ankle and right hand," Gabriel said.

· · · · · · · ·

He reflected that they had obviously upgraded the basic model ... the one he was familiar with. The spiders now had needles in their upper body... presumably to get around the evasive action that Dmitry had just tried. Dmitry laughed. "Fucking weapons techs. They build a fancy delivery system, they demo them, but they can't leave well enough alone."

· · · · · · · ·

"Ginny?" Gabriel said.

"Yep ... what?"

"What did you end up choosing?"

"How do you mean?"

"What did the spider have in it?"

"It was called 'WNF'."

"What does that stand for?"

"It's weaponised necrotising fasciitis," Vicky said.

"Isn't that the flesh-eating virus thing?" Gabriel said. "Been around for donkey's years? Dates to biblical times?"

"Possibly," said Vicky. "It's an infection of the soft tissue. It starts in the subcutaneous tissue. That's the tissue just below the skin. It spreads along the flat layers of fibrous tissue that separate the different layers of tissue."

"Sounds bloody horrible," Gabriel replied.

"The symptoms normally start as areas of localised redness, with warmth, swelling and pain ... normally a great deal of pain. Then the skin darkens, and blisters and black scabs appear. Although there is normally an enormous amount of pain during the progress of the disease, interestingly the pain may subsequently diminish ... that is because of the nerve damage caused by the ..."

"For God's sake," said Gabriel.

"And there are other symptoms associated with this disease," said Vicky.

"The fun never stops, does it?" Gabriel said.

"Typically, there is nausea, vomiting, weakness, dizziness, and confusion. Then, if left untreated, the infection spreads throughout the entire body... typically leading to sepsis, which spreads the infection to the bloodstream. At that point, death is inevitable," Vicky concluded.

"Sorry ... you say that this disgusting disease was 'weaponised' by ACME INC?" said Gabriel incredulously.

"ACME provided ... whatever its clients required," Vicky said. "And the requirement was to make the native disease faster-acting. What might otherwise take hours or even days was re-designed to take a maximum of about fifteen minutes."

"What the fuck would somebody want something like that for?" Gabriel said.

"Ask Ginny," Vicky said, nervously.

"I've no idea what other people wanted it for," Ginny said, "but it seemed appropriate for my use ... to kill this evil bastard."

Gabriel looked over to Ginny. She was holding onto the robot for balance. She was watching Dmitry intently. She had been listening to Gabriel's discussion with Vicky.

She looked very calm.

· · · · · · · ·

Within seconds of being injected by the spider, the pain in Dmitry's right hand and leg were excruciating. Blisters were erupting on the skin, and almost instantly they were cracking open, oozing a thick green fluid. He touched his right hand with his still un-affected left hand. Only that light contact caused pain to sear through the length of his right arm.

So now he realised he wouldn't be able to use his right arm or hand.

He bent down and rested the shotgun on the floor. He rotated the stock. The gun had been designed to be fired one-handed. You rotated the stock so it would fit under your forearm. And because he recognised he would not be able to use his right hand to re-load the gun using its manual pump action feature, he felt with his left hand for the firing-mode switch under the fore-grip. He selected gas-activated rather than pump-action.

He stood up, wincing as he put weight onto his right leg. He tucked the stock of the gun under his left forearm. He looked out of the window and across to the starship.

The robot in the starship doorway was just standing there. It had lowered its weapon. Beside it stood a boy and a girl. They were both about twenty years old. The boy looked about six feet tall, dark skinned, with tufty hair. She was shorter ... pretty, with long blonde hair.

Dmitry didn't recognise either of them.

He could barely put pressure on his right leg. Waves of pain were spreading through into his chest, into his groin. The boy was looking directly at him. The girl was grinning.

He grunted with the pain ... but then he began to laugh. When he saw (and recognised) the spider, he had expected worse ... much worse. He guessed he would have a great deal of pain ... and then die coughing his lungs up out of his mouth. Those little spider fuckers didn't deliver you a nice shot of whisky. It would be something unpleasant, you could guarantee that ... but if he had designed this toxin, he would definitely have got the weapons techs to incorporate fire into the equation.

People feared fire. Everybody feared fire. It always got results.

He remembered the time ... the tiny village in the mountains. He had taken all their young boys and girls. He had loosely bound them in coils of chicken wire.

He laughed again at the memory.

The smell had hung about the village for all that day. A gentle breeze from up in the mountains had drifted it to the surrounding villages. He had deliberately waited for that to happen ... even though his men were urging him to move on.

The other villages had put up no resistance.

Who else would want their kids to die in that way?

So, yes, if he were going to design weaponised toxins, he wouldn't make ones that gave you skin blemishes and blisters ... it just wasn't enough.

It wasn't enough to discourage the others.

The pain in both of his legs was intense now. His stomach turned over. He retched a gout of thick green bile, splattering down onto the floor. He automatically wiped his mouth with his right sleeve. He grimaced from the pain of moving his right arm.

He guessed that most other people would be screaming by now, but he had always had a high pain threshold.

Just as well.

The lift console showed it was on the 4th floor now. It was on its way back up. Maybe the lift would be here in 30 seconds. He knew it didn't matter now when it got here ... he guessed he didn't have long.

He hoped he didn't have long.

He lifted the gun with his left arm. It seemed heavier ... almost too heavy to lift. He was feeling dizzy, so he had to focus, to concentrate. He focussed his attention on the plexi-glass ... the section already drilled ... the section that the spider was pushed through.

His gun boomed and bucked ... a comforting feeling.

Three left.

And in semi-automatic mode, the shell was automatically pushed out of the ejector port. It clattered to the floor at his feet. He muttered a small prayer of thanks.

He fired again.

Two left.

So that was two shells fired directly into the plexi-glass window.

Into the same area that the hole was drilled.

And a five-foot by four-foot section of glass fell away.

It plummeted down into the plaza.

The lift was on the 23rd floor now.

He forced his body to take him to the window ... to the shattered section of glass. The boy and the girl were still standing there. They were holding on to the robot for security, their arms locked around its arms as their craft swayed in the turbulence. And it was the boy who had controlled the spider. He was still wearing the control gear and goggles.

The pain in Dmitry's right hand and arm was intense ... it looked as though his skin was literally falling off in front of his eyes.

He lifted the gun again.

He thought to pull the slide back ... but he realised that he didn't need to. The shell was in there already. He could barely keep the gun on target. He wasn't sure if that were because the starship was moving around, swaying in the tall building's turbulence, or because he couldn't manage to hold the five-kilo gun steady with one arm. He lifted the muzzle ... pointed the gun as best he could at the starship's open hatchway.

His gun boomed, and the used shell spun out and clattered away.

One left.

He wasn't sure if he could do it again. It seemed to have taken all his strength merely to hold the gun up and level for that last shot. And even then ... he had aimed for the boy... but he had hit the fucking robot. Those robots were stupidly strong and robust. They were built to take anything an off-world environment might throw at them. But he had just thrown a 28-gram piece of solid steel at it, from an awfully close range. The slug must have bounced off the robot's hardened outer shell, but it looked like it must have made some damage. He guessed that plasteel shards must have been sent spinning through the air. Spinning and striking the boy who was falling forwards, tumbling out of the cockpit door.

Dmitry watched as the robot leaned out. It grabbed the boy's arm, holding him securely over the immense drop.

The boy had blood dripping from his arm, but he had swung himself ... he had swung and caught hold of the robot with the arm that was dripping blood.

The robot was holding onto one of the boy's arms. The boy was holding on with the other.

He saw the boy nodding over to the girl ... gesturing that he was ok.

The girl reached back behind her. She pulled a gun from her back-pocket. She still had one arm locked around the robot's. She was using the robot for stability. She was taking great care. Dmitry watched her. She transfixed him.

She was controlling the robot. He knew because she was wearing one of the usual WORM-LYNK headsets used to control those things.

And he realised she had decided.

She needed the robot to be rock-solid. She realised the boy was dangling from the robot's arm, but she had made a conscious decision to leave him there, dangling. She would leave the boy hanging over the void rather than get the robot to turn and pull the boy back onboard.

He watched the pretty girl playing with a toy gun.

Taking careful aim. Not hiding in case Dmitry shot at them again.

She fired.

Dmitry felt the thud of impact in his right thigh. He grunted, though the pain from the bullet scarcely registered above his other pain.

The girl was taking aim again. She was trying to judge the shot to account for the swaying of the starship.

He wished he had had her working for him … instead of the fuckwits he had spoken to earlier.

She looked smart. She looked focussed. She looked committed to getting a job of work done. He admired her; admired her attitude … admired her professionalism.

She reminded him of someone, someone else.

Someone a long time ago.

He thought he should take another shot. He was aware he had one shell left. He thought his left hand still worked. Maybe he had enough strength to lift the gun again. Just enough, maybe. Just enough would do it. He was still holding the gun. But he didn't think he could hold the gun steady enough to make it worthwhile.

And besides, he didn't really want to risk shooting the girl.

He couldn't think why … it wasn't like he hadn't shot girls before.

Maybe …

"Shoot him again … shoot the bastard, Ginny," Gabriel said. "The fucker doesn't look like he will drop … I can't imagine what's holding him up. It looks like his skin is dropping off him."

Gabriel winced. The robot's grip on his good arm felt like he was being slowly cut in two. He was grateful he had got a secondary grip with his injured arm, even though it was hurting like fuck. At least it took a bit of pressure off ...

Ginny locked her arm in and against the robot.

This robot didn't have a name as such. It had a nameplate on its chest, but it said SURR4-B32.

Not like Bill or Ben.

She had told it where and when to shoot the weapon.

Then she had told it to lower the weapon and stand there ... just stand there in the hatchway.

So it stood there; stood there in the gently swaying starship.

She had seen Gabriel fall forwards ... she had instantly commanded the robot to catch him.

It had caught him.

But now, as Gabriel hung there, she needed the robot to just stand there, immobile, like they had welded it to the deck.

She eased in against the robot's arm, sighted. She gently squeezed the trigger of the small cream gun.

Dmitry howled.

"You've shot him in the balls," Gabriel said.

"Second time lucky," Ginny said.

Dmitry rocked forwards.

He instinctively grabbed right-handed at the jagged edge of the plexi-glass screen. It flexed under his grasp. He looked over. He looked directly at Ginny.

He swayed forwards, rolling out and down, tumbling through space.

Ginny looked down. Watching him fall. Fall into the plaza, forty-six storeys below.

A small group of people came to look.

"I think he's dead now," she said.

From the heads-up display came the sound of chiming.

"The lift's here," Ginny said.

The lift doors opened. After a few seconds, they closed again.

"Can you pull me in now, Ginny?" Gabriel said.

I guess it's over   12:30 pm 22nd Oct 2180

Baltimore

"I guess it's over," Ginny said.

"What about Flynn and Matthews?" Gabriel said. "Dmitry put them back on the case, remember."

"I saw them standing by Dmitry's body," Vicky said. "My guess would be they have suddenly lost interest in pursuing a course of action given to them by a now deceased employer."

"And given to them under considerable duress," said Ginny.

"I think you're probably right," said Gabriel.

"So, what do you want to do?" asked Vicky.

"I wouldn't mind getting my arm fixed up," Gabriel said.

"It's only a flesh wound," Ginny said. "A kiss better should put that right."

"Or ten minutes in the MED unit," suggested Vicky.

"And then I think we should get out of here," Gabriel said.

Ginny nodded.

"Seville?" asked Ship.

"You read my mind," Ginny said.

"On our way," said Ship.

BOOK FOUR

You did get rid of the bad guys 25th Oct 2180

In Seville

Gabriel and Ginny had contacted Sara and Zackery, who had made their way back to Seville.

Sara and Zackery felt, as Ginny did, that Flynn and Matthews were unlikely to want to finish a piece of work for a now dead employer. Flynn and Matthews hadn't seemed keen anyway, and what advantage could they possibly gain from it. So, Sara and Zackery had decided to stay in Seville. They had agreed to keep a watchful eye out, but otherwise to enjoy living in a city they both felt at home in.

And this was Gabriel and Ginny's last evening with them. They had all eaten in a little place that Sara and Zackery liked. A nice meal followed by nice wine. The streetlights had come on as the late afternoon lapsed into early evening. Waiters carried out candles in glass jars and placed them on their table.

"What are you going to do now?" Zackery asked.

"We always said we were doing this to get a STU for John's wife," Gabriel said.

"You would have to give it to her before her dementia set in," Sara said.

Sara and Zackery were both aware of the story of John Cullen and his wife, Mary. Gabriel and Ginny had talked it through with them, as they tried to decide what best to do.

"But," said Zackery, "if you go back and give a STU to Mary … if she lives longer, there is a serious likelihood that John's life will significantly change."

Gabriel and Ginny nodded. They had already talked about this.

"He might not, for example, go to the care home that you two guys met him in," Zackery continued. "And if that happened, you guys might never meet."

Sara looked across at Zackery. She looked like she wasn't sure that Zackery's thought process was helping Gabriel and Ginny.

"And," said Zackery, "… you understand about all this stuff about time resolves any anomalies."

"That's the sort of thing ACME INC tried hard to avoid," Vicky said.

"I really have an awful feeling about this," said Zackery.

"But," said Ginny, "if we don't go back and give a STU to Mary, what was the point of everything we did?"

"Well ... you did get rid of the bad guys," Sara said, looking pointedly at Zackery.

"And you certainly saved our bacon," said Zackery, "so ... whatever you two decide ... I'd like to propose a toast. To Gabriel and Ginny. To two good friends."

Zackery lifted his wine glass to them. Sara clicked hers against his.

Gabriel and Ginny smiled, lifted their wine glasses likewise.

"To good friends," Gabriel said.

It's what we said we were going to do 26th Oct 2180

In the starship, on the outskirts of Seville

They were sitting in the cockpit seats. The ship was cloaked. They were looking out at the stars. The night sky was noticeably clear. The stars looked very close.

"We keep talking about this, but we end up going round and round," Ginny said.

"I realise that," Gabriel said.

"We think there is a possibility that giving John's wife a STU will cause some sort of time anomaly," Ginny continued. "We understand there is a possibility that time will resolve itself …"

"To our detriment," Gabriel said.

"So, do you think we shouldn't do it?" she said.

"I'm worried," Gabriel said. "I don't want to lose you. I couldn't imagine my life without you. I just … I …"

Ginny leaned over and took hold of Gabriel's hand. She clasped it tightly.

"But it's what we said we would do, isn't it?" Gabriel said.

"Yes, it is," said Ginny.

Gabriel squeezed Ginny's hand. "Vicky?" he said.

"Yes, Gabriel?"

"What date would we need to go back to, to give John's wife the STU?"

"Do you mean before I identified she had the onset of dementia?"

"Yes."

"I first noticed the symptoms in March 1969."

"So, a couple of months before that … would that be sufficient to prevent her from getting the disease?" he said.

"November 1968 would probably be a better time," suggested Vicky. "Just in case."

"Where did they live, back then?" Ginny asked.

"They lived in John's mother's house in Walton-on-the-Naze," said Vicky. "John's mother had died much earlier … in 1952. John and Mary moved in there after they got married. They got married in 1951. And his mother died the following year."

"He lived there all his life ... before he moved into the care home," Ginny noted.

"Yes, he did," said Vicky.

"And you can take us back to Walton in November 1968?" Ginny asked.

"If you so wish it," said Vicky.

"But you don't think it's a good idea?" said Ginny.

"It is not for me to say," Vicky said. "I don't think I would have advised you to do many of the things that you in fact did."

Ginny looked quizzical.

"And at least," Vicky said, "there will be no possibility of meeting yourselves ... at a younger age, that is. You wouldn't have been born at the time we are going back to. That was always something that worried ACME. They thought it offered the greatest risk of causing a time anomaly."

"But," Gabriel said, "our presence then ... in 1968 ... it will mean that you, Vicky, you will exist twice at the same time. You will have come back with us, and you will also exist on John's wrist."

"I agree, Gabriel," Vicky replied, "but I will strive to stay out of any contact or communication with John. Hopefully, that will reduce the risk of creating an anomaly."

Gabriel looked worried.

"And anyway," Vicky continued, "in your travels so far, despite any reservations I may have had, I don't think anyone can say you did not achieve a great outcome ... and at no small costs to yourselves."

Ginny looked pleased.

"But, as we said, round and round," said Gabriel.

"So," Ginny said. "What should we do? We need to both agree."

Gabriel stared out of the cockpit screen. He remembered his vow he had made to himself. His vow to support Ginny. To be there for her. Whatever the cost to himself.

He loved her too much to stop her.

Even if ...

"We should do it," he said. "It's what we said we would do, right from the start."

Ginny smiled. She stood up, walked across to his seat, and lowered herself onto his lap. He put his arms around her. They cuddled up together, staring up at the night sky.

"What are you going to do about me," Ship said.

"Oh, of course," Ginny said. "You can't come back with us."

"What would you like to do?" Gabriel asked.

"No-one has asked me that before," Ship said.

Ginny smiled.

"I suppose I could go back to the ACME-HUB," said Ship. "That way I might get re-assigned. That's what seemed to happen last time."

"But what would you prefer to do?" said Gabriel.

"I think I would like to travel through space ... just keeping going. Seeing what there is to see."

"I thought you had a poetic side to you," Vicky said.

"But what if your Ramstat motors burn out again?" Ginny asked. "You would float out there forever."

"Sounds wonderful," said Ship.

Gabriel smiled. "We've seen and heard some strange things in our travels, haven't we?" he said to Ginny.

"Yes, you have," Ship concurred.

Ginny laughed, and Gabriel laughed with her.

"So, now Ship is sorted out," said Gabriel, "when do we set off?"

"How about first thing in the morning," Ginny said. "How about we get off to bed and have a nice cuddle. A nice cuddle before we do anything else."

Gabriel smiled and gave Ginny a tighter hug. Then she climbed up off him.

"Come on, Gabriel," she said.

He watched her leave the cockpit.

He loved her so much that it hurt.

I'm Mary, John's wife 13th Nov 1968

Walton-on-the-Naze

Vicky had teleported them to a quiet spot on the cliff-tops outside Walton-on-the-Naze. Gabriel was wearing cargo pants, a blue sweatshirt and sneakers. Ginny had on a pair of tight-fitting blue jeans, a white T-shirt, a green fluffy jacket, and hiking boots. Vicky had suggested their apparel wouldn't be considered out of place for the time and space.

"So, here we are," Gabriel said. "It's like we've never been away."

"John will be about 51 years old," Ginny said. "We're looking for a middle-aged man."

"He was sprightly when I last saw him," said Gabriel, "and he was twice that age then."

"I'll direct you to his house," Vicky said.

A thin yellow line appeared momentarily on the road in front of them.

"Off we go," Gabriel said.

· · · · · · · ·

John's house looked sweet. A small terraced cottage, with a small garden in the front.

They walked up the garden path and knocked on the door.

A middle-aged woman answered the door. She was slim, five feet four inches tall, wearing a cream-coloured dress detailed with deep-red poppies.

The woman smiled at them. "Can I help you?" she said.

"We were looking for John," Gabriel said.

The woman turned her head back into the house.

"John ... there's someone here to see you," she called.

"Coming ...," a man's voice in the distance.

"Won't you please come in," the woman said. "I'm Mary, John's wife."

She closed the door behind them, gesturing them into a room on the right.

They walked in. It was a small but very cosy living room.

"I'm Gabriel, and this is Ginny," said Gabriel.

"Pleased to meet you," Mary said. "John should be here in two ticks. He was in the garden doing ... oh ... here he is."

A middle-aged man came into the living room but was immediately ushered out again by Mary. They saw him taking his muddy shoes off in the hallway.

He came back in again.

He pointed to his feet on which he was wearing a pair of tartan socks.

He grinned across at them, as if apologising for his attire.

Gabriel grinned at him, holding his hands out in front of him, palms upwards. A sense of comradely understanding.

"They're called Gabriel and Ginny," came a voice from the back of the house. "And they're looking for you."

"And how can I ...?" John said.

"I'm just putting the kettle on," came Mary's voice again.

John smiled and sat down. He gestured for them to sit down.

Ginny sat down.

Gabriel remained standing.

We've come to see you 13th Nov 1968

Walton-on-the-Naze – in John's house

Mary had brought them in a tray. It was laden with a large pot of tea covered with a teapot cosy with roses on it. There were three china teacups and saucers, a small jug with milk in and some sugar lumps in a cup.

She put the tray down, went out and came back with a plate with biscuits on it.

"I'm off out into the garden," she said. "Lovely meeting you but ..."

"She made the biscuits herself," John said. Then, when he noticed their confusion, he said, "I think she assumed that since you said you had come to see me, that she would give me some space to talk to you."

"She didn't really need ...," said Ginny,

"We've come to see you ... and to see Vicky," Gabriel said.

John's mouth dropped open.

....

"... and so, we asked them if they would give us another STU ... and they did," Gabriel said, holding out the spare STU.

"You make it seem so very easy," John said, leaning across to accept the device.

Ginny looked at Gabriel. She knew John was not a stupid man. She guessed that he suspected their efforts to bring him back another STU had been trickier than Gabriel had inferred.

"There were a few 'bumps' along the way," Ginny said, hoping that would be enough to placate John's curiosity.

John nodded, as if would have expected no less. He stood up and walked over to the fireplace.

Ginny thought there was probably something on his mind. Something he was mulling over. Waiting until he had found the right way to say it.

"Do you realise," John said, "that when Mary started visiting me ... to take me for walks ... it was near the end of the Second World War. Back then, Walton, was considered a possible invasion target for German troops."

Gabriel gave Ginny a quizzical look. He remembered John telling him about this when he had gone to see him, not long after his 100th birthday.

"The entire area was fortified," John continued. "The beaches and the cliff-tops were heavily mined. There was even a secret radar installation built into the Naze Tower. It was extremely high security. Troops prevented anyone from walking around that area."

"But you said that you found Vicky when you were walking along the …," Gabriel said, playing along with John's train of thought.

"Yes, that is true," said John. "And do you understand how that was possible? It was because they had given Mary the job of Auxiliary Coastguard. It was a special position … with great responsibilities."

Ginny thought John looked enormously proud to think they had given his wife such a role.

"She had the job to monitor for an enemy invasion," John continued, "which meant she had access to the cliff-tops, including the high-security areas."

"And she took you with her," Ginny said, smiling.

"Yes … yes, she did," said John. "Who would stop her taking her imbecile friend for a walk on the cliff-tops, as she watched for enemy craft. But she had another duty …"

He looked up pointedly at them.

"They had given her a weapon. A revolver. No-one in the town was aware of it. And if there was an invasion, they had empowered her to shoot anyone who she thought was … was in favour of the Germans … anyone who was a collaborator."

"It sounds like they had a very responsible job, these auxiliary …," said Gabriel.

"She had the authority to shoot and kill anyone who she suspected, whether it be ordinary townsfolk or the local mayor, the chief of police, anybody."

Gabriel looked suitably shocked at the thought.

Ginny wondered where this was going.

"She said she never had to use that authority," John said. "She never had to kill anyone."

Gabriel nodded his understanding.

"But she always said she had been prepared to do it. That she had inwardly prepared herself. Just in case. She didn't want to face that situation and be unable to carry out her responsibility."

John turned and stared pointedly at Gabriel.

"Can you imagine that ... having to kill someone? Having to purposefully kill someone. Having to watch them die? And to live with the possibility that you were wrong ... that they were innocent. That they didn't deserve to die."

Ginny saw Gabriel's lips start to tremble. She leaned over and folded her arms around him. He tucked his head into her shoulder. She stroked his neck. "It wasn't your fault," she whispered. "It couldn't be helped."

She turned to look across at John, who was looking shocked and saddened.

"As we said, John," Ginny said, "there were a few bumps along the way."

Barney's wedding day   2:30 pm   15th Feb   2018

Frinton Registry Office

"This is where and when it should be," Vicky said.

Gabriel checked the board outside the registry office. There was no mention of a wedding that day.

"I'll go inside and check," he said.

Ginny stood outside. There was no-one about, certainly no-one running up the street, late for a particularly important date.

"They have no bookings for anyone with that name," said Gabriel, looking very worried.

"Perhaps they called it off," Ginny said.

"Yeah ..." Gabriel said.

Ginny scanned the street again.

"Maybe we fucked it up for them," Gabriel said.

"It looks like something went wrong ... something changed," Ginny said.

Gabriel looked about.

Ginny sensed an air of panic in him.

A realisation that for all their 'it should be all right ... that's what we came here to do in the first place' talk; maybe they really had screwed it up.

"Let's go back earlier," Ginny said. "Let's try to see what happened."

"Ok," Gabriel said, with a sense of hopelessness.

Want to talk about it? Monday 17th July 2017 morning

Outside the Gazette Office - Frinton

Ginny and Gabriel had teleported into a quiet Frinton backstreet. They turned up into the High Street, walking along in the direction of the Gazette office.

It was still there, between the florist and the charity shop.

Gabriel opened the familiar street doorway and walked up the stairs.

He heard Ginny's quiet footsteps behind him.

He stopped at the top of the stairs. The sign on the door still said:

> **Gazette**
> **please knock**
> **before entering**

Gabriel gave a quick knock on the door, then pushed it open.

Barney was sat at his desk, in his usual chair.

He looked up to see who it was.

"Hi, Barney," Gabriel said. "We've come to see how you're getting on."

"Is that the 'Royal We', mate," Barney said. "We usually means you and somebody else. You do realise that, don't you?"

Barney chuckled at his own small joke.

Gabriel looked behind him, at the open door, at the vacant staircase.

He ran down the stairs.

He scanned the street.

He felt a deep sense of loneliness overwhelm him ... and he didn't understand why.

He walked back up the stairs.

He went into the office and sat down at his desk. He opened his laptop and stared at it morosely.

"Want to talk about it, Gabriel?" Barney asked worriedly.

"Nothing to talk about, Barney."

"You never know," Barney replied, feeling even more worried.

"I think I've blown it," Gabriel said. "And I don't understand why. I don't know what I should have done. I don't even ..."

"I'll buy you a sandwich and a pint at lunchtime, mate," Barney offered, and Gabriel grunted in assent, but Barney took no consolation from it.

Who is Vicky?   Monday 17th July 2017 5:30 pm

The Gazette Office – Frinton

Barney and Gabriel got back from a solemn and quiet lunch. Barney had bought Gabriel a cheese and pickle sarnie and a coffee. Gabriel had said he wasn't in the mood for alcohol, so they had sat there watching the world go by. It looked as though someone had sucked the life out of him.

Back at the office, Barney stopped trying to make conversation, and decided to let Gabriel mull over whatever it was that he didn't want to talk about. It was obvious to Barney what it would be, but if the lad didn't want to discuss it, there was no point in trying. Eventually he would mention it, and then, well, perhaps Barney could offer some sort of advice.

Or just consolation, if that was all that was left.

At 5:30 pm Barney said he was finished for the day. "Whatever you've got left to do today, I'm sure it will keep until tomorrow," he said, in as jocular a tone as he could muster.

Gabriel flipped down the lid of his laptop, stood up and picked up his jacket and rucksack.

They both made their way down the stairs, Barney first, opening the door that faced onto the high street. He ushered Gabriel out, locking the door behind him.

As Barney turned to go, he saw a young woman standing directly in front of Gabriel. She was very pretty, noticeably confident. She looked self-assured. Gabriel obviously didn't recognise her. He had that look Barney had seen before when Gabriel was confronted by a pretty girl. He would be tongue-tied. He would blush. He would stammer some vague fragment of a sentence. Then he would stumble off, cursing himself for his shyness.

Barney guessed that the girl was going to introduce herself to Gabriel. Well, Gabriel was a nice lad, and maybe that was how it worked these days, but he felt fearful for the lad. She looked to be a nice girl, but even so ...

He turned to Gabriel; "I think I'd better get going" he said, but then he leaned over and whispered into the young woman's ear, "he's a good lad, and I wouldn't like to see him upset."

Barney turned and made his way off down the street.

Ginny turned to watch him go.

She turned back to Gabriel. He was looking frightened and confused.

"What did he say to you?" Gabriel asked.

"I think he likes you," Ginny replied.

"I guess so," Gabriel said.

Ginny stood watching Gabriel. He obviously didn't recognise her, but nor did he turn away.

"Do I know you?" he asked her.

"We've met before," Ginny said.

She could almost see the cogs whirring, as he tried to think where he might have met this girl before.

"Vicky suggested I meet you here," Ginny said. "She suggested this precise moment in time."

"Who is Vicky?" Gabriel asked.

Ginny leaned in toward Gabriel. She took hold of his hands, holding them between her own. He started to pull away from her. She pressed Vicky against Gabriel's left wrist. He flinched momentarily. She kept hold of his hands. He seemed to have become immobile.

"Are you all right, Gabriel?" she said.

He looked down into her eyes. He seemed to be drowning in her eyes.

He nuzzled his face down onto her shoulder. Into the nape of her neck.

He began to sob. Deep sobs, from the depths of his chest.

She let go of his hands and put her arms around him. He reciprocated, holding on to her as if she might leap away at any moment. She snuggled her face against his chest. She felt his heart beating.

He pulled her closer; closer until she could barely breathe. He didn't want to let her go.

A passer-by looking over smiled at them as they cuddled on the pavement. He noticed Gabriel's face light up, unaware it was Gabriel's first smile of the day.

It's nearly that day   17th Dec 2017

The offices of Bart, Smithson and Peters Associates

"It's nearly that day," Toby said.

"Never thought it would come around," Willoughby replied.

"Old Jones hoped he would still be working here," Toby said. "To be the one to take them."

"Yes ... shame that," said Willoughby. "He was looking forward to it."

"When was it?" Toby said.

"He died last year ... July I think it was," said Willoughby.

Toby walked over to the company safe. A huge thing. Three tumblers plus a complex and intricate key.

He took the key from its hook on the wall and inserted it into the keyhole on the safe door.

He gave the tumblers a spin.

Willoughby watched him with keen interest. They did this every few months. Somebody from the firm had probably been doing it for the last few years, ever since the deposit had been made in 1968.

Toby tugged at the big safe door. It opened grudgingly on its huge hinges.

The nameplate on the door proudly proclaimed the name

    ACME

written in big, bold, half-inch thick steel letters. The name was also inscribed in tiny script on the barrels of the hinges. A name to be mentioned proudly. It stood for safety, for security, for length of service.

Toby leaned into the safe and took out two packages that lay within.

Two identical packages. Both A4 sized. Both wrapped in sturdy brown parcel paper. Both neatly tied with strong twine and small tight knots. Both bearing blobs of what had probably once been bright red sealing gum; holding the twine together where it crossed over itself.

Toby handed one of the packages over to Willoughby. He handed it ceremonially.

Their client had paid a substantial sum of money for them to keep these packages safe … to hand them over when the time came.

Toby had handed Willoughby the one marked 'Ginny Peters, living in Clacton-on-Sea sometime in 2017 – about 20 years old'.

He kept the one labelled 'Gabriel Jones, living in Clacton-on-Sea sometime in 2017 – about 20 years old'.

As they had both done before, and as old Jones had also done (maybe with a particular fondness on his part, since he had felt he was a sort of namesake to one of the parties), they both gently bent the packages, listening to the sounds they made.

"It's some sort of a book," Willoughby said.

"That's what you said last time," Toby said, smiling.

"It's got to be," said Willoughby. "Just listen to it. It sort of creaks, and there's a crackly noise when you bend it. Sounds like some sort of leather-bound thing."

Toby held his package up to his nose. He sniffed it gently. There was no discernible smell, other than the slightly musty smell from the paper and the old twine. Then again, the packages had been stored in the company safe for over fifty years. And they weren't the only old things in there.

Willoughby handed his package back to Toby, who placed them both reverently back into the safe.

Toby closed the safe door. He always expected the door to make a thudding noise, but the door was so very heavy, the door-seal so very tight, so very precise.

It made a low noise … almost like a gasp. As if the very air was acting like a cushion, and the closing door slowly pushed it out.

"Have we got their current addresses?" Toby asked.

"Of course," Willoughby said. "They are both living in the same flat. It's in Clacton-on-Sea. Up until recently they were sharing the flat with a girl called Elizabeth Mothwell-Barrett, but she moved out."

"Maybe she thought they were needing more space," Toby said. "Maybe she thought they were 'nest building'," he said, chuckling.

Toby remembered when his own son had moved in with some young woman. They had bought themselves a cat. Then they had bought another cat. And then, finally, they …

"I wonder if our client realised they would be living together," Willoughby said.

"I don't suppose he can have been sure about that," said Toby, "otherwise he would have sent them one package between them."

"I suppose so," said Willoughby. "But what it means is that it only needs one of us to deliver both the packages."

Willoughby saw the look of disappointment on Toby's face.

"Only joking," said Willoughby. "We'll take one each. After all, it's a bit of a ceremony, isn't it?"

His wife survives him   18th Dec 2017

Ginny's flat – Clacton-on-Sea

"We will need some paint, and a gate-thing and …," Gabriel said.

"I realise that," Ginny said.

"Barney said he's got …"

"You mentioned it, already," Ginny said, smiling. "It's truly kind of him."

"I asked him if I might work some over-time, but he said he didn't think …"

"Don't worry," Ginny said. "We'll manage."

"I'm really sorry," Vicky said.

"What about?" Ginny said.

"Well … when we tried to request some money. It looks as though ACME INC have chosen not to provide any further currency requests," Vicky said.

"Well, they've obviously kept the system going for other things," Gabriel pointed out, "but the things they are happy to provide are not the sort of things we are going to need."

"We'll be ok," Ginny said. "Don't worry."

"Yeah … ok," Gabriel said, unconvinced.

"I checked again about John … I checked yesterday," Ginny said, trying to change the conversation.

"And?" said Gabriel.

"Nobody has heard of him," Ginny said. "He isn't in the records at all. It's like he never lived there."

"A time anomaly then?" Gabriel said.

"It might be," Vicky said. "ACME INC were always very reluctant to allow anyone to make fundamental changes to past events. You can never predict what might happen."

They heard a cautious knocking on the door of their flat. Not like the robust knocking of a postman or a delivery man, where time really matters. This sounded like someone altogether timider.

"Can you get it, please, Gabriel?" Ginny said.

Gabriel smiled. He dropped the washing-up sponge into the sink and picked up the small towel hanging on the hook next to the sink. He dried his hands whilst walking through to answer the door.

He opened the door.

Two old gentlemen were standing there. They were very formally dressed, in a very old-fashioned way. They were both carrying an umbrella in one hand and a briefcase in the other.

"Can I help you?" Gabriel said.

"Gabriel Jones?" asked one of the old men.

"Erm, yes, that's me," said Gabriel.

"And is Ginny Peters here also?" said the other old man.

"Ginny?" Gabriel shouted.

Ginny came through to the doorway.

"These gentlemen are here to see us," Gabriel explained.

"Please come in," Ginny said. She immediately dashed back into the small living room, hurriedly picking up and tidying away several teacups and newspapers.

The old gentlemen moved over to the sofa and sat down alongside each other.

Gabriel and Ginny pulled two simple wooden chairs across the room, so they could sit facing the two old men.

"We are here to represent …," said one of the old men.

"Just a minute," interrupted the other, smiling. Then, "My name is Mr. Willoughby, and this is my colleague Mr. Toby." He gestured back to the other man to continue.

"I am sorry," said Mr. Toby. "We are quite excited."

Gabriel smiled over to Ginny, who smiled back.

"We are here to represent the wishes," Mr. Toby continued, "of a long-standing client of ours. He wished to give you something."

"Who?" said Gabriel.

"There is a package for each of you," said Mr. Willoughby. "We don't have any idea what they contain."

"Though we have had many guesses over the years," Mr. Toby said.

"Yes ... quite," Mr. Willoughby said.

"Over how many years?" Ginny asked.

"The packages were deposited with us in 1968," said Mr. Willoughby. "I believe our company was chosen because of our long and dependable service to ..."

"Quite so," said Mr. Toby.

"Ah, yes," said Mr. Willoughby, colouring slightly.

"It's John," Ginny whispered to Gabriel.

"And so, without further ado," said Mr. Toby.

He pulled his briefcase onto his knee and unclipped the flap.

He took a package out of it.

He checked the label, then ceremonially handed it over to Ginny.

Mr. Willoughby watched this little scene, then took an identical package from his own briefcase.

He handed his to Gabriel.

Ginny watched as both the old men sat back into the sofa. They didn't appear to be preparing to get up or leave. They both seemed to be trembling with excitement.

"So, you don't have any idea what is in the packages?" Ginny asked.

The two old men shook their heads in acknowledgment.

"Well, you'd best be going," Gabriel said, chuckling to himself.

Both the old men looked close to tears.

Ginny gave Gabriel a wry look.

"I'm sorry, guys," Gabriel said. "I was only joking. I think the very least we can do is to let you see what's in the packages. After all, you've looked after them for us for all this time."

Mr. Toby pulled a small handkerchief from the breast pocket of his jacket and wiped his eyes.

Gabriel looked over at Ginny. "You first," he said.

She broke open the sealing wax, tugged on the tiny knot.

It remained firm.

"You might use this," said Mr. Willoughby, holding a small knife. He carefully prised out a small pair of scissors from a slot at the back of the blade.

He handed it over to Ginny.

Ginny snipped the twine with the miniature scissors. She handed the knife back to Mr. Willoughby. She pulled the twine free from the package. She gently pulled the brown wrapping paper open, revealing a leather-bound book. The leather was a very pale tan colour.

Inscribed in gothic black lettering on the front cover were the words.

Journal of Intergalactic Mining / Transhipment

Version 12.3.2   Published on June 2183 AD
Published by Steinberg & Scott,
Broadwater Square, Basildon.
United Kingdom. Earth.

There was a piece of paper loosely inserted into the first page. She lifted it out. It looked as though it had been written with an old-fashioned ink pen. The sort of pen you filled from a bottle. The sort where you dipped the nib into the ink bottle and then pulled a little plunger to draw in the liquid.

And it looked as though it had been written by someone in a time when penmanship counted for something.

The note read.

> To Ginny (I'm thinking Virginia, but you introduced yourself to me as Ginny, so that is what I shall refer to you as).
>
> It was wonderful to meet you (and your close friend Gabriel, both). Words fail me ... I can't begin to describe how I feel ... that you were prepared to go through so much, to bring back the means by which my wife, Mary, could remain fit and healthy.
>
> I don't know if we shall ever meet again. Vicky explained to me that 'time sorts itself out'. I worry now that what you have done for Mary and myself may well be detrimental to you. I have thought to give you this small gift (timed to be roughly when you said you knew me), partly so that I could re-iterate our sincere thanks, and partly because I don't know whether you will need assistance.

Anyway, I thought that, maybe … no … enough said (Mary always says I tend to ramble on).

With my very deepest thanks

John Cullen

"It's a note from John," Ginny said, handing the book and the note across to Gabriel, so he might read it too.

As she handed the book over, another piece of paper fell out onto the floor. Mr. Willoughby picked it up and handed it to Ginny. She looked at it.

"I don't understand it," she said, scanning the piece of paper.

"Shall I?" said Mr. Willoughby, holding out his hand.

Ginny handed him the piece of paper.

"It's a receipt for the purchase of stocks and bonds," said Mr. Willoughby. "A Mr. John Cullen deposited a large sum of money into a long-term managed fund. He did this in 1968. This note says the value of this fund, if any, should be put at your disposal on the … well … on the date that this package was delivered and formally received."

"If you so wish, I can use the details on this receipt to check for you," Mr. Willoughby suggested.

Ginny nodded her agreement.

Willoughby lifted his briefcase and pulled out a slim leather pouch. It opened, revealing a shiny computer tablet.

"I'm afraid that we need to use these sorts of things sometimes," Mr. Willoughby said apologetically.

He switched the tablet on. The screen lit up. It showed two young boys playing in a garden.

"My great-grandchildren …" he said, smiling. "They are called …"

"Mr. Willoughby?"

"Ah, yes … sorry," Willoughby said, looking apologetically over to Toby

Willoughby turned to the tablet. He clicked through a few screens until he found what he was looking for.

"It would seem," he said, "that the bulk of your managed fund was heavily invested into an initial public offering back in 1986."

Ginny looked downcast.

"It was an IPO for a company working in emerging technologies," continued Willoughby.

"Oh well," said Ginny, sadly. "You see, we've been trying to save up for ... well ... I was just wondering if it might be worth ..."

"Well, as it transpired, the company the fund was invested in was called the Microsoft Corporation. I believe that most people would have called that an exceptionally good investment," Willoughby said, chuckling to himself.

Willoughby clicked and dragged through a few further screens, referencing back to the account details on the receipt.

"It would seem," Willoughby continued, "that your funds are probably worth in the region of ... oh ... oh my word ..."

Toby looked across at his colleague, ready to assist if necessary.

"If you would allow me to say so," Willoughby continued, "our company would be incredibly pleased, indeed honoured, to assist you in redeeming and managing these funds."

Toby allowed himself a small smile. "Did you realise," he said, "that the same Mr. John Cullen who set up this managed fund was the very person, our client, who deposited these packages with us? I must say that I find it hard to understand how you might have known him ... or indeed that he can have known you would be here ... here in Clacton, at this very point in time."

"I met him a long time ago," Ginny said.

"I fear that you may be speaking of a different man," Toby said. "Our client died in 1998. He died in an automobile accident."

Ginny looked at Gabriel.

"He died sooner ... because of us," she whispered.

"His wife survives him still," Toby said.

"Mary is still alive?" Ginny said.

"Yes. She lives in a care home in Frinton."

"Sunny Vale?" Ginny said.

"Yes. How did you guess that?" Toby said.

Dead all these years   23rd Jan 2018

Sunny Vale Care Home – Frinton-on-Sea

"Hi Ginny," Monica said. "What are you doing down here? It's your day off."

"We've come down to see Mary ... Mary Sands," Ginny said.

"How do you know Mary?" Monica asked. "She's in a different unit to the one you normally work in. I didn't think you'd ever met her ... or worked with her."

"I think we might have met her some time back," Ginny said, smiling.

Ginny noticed Gabriel had politely turned away from them, allowing them to have their conversation. He was standing looking out into the front lawn.

"Tell you what Ginny ... we ought to get together sometime," Monica said. "Perhaps we could go for a drink or something."

"Sounds like a nice idea," said Ginny.

"And I've never had the chance to chat to your chap," Monica continued, "though he seems like a nice guy," this last in a slight whisper.

"Tell you what," Ginny said. "Why don't you come along this evening? Gabriel's boss is taking us both out for a drink and a bite to eat. He's a nice guy. You might like to meet him."

"Are you sure?" Monica said. "It sounds like a formal do."

"It's sort of like a little celebration," Ginny said, "but I don't think Barney would mind if you came. It's only a burger and chips in the Olde Swan. Nothing special."

"You said it was a celebration?" Monica said. "What are you celebrating?"

Ginny took hold of Monica's hand and placed it onto her stomach, cupping the small roundness.

"What? Really?" Monica said.

"Yes, really," Ginny said, smiling. "I wasn't sure about telling people yet, but this big blabber-mouth ...," she pointed affectionately to Gabriel, "he told his boss, Barney, and now Barney's really excited about it. He wanted to do something to celebrate."

"I don't really think I should come along to what is a very private celebration," Monica said. "Perhaps another time, eh?"

"I think it's a little celebration to be shared with good friends," said Ginny, "So I would like you to come along."

Monica looked a little embarrassed. She put her arms around Ginny and gave her a hug. "In that case, I would love to come," she said. "I just hope I don't say anything awkward in front of Gabriel's boss."

"I think he'll love to meet you," Ginny said.

Ginny leaned back and grabbed Gabriel's hand.

"C'mon Gabe," she said. "Let's go in. Let's go and meet Mary."

· · · · · · · ·

"This is the dementia unit," Monica said. "You won't have worked in this section yet."

"Does that mean Mary has dementia?" Ginny asked.

Monica seemed not to hear but continued down the corridor.

"All the doors have got wallpaper on," Gabriel said. "Seems a bit bizarre. You can't see them very easily, can you?"

"That's the point," explained Monica. "A lot of dementia clients feel the need to keep walking about. It's like their illness drives them. But if they see an exit, a door, they tend to congregate round it."

"I guess they want to get out," suggested Gabriel.

"Maybe," said Monica. "But when they see a door ... and they aren't allowed to go through it, they become very anxious. If we make the doors look like the corridor walls, they don't recognise them as doors. They keep on walking round and round. It's a simple visual trick, but it seems to keep them happier."

"So, has Mary got ...?" Ginny said.

"Mary's in here," Monica said, pointing to a door on the left.

On the door, it said

Mary Sands

Monica knocked on the door.

A woman's voice said, "Please come in."

Monica opened the door, ushering Ginny and Gabriel inside.

"There are two people here who would like to see you," Monica said. "They are called Ginny and Gabriel."

Monica whispered to Ginny, "I'll leave you to get on with it."

"See you later this evening," Ginny whispered back.

Monica showed herself out of the room.

An old lady was sitting in a straight-backed chair. It was next to a window which faced out onto the back gardens. She was dressed in a long cream dress. She had on cream shoes. Her hair was combed. She looked very alert. She was looking over towards them.

"Did she say Ginny?" the old lady asked.

"Yes," Ginny said. "It's Ginny and Gabriel."

"Ginny Peters?" Mary said.

"Do you remember me?" Ginny said.

"How can I forget? I remember you both."

"But it was so long ago," said Ginny.

"It was 1968," Mary said. "You said you had come to see John. I made you a pot of tea."

Gabriel looked at Ginny. His face showed enormous relief. They had expected her to have dementia. They had expected her to not remember anything.

"You and your boyfriend ... you brought us ... you brought us this," she said, rolling back her left sleeve to reveal a simple lady's wristwatch.

Ginny knelt in front of Mary to look at the watch. As she did so, Mary caught her arm. She pulled Ginny towards her. She gave Ginny a big hug.

"We never ever forgot you," Mary said. "I realise I only saw you briefly, but after you had gone ... after John told me ..."

Ginny stood up ... she walked over to stand by Gabriel.

"You are aware that John is dead, aren't you?" Mary said.

"Yes, we have heard," Ginny said.

"He died in a car accident," Mary said. "A stupid thing. It was in October 1998. He had been given a lift to ... well, anyway ... it was a stupid thing. He didn't suffer though, and that is a mercy."

"We were sorry to hear of it," Ginny said.

"Did you realise Vicky chose to be buried with him?" Mary said. "She asked me if ... she asked me if that would be all right. What could I say? Vicky had been with him for over fifty years. Of course, I agreed to her request."

Ginny looked at Gabriel. She saw that he was shocked. She was herself.

"I suppose you are wondering why I didn't register here under my married name," Mary said.

"I had wondered that," Ginny said. "If you had been registered under your married name, I would have spotted your name on the client roster."

"Well, the funny thing is ... I can't remember now why I did," said Mary. "And before you think, 'oh no, it's the dementia', let me tell you that I chose this room because of the view. Back in 2005, which is when I moved into this care home, this room wasn't in the dementia unit. They didn't have a dementia unit at that time. I picked the room because of its view over the gardens. I get beautiful colours, all the way through from the spring right into the autumn. John and I always loved a garden. It was a joy that we shared. Then they decided to have a dementia unit. They asked me to change rooms, but I decided to stay in here. I am happy and settled in here."

"Gabriel here ... he can't really remember meeting you," Ginny said. "We think it is because of the time anomalies that were generated when we went back to see you."

"John talked about that. He feared such a thing would happen," Mary said. "But Gabriel ... please understand that I remember you very well. John and I said that you both looked such a lovely couple."

Gabriel smiled.

"Is it all right if I speak now?" a young male voice said.

"Of course," Mary said. "Please do."

"My name is Arthur," the voice said. "I am pleased to meet you. I am Mary's companion."

"And you have been ever since my good friends here gave you to me," Mary said. "And, by the way, do you still have your ...?"

"As ever," Vicky said. "I am pleased to see you again, Mary."

"Vicky?" Mary said. "Would you be able to do me a great favour?"

"Anything," Vicky said.

"Your memories ... your memories of John and myself. Would you be able to ...?"

"Can I send them to Arthur, do you mean?" said Vicky. "So that you can view them again?"

"Yes, I would very much like ..." Mary said. "John used to play me memories ... of when we were younger. They were stored on the old Vicky. I never thought to transfer them to Arthur, and then, after John died ... and Vicky was buried with him ... it was too late."

Ginny felt her eyes prickling.

"I have some memories," said Vicky, "such as this one."

The room became a grassy meadow. Ginny and Gabriel felt the sun warming them. The meadow was alive with the sound of small insects and birds.

A couple in their early thirties were lying face down along-side each other on the soft grass.

The woman had tied up her hair with a red and white polka-dot scarf. She had plucked a daisy and was stroking its petals along her own cheek.

Another man, a friend, walked up towards them, a camera in his hand. He stooped and took a photograph of them. Then he wandered away.

The man lying on the grass watched his friend go. He turned to the girl and took hold of her hand. With a look of mock seriousness, he nuzzled his face against hers.

He whispered something to her. She smiled and said something in return.

"Can you please show that bit again, Vicky?" Mary said. "And please make it a little louder. My hearing isn't what it was."

The scene re-wound slightly, and they zoomed in closer to the couple lying on the grass.

The man nuzzled his face against the woman next to him. He said, "Mary, would you do me the great honour of ... would you ... would you marry me, Mary?"

The woman turned to face him. She put her mouth close to his ear. She whispered, "Yes, John ... of course."

Gabriel looked across at Ginny. She was crying.

The meadow scene dissolved. They were standing in Mary's room once more.

"I will transfer my memories across to Arthur, Mary," Vicky said. "They will be yours to view as you wish."

"I don't know how ... how I can ever ...," Mary said.

"I have them now," said Arthur.

"Mary?" Ginny said. "Did you realise that John left two ...?"

"Oh, the packages," said Mary. "Yes, John wanted to say thank you, and he didn't expect to see you again. Or, at least, if he did see you, he didn't expect that you would remember each other."

"Time anomaly," said Vicky. "That is why Gabriel can't remember meeting you or John. He wouldn't have been able to remember Ginny if I hadn't ..."

Ginny turned to Gabriel and gave him a hug and a kiss on the cheek.

"Thank you again, Vicky," Ginny said. "I can't imagine what I'd have done without this big lunk-head."

Gabriel smiled back at Ginny, a cheeky grin on his face.

Mary smiled at them; the indulgent smile of very old women for the young people that they love.

"Yes, John wanted to say thank you," she said. "Just some old book each and a bit of money put into some account or other. He hoped it would help you out, if ..."

"It's been a really big help," said Gabriel. "If only you knew ..."

He stopped. Ginny was looking at him. That 'say no more' type of look.

"It was very nice of John," he concluded lamely.

"I wish I could remember what he wrote to you," Mary said. "You don't remember, do you?"

Gabriel pulled out his wallet. It was an old leather one. Lots of little pockets in the front, and with a long pocket running down its entire length when it was opened fully. From the long pocket he carefully took out a slip of paper; the one that had been inserted into his copy of the Journal of Intergalactic Mining / Transhipment.

He read it out aloud.

> **Dear Gabriel,**
>
> **You probably don't remember me now. When you came back to give Mary a STU, your friend, Ginny ... she was wearing Vicky.**
>
> **I obviously still had my own Vicky.**

> That's time anomalies for you.
>
> While you were with me, I asked Ginny if she would let her Vicky send me some of her memories; the ones from when you and Ginny met me in the care home.
>
> I have watched those memories many times.
>
> It is ironic, I know, since you almost certainly won't remember me, and yet I feel that you are my very good friend.
>
> You and Ginny went through a lot, the both of you, all to bring back a STU for Mary.
>
> Whether that was wise or not, I could not really say.

Gabriel stopped reading. His voice was faltering He looked at Ginny, who took the paper from him.

Ginny continued reading from John's letter.

> All I know is that I am grateful ... grateful beyond belief. And so, I ask you, as my dear good friend, can you please accept these small gifts.
>
> From your very good friend
>
> **John Cullen**

Gabriel turned to Ginny, who wrapped her arms around him.

He sobbed quietly.

Ginny looked over at Mary Sands. Mary was sitting quietly, sitting calmly, sitting in her straight-backed chair which looked out into the rear gardens of the Sunny Vale Care Home.

She was smiling gently at hearing these words ... words written fifty years ago. Written by her husband, John ... her dear and close companion, who had been dead all these years.

THE END

About the author

David Griffiths was born in 1954 in a small mining town in South Yorkshire, England.

He moved to the south-east coast of England, where he still lives today.

He is married, with two children.

He plays bass guitar, and he is part-owner (with his younger son) of a Volkswagen T4 campervan.

He thinks there is nothing finer than to be able to pull up at the side of the road, put the kettle on and make a nice cup of tea (to which a Digestive biscuit is a nice accompaniment).

Acknowledgments

The term 'Ramstat' was first coined in the Radix Tetrad, written by A. A. Attanasio way back in the early 1980s. I would heartily recommend his works, as they gave me much pleasure.

The description of the Coca-Cola machine (referred to in the chapter called 'Coca-Cola light') came from an evocative photograph I once saw of an old Coca-Cola drinks machine on an old pier. I don't know what era the machine would have dated from, but the way that it glowed in the darkness stayed with me (long after the photograph itself was lost). Needless to say, the machine in my book refers to the Coca-Cola drinks machines which are manufactured for the supply of Coca-Cola (where the term Coca-Cola is owned and trademarked by the Coca-Cola Company).

Cover design/digital artwork courtesy of Stuart Hancock.

Stuart can be contacted at   stuart@hancockarchitecture.co.uk

Images used are under license from Shutterstock.com

Titles by David Griffiths

Acme Time Travel Incorporated - Volume 1

John Cullen was born in 1917 in a small coastal town on the southeast of England. Diagnosed with catatonia from birth, he is unable to speak or move voluntarily. He is labelled 'an imbecile' by the medical community of the time. He can only silently observe as his younger brother grows up, finds love, goes to war, and dies in the conflict.

In 1945, John, aged 28 years old, is given an old watch, found on the nearby grassy cliff top. It proves to be a time-travel device, mislaid by a now-dead traveller. The device's artificial intelligence promises John that it can provide a lifelong cure for John's illness. It promises that it can change his life for the better. But it did mention that its last client died whilst under its care.

Should he take the risk of using this strange device from the future, or perhaps more pertinently, can he afford not to?

Acme Time Travel Incorporated- Volume 2

John Cullen (see volume 1), now 100 years old, has passed his old watch onto a young man named Gabriel, a shy boy with a troubled background. John says he has no further use for the watch but thinks that it may be of assistance to Gabriel. John has explained to Gabriel that the device is a time-machine, left there by accident in 1945 by a long-dead time-traveller. He says that bits of the time-machine's functionality work, and others don't. He thinks that it may be of use to Gabriel. Gabriel is sceptical of what John has told him, but . . .

What if it really did work?

What if it really can transport you through time and space?

What if it can somehow improve his confusing and lonely life?

Getting Book Reviews

Getting book reviews is a bugger. Nobody wants to do them. Ok, you enjoyed the book (or you really hated it), but do you really want to spend time logging onto Amazon (or wherever) and start explaining how you feel about it. You might tell your friends (over coffee or a beer) . . . especially if you hated it . . . if just to warn them not to waste the three hours that you spent (and will never get back again). But who really has the time / enthusiasm / inclination to try to explain why you hold the view you have?

Sadly, with that in mind, it is maybe worth mentioning that reviews are important to authors. They might fear them (nobody wants to see the "this book is an utter pile of poo" review comment), but unfortunately, they are important. For indie authors (like myself) who can't necessarily afford to pay for expensive professional editing services, good constructive reviews are particularly important. Authors can often be too close to their books to spot the glaring issues. Good criticism lets an author know where the problems lie. They learn from that sort of feedback. They might even write better books ongoing.

Anyway, if you can be bothered to write a review of my books, I would be deeply grateful.

Printed in Great Britain
by Amazon